FEASTS OF PHANTOMS

Kehinde Adeola Ayeni

This is a work of fiction. Names, characters, places, and incidents either are the product of the author's imagination or are used fictitiously, and any resemblance to actual persons, living or dead, business establishments, events or locales is entirely coincidental.

Genoa House
www.genoahouse.com
books@genoahouse.com

Feasts of Phantoms
Copyright © 2010 by Kehinde Adeola Ayeni
First Edition

All rights reserved. No part of this publication may be used or reproduced by any means, graphic, electronic, or mechanical, including photocopying, recording, taping or by any information storage retrieval system without the written permission of the publisher except in the case of brief quotations embodied in critical articles and reviews.

Published simultaneously in Canada, the United Kingdom, and the United States of America. For information on obtaining permission for use of material from this work, please submit a written request to:
books@genoahouse.com

ISBN 978-0-9813939-2-6

To the grace in my life, my children, Segilola and Mobolaji

Many thanks to Daryl Sharp (www.innercitybooks.net) and to Patty Cabanas of Genoa House for editing *Feasts of Phantoms*, and to Jimoh Ighodalo (Ibadan, Nigeria) for granting permission to use the sculpture as a front cover image.

1

"Doctor, I have terrible news. The girls from Gari village that you treated two years ago, do you remember them?"

Ranti nodded on the phone without speaking.

"They are dead." Fausa paused. "Hello?" She checked to be sure they had not been disconnected. "Doctor, are you there?"

"Yes, I'm here," she whispered.

"I'm sorry doctor. The police said some neighbors killed them because they became prostitutes. They accused them of being prostitutes simply because they did not smell of urine and feces anymore, and they started to make themselves pretty the way normal girls would. Is that a reason to kill someone?

"The police might trace them to us since we have been paying their rent. You know how hostile people have been to us because of our work. We don't know what to do."

Ranti still could not speak because of the freezing towel squeezing her heart. "I will never be a normal woman and neither will the women I try to help. We are scapegoats of our culture, playthings for men," she muttered under her breath.

"Doctor, are you there?" Fausa checked again.

"I'm here, Fausa, I'm sorry I'm not there to comfort everyone. Who else is there with you?" She tried to transmit a calm she did not feel.

"No one doctor, I asked everyone to go home. We will be visiting the women secretly. It's like we have to go underground. I'm sorry I have to call you with the news, with your difficult pregnancy and all, but I thought you would want to know immediately. How are you?"

"I'm doing okay. It's good you closed the office. Tell everyone to stay home until I say otherwise and that they still have jobs with me. Visit the women the best way you can, but please be very careful, we will be of no use to them if we are dead too. I'll call you soon."

Her heart started to race as she had anticipated and she started to breathe heavily. She told herself to call Depo. Her throat tightened as the feeling of impending doom arrived. She threw on her coat, pulled on her pair of Ugg boots, grabbed her purse and fled the apartment.

"Death begets deaths." She nodded, agreeing with herself. "Why now? I don't want to go back into that hellhole. God please help me."

It was four months into the pregnancy that January of 2006 after she had been told she was carrying a set of twins; she had plunged into anguish such as she had never known before, and though she had been in that hole that is depression before, she feared to go back.

The anxiety attacks and sense of impending doom had been descending on her without any obvious provocations, and she would anticipate disaster she could not articulate. She knew foremost was the fear she would not carry the babies to term, that she would do something to kill them as she had killed her unborn child thirteen years before. They were unfinished business she had less than six months to finish or at the least get a firm handle on. They were the same business responsible for her remaining childless in spite of burning desires all her life to be a mother, *her* ghosts and evil spirits.

She suffered through the unforgiving morning sickness of early pregnancy, and as the pregnancy rolled into its second trimester, the nausea lifted significantly and the vomiting abated to only once or twice a week, from the three to four times daily that had prevented her from eating, and drained her of over twenty pounds she could not afford to lose.

But she survived it with the help of Depo, the father of the babies, and of Grant, and her two 'sisters' Moradeke and Gboye. Boris had not been left out; he provided his comforting presence in the many forms of food he tried to tantalize her palate with.

With the release from the morning sickness came the realization she was not in control of anything. She felt loose, not in control of her muscles, as she had been dropping and breaking things, nor of her bladder; she had wet the bed on many occasions, and had been leaking urine again, but this time, as her obstetrician reassured her, it was not as a result of any holes in her genitals.

The cruelest of the ghosts was the genital pain that returned. It was difficult to describe because it was a combination of discomfort, burning and a tearing sensation she used to experience when she had the keloid joining her labia majora together, but she had the corrective surgery twenty-four years before.

But she was not in control of her mind. She was full of despair and she felt disconnected from everything. She found herself lapsing into a state that was a cross between daydreaming and hallucination, with her seeing things that happened to her as a little girl growing up in Ibadan, while she was wide awake in New York City.

These visions scared her, but she realized they were the ghosts that her mind had to lay to rest, and her body had to stop feeling in the forms of leaking of urine, genital pain, smelling urine and feces, or anticipating rape where it is cherishment beckoning to her so new life could be born and nurtured in freedom. They were the ones acting out their scripts that should be dead but were still very much alive.

In spite of the fear of completely losing her mind, she had decided to wade into the ocean of her mind and take care of business this time, before she became responsible for two additional people; otherwise, she might end up like her grandmother, and do terrible things to her children when those demons nevertheless take possession of her.

The messages from the books she read were of the need to take the plunge, go into the depth of the sea or the cave, or descend into hell, go into the forest or into the hills, or answer the call to adventure, or go on that journey. Dante did it, Odysseus did it, Hercules had to do it for his own redemption; she could go on and on, and at the end they had come back with the Golden Fleece, Medusa had been beheaded and out of it was born Pegasus, the Muses and all arts, the Minotaur had been killed putting an end to the sacrifice of hope.

She understood the mythological stories as metaphors to guide everyone with their lives, so with the hope of reward of peace, she had been letting the hallucinations play out without freaking out too much, but she had not told her friends. She did not want to end up in a psychiatric hospital.

The mercy from shedding those assuaging tears had deserted her. It was an inheritance from her grandmother. Esho at her best would say to her, "Iranti, cry all you want, cry rivers of blood and not just tears, it will not make a difference." And when she was at her worst, she had given her thorough lashings for crying.

She thought of calling Depo again, but decided she would wait till he got home even though he would be angry with her for not calling him.

She felt unnecessary, worse than unnecessary, dangerous to the people close to her and the people she claimed to want to help. "But I don't know how to do any other job. The only profession I have learnt very well and have become an expert at is repairing female genitals damaged from over-enthusiastic circumcision and those that resulted in fistula from childbirth that should have been intervened with, but were not. I am jeopardizing other people's lives. This is the second time this kind of tragedy has happened to my patients.

"It's as if we are not entitled to healthy vaginas, me and the thousands of women who have come to be my patients in the past twelve years, those on whom I have performed the corrective surgery to help them restore their vagina, and thus their femininity, so they too can cross the thresholds into motherhood, lovers or just women with dignity.

"This curse born out of the cruelty of ignorance and the malignancy of fear that Esho pronounced to have been hers and her ancestors has continued to dodge my steps, no matter how much I try to overcome it."

"These things are not for us Iranti, maybe for other women but not for us,"

Esho used to say to me, and I continue to fight it, "No Esho, they can be ours too. We can be women who know we are beautiful and desirable, and that knowledge would not put us in danger or make us playthings for men. Too many books have told me that."

She recalled the phone conversation as she stood on the street and sucked in the cold air, hoping that the shock of it would still her racing heart. She started to walk briskly down the street as she told herself to transfer the anxiety to her legs.

She did not know in which direction she was going, and she was almost running when a woman coming in the opposite direction put out her left hand to stop her. "Honey, don't run in your condition, it's not good for you or the baby and the side-walks are sometimes slippery." The woman said as she came abreast of her.

She stopped and watched as the woman walked by her; she squeezed 'thanks' through her tight throat. She stood rooted to the spot and continued to stare at the woman until she rounded a corner and disappeared.

She could hear her grandmother. "Life is full of short, short stories," Esho was fond of saying. But all her stories had been tragic. As an adult, she realized it was her grandmother's way of ordering and making sense of her chaotic life. She formed it into little stories that she kept alive in her mind, so she would not forget, hoping that the not forgetting would guard her against future trauma. "And she had imparted it to me, not just the words, but the horror too, and I have learnt not to forget as well, but the not forgetting is not enough. I have known for a long time that like Esho, I have been casting angels into the roles of demons."

The wraiths between her thighs shot a harrowing pain into her brain. She twisted her thighs together in an attempt to stop it. "It is a phantom pain," she tried to reassure herself. "The phantom that replaced the keloid that replaced the fire that was supposed to be between my thighs, the fire that should have made me into a passionate woman, into a lover, into a woman who believed she is truly beautiful, but Esho removed the fire and gave me a scar in its stead."

"A few stories just happened here now," she said aloud. "The news from Fausa is one story, and the woman asking me not to run in my condition is another story.

"My head is full of stories, my great-grandmother, grandmother, mother and mine –an expectant mother. They are stories of Mothers, but tragic ones.

"Do I want the world to witness my anguish? Is that why I'm now wandering the streets? Yes. I want the world to see what I'm going through. That must be why psychotics take to the streets."

She remembered numerous vagrant psychotics in Nigeria. "They need to tell their stories. We all need witnesses and we are all looking for advocates. To be heard and understood." She shook her head in dismay.

She kept telling herself to call Depo, that he would drop whatever he was doing and come comfort her. She stopped in front of a coffee shop and looked down at what she could see of herself over her bulging abdomen. She turned around to look at her reflection through the shop window, and she acknowledged she did look crazy.

Her short cotton nightshirt was above her knees, the boots were mid calf and the short suede coat more like a jacket, did not cover much, she could not button it. Her uncombed hair was in disarray and she looked scared as she clutched her purse under her left arm. Her lips were parched. She ran her tongue over them and thought of going into the shop to get a cup of coffee.

"They will not serve me." She said aloud. "They will say to me, 'Go away please, get out of here, we do not want the likes of you in our shop.' And then they will laugh, and point at me and sing songs to ridicule me."

She stood there, trying to convince herself they would serve her, as long as she could pay for her coffee. But then the smell arrived!

"Oh God, I'm in serious trouble. God please help me, help me become a mother." She slapped her right palm against her forehead.

She stood still as people hurried past her in every direction. "Where are they going? So many stories, these people's lives are stories," she wondered as she slowly turned to look all around her.

The smell arrives like a demanding and cruel dignitary when she is at her lowest to crown her despair. Its last visit was ten years ago when her grandmother died suddenly; after she had suffered such betrayal from the man she yearned so much to have recognize her as a daughter. The smell had stayed for a year and a half, and she had dropped some thirty pounds because with her constantly smelling feces and urine, she was unable to eat.

"I need to eat this time, I'm pregnant. I can't afford not to eat."

She stood in front of the coffee shop staring at her reflection in the window as she prayed. She could hear herself sounding hollow. She did not think her prayers would be answered because she did not have Moradeke's faith. Her friend describes God as her personal friend and savior, there to help her whenever she was in difficulties.

Esho had taught her differently about God because to her we live in an impersonal universe. Her grandmother's 'god' was a combination of her destiny and fate and not someone somewhere who granted wishes. Nevertheless, she prayed she would carry the babies to term and become a mother. She desperately needed that stamp to convince herself she was a woman after all.

A police officer came up to her. In a gentle manner he took hold of her right hand. "Are you okay ma'am?" he asked.

She wanted to snatch her hand from his. That is what Esho had taught her to do. "Be careful around men, they are out to do just one thing, one thing only, and that is, ruin your life!"

Her friend Gboye had repeatedly told her, "Ranti, there are lots of kind men in the world," and Gboye would know, she grew up in a house full of men.

She looked up at the policeman and noted that he had a gentle face, not the face of a villain or someone out to ruin her life.

"I'll like to buy a cup of decaffeinated coffee, but I'm afraid they won't sell it to me."

She looked into the coffee shop and could see people looking at her with interest. "They think I am a crazy woman, *a crazy pregnant woman,* so they called the police to remove me so their customers can come in and buy coffee."

She looked at the policeman and repeated, "I will like to buy a cup of coffee, but I don't think I would be welcomed in that shop."

She did not tell him it was because she smelled of urine and feces. Gboye had advised her, "Ranti, no one can smell you, it's all in your head, but don't go around telling people that you smell, because some people could use that as a weapon against you." And Gboye had been right. It had been her ex-husband's favorite weapon against her.

"I understand. Is there someone I can call for you? It's very cold ma'am and you've been standing here for the past hour," the officer informed her.

"An hour?" she stared at him in shock as she realized that if she did not snap out of the fog quickly, she could end up in an asylum. "That will definitely kill me, especially with these panic attacks. I don't need to be locked up, I need to be free; to fly like a bird, and the other patients will just hate my guts because of this smell. You do not smell Ranti, it is a hallucination," she snapped at herself.

She looked at the officer. "I'm okay, I'm a doctor in Nigeria and some of my patients were killed. I heard the news this morning and I couldn't stay at home alone." She brought her cell phone out of her purse and showed him as if he could read the news on it. "My friends have gone to work so I came to get some coffee."

He moved closer to her as he put his left arm around her shoulder, "I'll get the coffee for you, but I have to take you to the station. It's not safe for you to stand in the streets, especially in your condition."

He escorted her to his car, opened the door and guided her into the backseat. She did not protest. He went around to the driver's seat and spoke into his phone, ordering her coffee.

A few moments later, he turned around to look at her as he handed her the coffee, at the same time asking her what happened to her patients.

She recounted her assistant's phone conversation to him.

He gave her a long look. "Good luck ma'am," he said as he turned back to the steering wheel and started to drive.

"Another story just took place between me and the officer, but it's a good story, he is not going to rape me or lock me up. See, Ranti, not all men are horrible," she reassured herself.

"Why didn't you call me?" Depo hugged her thirty minutes later when he arrived at the police station. "Ranti, you can't shut me out, we are in this together. It's not fair of you to shut me out? I'm sorry about the girls"

She stared at him, "Depo, the smell is back. And the pain in my vagina as if the keloid is still there, I smell of urine and feces."

"Oh Ranti, Ranti," Depo hugged her more to him.

2

The technician coursed the paddle over Ranti's abdomen as she pointed out the different parts of her unborn babies to her and Depo. He was excited as he tenderly caressed her left hand held in his.

He smiled at her but she nodded as she looked away from the monitor. She could not share his excitement. She did not want to see the babies because her trained eyes might pick out their gender, and she did not want to know.

The technician informed them the babies were doing as well as could be expected at their age of eighteen weeks, as she concluded her examination. They thanked her as she left the room. Depo helped her down from the couch and into her clothes. She smiled her gratitude to him, especially for not insisting this time as he had at the other times that they be told the gender of the babies.

He had told her it would help him begin to bond with them if he knew if they were he or she. Then, they could pick out names and start to address them by the names as well as developing mental pictures, but she was afraid that if she knew the sex of the babies, it might jeopardize their wellbeing. She unsuccessfully tried to explain this to him.

They walked out of the hospital into the cold air. Depo wrapped his arms around her, "Let me take you home and stay with you today Ranti," he offered again.

She knew he was afraid that if he left her alone, he would get another call from the police that they picked her off the streets again. She still had not cried and the anxiety attacks had stayed put as well as the smell. If she had cried, it would have reassured Depo who had been saying repeatedly, "It's okay to cry in a situation like this."

Grant had actually wept when he arrived home and they told him the news. Ranti had wondered, '*Crying more than the bereaved.*'

"Depo, I'll be fine, you can't baby-sit me forever, you've got to work, don't worry, the police won't pick me off the street again, I'll walk to Boris' diner and if anything happens, I promise, I will call you."

He looked at her for a moment, flagged down a taxi and ushered her into it. "I will take you to Boris and personally hand you over to him."

Depo recounted the tragic news and the event of the previous day to Boris as he left Ranti with him. The older man gave her a comforting hug. Ranti kissed him on the cheek and got out of his way to sit in her corner of the diner.

Boris was busy with the lunch crowd who were filing in already, and Ranti watched him as he maneuvered himself around his customers with a kind word here, a hug there, a pat on the back over there. He moved around briskly for his eighty-four years. She kept staring at him and at some point he caught her eyes and winked at her. She gave him a weak smile.

She wished he was not busy so he could sit with her. She loved his comforting presence. Boris was one of those people you could be with for a whole day, not exchange a word, and you still know they were holding you in their mind, and he was a man of very few words.

Her phone rang, startling her out of her reverie. She fished it out of her purse. Gboye was hysterical. It took Ranti a while to comprehend what she was saying and she became alarmed because Gboye never panicked. She liked to think of herself as a 'cool man' in control of her situation.

Ranti blames her name for that attitude. Gboye's parents gave her a traditionally boy's name, and she believed she had to live up to the name by detesting all things gentle and kind which to her were 'feminine and weak.'

"Where are you?" she yelled, "We are coming into the city later today. We need to talk, my life as I know it is over. I'm on the train and Moradeke said she would be there at about three- thirty. Where are you?" she demanded again.

"I'm here in New York City, the place where you are headed." Ranti wondered, "Why is she not flying?" She answered herself. "She does not fly when she is pregnant."

"You are pregnant!" she shouted accusingly into the phone but Gboye cut her off, "I will see you at about three, where are you? You know I'm not coming to that den of sodomites so we have to meet somewhere acceptable to me."

"I'm at Boris' diner, you know where that is, don't you?" Ranti snapped at her with a lot of irritation as she disconnected. She asked herself again, why she had remained friends with Gboye. "She is such a bully. She is the most arrogant, opinionated, close-minded person I know. She hardly ever has a kind word to say about anyone or anything. I must have some deep masochistic needs," she concluded.

"No, at the lowest points of my life, she has always been there for me, taking care of me even though it is in her crude manner." She remembered that time at the age of seven. Gboye had been the only person in the whole school who would speak to her. "That is why I will always be her friend."

She got up to get some coffee and waddled back to her seat as she looked out into the street. The man was outside again with his dogs. He was in a pair of faded jeans, a brown turtle neck sweater and brown boots. Ranti admired his muscular broad shoulder as they stretched out the sweater.

"He is about five eleven at the least. He is about Depo's height. I love his face; it is so gentle, such a calm face. He is a handsome man, and he is so dark, in fact he has Depo's complexion. Gosh!" she caressed her throat with her right hand, "I have a crush on another Depo! That is pathetic, Ranti, just pathetic!" She sighed in resignation.

He tied the leash on the dogs to a post and came into the diner. She kept staring at him and he stared back at her. She averted her gaze. He chatted with Boris as he paid for his takeout food and coffee, but this time instead of leaving like he usually did, he came toward her corner. Her heart started to race.

She had been hoping he would speak to her since the first time she saw him at the diner. That was about eight months ago, but then she had become pregnant and had given up any hope he would ever talk to her. Besides she had told herself she was dreaming. "Men who look like him do not talk to women who look like me."

But each time that thought had come to her, she knew she was being irrational. The world had continued to tell her she was a beautiful woman, even though it was unbelievable to her. Then she concluded he would think she was married. "Who dates a pregnant woman anyway?"

"Hello, what are you having?" he asked in a friendly manner.

Her heart jumped again, and so did the babies. She looked at him and out at his dogs; they were restlessly moving around, in all shapes, colors and sizes. He was holding a bag and disposable gloves. "Dog walker," she informed herself. "Just decaf latte," she answered him.

"No, I mean the baby, boy or girl?" He pointed to her abdomen.

Ranti looked down at her abdomen and caressed it. "I don't know. I don't want to know." She shook her head. "There are two of them in there."

"Oh? Why not, you want to be surprised?"

"I guess," she shrugged.

"When are you due?" He made himself comfortable sitting across from her.

"In twenty weeks."

"That's like four, no five months."

"Uhn," she nodded.

"Good luck, you should do it more often, I mean, get pregnant more often. It looks great on you."

Ranti nodded. "Be careful! No!" She snapped at herself trying to shake her grandmother's voice loose from where it was lodged in her head. "There are lots of good men in the world, Esho," she informed her deceased grandmother in her mind.

"You mind if I sit? I see you here a lot, and I feel bad that we haven't talked. I've been watching you for the past few months, it's like you bloom more and more each time I see you. Boris says you are his friend."

She stared at him and nodded again, "Yes, he baby-sits me during the day."

"No wedding ring eh?'

She shook her head, "I'm pregnant out of wedlock."

"Sorry. I say stupid things sometimes." He hesitated. "I might as well come out with it. I was just trying to find out if you are seeing someone. I have wanted to ask you out since the first time I saw you here about nine months ago, but I was slow. I am slow, then I noticed the pregnancy and I concluded you must be in a committed relationship, but then I asked Boris and he told me you were not seeing anyone. Maybe you'll like to have coffee with me sometimes. Oh, we're having coffee together now," he smiled. "So, maybe dinner some time. That's all."

Ranti continued to stare at him. She was feeling light headed from the heart palpitations and from not having eaten in two days. She could not believe her ears. "He actually asked me out. He dates pregnant women!" she informed herself.

"You must eat, right? You have to eat for the babies at least," he smiled encouragingly at her.

"I should but I'm not, I've always had an ambivalent relationship with food and that has never been a good thing. My doctor is not happy with me. This is a time to have a good relationship with food." She stopped herself before she told him about the smell.

"Jack." He offered her his right hand as he transferred his plastic bag and gloves to his left hand.

Ranti stared at his hands as she thought of him picking up after his dogs. "What the hell," she said to herself, "I smell of urine and feces anyway." She offered him her right hand as she told him her name.

"I know, and you are from Nigeria. Boris told me," he smiled.

She stared out at his dogs and passersby. He looked out the window as well.

"So what do you say? About that dinner, it's got to be somewhere else, not here, you know Boris closes at four and besides this is practically home for you. What kinds of food do you like, Italian, Chinese?"

She drank some more of her lukewarm coffee and continued to stare at the people on the street. She wanted to tell him the only thing she put into her stomach these days was decaffeinated coffee, in gallons.

She remembered as a little girl how she had hated to eat because the food made her sick. Esho would yell at her to eat, and then she would become frustrated with her and force-feed her.

Esho would sit on a low stool and spread her legs apart. She would tuck her wrapper under her butt to cover her underwear. She would then grab Ranti and sling her across her lap, pin the lower half of her body under her left armpit, and with her right hand block off her nostrils so she would not be able to breathe; that would force her to open her mouth and Esho would pour in the cornmeal.

Ranti would gulp down the liquid meal so she could breathe through her mouth. The feeding usually lasted less than a minute, but to her it felt like an eternity because she was convinced she would die from asphyxiation.

Esho had continued to feed her in this way until she was seven years old, when she grew too big and would struggle so hard that Esho could not restrain her anymore, and she had come to hate the liquid cornmeal and had never tasted it again.

In medical school she appreciated that the force-feeding saved her from malnutrition, as she saw many children who had either Marasmus or Kwashiorkor, but she also realized how dangerous it was, because several children brought to the emergency room died when they aspirated the food being forced into them.

"I want to eat so I can carry these babies to term without any complications. The sun is coming out more it seems," she observed, still looking out the window. "I miss the hot sun on my skin, and I miss the sky and open space you can see for miles as in the savannah of northern Nigeria. I don't like New York City," she concluded, "It's so cluttered with all these skyscrapers that I can't even think."

She turned her attention back to the man in front of her. "I don't know, Jack. I'm not feeling too well. I'll see you around here won't I? We can talk some more about having that dinner, okay?"

"Are you doing this pregnancy thing by yourself? I just want to get to know you. You are a very beautiful woman, and I might miss my chance and regret it for the rest of my life," he apologetically explained to her.

"Yes Ranti, he's right, and Esho was wrong, you are a beautiful woman, and he's not a pervert or out to rape you, this is what normal men and women do. They speak to one another and go on dates with one another, and if it works out, they become lovers," she lectured herself.

She said aloud, "No, it's okay; I'll like to go out with you, just not now. I'm not up to it."

"Good enough for me, take it easy and if there is anything I can do, like lift heavy furniture, walk the dog, grocery shopping, accompany you to the doctors, walk with you to the museum, keep undeserving men away, anything, I will be happy to do it for you." He smiled at her and digging into his pocket he gave her his card.

Ranti smiled and thanked him as he left. She looked in Boris' direction and he winked at her. She shook her head at him.

"See, men who look like that do talk to women who look like me," she informed herself as she watched Jack leave with his dogs.

3

"I know why I feel terrible, it's because I've not worked in seventeen months. I've got too much time to think." Ranti agonized. She knew the hallucination/skits were connected to her anxiety. She was in full possession of all her history. That had been one gift from her grandmother. Moradeke and Gboye told her it's a bad quality to have though.

"Yes, it helped you in medical school to have a photographic memory but in life it's good to forget some things, sometimes." They told her many times.

"Iranti, don't forget that this happened to you today, do you hear me? Don't you ever forget it! That is why I gave you the name 'Memory.' If you forget anything that ever happened to you in this life you are as good as dead." Her grandmother had drummed into her ears and Ranti had not been able to forget anything. "It would be good to forget some things, sometimes, like the cause of these smells," she thought as tears welled up in her eyes.

Boris signaled to her from behind the cash register to come with him. The crowd had dwindled down to a few people his assistants could manage. She pulled herself up from her chair and went to meet him. He pulled her along with him toward the back of the diner and up the stairs to his apartment. He helped her into a chair in his living room as he draped a blanket over her knees. He sat next to her.

He looked at her for a moment and stood up, went to the record player and put an album on. He came toward her but he did not sit. He towered over her with his five feet ten inches frame, slightly bent with age.

Ranti looked up at him and felt such a warm rush of affection for him. She had the urge to caress his face that was full of lines, and trace out each one of them so they could tell her their story. Tears stood in her eyes.

The record started to play.

"Dance with me Ranti." Boris gave her a bow.

She smiled, but shook her head no, pointing to her big abdomen.

"Okay, I dance with Ranti and the babies then," he said in his Russian accent.

He helped her up and took her in his arms. He started to move her around the room ever so gently, and the tears started to stream down her face. She was grateful that the tears finally came.

Boris looked down at her and smiled. "You look like my mother when you cry, Ranti. You look so much like her. She was beautiful with so much pain. Oh, so much pain. She was a beautiful woman, very beautiful woman."

He continued to move her gently around the floor, and Ranti settled into his arms with her head on his chest. She continued to cry. The music was poignant, the lyric was in Russian, so she did not know what the woman was saying but it was dripping with pain.

The song ended. The album scratched to an end from being old. Boris disengaged her from his arms and kissed the top of her head. "It is good to dance with beautiful woman, thank you."

Ranti sat down and Boris slowly walked over to the record player, took off the record and put it back into its jacket. He came back and sat next to her. "Ranti, so much pain, I'll tell you a story. My mother was a very beautiful woman, and so was my wife, Anya. Beautiful here and beautiful here," he touched his face and his chest.

"We were married for fifty-eight years, but no children. She wanted children, but we didn't have children. I loved her so much. But today, I'll tell you about my mother. She knew about pain. She used to say to me, 'Boris, you go to America, there you will become a good man.' I didn't know how I will go to America but she told me every day." He paused.

"Now, my father," he shook his head regretfully. "He was a big man, and a very angry man. Everyday he would hit my mother. He did not drink so it was not the bottle that turned his head. He would come home very angry and hit her.

"Every morning she would cry with so much pain, not pain in her body, but pain in her heart, and she would say to me, 'Boris go to America and become a good man,' and I would say to her, 'okay Ma, I will go to America and become a good man.'

"I was sixteen, I came home and she was there as usual sitting at the table, but she was dead. She just died. Her heart that knew so much pain just broke and she died."

He paused for a moment and Ranti stared at him.

"The next thing I know Ranti, I am twenty years old and I am in America. I was in an asylum. It was like I just woke up." He snapped his fingers to emphasize his point. "I thought I was sixteen but they told me I couldn't be sixteen because when I came to them four years before, I told them I was sixteen.

"Four years and I don't remember! I remember the day I came home from school and my mother was sitting at the table and her heart had broken, and then

I remembered being told I am not sixteen anymore and I had been in America for four years.

"They were playing this record I just played for you, the day I started to remember again. My mother, she would play it and she would dance with me and she would cry, and she would cook for me. I remembered my name, Boris. How I came to America, I did not know.

"In the asylum they asked me what I could do. I said I could cook, so they put me in the kitchen and I cooked. They liked my food. One year after I started to remember and I was told I was not sixteen anymore but twenty, they told me I could go. They found a job for me at a restaurant and I cook at the restaurant.

"Anya came to eat at the restaurant with her friends and I cook for her. She liked my food, so I played the record for her and she cried. I decided to marry her and two years later we got married.

"I tried to be a good man like I promised my Ma. I worked very hard. Anya and me, we bought the diner in 1955. I cook for people every day and they like it and I am happy.

"Anya before she died, she told me she loved me. She said to me, "You are a great man Boris." She died and my heart broke but I did not forget like when my mother died. I told myself I will never forget again. So my heart broke and it hurts and I cried every day, and so what?

"Then one day, two years to the day my Anya died, you," he pointed to her, "Ranti, you stand in the rain in front of the diner, crying. I came out to meet you and I asked you to come in from the rain. You said it was okay, that you were fine. You were mugged. You had a cut on your arm and it was bleeding. It was very heavy rain, and you did not have a coat. I begged you to come in, and you refused. I said to you, okay, I will stand in the rain with you. You looked at me and you came in and I cooked for you and you ate everything and you cried. I said to myself, my dear wife Anya sent her to me, she wants me to take care of her."

The tears continued to stream down Ranti's face. Boris looked at her for a while. "Agh! Life!" he shook his head. "You weep for so much in life but in the end it all makes sense. Like you, like Depo and Grant, like the babies." He paused again.

"You know cross-word puzzle? My Anya, she liked crossword puzzle, every day she did crossword puzzle. You see, life is like crossword puzzle, things happen to you and they hurt and then they scatter around, because you don't like them and you want to forget them. But, you have to pick them and not forget them and put them back together. You connect them and then life, it makes sense and you understand and then it doesn't hurt so much.

"If not for my Ma, Anya would not have come into my life. If I did not connect the dots after Anya died, Ranti, I would have forgotten again, and I would not have found you when Anya sent you to me." He moved over to Ranti and kissed her on the cheek.

Her phone rang jarringly, interrupting them. She looked at Boris and he signaled to her to take the call. It was Depo checking on her.

Boris suggested she lay on the couch and rest, because he needed to return to the diner.

Ranti thought, "Always complete a narrative by connecting all the little, little stories together. Don't let them stand alone by themselves, unrelated and unconnected, because that is when they become ghosts and demons that scare the hell out of everyone, like these smell of urine and feces, like this pain in my vagina, like this anxiety attack, and like this fear of not carrying this pregnancy to term or of giving birth to one or two baby girls, or the fears of allowing a man hold me. I will like Jack to hold me and make love to me."

She remembered: *"It did not seem so difficult. Only connect! Only connect the prose and the passion, and both will be exalted, and human love will be seen at its highest. Live in fragments no longer. Only connect, and the beast and the monk, robbed of the isolation that is life to either, will die."*

She knew that until she connected her little, little stories and her grandmother's little, little stories as well as her mother's little, little stories together into one full tale, including the pain and the tears, she will continue to smell feces and urine, and have anxiety attacks, because, by not connecting the dots, she continues to live in fragments.

"Boris forgot when his mother died. I have not forgotten, but I'm still living in fragments, and in the same way I am being told *'you are not sixteen anymore, you are twenty.'*

"Esho, you would have loved Boris if you had met him. He belonged to the category of men you did not believe existed. He is a very kind man." She told her grandmother in her mind again.

4

"What is the big emergency?" Moradeke demanded of Ranti an hour later as she burst into Boris' living room. "I had to cancel a room full of patients in the middle of the week, and I drove three hours from Delaware. This had better be good because I'm losing money."

Ranti smiled at her, "It's good to see you Moradeke." She stood up to hug her and help her out of her coat.

Moradeke gave her a quick hug and a peck on the cheek. She dropped her purse on the floor and stood across from Ranti with her hands on her hips, inspecting her.

Ranti looked at her friend whom she had not seen in over a month. Moradeke had always been beautiful to her; right from the first time they met in their all-girl secondary school at the age of ten. She had maintained her girlish figure over the years with her height of five feet six inches, and at the age of forty-one she still had the sparkle in her eyes as well, but she had lost her flawless complexion that would have made you yearn for a cup of hot chocolate on a cold night.

For some reasons, Moradeke believed she would be even more beautiful if she was light complexioned and her husband would find her more attractive, and so had always bleached her skin. Her friends hated this about her, and Ranti had always been confounded by the idea because she just could not get it.

"What did Gboye tell you?" Moradeke interrupted her thoughts.

"She said she was on the train coming in from Boston and you were on your way. I think she's pregnant again. She said her life as she knew it was over, whatever that means."

"That doesn't mean she's pregnant. Did she tell you she was pregnant?" Moradeke snapped.

"No, she's coming by train; you know, when she's pregnant, she's afraid of flying."

Moradeke looked preoccupied as she continued to inspect Ranti. "That doesn't mean she's pregnant, maybe she couldn't get a flight. Are you still losing weight?" She yelled at her. "You are pregnant with twins and you keep losing weight, this is your chance to eat whatever you like and get away with it. Are you okay? You look terrible, and scared. Ranti, what's going on? And why are you at Boris' and not at Depo's?"

Ranti sat on the couch and pulled the blanket over her legs. "I'm having anxiety attacks, and I smell of feces and urine again and so I haven't been eating."

"No you do not smell darling, we've told you many times that it's a delusion. You do not smell of urine or feces. I love you and you know I won't lie to you and neither will Gboye. You know her, even at times when a white lie could help; she will let you have it. You don't smell darling. It's the depression coming back again. Why?" Moradeke sat down next to her and took her left hand in hers.

Ranti shook her head in resignation as she sighed. "I feel so unnecessary Moradeke. I feel like I'm taking up useful space on the face of the earth and a danger to people. Three years ago I operated on these girls, four lovely girls, they were in their late teens, two of them had fistulae, they had babies at the ages of thirteen and fourteen years and the other two had infibulations.

"They were doing well, we enrolled them in trade school and got them an apartment; anyway they were murdered two days ago. The neighbors accused them of prostitution. I gave them their sexual freedom and they were killed for it. What am I doing? This is the second time this has happened. What is the point of it all? I just want to matter, that is all I ask of life. I just want to matter, to be somebody."

"Why didn't you call me? Oh Ranti. Jeez." Moradeke hugged her.

Gboye exploded into the room at that moment, because she does not walk into a room, at a height of six feet, carrying some two hundred and sixty pounds; she made sure everyone knew when she arrived on the scene.

"Let's get out of here," she announced. "You know Boris closes at four and I'm not sitting in this cramped room. Let's go eat. I'm starving."

Ranti and Moradeke looked at her and she stared back at them, taking them in one at a time. She zeroed in on Ranti.

"You keep losing weight!" She accused her in disgust as she pointed her right index finger at her. "What is wrong with you, don't you want these babies, you want to have another miscarriage?"

"Her patients were killed, Gboye, she's upset about that." Moradeke yelled at her.

"I've told you many times to quit that charity nonsense. It isn't going to change anything. I keep telling you but you won't listen to me. People don't change. Those people will keep cutting off their daughters cunts, get that into your head. They hate women in that part of the world. Do you think you can go amongst them and change what they've been doing since the beginning of time?

"As far as I'm concerned that whole country is cursed. The last time I was there, I brought some earth back with me. You know what that means don't you? It means, I am never going back there, never! You were about the most brilliant student in our class in medical school, Ranti, what have you done with all that brain?"

She paused to take a deep breath. Moradeke stood up to try to stop her tirade but she would not let her. Gboye put up her left hand as a warning for her to stay away and Moradeke backed down.

"Do you guys remember Daniel? He failed every exam when we were in school, well so much for that. He's a pediatrician now, and doing very well too, he has a thriving practice in Mississippi, or somewhere down there, the only pediatrician for miles. He is making a killing and what are you doing? You are being a martyr for Nigeria.

"Mark my word, the next time you show your face in that place, they will lynch you for trying to corrupt their girls, because that is how they see it. Any girl that hasn't had her cunt cut and sewn together to make sure she is not having sex, or tries to go to school and be a person in her own right, is corrupt.

"I don't know how you can even go amongst those people. I don't know what to call them, barbaric? These are the same people who wanted to stone a woman of childbearing age to death, for becoming pregnant! Have you forgotten? Other people in the world are splitting atoms, discovering new planets and finding cures for deadly diseases, but what are they doing in Nigeria? They are cutting baby girls' vaginas.

"Do you know what their destiny in this world is?" She paused and stared at her friends. She continued, "Their destiny is to be the museum for the rest of the world. Very soon, when developed and progressive people want to remember how life was centuries long gone, they will travel to Nigeria. They wouldn't have to go to the Louvre or the Smithsonian anymore. They will just travel to Nigeria and watch the barbarians go at it.

"They are worse than animals. I have never heard of any group of animals cutting off each other's genitals. You can argue that it's because they don't have opposable thumbs, but they have fangs and claws, yet they don't do it. I'm grateful I'm from a home where they don't practice that nonsense because unlike you Ranti, I am not a saint. If anyone had done that to me, I would have burnt down the whole town when I grew up. For someone to deprive me of the ability to enjoy sex? The whole ethnic group would have paid because I would have killed people."

She lowered her voice and attempted to sound gentle, "You are a fine surgeon Ranti, you are Board certified to practice as an Obstetrician and a Gynecologist in this country; you graduated from your residency training thirteen years ago, you could be making millions of dollars by now, but what do you have to your name? You rely on Depo for money, and you spend your life doing a thankless job that is getting people killed and putting your life in danger." She took another deep breath. "Tell me something, how much are you worth and what do you have to your name? Uhn?"

Ranti and Moradeke were quiet.

"I thought as much, not a dime. That is how Nigeria thanks you for trying to help. Kill your patients and if you are there, they will kill you too, just like they tried to do ten years ago. You have yourself to blame."

"Those are comforting words Gboye," Moradeke interrupted in a sarcastic tone of voice. "We can always count on you to put things in perspective for us since you are an authority on everything, but the important thing is Ranti is hurting, and yelling at her and calling her a failure is not what she needs now. Besides she might not be as rich as you are, but what she is doing is commendable and more of us should do that. It wouldn't hurt you, if once in a while you go to Gbobi orthopedic hospital in Lagos to volunteer your time, or if I go once in a while to volunteer my time as an internist.

"It wouldn't hurt, Gboye, and remember that our escape from genital mutilation was just a chance of geography. People in our part of the country mutilate their daughters' genitals too. Ranti is a Yoruba girl, and that was her experience. So if someone is doing more of what all of us should be doing, I think we should be a little bit more supportive of her."

"No," Gboye shook her head, wagging her right index finger at Moradeke, "you are not going to get me to feel guilty, no way. I don't care about Nigeria; do you know why? Because Nigeria doesn't give a chicken shit about me! And I have paid my dues with the lives of people who are dear to me, and that is enough payments.

"When armed robbers killed my cousin, I paid whatever debt I owed Nigeria there and then. And if Ranti chooses to continue to go there, that's her problem. I have bigger fish to fry and that's why I asked you to meet me here for some support."

She turned to Ranti, "I didn't mean to be so cold but I don't care about Nigeria and that's the truth."

They were quiet for a while. Gboye stayed on her feet and they could hear Boris closing the diner. "Let's get out of here, I'm starving and I need to talk to the two of you, let's go to Guilds." She said again.

5

"So what's the big news?" Moradeke asked after they were seated and had ordered their food at the restaurant.

Gboye looked at her friends as she announced, "I'm pregnant."

Ranti was busy with her palpitations and trying to concentrate on her breathing. She had started to feel light headed after Gboye yelled at her. She was afraid she would faint, so she promised herself that when her food arrived, she would force herself to eat some of it.

"Please tell me you didn't drag me down here to tell me that, because if it is so, you owe me four thousand dollars and I will kill you! What is news about you being pregnant again? You have six boys already! And it's time you started giving birth control some serious thoughts, oh gosh Gboye, what is wrong with you? You just have to overdo everything don't you?" Moradeke was livid with anger.

"I'm really scared here. I think Olu will leave me. I don't want to lose him, he's a good man."

"And why would he do a crazy thing like that, is he out of his mind? You have been cheating on him all of your married life, sleeping with anything in pants and bringing home illegitimate children and he has been taking care of them, not suspecting a thing...." Moradeke started, but Gboye bursting into tears stopped her.

Ranti was shocked as well, and her palpitations took a pause as she stared at Gboye. "Gosh! What a strange day," she thought.

"I'm about two months pregnant and the baby is not Olu's. The baby is Chinese." Gboye blurted out between sobs.

"Actually, God is a Chinese woman," Ranti quoted to herself as she remembered a colleague telling her when she was in residency training. His argument had been that since the Chinese were the most populous race in the world, God must be Chinese, and since women were more numerous than men, so God is a woman.

Ranti stared at Gboye as Moradeke's jaw dropped in disbelief. They remained speechless as the waiter arrived with their food and arranged it in front of them. Ranti could not feel her legs. She wondered how she would get up and walk when the time came for her to go home.

"I can't pass this baby off as his. I've overdone it this time," Gboye lamented. "He will leave me and take the children. The court will give him custody because he stayed home to take care of them, and has been working part time since Jide started preschool." She paused. "None of those kids are his and he's going to win them."

"What? Not one of those kids is his?" Moradeke asked in shock. "Did you know this Ranti, and how come I don't know this?" she gave Ranti a questioning look. "Gboye, you mean, not even one of your children is Olu's?" She asked again.

Moradeke could not hide her triumph. "Well, you need some punishment for all your sins. Do you think it feels good to be cheated on? The wages of sin is death, Gboye, and you just died a little this time. I'm not sorry for you. You had it coming. You've had it coming for a very long time." She paused for a moment. "You know what? I quit this job! I quit this job of being friends with the two of you, I've had it." She raised her hands in resignation. "I don't even know what I'm doing with the two of you, honestly I don't. What is wrong with you two? Ranti, I'm talking to you as well. What is the matter with you and Gboye? Can't I just have normal women as friends? Gboye, you are worse than a prostitute and Ranti, you condone her lifestyle. God forbid you should 'judge' anyone. You live with two gay men, and your best friend is a fornicator, oh no, you cannot judge anyone, can you Iranti Jare?"

By this time Ranti's heart was pounding so much it felt as if her head was bobbing up and down in a jackhammer manner, in sync with her pounding heart. Her ears were roaring. She held her hands to the sides of her head to hold it in place. She thought of asking them if her head was actually bobbing up and down. Gboye was in tears and it is scary to see Gboye in tears. Moradeke looked sick.

Ranti wondered again why the two of them continued to be friends. They were the exact opposite of one another. Gboye had always cheated on her husband and boyfriends before then. Ranti had never been able to comprehend the behavior, but she saw her difficulties as a variant of her own. She does not have sex at all while Gboye cannot seem to get enough sex.

Moradeke hated Gboye for her affairs, because she was a devout born-again Christian, and to her, having extramarital affairs ranked high on the list of sins that were unforgivable. Ranti wanted to say something to comfort Gboye, but as usual, she could not find the words. She was terrified that Gboye was in tears because she had always been the one to take charge of situations, even though she had always gone overboard. She finally convinced her right hand to take hold of Gboye's left hand in a comforting gesture. Her heart continued to race and she was finding it more and more difficult to breath. They did not touch their food.

"This is a wicked hallucination, no one deserves this," Ranti said to herself, convinced that the whole scene was part of her delusions like the smell.

All of a sudden Gboye exclaimed as she quickly dried her tears, "Don't look but incoming at three o'clock."

Moradeke spontaneously snapped her head to three o'clock.

Ranti pushed back her chair to give her abdomen room as she laid her head on her arms on the table. She was feeling dizzy. She rummaged in her purse for her phone to call Depo to come get her from the restaurant immediately.

"I told you not to look," Gboye yelled at Moradeke, "now he's coming over."

"Well, well, well, what a surprise. Females, I won't call you ladies, and we all know why. Anyway, whenever I see three or more ladies together in a restaurant, especially in New York City I think of Sex and the City. But seeing the three of you together, the thought that popped into my head is 'Tragedy in the City.'" Brian laughed at his play of words.

"Jesus, I have really lost my mind. Now my hallucination is of my ex-husband too." Ranti started to weep.

"No, Irish, you are the Tragedy in the City." Gboye shot back at him, her tears forgotten. She had always called him Irish because he was a Yoruba man with Irish names.

"I've been hoping to run into my ex-wife at the least. I keep saying to myself, New York City isn't that big, I'm bound to run into her sometimes and I just had to see her pregnant. You know it digs into some deep part for a man when his wife refuses to carry his child to term, and goes ahead to get pregnant for her gay best friend.

"I thought she was as barren as the desert, you know with all the cutting and messing around her grandmother did on her vagina, and the times we were together, she was as frigid as the north pole, nothing there, but then I started to hear this rumor that she was pregnant, and I said to myself, four years of marriage and she didn't give me a child. The only time she became pregnant, what did she do? She lost the pregnancy. This, I've got to see with my eyes. People have been wondering how you did it, Ranti. Some said you and Depo finally had sex, but I said No, Depo couldn't get it up. Not for any woman. Not if his life depended on it. Some said you had in-vitro fertilization, or even an egg donor." He laughed again.

"There you are, darling. I've been looking for you." A sultry voice said to Brian.

"Oh this is your latest trophy wife. They keep getting younger and younger. You know, Irish, one of these days an irate father is going to get the police to charge you with statutory rape, or even shoot you himself," Gboye warned him.

"Honey," Brian said to his wife. "I want you to meet the three most tragic women in history. They are physicians; really smart women. But you know what? Their lives are pathetic. This one here," he pointed at Gboye, "she is an orthopedic surgeon in Boston, on staff at Harvard medical school, one of the best in the world."

Gboye gave a mock bow as she said, "thank you."

He continued, "But personally, I think she's a man under all that façade. Her husband stays at home and she earns the bacon. She has six boys, but none from her weakling of a husband, and she sleeps with anything in pants. She begged me once in medical school to sleep with her but I have better taste.

"This one, her name is Moradeke. She is an internist, in private practice somewhere in Delaware, makes well over half a million dollars a year, I hear. She has three beautiful children, but she is a religious fanatic and she would like to be a white woman. She had the most gorgeous skin when she was younger but that's history now.

"And here is my ex-wife, she has a photographic memory; incidentally, her name means 'Memory,' so go figure. And she is amazing with a knife. I told you her story already. She is pregnant for her gay best friend. Ranti is in love with the one man in the world who can never marry her or have sex with her." He paused. "Cat got your tongue, Gboye?"

"What is your name, peroxide, and how old are you?" Gboye asked Brian's wife as she tried to imitate her sultry voice. She did not wait for an answer. "Do you know that your husband is a rapist?"

Ranti's head snapped up so fast that it made her dizzy for about half of a minute, as Moradeke yelled, "Are you out of your mind, Gboye, don't you have any self-control?"

"Oh yes, I have a lot of self-control otherwise I would have given Irish a repeat of the performance I gave him thirteen years ago when I beat the crap out of him. Oh yes I have a lot of self-control. His wife should know he's a rapist. How many times did you rape my friend? Answer me. How many times? Until she stabbed you, do you want me to give her details? You are right; Ranti is *great* with knives. You know very well how great she is with knives."

"Gboye, please," Ranti managed to squeeze out, "please stop. Enough."

"And you raped your second wife too. I met her in Boston, she told me. You also raped your third wife, I'm sure of that."

"She's lying, she's a crazy woman and she's lying," Brian started, but Gboye was not done.

She was snapping her fingers and shaking her head furiously as she continued, "Do you know why he wasn't convicted when he cut my friend's vagina? Because Ranti stabbed him, and he almost died. The prosecutor advised the two of them to drop the whole thing. I told Ranti at the time, he's a sex offender, I'll get the best lawyer in this country for you and we will send his smelling ass to prison for a long time. You should know what your husband is capable of."

Brian's wife had heard enough; she made for the door. Brian out of sheer frustration snapped his fingers at Gboye as he started running after his wife.

"What you are going do to get even with me? I'll kick your ass again, rapist." She yelled after him.

People in the restaurant were staring at them. Their waiter came to ask if there was a problem. Gboye told him Brian was just leaving.

Ranti was sweating profusely. The smell of urine and feces became so intense that she started to gag. She felt stifled and had difficulty breathing. She looked at her food and the fries looked like golden worms. She gagged, and tried to swallow hard.

"How bizarre," she kept saying over and over again, "How bizarre, it's as if my whole life has been condensed into the past two days. Guys, I think I'm going to faint," was the last thing she remembered saying.

6

Ranti panicked on waking up and finding herself in the hospital. She quickly ran her hand over her abdomen to check if she was still pregnant. The babies kicked to reassure her. The clock said it was two in the afternoon. The palpitations and the smell were still there.

"They brought you in the night before. Your blood sugar was very low, and you were dehydrated," a nurse informed her half an hour later.

Ranti remembered her friends and all the bizarreness of the day before. She was dismayed at her choice of hallucination—Gboye pregnant with a Chinese baby? Running into her ex-husband and Gboye telling his wife how he tore up her vagina? She shuddered.

She dozed off. Depo kissing her on the cheek woke her an hour later. He and Grant were in the room. They took turns to hug her.

"You gave us a scare yesterday, Ranti. I came to get you, and you had just fainted. Gboye was screaming. I have never seen her like that. Her massive frame was heaving as she sobbed, hooofff, what a sight? I didn't know anything could scare that Amazon of a woman. She and I stayed the night with you, but she left this morning, she said it was her surgery day. Moradeke said she would be back later tonight.

"Ranti, the doctors are giving you nutrition through the veins again, you have to start eating. You've lost twenty pounds since the beginning of this pregnancy and it's dangerous for you and the babies. Please honey, you have to eat."

"I'm sorry Depo, I'm trying, but with this anxiety and now this smell, I don't know." She trailed off.

"Ranti, they will keep you here until you start to eat on your own because you can't afford to lose any more weight. Just try honey, maybe something small at first, you used to love to drink Coke, why don't we start with that?" He paused, "I told the doctor about the panic attacks and he said he would send a psychiatrist to see you, so I called Dr O, and he said he would be in early tomorrow to see you."

Ranti thought of Boris in an asylum for four years because he did not remember after his mother died. "I remember, so it will be horrible for me if they send me to an asylum."

She was very hungry and would like to eat, but each time she imagined herself eating, it was as if she was feeding herself feces, and then she began to gag. "I can't be locked up, if they lock me up my heart will break and I will die, just like Boris' mother," she thought.

"Depo, I want to go back to northern Nigeria." She announced. "I know what's giving me these anxiety attacks, it's this city. It's too cluttered and I am choking here. I miss Nigeria with the space and the sky you can see for miles. Just let me go back, I'll be fine, the babies will be fine and I'll come back in time to have them. Please."

Depo lay on the bed next to her. Grant went to sit on the single chair across from them. "I can't let you go, Ranti. It's not safe, not just because you are pregnant. Your assistant called this morning to warn you that you can't come back for now. Some people broke into your office and destroyed your furniture and burnt your records. They assaulted the chief surgeon at the hospital who has been very helpful to you.

"She left for the south with a lot of your patients she could round up within twenty-four hours, they had to run out of town. The police and the religious leaders are blaming you for subjecting these girls to these assaults. They said you are endangering their lives because by repairing their damaged genitals, you are giving them sexual license. I can't let you go back, I just can't."

Grant interrupted, "I hope you have your records on electronic files like I taught you. I hope you didn't leave them in your offices because they must have been destroyed. You can fight this, Ranti; your records of the work you've been doing are vital documents.

"It may not be the time to talk about this but you could make a presentation to the United Nations or Amnesty International, and lots of women's organizations all over the world will listen to you and fund you in ways that these girls will be safer; and if these killers are brought to justice, and they must be brought to justice, you wouldn't feel this hopeless."

Ranti closed her eyes. Grant had been encouraging her since they met ten years ago to let the world know about her work. As a human rights lawyer, he was very passionate about her work and had even bought her a laptop after her last one was broken, and taught her electronic filing. But she had remained terrified.

She knew she had been doing some remarkable work in Nigeria that her colleagues would definitely want to hear about, but she was afraid she would be laughed at, that she would not be welcomed, she did not deserve to rub shoulders with other physicians. They would smell her and ostracize her. She gave Grant a weak smile.

"Depo, the other day I caught a movie on television. I can't remember the name of the movie, and I didn't watch the whole thing, but this young woman had a date with this man and they started to have sex. He was so eager. In his excitement he was done within a minute or so; she became frustrated and started to sulk. He asked her what the problem was, and she told him how she wanted to be touched. He was a good student and he learnt very fast. He held her and loved her. Afterward, she said she felt like silk." She paused.

"I have never felt like silk when a man held me, Depo. You've been holding me since I was sixteen years old, and I do love the ways you hold me. Grant has been holding me since I met him. Boris holds me in his own way, but none of you has made me feel like silk.

"I want what that girl in the movie felt. I don't even know what it feels like, but I hope I'll be able to tell the difference between the way Brian used to have sex with me, and someone making love to me. I didn't know until I left Brian that for those five years I was with him, he was raping me. He was never tender, and he was never gentle. I didn't know the difference." She shook her head.

"For someone that Esho warned all her life to avoid rapists; isn't it ironic that the one man I chose to marry is a rapist? I have always been an outsider looking in on other people's happiness. Even my friends Gboye and Moradeke in their crazy ways are insiders. Olu holds Gboye when she allows him, and Moradeke's husband holds her all the time. I live with you and I watch you and Grant hold each other. I want to have that.

"The other day at Boris', a man asked me out. I've seen him there many times, and he has a kind face. He said he has been watching me for the past eight months and that I'm a beautiful woman. I want to go out with him, and maybe after, he would hold me like that woman in the movie was held, and maybe for the first time in my life I will feel like silk, I will feel alive, and I will feel that I can make life possible, because I am surrounded by so much death.

"A beautiful woman?' I asked myself. I've been called beautiful many times but you know I don't believe it. It's like a delusion coming from out there, from a world trying to force its way into my head, just like I have this delusion in my head that I smell of urine and feces, and there is a painful mass between my legs, but you, Moradeke and Gboye have been telling me for years that these are delusions.

"I believe you that I don't smell, but it is very real to me, it keeps me from eating because I feel I'm ingesting feces. It keeps me away from being with the people who want to be with me, because I expect rejection and ridicule. It keeps me from advancing in my career and giving my all to these women I want to help so much, since I'm not able to solicit funds to give them a more comprehensive help that would not jeopardize their lives, like better education so they can move away from the places that have traumatized them so much. Just like Grant has been urging me, I'm afraid that if I apply for a big grant, and I go for the interview, they would smell me and laugh at me, and I can't subject myself to that, Depo. And see what happened the last time I received a big grant. It cost my grandmother her life. I am always afraid.

"I know the fears are delusions and they are not real but at the same time they are very real to me. It's the same way, when a man says to me 'You are a beautiful woman, and I will like to be with you.' I say to myself, he is deluded or he is a pervert, or he is a rapist out to ruin my life. I'm a big girl now, I'm not ten or twelve years old anymore and having sex now won't ruin my life, but I can't believe otherwise." She paused. "I'm not making any sense." Depo turned sideways, supporting himself on his left elbow as he looked into her face.

"I'm not going to have these babies, I won't last that long if you keep me here, Depo. My heart will break and I'll die. I feel caged in here. I'm not a whole person, I'm made up of wraiths, with bits and pieces of me scattered all over the place. I feel incomplete and inadequate and unnecessary.

"I know having these babies is very important to you. Believe me I want to have them too. Maybe if I become a mother, it will let me enter into the fellowship of women. I'll have something to show myself that I have the right, that I'm a woman after all, a woman who can make life possible, and that there is more to me than death.

"Gboye said I repair damaged genitals to cure myself. I don't know if she is right or not and I don't know if it's important, but it has made me feel like a woman. I can help other women feel like women and I have helped many, so far

I have tried to help over two thousand women restore their femininity and about eighty percent of the time I have succeeded. I can't give that up. But I want to go all the way. I want to be a mother and a lover. I want to believe I'm beautiful when people tell me I am. There is no reason I shouldn't have that.

"Gboye also said a beautiful woman who doesn't know she is beautiful is like a millionaire who thinks she's a pauper. I want to feel rich and I want to be held in a way that would make me feel like silk."

Moradeke knocked and came in. She hugged Depo as she reached across him on the bed to hug Ranti, and she waved a greeting at Grant. "Ranti my dear, I'm so sorry, there you were trying to tell us you weren't feeling well, and I was just yelling and cursing at you. I'm sorry. I had no right to say the things I said to you." She looked subdued. "I can't stay long, I haven't been home in two days, but I just had to come and see how you are doing."

She lowered her voice, "Ranti, you have to start to eat. Please do this for all of us. Your blood sugar was thirty yesterday, that is too low. I brought your favorite food, *mixed okro soup*. I made the soup very hot and spicy. It helps the nausea. Why don't you try a little? I'll put a drop on your tongue. It can overpower the other…smell."

Ranti shook her head. Depo joined Moradeke in urging her to put a drop of the soup on her tongue.

She gave in and Moradeke dug into her purse and brought out the bowl of soup. She scooped some with a spoon putting a few drops on Ranti's tongue. "See," she said encouragingly, "just a few drops."

Ranti closed her mouth and the soup was as spicy hot as Moradeke promised. It stung her tongue and for the moment the smell of feces and urine disappeared. It also reminded her how hungry she was. She decided to eat as much of the soup as she could get in, capitalizing on the smell being gone. She opened her mouth and Moradeke slowly fed her the soup.

Depo got off the bed to give Moradeke room. He went to sit on the arm of Grant's chair. A few moments later Moradeke asked the men to excuse them so she could help Ranti wash up.

"Moradeke, is it true? I'm afraid I've gone crazy and I'm imagining things. Is it true that Gboye said she is pregnant with a Chinese baby or did I imagine that, and did we run into Brian?"

Moradeke rolled her eyes in disgust as if Gboye was in the room and she was giving her the dirty looks. "No, Ranti my dear, you are not crazy and you didn't imagine any of it. Everything happened! She *is* pregnant with a Chinese baby! I have never heard anything like it in my life," she said in exasperation.

"It's like she's possessed, and I don't even know what to make of it. She is a nymphomaniac. Is she trying to destroy herself? Maybe she wants to get caught. The whole thing is unbelievable to me. She has always been unbelievable to me.

It's like madness. I don't want to start again and go off like I did yesterday. I've been tempted on many occasions to tell her husband that she cheats on him but the thing is, I love her. She is my friend and she is a good friend. She looks out for me and she is very loyal. It's a big torture for me, Ranti.

"I've been trying not to think about it. Of course, she can't have an abortion because that would just be a worse sin God will not forgive, and I made that clear to her. I don't know what she will do, Ranti." She sighed in resignation.

"I called her several times already, without any response. Yesterday I was very angry but I've calmed down. She is scared and I'll be there for her the best way I can. I will try again later today."

"Today is her operating day, she is probably still in the operating room." Ranti offered.

"And those poor children, of course they are better off with Olu. He should get custody of them. It just breaks my heart. There is nothing I detest more than a cheating person." Moradeke twisted her face in disgust again.

Later in the day, as Moradeke was leaving with a promise to come back on Sunday, Grant started to take his leave as well. Depo wanted to spend the night with Ranti, but she felt she had taken him away from Grant enough.

"Please go with him, I'll be fine. Don't neglect him, go, I'll be fine, I promise." She pushed him away from her toward the door.

He checked with her but she waved him off. He picked up his coat, and after giving her a quick peck on the cheek, followed Grant and Moradeke.

7

By the next morning, Ranti had resolved to leave the city before she was stifled to death. The anxiety attacks were still raging on. She remembered that time ten years before, when she had the smell for eighteen months following her grandmother's death. She had accompanied Depo to some architectural conference in Florida, and while he was at his meetings she went to the beach. She took in one big gulp of the salty ocean air and the smell disappeared, until three days ago. So she decided to move to a quiet beach, one not too busy with tourists, till the babies arrived.

She thought of money. She did not want to beg her friends for money, but living on the beach for four to five months would be expensive, so she decided to cash in her retirement fund. She planned to send money to her assistant to take care of her patients she was able to leave town with, as well as the salary for her staff. She decided to make a list of all the things she had to do and tackle them one at a time.

Her obstetrician visited for a few minutes and was pleased she had some soup the night before. He encouraged her to eat a little at a time, but they would continue the intravenous feeding and if she were able to keep more food down, they would discharge her in a few days, and have a visiting nurse monitor her progress.

Dr. Obed came at about noon. Ranti was happy to see his reassuring face. He had for the past ten years been untiringly sitting with her, listening to her make sense of her chaos. She gave him a grateful smile.

She told him of her decision to go away because she believed it would help her. He agreed with her. "Ranti, try to write down the way you feel in an uncensored manner. The same way I have always encouraged you to say whatever comes to your mind. I know it's not an easy thing to do, but it can be learnt with a lot of practice." He paused and gave her that reassuring look again.

"I know it has been difficult for you to tell me a lot of things. Its okay, you are keeping them to yourself for reasons we need to respect, but sometimes picking up a pen and writing helps. You may be able to access them in other ways like in metaphors or in fiction. That is why I always encourage my patients to write or draw or make whatever art they can. And if anything comes up, you know you can always call me. We can have phone sessions."

Depo came in at his lunch hour. He urged Ranti to have some of Moradeke's soup from the day before that he had kept in the refrigerator. She agreed and he fed her about a dozen spoonfuls.

The soup helped again as the smell disappeared, or, as it later occurred to her, the spiciness of the soup numbed her sense of smell so that she could not smell anything for a while. She was grateful for the break from the smell. As he was clearing the bowl away, she announced, "Depo, I need to go away."

He looked at her for a while. "I know, Ranti, I know you want to go back to Nigeria, you've never felt at home here, and I know I'm the reason you return to New York when you do. If going back to Nigeria will help us until the babies are born, by all means go but I'm coming with you. We are not going to northern Nigeria though. We will go to my mother in Lagos. Grant and I talked about it last night and he is all for it; he will come visit."

Ranti looked at him for half a minute and tears sprang from her eyes. She opened her arms to him; he came to her and they embraced.

"You don't have to come with me," she said. "I will not go to Nigeria. I'll go to the Caribbean. It's warm there at this time of the year and the salty sea air will help me. Remember in 1996 when I went with you to Florida? That was when the smell disappeared at the time. I'm hoping for that cure again."

Depo disengaged himself and looked at her. She smiled at him. "I don't have to go that far away. I just need space, Depo." She told him the details of her plans.

He offered to find a place for her, and that she should not have to tap into her savings.

She shook her head at his suggestions. "I need to start to take care of myself, Depo. I'm almost forty-one years old. I'm going to be mother to two children and I have to be able to take care of myself and the children…"

"And I am their father," he interrupted her.

"Yes, you are, and you will do your part. See, Depo, all my life I have never been able to stand up for myself. Gboye was my protector in primary school. Moradeke did it in secondary school and the three of you since then. Let me do this for me. Let me go away and take care of myself for once, let me know I can do it before I become responsible for two people's lives.

"I was bitching about a lot of things yesterday, and I think I meant most of them, though the low blood sugar could have been responsible for some of them, but the truth is, I have been a very lucky woman, luckier than my mother or grandmother. I have had friends always there and ready to catch me when I'm falling, I should be the happiest person in the world, but apparently there are some things one has got to do for one-self, some things that no amount of love coming from the outside can cure.

"You, Gboye, Moradeke, Grant and Boris love me, but I don't love myself, and that is the tragedy. I feel scattered, I need to find all of myself, and put them together. Boris calls it crossword puzzle. Dr. Obed calls it mourning and burying the past, so the present can be and we can have a future. It's like those diagrams in Gboye's son's books where there are series of numbers, and the child connects one to two to three to four and at the end you have a diagram of a car or a house or a monster. I need to do that and see what I have. And maybe I might just love it.

"I need to go to the ocean alone. You can visit me on weekends, and I need to pay my way."

8

Ranti looked out of the window of the plane as it started to descend to the small airstrip on the Island. She liked the small buildings that were neatly lined on the beach. The oceans gleamed and beckoned to her. She felt like a schoolgirl released from the prison of a classroom and on a field trip. She smiled at Depo who was sitting next to her and she could feel her eyes dancing. She wanted to jump up and down in her excitement. She felt weird. It was a joyful anticipation. "Of what?" she wondered.

Depo looked at her in surprise and she burst out laughing. He leant over to her and kissed her on the cheek. Her eyes continued to dance.

"I should have been bringing you to the ocean. Why didn't you tell me it means so much to you?"

"Because I didn't know," she laughed out loud again. She could hear her voice ringing with delight and it felt strange to her ears.

They cleared immigration, and the elderly couple who owned the cottage they would be renting was there to meet them.

Mr. Sanchez, a gray-haired petite man with a cute moustache helped Depo with the bags while his wife, equally petite and gray haired and in her sixties like her husband hugged Ranti in a warm and motherly manner. She caressed her abdomen and her cheeks with both her hands. She took her purse from her and pulled her along with her toward their car.

The couple pointed out important landmarks as they drove through the small town, though they did not have to, because the landmarks spoke for themselves with signs like 'Church,' 'Post-Office,' 'School,' 'Store,' and 'Hospital.' The island had just one of each.

The island also boasted of an obstetrician who was board certified in the U.S.A., and Depo had interviewed him on the phone before renting the cottage from the Sanchezes.

Mr. Sanchez pointed out the doctor's office and that it was a walking distance from the cottage. Everything was a walking distance from the cottage.

When they rounded a bend on the hill and the ocean opened up to them in a glorious manner, Ranti caught her breath. She wanted to be let out of the car as she wished for wings to fly over the ocean. "That's what I have always wanted to do, be able to fly." She informed herself as if the career choice she should have made all her life just dawned on her. "Fly, fly and soar like an eagle, oh freedom!"

She remembered a song she loved to sing in elementary school—"*If I have wings like a bird, if I have wings like a bird, I will fly, far away, over the hills and mountains and oceans.*" She sang to herself.

"I let off here!" She blurted out suddenly.

"You okay, honey?" Depo turned around to look at her.

"I just want to walk on the beach. Please, I need to get out, now."

Mr. Sanchez stopped the car and she almost tripped over her right foot as she hurried out of the car. Depo had hurried out from the passenger seat where he was sitting next to Mr. Sanchez in time to catch her.

"Where is the cottage? I will walk there," she announced to them.

Depo encouraged her to let the Sanchezes take them to the cottage first, then they could walk on the beach later, but she had started to walk toward the ocean.

At some point she took off her shoes and walked bare feet. Depo walked behind her. She stopped and swung her arms around to embrace the ocean, "Thank you, thank you very much."

She sucked in the fresh sea air, and she could feel it coursing through her lungs and into her bloodstream. She sucked in more in rapid succession and it calmed her racing heart. She took in big gulps of air and held it in for a moment and slowly let it out. As she exhaled she burst out laughing. Tears stood in her eyes. She swung around to look at Depo who was a few steps behind her, ran up to him and hugged him.

"It's so beautiful here Depo. I wish I were a bird. If only I were a bird, I would find such peace. I would fly there and fly here. I love you Depo, I love you so much, thank you, thank you." She kissed him on both cheeks and on his lips.

She held on to Depo as she stared into the horizon, and that sense of calm continued to course through her body. There was something familiar to her about the water, a feeling she could not understand because she had never lived close to an ocean. She felt as if she was home after she had been gone for a very long time. The smell was still there. It did not disappear as she had hoped it would, but she felt good.

Later in the afternoon, as Depo unpacked her bags for her, Ranti sat in the big living room with huge windows that opened to the view of the beach and the ocean. It was very warm but the breeze helped. He planned to stay for two days, accompany her on a visit to the obstetrician and fill in the Sanchezes as to the ways to take care of her. He had wanted to stay a week but she refused. Mr. or Mrs. Sanchez came in from time to time to try to suggest or explain things to Depo. It was a lot of struggle on both their parts because of the language barrier.

She had been eating just a few spoonfuls of Moradeke's soup a day and she had continued to receive the intravenous nutrition. Depo offered her some of the soup. She started to drink it but somehow it was too spicy for her. Even though the smell was still there, she did not need to numb her senses as much as before.

When Ranti awoke about ten the next morning, it took her a while to get her bearing. When she remembered she was on the island, she rushed to the window to open the curtains. She watched for a while as the waves crashed onto the beach. The smell was still very much there but for some reason that morning, she believed that it was a delusion. It did not feel as real as before, but the anxiety was gone, even though there was still the apprehensive feeling of impending doom. She was thankful for that. "One down," she said aloud.

She stood in front of the full-length mirror and looked at herself. She turned sideways to check out her abdomen. She took off her nightshirt and caressed her abdomen, "Good morning to you two," she said to the babies when they kicked.

She surveyed her body critically and thought perhaps those people who think her beautiful might be right after all. At a height of five feet four inches, she weighed one hundred and fifteen pounds, pregnant. She shook her head disapprovingly and agreed with everyone that she needed to add on more pounds.

She zeroed in on her face trying to see what people called beautiful about it. As far as she was concerned she had eyes and a nose and a mouth like other people. She stared at herself for a while, but she did not see it.

She heard Esho's voice telling her when she was nine that she was not beautiful, and the people who had been calling her beautiful were liars. She had believed her grandmother, and disbelieved the rest of the world.

She moved closer to the mirror and stared at her lips for a long time. They were full. Her grandmother had told her they were too thick and so, she was not beautiful. She smiled at the fact that these days, women all over the world spent fortunes to have lips like hers.

"Esho, you were wrong about a lot of things because of your fears. These lips are beautiful and it is not about being full or not, but because they are my lips," she said to her grandmother in her mind, and sighed.

She looked at her abdomen, and caressed it again. Her eyes traveled down to her legs and she touched the deep big gash on her left thigh. She sighed again.

Depo knocked and came in. He was surprised to find her naked in front of the mirror. She swung around. "Why do you think I'm beautiful, Depo?" She demanded of him.

He came up to her and hugged her. "Because you are, that was my impression the first time I saw you at the university. I remember thinking, what a beautiful girl, but your eyes were so sad. I don't know, Ranti, I'm happy when I see you, and I look forward to seeing you and I'm happy you have remained my friend all these years. I love you and to me you are the most beautiful woman I know."

"The smell is not as intense, Depo, and the anxiety is gone. Today I believe you that the smell is not real. I haven't felt this good in a long time. I'm just afraid it will not last so I have this apprehensive feeling."

He hugged her again, "We will not think of the future; we will enjoy now. Let's get you into some clothes and get some breakfast into you. We have an appointment with the doctor in two hours."

Depo left on Tuesday morning with plans to return on Friday. He suggested again that he send for his mother, but Ranti reminded him they had recruited her for when the babies come.

9

Ranti spent most of her day on the beach walking very slowly up and down, not venturing too far from the cottage. She soaked in the sun and she sucked in the sea air. She believed she needed to suck in the sea air many times a day to make the smell go away. It was like doses of medication she had to take four or more times a day.

Mrs. Sanchez was worried that she was getting too much sun, but Ranti ignored her. She did not want to encourage her protectiveness, and the language barrier was to her liking, as the Sanchezes spoke only Spanish, a word of which she did not understand, so it limited the amount of nagging and talking.

Mrs. Sanchez and her husband lived in a two-bedroom building at the back of the cottage. Their cottage faced the road while the one they rented out faced the ocean. She came in three or four times a day to bring Ranti her meals, clean the cottage and check on her.

Ranti spent the evenings sitting in the living room, watching the ocean through the huge windows. The openness and the airiness made her feel uncluttered. When it became dark she watched the television. The programs were in Spanish, but she watched anyway; she tried to follow the story line by the people's actions or made up her own.

She was happy to see Depo and Grant when they arrived the following Friday, and they were pleased to see her eating more. Ranti told them she had been sleeping from ten to twelve hours a day, usually tired from the long walks on the beach.

Grant, as characteristic of him, continued to encourage her to make some presentations about her work in Nigeria. He was of the opinion that the world should know what was going on, and the killers should be brought to justice. He told her that through his law firm, and his connections with the World Health Organization, he could arrange for her to address the United Nations on the issue.

Ranti looked at him and wondered if he had gone mad. "Me? In United Nations, one whiff of me and they will have me arrested," she thought. She looked at Grant but he was very serious. Depo nodded in agreement with him.

"Iranti, it's the delusions again," she snapped at herself. "You are a good surgeon, you were the best in your class in medical school for goodness sake, and you won awards for outstanding performance in your residency training."

The following Monday, after Depo and Grant left, Ranti decided to do some things on her list, especially about her work in northern Nigeria and write a proposal for serious funding. She reminded herself of her plans when she started the project some twelve years before.

She had known that just repairing the damaged genitals was not enough to help the women. They needed education and empowerment to be self-reliant and not remain at the mercy of their culture, which did not recognize women as human beings. She formulated her plan at the time, but there were no funds for its implementation.

Also, what most of the women had cared about was having the surgical repair. It was much later that many of them realized they needed more than just surgical correction of their genitals, usually some five to six years later when they had been re-traumatized in similar ways.

So, she decided to write a comprehensive proposal and send copies to as many funding organizations as were out there. Most of the funding she had been working with had been small grants from the World Health Organization, other smaller organizations and her friends.

She had breakfast that Mrs. Sanchez prepared, pleasing the woman very much by eating more of the food. She got out her laptop, sat on the deck overlooking the ocean and proceeded to work on the proposal but not a word occurred to her. Not even the title. She was blank.

She got up and went into the house. She used the bathroom, took a bottle of water out of the refrigerator, scanned the channels on the television and looked through the pile of books and movies Grant had brought for her. An hour later she returned to the balcony and the laptop, and still nothing.

She sat there for another thirty minutes and then decided to go for a walk. She changed from her nightshirt into white cotton loose pants and a sleeveless top, and she wore a wide brim straw hat as well as sunglasses. She walked up and down in her usual slow manner for an hour and returned to the house. Mrs. Sanchez brought her lemonade and disapprovingly clucked at her for walking in the hot sun.

Ranti sat on the deck again and turned on the laptop, nothing.

She turned it off and took it back to her room. She went back to the beach and walked up and down many times for another hour. She watched the birds as they flew everywhere, envying them their freedom as she tried not to become frustrated that she could not write the proposal.

"I might have to hire a professional to write the proposal for me," she decided and felt relieved.

At the cottage, she decided to start on one of Grant's movies he brought for her. Grant was addicted to movies and they were the metaphors by which he spoke. If a movie made an impression on him, he bought it on DVD and had been known to watch such movies several times. He always found Ranti uneducated about movies so he brought ten DVDs with him with a promise to bring more the next time he came to visit.

She decided on *The English Patient*, because she had read the book many years before, and she felt a bond with the hero.

She settled down on the comfortable sofa, and when Mrs. Sanchez brought her supper and saw her cuddled in front of the television, she nodded her approval and brought the food to her on a tray.

The next day, she decided to take a walk first, to get her brain cells firing, and try to write the proposal again, but it was a repeat performance of the day before.

She reminded herself that she was going to use a professional, but she felt that another person would not be able to convey the pain and the anguish of genital mutilation like she could, since it was her personal experience.

She suffered through the second day of trying to work on the proposal with the same result as the day before. She simply did not have the words. She finally gave up and continued with *The English Patient,* which she had not finished.

On Wednesday, she took her morning walk, showered, ate breakfast and settled down on the balcony with her laptop to write the proposal. The words did not materialize.

She sat there stunned, and wondered if the pregnancy was making her brain dead.

She reminded herself that her brain had always obeyed her. She admitted that she had never been a person who always had the words to convey what she needed to convey, and had always relied on other people's words, but even those seem to have deserted her.

The babies kicked; she caressed her abdomen and talked to them.

After an hour of sitting on the balcony trying to find the words, she went for a walk again and watched the birds. She wished she could identify the birds. She imagined herself flying. "I will ask Depo to bring me a book on birds," she said aloud.

She returned to her computer after lunch and her intravenous fluid session, and for thirty minutes, no words. She lifted up her loose shirt and caressed her abdomen because it seemed as if the babies were having a fight. "Take it easy you guys," she said to them.

She walked around the deck for a while. She leaned against the doorpost and wondered at what was happening to her mind. Then it hit her, "I should write about me, my own experience! I am a victim of genital mutilation as much as the next girl who has been through the horrible experience. Isn't that what Dr. Obed told me to do just a few days ago? He said to me, 'write down the way you feel in an uncensored manner." She yelled at herself, "It will not be typical for most of the women afflicted by this trauma because most of them are not doctors. In fact some ninety percent of them do not even have elementary school education, but if I, who had the opportunity of a good education, could have suffered this much from the consequences of genital mutilation, one could only imagine what it must be for these women."

She felt so relieved as this insight dawned on her that she sat down and started to write, and she wrote for four hours without stopping. It was as if her fingers grew a life of their own, independent of her brain. She was also afraid that if she stopped writing, the insight would disappear and she would not have the words anymore.

10

"In an attempt to save myself from these recurring deaths, I have to find myself, and in order to find myself, I first have to find my mother.

Esho was born on November 20, 1935. Her birthday was tattooed on her chest, because that was the only form of record keeping available in her part of the world at the time. Esho's mother died giving birth to her because the placenta did not separate. Her family told her it was because she had a cursed head. And Esho did believe she had a cursed head that she carried around till she died at the age of sixty-one." Ranti started, and as she typed, she began to feel loose all over, as if she was losing muscle control, for a split second she felt dizzy and disoriented, but she continued to type.

Time and walls collapsed into one another and she was transported back to the 1930s and she was her grandmother. Ranti stopped typing and gripped the edge of the table with both hands for a sense of grounding. Her heart started to race, but the feeling would not leave her. "I should go there, that is the only way I can connect the prose with the passion; I have to go there," she insisted.

She paused and looked around as she was spiraled back in time in the eye of a vortex. Unknown doors flew open as she approached them, and she flew through rooms after rooms and these cells of memory vomited their prisoners.

"Penguins fly underwater but not in the air," she said aloud and she was in the middle of an unfolding drama, the drama to which she had a thousand percent claim, because it was her drama too. She had been there, but only as a future, a future whose life was compromised because of this past, a future that would not really be for another thirty years, but as it was in the beginning is now and ever shall be. But the future was the past and the past is the present and this present is the coming future, which was and is and would be. That was why those cells were so eager to vomit those convicts housed inside of them.

Esho's father and the extended family did not want her because of the curse which they were afraid would afflict more women in the family. The elderly traditional healer that attended the birth took the baby home to his equally elderly wife. He did not believe she would last the week, as was the case with babies who 'killed' their mothers in childbirth.

The elderly couple fed her goat milk from one of the mammy goats. When she was seven days old they gave her the name Esho which means 'Treasure,' with the hope of neutralizing her disastrous beginning.

At a tender age Esho knew what it was to be an outcast in her home as she was repeatedly told that she was not a Treasure, but that she was trash.

When she was five years old, her adopted father died and his wife followed him a few months later. The villagers appealed to her biological father to take her. By this time he had remarried and his new wife had given him two sons. They reluctantly took Esho in. Her stepmother turned her into a servant who had to do all the chores.

By age nine, Esho's body started to change into that of a young woman with high full breasts and wide hips. This displeased her stepmother a great deal, and she used every opportunity to make her life miserable, accusing her of being a whore who used her changing body to seduce men. She gave her a beating at every turn, most of the time without any need for it.

The first time her father raped her, Esho must have been about ten or eleven years old. She did not know for sure but like she told Ranti, "Hitler's war had been raging on for some time and it ended shortly after." That was how she kept records, by tying the time period to historical events.

Esho did not know what to do, but somehow she knew it was inappropriate, a father should not have sex with his daughter. She wanted to talk to someone but she did not have any confidant in the village, not even girls of her age that she met at the well all the time. The girls would start to whisper whenever they see her coming.

She wished her adopted mother was still alive, because she had taken care of her to the extent of her ability, trying to undo the curse the whole village tried to impress on her by saying to people in her defense each time she was called a 'mother-killer,' that she survived, and usually, children who 'killed' their mothers in childbirth do not survive past infancy.

A few weeks later, her father raped her again. Esho thought of running away but was afraid of what would happen to her. She had never been outside of the village, and she had heard stories of horrible things that happen to runaway children; they were either used for black magic or devoured by wild animals.

The third time her father came at her, she appealed to him not to rape her. He slapped her hard across her face and raped her.

The following day, as she was returning from the well with a clay pot full of water on her head, she stubbed her left big toe against a stone and she and the water pot ended on the ground, with the water pot shattering to pieces.

Her stepmother gave her a severe beating for this, but Esho took the longest piece of the broken pot, filed it into a sharp point and hid it in her clothes.

A few days later, her father came to her again but this time instead of pleading with him not to rape her, she fought him. She wanted to wake the household so they could see what had been going on for months.

Her father hit her hard across the face again overpowering her. She brought out the pointed shard from the earthenware pot and stabbed him in the chest with all her strength. The shard lodged in his chest as he cried out, yelling on top of his lungs.

Esho knelt next to him as he continued to roll around on the ground in agony, she removed the potsherd, and he screamed even louder from the pain. She plunged it into him again with all her strength, and removed it a second time.

As she plunged it in a third time, she could hear the household stirring, as people started to run toward the noise, which was in the hallway where she slept.

Her grandfather, on assessing the situation, yelled for the people to get hold of the girl with the cursed head because she had brought evil into the house and must be killed.

Esho took to her heels and fled into the night with only the torn dress she had on her. She ran through the night not stopping until day started to break. She had known for a while that she was not pursued, but the anticipated terror from the forest gave flight to her legs.

She walked all day, not daring to stop and kept on walking through the jungle at night with all the imaginary evil spirit and demons her mind could conjure as company. She sang songs she had been told would keep evil spirits away, and continued on until it was daybreak again.

She found some oranges hanging low on a tree, and ate till she was full, after which she found some shade and fell into a very deep sleep.

She dreamt of varieties of evil spirit, trolls, fairies, ghosts and ghouls. They were trying to take her away. They started to fight amongst one another for ownership of her. She tried to run away but her legs would not move. She started to cry and to beg them. She told them she was a motherless child and she had suffered too much, and they should spare her life so she would not suffer anymore.

She awoke with a start to find a lot of people towering over her. She struggled to her feet and was ready to take off but one of the men caught her in a firm grip. She begged them to let her go, that she was sorry if she was in their way.

They interrogated her and she told them her story. The women lamented and cursed her father. They asked her where she was going, and if she had family in another part of the region. She told them she was going to the major city, Ilesa.

The people whose village was close by took her home and fed her. They gave her some clothes, and the next morning, they entrusted her to the care of some traders who were traveling to Ilesa.

Esho walked with these people for a week until they arrived in the big city and she was astounded at what she saw. She had never seen so many people in her life, and she was amazed that such a large number of human beings existed on the face of the earth.

She remembered hearing the villagers back at home speak of Ilesa, they had said all the people there could not be alive, that the world could not possibly contain such a large number of human beings, and that most of them were ghosts, because ghosts were known to love to go to the markets to mingle with the living.

She believed the villagers back at home and warned herself to be very careful so a ghost would not harm her, unless they were the ghosts of her dead mother and adopted parents.

The travelers pointed the way to the convent to her, telling her the nuns help runaway children. At the convent the head nun who did not speak Yoruba interviewed her through one of the student nuns.

Esho told them her story.

The student nun gave her a look of contempt and spoke to the head nun. They started to argue. The head nun spoke sharply to the student nun and the latter kept quiet.

The head nun patted Esho on the head and smiled at her as she left the room.

The student nun took her to the kitchen and told the cook she was the new maid. The cook was a very big woman and she looked at Esho with unconcealed disgust.

"She is an *Asewo*, they start their career early in life and they lie that men raped them. Look at her body. She claimed she is just eleven years old but look at the breasts on her." The student nun hissed in disgust as she left the kitchen.

Esho did not know what to do. She did not feel welcomed at the convent, but where would she go? She wanted to tell them she was not a prostitute as the student nun accused her, but she realized that it was pointless. They had made up their minds, just like the people in her village labeled her a 'mother-killer.' "What wouldn't I give to have my mother alive?" She thought.

The cook did not speak to her, so she stood where she was until it was dark. The cook finally gave her some food and told her she could sleep in the kitchen.

Esho started to live at the convent and to help the cook around the kitchen. After she had been there for one month, the cook started to warm up to her because she was a very responsible and hard working girl. She did whatever she was asked to do without a word of complaint, and she stayed out of everyone's way.

From time to time the cook would ask her questions about her life, and Esho would tell her the story she told the head nun when she first came to the convent.

The cook would shake her head sadly and make comments like, "Life could be unbearable for a child who doesn't have a mother." Sometimes she would pray for Esho that the spirit of her dead mother would continue to watch over her and would not forget her.

Esho did everything in her power to remain on favorable terms with the cook.

A year later, the head nun came to the kitchen to ask the cook to spare Esho for just one hour on Sundays, so she could attend the children's Sunday school to learn about the Lord Jesus Christ.

So every Sunday at eleven in the morning, Esho would wear her one good dress and go to the Sunday school to listen to the stories of the bible. She enjoyed the stories as she found them very entertaining, but she did not believe there was any special god anywhere looking out for her.

Fifteen months after she arrived at the convent, the cook started to take her to the market, to teach her about quality of food and how to get a good bargain. "Haggle with the traders until they curse you out, in that way you know you are getting the best deal possible." She told Esho repeatedly. Esho paid close attention and learnt very well.

A year later, the cook decided she had been trained well enough to go shopping on her own. So Esho started to go to the market alone to buy the foodstuffs for the convent. Every morning she would wake up as early as five in the morning while it was still dark so she would arrive at the market at about the same time as the traders, to ensure she got the best of the food items.

The convent was built on the outskirt of the town, so, she had to walk for about thirty minutes through a deserted path in the forest to get to the market in the center of the town.

Initially this used to scare her, because of fears of evil spirits, but after a while she grew bold and she would sing to herself to drive away the fears.

Nine months after she started to go to the market alone, a man jumped on her out of the shadows of the forest. Esho fought back but she was not a match for the man. He dragged her into the bushes and covered her mouth with his hand. He had a knife that he used to knick at her throat drawing blood to convince her that he would kill her. Esho fought him and the knife cut her in several parts of her body. The man hit her hard across her face and she lost consciousness. He raped her.

When she regained consciousness and realized she had been raped again, she sat in the bush and cried for a long time. Then, she dried her tears and promised herself that she would never cry again for as long as she lived. "I have been shedding rivers of tears as far back as I can remember, wishing for my dead mother to protect me but it has not happened, neither has the Jesus Christ they talked about in Sunday school."

It dawned on her almost thirteen-year-old mind at that moment that she was alone in a hostile world, and it was up to her to protect herself. She got up and cleaned herself as much as she could. She was grateful she was not given cash because the rapist would have stolen it. The traders sold to the convent on credit, and collected their money directly from the head nun at the end of the week.

She continued on to the market and bought the food items; then she went to the hardware section of the market. There she eyed a glinting knife with a blade about ten inches long. She hung around the trader's stall pretending to look at the items on display. When the trader was attending to a customer and her attention was in another part of the stall, Esho quickly swiped the knife and hid it in the basket containing the food items on her head. She slowly walked back to the convent.

The cook started to yell at her for being late but Esho only apologized. She did not tell her she was assaulted and raped. She knew it was not a story they wanted to hear at the convent. She remembered the student nun calling her a prostitute on her first day at the convent, and that she had brought the rape on herself because of her big breasts.

The next morning she woke up as usual before it was daylight and started for the market, but this time she did not sing. She walked purposefully with determination and did not entertain all the fantasies about fairies, evil spirit or trolls of the forest she used to scare herself with. She stopped believing that such creatures existed.

The man did not come at her. Each morning she went to the market, she held the knife in her hand daring him to come at her.

Two weeks later, as she was walking to the market, he pounced on her again. Esho was ready, and though he knocked her off her feet and sent her knife flying off, she recovered quickly and made in the direction she heard her knife fall. She groped for it in the dark and grasped the blade. It cut into her palm.

She quickly transferred the knife, grasping the handle. As the man came at her again, she tried to plunge it into him, but she missed. He slapped her hard across her face and asked her if she wanted him to cut her like the other time. He continued to slap her face, and Esho realizing that he would keep hitting her until she passed out, calmed herself and laid still.

He stopped hitting her and raped her. As he was making to get off her, she brought up the knife in her right hand and plunged it into his back. He screamed in agony. She extracted the knife, pushed him off her, got on her knees. He was on his back rolling around in pain. Esho brought the knife down on his chest. She plunged it in, and twisted it around for a few moments.

He started to shriek in pain, just like her father had done three years before, but Esho would not let go of him. She removed the knife and plunged it into him again. She repeated this until he stopped moving.

She stood up, walked to a stream close by to wash the blood and grime off her face, arms and legs; then she went back onto the deserted path and continued on her way to the market.

Later in the day, the body of the man was discovered and there was a lot of excitement in the convent as people talked about what they described as a gory murder. They speculated that it was a ritual killing; that the man must have been killed for black magic.

The police came to the convent later in the day to talk to the head nun. She brought them to the kitchen, since that was the path Esho and the cook took to the market, in case they had seen anything unusual. Esho was questioned, but she denied hearing or seeing anything.

The police warned her and the cook to be careful when they went to the market. From that day on, the cook did not let Esho go to the market while it was still dark.

Three months later when Esho returned from the market, she found the head nun, a student nun and the cook in the kitchen, they looked very angry.

She put down the food items she carried in a basket on her head, and the cook accusingly told her she was pregnant. She said she had been watching her for the past six weeks and her abdomen was protruding.

Esho stood across from them and stared at them.

"You have to leave this place. We don't want prostitutes here because we are doing the work of God. You are a child of the devil and you are going to rot in hell, you and your unborn baby. Get out!" yelled the student nun.

Esho stood where she was and stared at them. She knew something was wrong with her body, but she did not know it was pregnancy.

The head nun spoke angrily to the student nun for a long time while the cook kept looking at Esho as she continued to shake her head in sorrow. "Why would you do this to yourself? When you know you are a motherless child. You have a good life here. They feed you, clothe you and have given you shelter, is this a way to repay these good people?"

Esho stared at the head nun and the Yoruba nun as they argued. She had always known the head nun liked her. She wished she could speak English, so she could talk directly to the white woman, maybe she would understand her.

The student nun calmed down as the head nun had apparently chastised her.

She gave Esho a dirty look and asked gruffly, "Who is the father of the baby? Who have you been fornicating with? You are going to hell you know."

Esho kept quiet.

The head nun spoke again, for a long time, explaining something to the student nun.

"Reverend Mother would like to know who the father of the baby is. She said he will have to help you and take care of the baby. He will have to pay for your medical care. She said you should tell her, she will not send you away. So don't be afraid, she said she is not angry with you, because you are a very young girl who had been taken advantage of and you will always have a home here with us. So speak."

Esho remembered when she stabbed her father; her grandfather said she should be killed. If she told them she already killed the father of this baby, they will definitely kill her. So she did not say a word.

"Don't lie because you know what happens to liars." The younger nun reminded her, "They burn in hell!"

The head nun spoke again.

"Reverend Mother said you will be taken to the doctor tomorrow to make sure you are okay since you are such a young girl. She said that perhaps you will not be afraid of her and will tell her who the man is, and the convent will help you."

The cook continued to cluck and to shake her head sorrowfully.

They took Esho to the doctor the next day. First, she had to speak to an impatient record clerk. He kept yelling at the people ahead of her in line, and many of them were trembling as they spoke to him.

When it was her turn, Esho gave him a fearless and as cold a look as he gave her.

He asked her for her name and she told him, "Esho."

He asked for her last name and she told him she did not have any.

"What is your father's name? He must have a name." He yelled at her.

Esho thought for a while, "*Oloriburuku.*"

The clerk and the people around him stared at her in shock.

"Your father's name is *'the one with the cursed head?'*"

Esho nodded. "Yes, *Oloriburuku,* that's his name."

"Where is he?"

"He's burning in the Christian hell."

The clerk dropped his pen and continued to stare at her. He sat back in his chair.

"Where is your mother?"

"She is dead."

"What was her name?"

Esho kept quiet.

"You have got to have a last name, for the record," the clerk patiently explained to her, his gruff manner gone.

Esho thought for a long time and the clerk waited. Some people in line behind her were impatient but the clerk yelled at them to be quiet. Something in Esho's manner scared him because she was not afraid anymore.

"I don't have any and I don't want any," Esho finally declared.

The clerk looked at her for a moment; he asked her to have a seat near by and think of a last name. "Everybody must have a last name, it's the law. They can lock you up for not having a last name."

Esho sat on the bench and looked around her. After a while she decided to give herself a last name so they would leave her alone. Besides, she did not want to go to prison.

She thought long and hard for a name that would describe her situation in life. Her deceased mother's name was *Wura,* but she did not feel like 'Gold.' It would be ridiculous for her names to be Treasure and Gold because she was far from either.

"*Kosoluranlowo,*" she announced to the clerk fifteen minutes later when he asked her if she had thought of a name.

He stared at her again. "No, you can't call yourself that, there is always help in this world for you. You just have to find a way to get to it."

"*Modaduro.*"

"No, you are not alone, God is always with you."

Esho gave him a baleful look.

"*Iyayanmi.*"

"Anguish chose you? Hah! You are the one bringing bad luck on your head with all these names you are coming up with." The clerk said to her in exasperation.

"No, I am not, I'm innocent of everything but this is my lot," Esho told him.

"That is it!" the clerk exclaimed. "*Jare*! 'Innocence!' That will be your last name. It's the truth of your situation, but it is better than all those other names. I know life has been cruel to you, but we should always have a prayer and a way to pray is in the choice of our names. See, someone gave you the name Esho. They want your life to be full of Treasures. They see you as a Treasure." The clerk tried to convince her.

Esho shrugged and the clerk wrote her name on the clinic chart as Esho Jare. As she was leaving, he advised her to begin to think of a name for her unborn child.

The white doctor had a Yoruba man with him to translate. The Yoruba man looked at Esho disapprovingly. They too wanted to know who the father of the baby was. Esho kept quiet.

The doctor wanted her to lie on a table so he could examine her but she refused. She had vowed to herself that she will never lie down for any man again in her life.

The doctor touched her arm and she ran out of the room. The Yoruba man followed her and pleaded with her to return. She ran all the way back to the convent.

The cook later explained to her that she had to let the doctor take care of her. She too had been trying to extract the information about the father of the baby from Esho without any success.

Esho continued to do her chores in the convent as she had been doing all along without getting in anybody's way.

About two months before the baby was due to be born, the cook woke her up in the middle of the night and giving her some money and a package, she asked her to leave the convent immediately, because the nuns had been discussing amongst themselves that when her baby arrived, they would take it from her and put it in an orphanage.

"The orphanage is for children without mothers. Your child will have a mother, but these white people have all the power. You didn't have a mother and I'm sure you don't want to do that to your child. Think of the anguish you have been through; please don't let them take your child from you.

"Here is some money. This is all I have, and in the package is food, and some clothes, go to Oshogbo and ask for the priestess of Oshun. She will take you in and take care of you. Leave now before they wake up." The cook pulled her up from the sleeping mat.

Esho stared at the cook as she pushed the package at her and pushed her toward the door. Esho kept looking at her, and the woman said to her, "Go in peace and may the spirit of your dead mother watch over you." She pushed her out of the kitchen into the darkness of the night.

Esho walked to the market through the forest where she was raped and where she killed the rapist. She arrived in the deserted market and found a spot where she slept till morning when the traders arrived.

She asked the fish seller for the direction to Oshogbo. The woman told her some people would be leaving at dusk. She expressed concern that in her condition she would not be able to trek to the neighboring town, as she might have the baby on the way.

The walk to Osogbo took her three weeks, but she walked most of it on her own. She was too slow for the people she started the journey with so they left her behind, as she needed to rest for a whole day sometimes.

The priestess welcomed her and she was given a corner in the open courtyard to sleep and was fed without being asked to do any chores.

A week after she arrived in Osogbo, she had a baby girl.

Esho had not thought of a name for the baby like she was advised by the clerk at the clinic and she had a repeat conversation with the priestess about naming the baby.

The older woman, finally frustrated with Esho after the baby was three weeks old and did not have a name, named her Oshun, after the goddess whose priestess she was.

She explained to Esho that Oshun, the goddess, was a helper of women and had given her the baby girl.

"A mad man gave me this baby," Esho said to herself.

The priestess helped Esho as much as she could in caring for the baby and Esho, as characteristic of her, worked hard to help around the shrine and the household.

A lot of people came to consult with the priestess on a lot of issues. Most of them would sleep in the shrine for weeks or even months, depending on what the goddess through her priestess prescribed as the solution to their problems, which usually involved taking several baths a day in the River Oshun whose water was believed to be curative.

Six weeks after Oshun was born, the priestess invited Esho to the shrine to speak with her in confidence. Esho went with the baby strapped to her back.

"Esho, the goddess Oshun loves you very much and is happy that you are here. She saw you through the birth of your child and made sure you and the baby are in good health."

Esho stood silently and watched the priestess.

"Oshun wants to use you as her vessel to do a lot of good work she's not able to do directly as she is in heaven. So she instructed me to tell you what she wants you to do," the priestess paused and continued.

"There are lots of people who come to her as you have noticed since you have been here with us. Many of them come to ask Oshun for things like good health for them or their family members, prosperity and children.

"Oshun is not able to do much about the requests for money because she believes that prosperity comes to those who deserve it by working hard. Sometimes she grants the wishes for good health but if the person's time on earth is up, she cannot overturn the work of God almighty.

"She is able to grant the wishes for children most of the time, but she does it through other people. You are a very beautiful woman with a very fertile body. That is the gift of Oshun to you. Sometimes, the only thing these childless couples need is for the man to sleep with a fertile woman like you, and in that way you transmit some of the fertility to him, which he is then able to pass on to his wife and then they will be able to have children.

"There are some men who have expressed the desire to sleep with you, and they have promised to make it worth your while. You can make a lot of money in this way because they will reward you, and one of them might even marry you because you are a very beautiful woman. So what do you say? Will you do it? Help these desperate people by giving them some of the fullness that God in his infinite mercy has given you?"

Esho slowly shook her head from left to right.

The priestess appealed to her, "You don't have to give me an answer today, just think about it. Take your time. Remember I have been very good to you. I took you in when you were in danger of losing your baby and I took good care of you and I have been like a mother to you, helping you with your newborn baby. You don't want to be ungrateful do you?"

Esho assured her that she was very grateful for her help and promised to think about the proposition.

In the middle of the night, she packed her little belongings and strapping her baby to her back, walked out of the priestess' house.

She walked through the night until she was tired and she slept only during the day hiding in the bushes. She ate fruits from people's farms, and one week later arrived in Iwo, the neighboring town.

She went to the market to look for a job, and a woman who had a restaurant employed her to help with the cooking. She gave her two meals a day as payment.

Esho slept in the restaurant in the market at night, and saved her tips until she could rent a room.

A year after she arrived in the town, the very old and gray-haired Imam of the predominantly Muslim town, who came to the restaurant every day, asked her to marry him.

Esho had wondered if she would have to kill him because for the previous six months, he had been using every opportunity to grab her butt or pull her breasts when she served him. She had promised herself that if he came after her in one way or the other, she would just let him have it.

A lot of the younger men had been approaching her as well, asking for her hand in marriage but she made it clear she was not interested. She told the Imam she would not marry him.

Her boss appealed to her to accept the offer, which she called a good prospect. She reminded Esho that the Imam was very learned in the Holy Koran and had made a pilgrimage to Mecca. The other women who worked with Esho started to mount pressure on her as well.

Three months later, her boss informed her that she could not be allowed to remain single because single women on the loose were not good for the stability of any town. They usually become prostitutes and lure respectable men away from their homes and marriages. Such women, she explained to Esho, corrupt the morals of a community, so therefore she had an ultimatum. She had to marry the Imam.

Very early the next morning, she strapped her seventeen-month-old daughter to her back and left town on one of the Lorries that had become available. The lorry took her to Ibadan.

In Ibadan she got a job with a builder who was building a house, and she carried cement on her head for him from one part of the grounds where the cement was mixed with sand and water to the site of the building.

At this job as well, men approached her, asking for her hand in marriage.

After two years of working with the builder who had continued to get many contracts to build many houses, and had continued to take Esho to work for him, a carpenter on the job started to show interest in her.

He initially started by complimenting her on her looks and admiring her daughter. Esho ignored him.

Then he asked her to sleep with him. Esho told him no. He made the request many times. Then he grew nasty and started to make crude remarks about her body. He accused her of using her curvaceous body to seduce men and then she would not deliver. He called her a witch and a whore each time she came around him. When he made these remarks other men on the job would laugh at her. Esho ignored them.

Two months later, he accosted her on her way home and demanded that she sleep with him. Esho calmly explained to him with her very cold eyes that if she slept with him then she would have to kill him. She showed him her knife and waited. He quietly moved out of her way and did not bother her again.

Esho continued to work with the builder who continued to build homes all over the big city, and to raise her daughter.

11

Oshun grew into a girl who was always at loggerheads with her mother. Esho could not understand this, but it felt to her as though Oshun had to fight her on everything, and so Esho fought back. There was constant screaming and cursing between mother and daughter. Oshun was lazy and would refuse to do her chores, so Esho would retaliate by giving her thorough beatings almost every day.

By the time she was nine years old, her body started to change to that of a young woman like Esho's body had changed early too. When Esho saw her daughter's body changing, she panicked. She remembered her stepmother's reaction to her body at that stage in her life, and how she had predicted it would get her into serious trouble, and she had been right. So she decided to keep a firm grip on Oshun in order to keep her safe from men.

She became very strict with Oshun, especially when soon after she started to notice men looking at her. She had enrolled her in school at the age of six, but she entertained the idea of withdrawing her from school to monitor her closely, but realized if there was going to be any hope of them getting out of poverty, Oshun had to stay in school.

She told Oshun the story of her life. Of how she was raped by her own father when she was eleven years old, and that she eventually killed him. She also told her she killed the man who fathered her as well. Prior to this, she had told Oshun that her father died of some illness.

"You killed my father?" was Oshun's shocked reaction to the news, "You told me he died of an illness. You are a witch! That is what people have been saying of you. They say, 'she is such a beautiful woman but no man will go near her; all the men that have tried to touch her, she killed them.' So they are right, you kill men, you killed my father!"

Esho tried to explain to her daughter that it was in self-defense but Oshun would not listen. The fights continued as well as the beatings from mother to daughter.

Oshun bloomed into a beautiful adolescent and the attention from men increased. Oshun took all the attention in stride like it was her due. By the time she was twelve years old, she had started to stay out later than her curfew of eight o'clock and all the beatings and cursing from Esho did not make an impact on her.

By age thirteen, she was much taller and bigger than her mother. Once, when Esho tried to discipline her by whipping her, Oshun overpowered her, took the whip from her and whipped her instead.

Esho rained curses on her, accusing her of being a prostitute and telling her she was not surprised, as her father was a rapist. Oshun ran away from home that night.

Esho scanned the neighborhood all night looking for her daughter, and for the first time she noticed her neighbors laughing at her.

Early the next morning, a woman who was much older than Esho knocked on her door to inform her that Oshun had been shacking up with her husband, Akanbi, who lived down the street from them. She asked Esho to warn her wayward daughter to stay away from her husband; otherwise she would do her some terrible harm.

Akanbi and his family had been their neighbors for years. He worked as a school superintendent. He was the richest man in the neighborhood and he lived on the second floor of his big house, while he rented out the first floor to many tenants. He was one of the few people in the area who had a car.

Esho went with the woman to retrieve her daughter who was in bed with Akanbi early that morning. She tried to appeal to Oshun to stay away from men and that it could only bring disaster.

Six months later Oshun was pregnant. Esho became so enraged that she started to hit her, and the neighbors had to intervene to separate the two of them. Oshun dropped out of school. Esho tried to get Akanbi to marry her daughter so she would not have to suffer as she had, but Akanbi refused, claiming the baby was not his because Oshun went with other men.

Oshun gave birth to a baby boy in 1962 and Esho was relieved it was not a baby girl who would have been born into the life of suffering, because as a boy he would stay in school since he cannot become pregnant, and he would go on to get a good job and protect them from the men who had been exploiting them, and so with these hopes, she named him Lana—'the one who paves the way' for the women in his family. Esho doted on him. Oshun continued her characteristic behavior of being recalcitrant and going away from home for days, and Esho finally left her alone.

Oshun continued to see Akanbi and from time to time she would go away with other men, and would be gone for weeks and even months.

When Lana was two years old, Oshun suddenly reappeared from one of her long absences and started to hang out with Akanbi again.

Esho was not happy about this, especially that Akanbi had not raised a finger to help her with Lana's care. Esho had approached him on many occasions when she desperately needed money especially for the doctors, when Lana was ill. Akanbi had refused to help her, claiming the boy was not his son even though he was a spitting image of him.

Three months after Oshun came back and started to hang around Akanbi, she became pregnant again. She gave birth to a baby girl in 1965, and Esho was thrown into despair again because she was convinced the baby girl was damned, just like she was and her mother had been.

Oshun disappeared three days after the baby was born. Esho did not have money for milk. She approached Akanbi for help, but as usual he refused to help, claiming the second baby was not his either.

Esho did the best she could to care for the baby and she felt a bond with her in that she had been a motherless child who was rejected by her father, and this new-born baby girl had been rejected by both her mother and father, even though they were alive and well.

She could not afford to feed the baby as she should have been fed, and many nights when it cried inconsolably from hunger, Esho would offer it her breasts, and the baby would hungrily latch on and suck at the dry breasts.

She was determined to tell this baby the story of her life right away, so she would grow up knowing who she was and be careful around men. She decided that *Memory* would have to be her constant companion and so she named her Iranti, which was later shortened to Ranti by neighbors, but each time anyone called her Ranti, Esho would correct them explaining to them the big difference between the names Ranti, which is a shortened form of Oluranti. And as she later explained to Ranti, with 'Oluranti,' you are asking a power out there to remember you. You are placing your life in the hands of an indifferent agent, whereas with the name, 'Iranti,' you are the one who is actively remembering yourself, and placing your life in your own hands.

Ranti was a precocious little girl who talked all the time. She stood up and walked at the age of seven months, which scared Esho a lot. She was afraid that this girl too would get into trouble prematurely because she was very forward. She decided to clip her wings before they expanded and took flights, flying her into disaster.

Ranti remembered the admonitions of her early life, with slaps, knocks on the head, and being hit. 'Don't speak unless you are spoken to Iranti.' 'Who asked for your opinion, why are you always hanging around when adults are talking?' 'Don't follow those children; it is none of your business.' 'You don't have to help every old person you see carrying a heavy load.' 'You have to learn to mind your own business, who made you the police of the neighborhood?' 'Why are you dancing in such a seductive manner? What are you showing off already, you don't have the body of a woman yet! *Are you planning to fetch water before you arrive at the well?*'

More knocks on the head and more spanking. 'Don't ask so many questions.' 'You are too wild Iranti.' 'It is my cursed head, where did this wild child come from?' 'What am I to do to keep this child safe from herself?' 'Why are you staring at the rain? What do you mean it is beautiful? It is the rain, what can be beautiful about it?' 'Iranti stop running all over the place.'

Esho in many ways tried to clip her wings to keep her earthbound.

Lana loved his little sister and doted on her. He took her everywhere with him and taught her a lot of things. At eighteen months, Ranti wanted a doll and would cry when she saw other little girls playing with their dolls, but their grandmother could not afford one, so Lana carved a doll out of a plank of wood for her, and this Ranti christened 'Lana' and would proudly tie to her back, as mothers in the neighborhood did with their babies, as she ran after her brother to play with him.

Esho enrolled Lana in school when he was the right age, determined that he would get an education. She was grateful that Obafemi Awolowo was the premier of the region at the time. He was a visionary who wanted every child of school age to be in school, and made that his policy, so education was free and accessible to the likes of Esho who were very poor.

Oshun returned when Ranti was four years old, and as characteristic of her started to hang around Akanbi again. She was irritable toward the children and whenever they came around her she would yell at them or smack them on the head. They learnt to stay out of her way.

Three months later she became pregnant for Akanbi again and this time was very sick. Esho appealed to Akanbi on many occasions to give her money so she could take Oshun to the hospital, but he refused, claiming he did not have money and as usual the baby was not his.

Oshun died in her sleep when she was about six month pregnant. She was just twenty-one years old, and Esho was thirty-four.

Esho did not cry. She was relieved Oshun did not have the baby before she died because it would have meant one more mouth to feed.

A world where a young person's death, a young mother's death, a daughter's death is greeted with relief of "one less mouth to feed" is a world that no human being should inhabit. But it was Esho's world and she did not weep for her daughter.

The neighbors helped her bury Oshun. The night Oshun died, before Ranti who shared the sleeping mat with her grandmother fell asleep, Esho explained to the four year old that men and sex killed her mother because she did not fight back. She told her she had learnt to fight back and had used a knife when it was necessary.

Esho focused her attention on Lana and Ranti. She was determined that Ranti would not endure the trauma she and her mother endured from men. She continued to tell her the stories of their lives, the way other mothers told their children bedtime stories.

12

Ranti joined her brother in elementary school at the age of six and Lana continued to take care of his sister. He was growing tall and was very smart in school. Esho was very proud of him and she would boast about him to the neighbors. To Ranti, she would speak endlessly of when he was born, and how he had been a very beautiful baby, with big curls of hair like that of a white person, and how she used to love to comb his hair.

Ranti realized the difference in the affection her grandmother had for her brother and for her. She knew Esho was disappointed she was a girl and felt it burdensome to have to raise her, but she too adored her brother.

Ranti loved going on adventures with her brother. They mostly roamed the neighborhood, and to her it was the most beautiful place in the world. They would walk on the dusty un-tarred roads and run into women coming back from the farm with produce in baskets on their heads; most of them would not have on tops because of the tropical heat, and would tie their wrapper across their chest above their breasts, while some who did not care would leave their sometimes long breasts dangling.

She loved to look at mothers with their babies tied to their backs, and the heavy baskets of yams and fruits on their heads. When the babies cried and wanted to be fed, they would just loosen their wrapper and the babies would maneuver their way under their mother's arm to get to the breasts. She remembered the times Esho used to carry her on her back like that and she missed it. She would wonder if Lana could carry her on his back, but then she would remind herself that Lana was a boy, and boys and men do not carry babies in that manner.

Ranti would look at the women with a lot of yearning. She would put her doll on her back and imitate them as they walked with the heavy load on their heads, the babies on their backs and the manner in which they swayed their hips.

When Lana saw her imitating the women, he asked her what she was doing, and she told him she would like to be like the women when she grew up, with babies on her back, swaying her hips as she returned from the farm on her way to the market.

Lana had looked at her and laughed out loud. He warned her that Esho must not hear her say that because it would make her very angry. Esho wanted them to go to college and be big people, not poor people who would carry heavy loads on their heads.

Ranti nodded, disappointed, but she thought the women with the babies on their backs were the most beautiful things she ever saw.

They loved to visit the old woman who sold palm oil. Her shack was very dirty because of the red thick oil that had spilled on the floor and walls, and it stuck to their feet after they left.

The old woman adored Lana like a lot of women in the neighborhood, and she called him "my husband." Lana explained to Ranti that she did not really want to marry him but it was an affectionate way of addressing him.

The woman would give them very ripe spongy and yellow mangoes, and they were delicious. She would ask Lana if he was studying hard in school and she would remind him that when he became a doctor, he would take care of her because she was his wife. Lana would nod his head as he promised her that he would remove the swelling in her neck.

The first time Ranti saw the woman's neck, she had been scared because of the big mass, but Lana had assured her that it was not a thing to be afraid of, that the woman was not eating some of the foods she was supposed to eat, and she developed the goiter. He read it in a health science book in school.

Lana and his sister who did not have shoes because Esho could not afford them, would go on expenditures after school, going into the bushes and the open community dumpsite where all the garbage ended up, pretending to look for treasures, as they went through the trash and dirt, sometimes stepping on animal droppings and human feces.

When this happened they would shriek loudly and race each other to the fast flowing river, jumping in to wash off the feces and other dirt.

The flies, ants and mosquitoes were constant companions, biting them and leaving bumps, sores and welts on their bodies. Esho made them take a medication that she called *"Sunday-Sunday"* every Sunday to prevent malaria.

Ranti loved this colorful landscape of her childhood with the smell though not pleasant most of the time and the noise. The cacophony of sound was amazing. Hawkers screamed as they walked by advertising their wares; everyone's radio would be competing with one another along with the screaming of babies, horns of cars and fighting couples in their heavily congested neighborhood.

Sometimes they got into trouble with neighbors who would find them at the dumpsite going through the trash. Some neighbors would hit them and later report them to Esho who would beat them again. So whenever they saw a neighbor coming, they would run away as fast as they could.

Lana told Ranti that it should be against the law to beat other people's children, but Esho did not have a problem with that; she would tell Lana and Ranti that "*It takes a village to raise a child,*" and that her neighbors were helping her since she was a very busy woman.

Lana would argue with her and tell her he read in a book that you should not beat other people's children and that Esho should not allow it.

Esho would beam, "Uhn Lana, you and your books, you should become a lawyer and not a doctor. You are so brilliant that you make me so proud."

Lana would smile and wink at Ranti, who would smile at her brother too.

Lana loved to read and he would tell his sister the stories he read from the books in the little school library, and sometimes after school they would stop by the big bookshop on their way home, and pretending to look at the books would hide behind the shelves and read them. A few times the attendants would catch them and throw them out, but they would be back within a few days.

They would also go to the fast-flowing river close to their house and swim for hours as they talked about a lot of things, with mostly Lana telling his sister his dreams and the places he hoped to visit, the places he had read to her from the books at the bookshop.

On a June Tuesday in 1972, three years after Oshun died, an assistant discovered Lana and Ranti hiding behind a big shelf in the bookshop as Lana was reading *Jason and the Golden Fleece* to Ranti.

The assistant grabbed Lana by the scruff of his shirt and dragged him to the manager's office. He told the manager that he found Lana trying to steal books.

Lana and Ranti protested that they were not stealing books, but were just reading them.

The assistant told the manager he had caught them behind the bookshelves on several occasions and he had warned them not to return to the bookshop.

The manager was very angry. He yelled at them and called them little thieves. He said they would grow up to be big thieves, and they were the ones destroying the country. He lectured them for a very long time. He threatened that if they came back to the bookshop at all, he would hand them over to the police and they would be sent away from their mother to the homes for wayward children. They threw them out on to the street and the assistant said they smelt because they wore rags.

Ranti was afraid. She did not want to be sent away, not from Esho and not from Lana. But Lana told her they were bluffing. "We did not break any laws. We didn't steal the books, we just read them and we were very careful and did not ruin or make them dirty in any way. Books are such treasures, like our grandmother and no one should own books exclusively. Books should be made available for anyone who wants to read them to have access to them, even if the person doesn't have money."

Ranti was afraid to go back to the bookshop but a few days later, Lana convinced her they should go back and finish the story of *Jason and the Golden Fleece*. He speculated about the ending of the book.

Four days later, on their way back from school, they snuck into the bookshop again. They hid behind the shelf and continued the story of Jason. As Lana got to the last chapter of the book, whispering as he read to his sister, the assistant who had thrown them out earlier in the week appeared. Ranti panicked and started to cry.

The assistant was very angry. "You stinking children, you dirt, didn't I tell you not to come back here? You and your witch of a grandmother are going to prison. I will spank you myself and then call the police on you and they will send you to prison." He yelled at them as he frothed at the corners of his mouth in frustration.

He tried to grab Lana but he eluded him. Lana grabbed Ranti and pulled her with him as he ran out of the bookshop dragging her behind him. They could hear the assistant cursing and screaming at them. They ran all the way to the forest and on to the dumpsite.

Lana screamed all of a sudden and stopped. He had stepped on a broken bottle and there was a big gash on the sole of his left foot spurting out blood.

Esho went to Akanbi to beg for money so she could take Lana to the hospital but as usual, he called her a crazy witch and said he was not Lana's father.

Esho tried to treat Lana's foot at home with herbs that neighbors suggested but it grew worse, with the foot becoming so swollen that he could not walk. He developed a very high fever, and about seven days later became very stiff, and his whole body would go into spasms.

This frightened Esho so much that she took him to the hospital even though she did not have money to pay them, but she begged them to treat him and that she would pay whichever way she could.

Lana was admitted to the hospital and Ranti and Esho would go visit him very early in the mornings and late in the evenings. His condition continued to get worse.

Five days after he was admitted to the hospital, he asked Ranti if she had gone back to the bookshop to finish *Jason and the Golden Fleece.*

Ranti shook her head.

In spite of the pain that was obvious on his face from the spasms, Lana excitedly said to his sister, "You have to go back and finish the story and come tell me how it ended. I'm sure Jason was able to get the Golden Fleece. He is so strong and smart. He does not let anything frighten him.

"You have to go back, Ranti. Don't worry about that assistant. He's just mean because he's surrounded by so many books, yet he cannot read. Books are treasures, like Esho. Don't you ever allow anyone stop you from reading books or finishing a story!

"The police can't arrest you, you are too young and that's the law. I read it in a book. The police can't do anything to you until you are eighteen years old and that is if you commit a crime. Don't let anyone scare you away from books, Ranti, okay? So go and finish that story and tell me when you and Esho come back tomorrow. Always finish a story, Ranti!" He insisted.

The doctor asked Ranti if she received immunizations each time the big trucks from the Health Department came to their school but Ranti stared at him. He advised her to always let them give her the immunizations. He said it would protect her from getting sick like her brother. He also advised Esho to buy shoes for her children.

Ranti missed her brother terribly since she had to walk to school alone, and he was not there to take her on their little expeditions anymore.

A week after Lana was admitted to the hospital, Ranti and Esho woke up very early in the morning to go and visit him, but they were told that he died during the night. The Nurses took them to the morgue where his body was kept, and they told Esho she had to pay a lot of money to keep his body there.

Esho asked them to give her Lana's body, that she would take him home to her people to bury, because she could not afford to keep him in the morgue.

She carried Lana's body on her back and strapped him in place with her wrapper and head tie. She held Ranti firmly by her left hand, and started to walk briskly.

A policeman stopped them on the street and said he would take Esho to jail because she was breaking a law. She had a dead child on her back, and a dead child belonged in the morgue, not on people's back, that it was a health hazard. He asked her to put Lana's body on the ground.

Esho started to shriek and to rain curses on the policeman. She told him that if she took Lana's body off her back she would give it to him and it would become his problem, because then he would have to bury him. She continued to walk briskly away and to pull Ranti behind her.

Ranti was afraid the policeman would arrest Esho and send her to prison. But he did not. He left them alone.

Esho went straight to Akanbi's house and told him that Lana was dead. She showed him the dead child.

Akanbi called her a witch; he asked her to leave his house, and said that he was not Lana's father.

Esho left Akanbi's house, and while still dragging Ranti with her, started to walk around the neighborhood, shrieking.

She asked the neighbors to witness her anguish. She said she had a cursed head from the very first day of her life, and the cursed head had continued to dodge her steps. She wailed but she did not shed any tears.

Ranti started to cry. She was afraid. She wanted Lana to come down from Esho's back and tell her that things would be fine, but he did not.

Some men came to them on the street as Esho was walking around cursing herself and Akanbi. They forcefully took Lana's body from Esho and two women started to take her and Ranti home.

The men started to go away with Lana's body. Ranti asked them where they were taking her brother but they ignored her. She started to cry and to beg Lana to come back to her, but he did not.

She ran after the men taking Lana away but the women grabbed her. She pleaded with the men to be gentle with Lana, that he had been very ill, and he needed people to take care of him. She promised them that if they gave her Lana, she would take good care of him. She promised to be a very good girl and would not go to the bookshop anymore, and that Lana too would become obedient and not go to the bookshop anymore.

She started to scream loudly and Esho turned to her and slapped her hard across her face. "You will never cry again," she commanded. "If you cry rivers of blood it will do no good; we are cursed. This line is cursed."

The women took Esho and Ranti home.

Esho went and laid on her mat. She looked at Ranti and pronounced, "We will never mention his name again. Do you hear me? Never again! It is over, it is done!"

Esho did not get off the sleeping mat for six months.

13

Ranti did not know what to do, so each day she would get up in the morning and cook for her grandmother; she would appeal to her to eat the food and sometimes Esho would eat.

Ranti continued to go to school because Esho had told her many times that it was the only cure for poverty and suffering, and that she and Lana going to school was the hope of the family.

When she came back from school, she would appeal to her grandmother to get up from the mat. Sometimes Esho would get up and go to the bathroom, only to return to the mat.

After one week, they ran out of food, and there was no money to buy more food. Ranti informed Esho of this, but Esho just stared at her.

Ranti started to beg the neighbors for food, which she would encourage her grandmother to eat and she would eat some of it too.

She went to Akanbi and told him that Esho had been sleeping for the past week, and there was no food in the house.

"And why is that any of my business?" Akanbi asked her in a very cold voice.

"Because you are my father, and you were Lana's father." Ranti informed him.

He pulled her into the room and closed the door after her. "Now listen, you bastard, I am not your father. Only God knows where your prostitute of a mother got all of you. I didn't have anything to do with it, and don't you go listening to your crazy grandmother. Don't you ever call me your father for as long as you live! Now get out."

After a week of the neighbors contributing food to them, they started to say no, because they were equally poor. Ranti went to the construction site where her grandmother worked carrying mixed cement, and offered to take her grandmother's place, so she would earn money for food, but the builder would not hire her because she was too young and too small.

Ranti started to go around the neighborhood looking for jobs she could do to feed herself and her grandmother, and a neighbor about ten doors away offered her the job of *agbepo*. It would be her job to empty the bucket used to collect the feces in the latrine at the back of his house and that had to be emptied every night.

Ranti accepted the job and the man paid her enough money to feed her and her grandmother each day. She did not tell Esho about the job, and Esho continued to be withdrawn and to stare into space all the time.

Ranti would go and collect the bucket of feces at about nine o'clock at night. She would go and dump it in the designated dumping place about fifteen minutes walk away, come back to the river and wash the bucket in the fast flowing water, after which she would jump into the river and soak herself in it for about twenty minutes, hoping that the smell of feces would not stick to her body. She would then return home.

After a week of emptying the bucket of feces, it seemed as if the smell of feces was stuck to her, so every chance she got, she would jump into the river and swim, hoping to wash the smell away.

She missed her brother dreadfully as swimming had been one of the things they enjoyed doing together.

Three months later, one of her classmates saw her carrying the bucket of feces on her way to empty it. He announced to the class the next day, and other students started to laugh at her and to call her, "feces." They also started to say she smelt of feces, even though for the previous months, no one had said she smelt of feces. The girls who had been her friends stopped playing with her.

Ranti kept to herself and missed her brother even more.

One day at recess, she was standing alone and apart from the other children on the playground when a group of boys came toward her. They called her "feces," and one of them asked her to wipe his anus for him. He pulled down his pants and showed her his butt.

Ranti started to walk away from them. Esho's warnings were ringing in her ears. Another boy showed her his penis and asked her to lick it. She tried to run away when a third boy pushed her and she fell on her back. She panicked and started to scream for help, hoping the teachers would hear her, but she knew it was not likely since the teachers stayed in the staff room during recess.

The boys started to drag her, as she was still on her back, toward the bushes at the edge of the playground when all of a sudden a rock hit one of them in the head.

He turned around and more rocks rained down on them. They started to yell and curse Gboye who was running toward them as she continued to throw rocks at them. The boys ran away and she came to help Ranti to her feet.

Gboye asked her if it was true that she carried feces and Ranti nodded. She told her that her grandmother was sick and had not been able to work, and that was the only way to get food.

Gboye was sympathetic and she asked Ranti to stay close to her at all times, that she would protect her.

The next day at recess, Gboye told Ranti that she spoke to her father about her situation and her father said she was a good girl who was not afraid to do any work to help her family, and that he would give her grandmother a job at his factory where foam was made.

Four months after Lana died, the big truck from the Health Department came to the school to give the children immunizations. Ranti remembered the doctor at the hospital telling her to always receive the immunizations, so she stood in line even though she was scared, and a lot of the children were crying and some ran away.

Gboye ran home to get her mother who came to school with her. Gboye's mother spoke to the people who wore white coats and were giving them the shots, and she convinced Gboye to get the shot. Her mother stayed in line with her till it was her turn and took her home after.

Three weeks later, the neighbor refused to pay Ranti for her work of emptying his bucket of feces. She begged him to pay her so she and her grandmother could eat but he refused. He started to pay her every other day but would pay her half of what he had been paying her before.

A month after he started to cheat her in this way, when she arrived to empty the bucket for the day and to collect the money for the previous two days work, he asked her to come into his bedroom. Ranti refused. She stood outside on his balcony and begged him to pay her. She explained to him that if she went to his room, she would be disobeying her grandmother who had strictly forbidden her to go with a man to his room.

He came out to meet her on the balcony. He ran his hands over her chest. Ranti pulled back. He told her that her breasts were already budding, and he hoped she would grow to be like her grandmother and mother who had bodies for pleasing a man. He promised to pay her double the amount of money he had been paying her, if she came to his room.

Ranti turned around and left. The man shouted after her that she was fired, and he would get someone else to empty his bucket of feces.

She went to the fast river and swam for a long time. She missed her brother so much that her heart ached. There was no money for food and they would have to go hungry.

When she arrived home, she found her grandmother standing outside in front of the house. Ranti was very happy to see her out of the room, a thing that had not happened since Lana died. She ran to embrace her out of sheer relief, but Esho had a stony expression on her face. Ranti stopped and stood in front of her.

"Where have you been?" Esho demanded of her. "The neighbors told me that every night while I sleep, you go out and come back home very, very late. It is after ten o'clock, where have you been?" She did not wait for Ranti to answer. She moved closer to her and slapped her hard across her face.

Ranti started to cry, she tried to explain that she had to go to work, to bring home money for their food, but Esho would not listen to her.

Esho started to rant and rave. She called Ranti a whore and said she was going to ruin her life just like Oshun. She kept trying to hit her, but Ranti evaded her blows.

Ranti was upset that Esho did not believe her but grateful that she was her old cursing and angry self again.

The next morning, Ranti went to school without food, but Gboye shared her lunch with her and reminded her that the offer of the job from her father still stood.

When Ranti arrived home in the afternoon, Esho was busy cleaning their one room and washing their clothes. She also handed Ranti her first pair of shoes. They were made of plastic but they looked almost like the sandals that Gboye wore which were made of leather.

The next morning as she was leaving for school, Ranti ensured that she was standing far away from the reach of Esho's hands to avoid her blows as she announced to her that her friend's father would give her a job at the Foam factory if she was interested.

Esho stopped what she was doing and started toward Ranti, who seeing the firm set of her jaw knew that a beating was coming, so she grabbed her school bag and fled. Esho yelled after her, calling her a whore and asking her if her friend's father had been sleeping with her, and was that why he offered her the job?

Esho became crazy in these many ways toward Ranti, constantly yelling at her, hitting her and calling her a whore who was going to end up like her mother— "Dead!" She would shriek at her, "Do you hear me, you will die!"

On the streets as well, each time she and Esho walked by Akanbi's house and saw his wife and children, Esho would start to curse them out, and on many occasions she would wake up in the middle of the night and send curses out to Akanbi.

Whenever she caught Ranti staring at her, she would yell at her too. "He is your father but he has disowned you, just like mine disowned me. Men are terrible, Iranti, I keep warning you, stay away from them; they are a terrible species."

Ranti was at a loss, but she was determined that she would not die like Lana and Oshun died. "I will stay alive and I will not let any man touch me to ruin me or kill me. I will go to the university to become a doctor. I will do that for Lana," she would promise herself.

Esho returned to her old job and there was at least one meal a day. The jobs took her away for most of the day and Ranti was grateful for this because it gave her time to go to the river to swim. She had stopped going into the forest and the dumpsite since her brother died, because that was where he got injured when he stepped on a broken bottle.

She ached to go to the bookshop to read the interesting books but she was afraid of the assistant who had threatened to hand them over to the police, and besides her brother died because he was running away from the bookshop. But Lana's advice kept ringing in her ears. His last words to her were that she should not let anyone scare her from books, and that books are treasures, like Esho. "Always finish a story," he had insisted.

She promised herself that she would go back to the bookshop. She told herself she would do that as a memorial to her brother. She would continue to read books for the two of them, because Lana had loved books so much, and she would always finish a story.

She did not play with the neighborhood children who knew of her work of emptying the bucket of feces, and were always calling her "*feces.*"

In school, Ranti and Gboye became good friends. Gboye on her part was ostracized by the other children because her family was the richest in the school, as her father's foam factory which was started five years before was doing very well. A lot of the children's parents worked at the factory and they hated Gboye's father, claiming he did not pay their parents enough money. But they dared not taunt Gboye because, at the age of seven, she was the biggest student in the whole school aside from her three brothers who were in fourth, fifth and sixth grades.

On a few occasions Gboye invited Ranti home with her and she met her grandmother and her other two brothers. Gboye was the only girl and the youngest.

Going to Gboye's house was always an overwhelming experience for Ranti. They lived in a very big house with lots of rooms, and they had lots of servants. Gboye's mother was a very big and warm woman who would hug Ranti in such a way that made her feel that she would crush her to death.

She would also hug her each time their eyes met and sometimes she would have tears in her eyes. She would repeatedly say to Ranti, "I know what you are going through my good child, but one day it will all pass, because you won't stay a child forever; it will all be over one day."

Ranti would nod her thanks.

Gboye's grandmother was a busy woman who managed a poultry and she worried constantly about her chicken and eggs. She would give Ranti a boiled egg and insisted she ate it in front of her. There was always food cooking on the stove in Gboye's kitchen.

Gboye's brothers were big and rowdy. They made too much noise and even when they played with one another it seemed as if there was a battle going on. They played rough games with Gboye too, and she was a match for them.

Ranti made sure Esho did not know she went to Gboye's house, especially because it was full of boys and men. She also learnt to avoid Esho and her unprovoked blows at other times too, and felt lucky that Esho worked until late in the day.

Esho restarted to force-feed Ranti, which she had stopped two years before when she grew too big and would struggle with her. But this time she complained that Ranti was getting too thin.

Ranti was not eating, not even the one meal a day Esho was able to provide because the food made her sick. On many occasions, after eating she would run to the forest close to their house to throw up, so Esho would not see her. At other times, her stomach would just hurt her for a long time.

Esho took Ranti to the dispensary. They were told she had intestinal worms, and they were eating what little food she ate, that's why she was getting thinner. They gave her some green liquid medication.

Esho became very angry at the worms. She cursed at them the same way she had been cursing Akanbi. "I refuse to work hard to feed worms. Worms do not belong inside a person! They belong in the soil. Akanbi is the one who should be afflicted with worms because those are the things that will eat him alive when smallpox finally infects him." She cursed all the way home.

Ranti refused to take the medication because of its terrible taste and smell, so Esho asked a neighbor to hold her down, three times a day, while she forced into her the medication mixed in cornmeal she hated so much.

When she went to the bathroom at the back of the house the day after she started the medication, worms came out of her. She screamed and ran out of the bathroom toward Esho because some of the worms were still alive and they were dangling in her behind.

Esho slapped her hard across the face to calm her. She took her back to the bathroom and slowly extracted the worms from her behind.

For two weeks, each time she went to the bathroom she passed out worms. The thoughts of going to the bathroom started to terrify her so she started to obey all the instructions at the health science class, about hand-washing and of proper handling and preparation of foods and cooking them very well before you ate them, so you could avoid getting worms.

She realized that she must have been infected with the worms when she did the work of carrying feces on her head, so she and Esho could eat after Lana died and Esho would not die.

14

Ranti's changing body scared her because this is the story Esho told her about Oshun. She would stare at her breasts whenever she went to swim in the river alone, and she started to pray that her body would not change and put her in the kind of danger Oshun and Esho endured.

She confided in Gboye who said her mother told her it was a good thing for a girl's body to change. It meant she would become a woman and would be able to have babies, and that they are wonderful things. Ranti did not agree with her friend.

Ranti, who always stayed as far away as possible from Esho to avoid unanticipated blows had noticed her grandmother inspecting her body and shaking her head in sorrow. At other times she would lament that there was a curse on Ranti's head too, and then she would go crazy and start to shriek and scream at her to stay away from men, otherwise they would ruin her life or kill her.

Ranti was constantly afraid and confused as her body that seemed to have a will of its own continued to change nevertheless. She too started to notice boys and men staring at her more than usual, and at times while walking down the streets, men would call to her.

She started to run everywhere she had to go on errands and to run to school and home instead of walking, and she stopped eating. She knew that eating made one fat, so she would eat just one meal every other day. She hoped it would stop her body from growing, but it did not.

A year after Lana died, she braved her fears of returning to the bookshop because she needed somewhere to hide from the men who kept staring at her body, and whom she was afraid would ruin her life or kill her like they killed Oshun. So one day after school, she casually walked into the bookshop though her heart was about to jump out of her throat. She scanned for the mean assistant who threw them out the year before, but he was not there. Most of the assistants at the bookshop were new.

She was happy about this and slowly walked over to the section of children's books. She picked-up a copy of the book, *Jason and the Golden Fleece*, which she and her brother did not read to the end. She stood there without hiding and read the rest of the story.

She returned to the bookshop the next day and picked another book. She sat on the stairs and started to read it. After about ten minutes, an assistant asked her to leave if she was not buying the book.

"I'm trying to make up my mind if I want to buy it." She told him.

"Trying to make up your mind by reading the book first? If you've read it, why would you buy it? You have to leave now."

Ranti stood up and gave him the book. She walked slowly out of the bookshop, embarrassed. She walked to the river and sat on the bank for a long time. "It's not fair. It's not fair that I can't read books because we don't have money. I want to learn and know a lot of things and there are so many books in the bookshop that it doesn't matter if I read some of them. Life is not fair at all." She started to cry.

She remembered Lana telling her that books should not be owned by anyone, so that anyone who wants to read a book should have access to it. She stood up and wiped her face with the skirt of her dress. She returned to the bookshop.

"I'm going to read a lot of books and become knowledgeable so bad things will not happen to us anymore, because knowledge is power. I will return to the bookshop and read the books in there, all of them, and I will not let anyone stop me. I'm not stealing them; I'm just reading them. No one has the power to keep knowledge from another person. That is what Lana told me. No one should have that power and I'm not going to let the bookshop have that power over me."

She was too afraid to walk into the bookshop or even stand by the front entrance in case the assistant who threw her out saw her. She went to the back and hid behind a shack. She did not know how she would get into the bookshop but she was determined to get in.

She stood behind the shack for over an hour thinking of the different ways she could sneak into the bookshop. It was as if the books were pulling at her the way a magnet pulls at metallic objects. At some point she started to think of returning home because Esho would be getting home from her job soon, but she stood where she was.

All of a sudden, the big metallic door at the back of the bookshop was flung open and the manager came out. Ranti's heart almost stopped as she recognized him. He had threatened to send her and her brother to jail the year before. He walked away as the door slammed shut with a loud thud.

She waited and watched. He returned about ten minutes later with another man; he opened the door with a big key but he left the key in the keyhole as he and the second man went into the bookshop.

Ranti's heart started to race with excitement but she ran to the door and jiggled the key out of the keyhole and ran back to her hiding place.

The two men came out of the door fifteen minutes later and whispered to one another for another five minutes, then, the second man left. The manager tried to go back into the bookshop but he could not find his key. He searched in the many pockets of his clothes for a long time. He ran after his departing friend, calling to him. They both returned and searched for the key.

"I must have lost it," he concluded, though he was not convinced. "But I opened the door with it when we came back." They searched some more and finally they gave up. "I have a spare in my office." He told his friend who left with a promise to see him in a few days. The manager went around the building to the front of the bookshop.

Ranti ran home and hid the key in the shrub behind the house. She could not get up the courage to return to the bookshop until the following week. The bookshop was closed on Sundays, so after she finished her chores, she told Esho she was going to the river to swim as she left the house. She knew Esho would not miss her for about five hours. Her grandmother who worked twelve hours a day, six days a week at her hard manual labor job spent her Sunday afternoons sleeping.

She retrieved the big key from its hiding place and walked to the back of the bookshop. She was afraid the manager might have changed the lock, but was pleasantly surprised when the key turned and the big metal door swung open. Making sure she had the key, she hurried inside and closed the door.

She switched on the light and for a moment almost fainted because in the room were lots of scary animal parts. There was a huge cow horn, clay pots with dead rats, lizards, chameleons and snakes inside them. To a corner was the skull of a human being and to another corner of the room was palm oil split on the ground. Ranti knew immediately that it was a ritual room for black magic.

To one side on the wall was written: [BEWARE THIEF! THIS BLACK MAGIC PROTECTS THIS BOOKSHOP. IF YOU THINK YOU CAN STEAL FROM THIS BOOKSHOP AND NOT GET CAUGHT, THINK AGAIN BECAUSE THIS POWERFUL MAGIC IS WATCHING YOU. AND WHATEVER BEFALLS YOU; KNOW THAT YOU BROUGHT IT UPON YOURSELF WITH YOUR GREED].

She had heard stories about these things from her classmates and they always warned one another not to hang around such places as they could be used as a sacrifice for black magic.

She shuddered in fear, but she did not run out of the room. She also remembered Esho telling her that belief in black magic was a "load of crap," that such black magic did not work unless the targeted person believed in it, and it was more of mental poisoning than actual harm done to people.

Esho believed your god is in your head, and you have to work hard with your hands and brain through a good education to achieve things in life and not rely on some magical thinking to get them for you.

"Black magic, witchcraft and *juju* are illusory weapons of cowards and the powerless. Your god is in your head, Iranti. It is not in some Christian God or Muslim God or even in the indigenous gods like Ogun, Oshun or Obatala. It is up to you what you do with your head.

"There is no black magic anywhere unless you buy into that crap. It's a way

68   *Feasts of Phantoms*

for powerless people to feel they have some power, and the so called *Babalawo* exploit them and take all their money when they promise to give them powerful magic.

"No one has the power to control the world or other people unless you give them the power to control you. Do you hear me? Don't hang around people who think that way, the same way I don't want you going to their church. Your god is in your head and it is up to you and your head. If you let men ruin your life, that is what you have asked of your god, but if you stay in school and read all the books you can lay your hands on and get a very good education, that is what you have asked of your god.

"When my father first raped me, I called on God to save me. Did he? I had to take matters into my own hands to stop him. When the mad man that gave me Oshun before I was ready first raped me, I was too distracted thinking of trolls and fairies and Jesus and even my dead mother hoping they would come and take care of me. I didn't have all my wits with me. But the second time he came at me, I killed him.

"I know I have a cursed head and I'm working hard with my cursed head to make the best of what I have. I take matters into my own hands now. I will not go to someone to make black magic for me so I would become rich, or so that someone would give me the money they worked hard to get. I am working hard in the only job I could get because I don't have an education, and that is why you are going to get the best education out there, Iranti. That is what you are asking of your head and your god. That is the only magic that works; hard work and perseverance.

"If you want to harm someone, you take a knife and go at them; you do not dance around some dead animals or carve some plank of wood thinking that if you stick a needle into the wood the person will die." Ranti repeated Esho's admonition to herself as a reassurance not to be afraid.

She walked out of the room through a door that led into the bookshop. She wedged the door so it would not close on her since she did not have the key to it. The bookshop was strangely quiet and for a moment she was afraid.

"There are no ghosts, no trolls, no spirit, no magic, it's all people's imagination to scare themselves or to make them feel that they have power over other people, it is all magical thinking," she repeated to herself, quoting Esho.

She walked over to the children's section of the bookshop, got some books, sat on the stairs by the window for the sunlight and disappeared into the wonderful world of books.

Ranti started to go to the bookshop on Sundays, going through the 'fetish' room as she named the room with the black magic and making sure she wedged the door that led into the bookshop, and reading all the interesting books about faraway places and other people whose lives had been very hard too. She would also go to the river that was mostly deserted and swim in her clothes, taking a change of clothes with her.

15

One Saturday morning, a few months after Ranti turned nine, she and Esho had to go to the market. As they walked on the streets in their low-income heavily congested neighborhood, Esho noticed a lot of men looking at Ranti, and some of them even called to her. One man called her Oshun.

Esho went crazy and started to shriek. The man laughed and said Ranti looked exactly like Oshun, who had been his classmate in elementary school.

On the way home from the market, another man stopped them. He complimented Esho on the fact that Ranti was blooming into a young flower and he was sure she would grow up to be as beautiful as her mother of blessed memory had been.

Esho stopped walking and stared at the man for a moment. Ranti started to panic and wondered why people would not leave Esho alone. "Why do they have to speak to her at all?"

Esho started to scream at the man. "Beautiful flower eh? And you think you are the one to pluck it? Is that so? If I see you near Iranti, I swear on my life that I will kill you. You rapist! You child molester!"

She untied her headgear inside where she kept her knife, and showed it to the man. "Look at this knife because this is what I will use to kill you," she promised him.

He gave her a strange look and got out of her way.

Esho grasped Ranti's left hand and started to walk very fast. When they were out of the man's earshot, she started to pull her by her right ear and to slap her face. She asked her if she had been prostituting herself and Ranti tried to convince her grandmother that she had not. She said she had been obeying her, because she did not want to ruin her life. She wanted to go to the university, and like she promised, she would not let any man touch her.

Esho gave her lectures all the way home on the perils of talking to men. The lectures she had been giving her all her life. Once at home, she took a pair of scissors and cut off all of Ranti's beautiful long hair without any explanations. Ranti started to cry.

Esho yelled at her and threatened her with a beating as she explained to her,

"When a man wants to ruin your life, he will tell you that you are beautiful. It is a lie because you are not beautiful at all. You are too thin, and your lips are too big such that they are not beautiful, so hear the truth from me now. You are not a beautiful girl at all. In fact you are ugly, and it is because of the genes you inherited from that Akanbi with a head like that of a tortoise. Smallpox will afflict him and his bastards and ugly wife and will kill all of them.

"Do you hear me? You are an ugly girl, just like Akanbi, so don't believe anyone who calls you beautiful because they have one desire and one desire only, and that is to ruin your life."

She borrowed a full- length mirror from a neighbor. She stood behind Ranti in front of the mirror. "Iranti, take a good look at yourself and I will tell you the truth," she started. "You are not beautiful at all and that is the truth. Don't believe anyone who tells you that you are beautiful because what they want to do is kill you. Do you want to die or stay alive? Answer me and stop crying otherwise I will really give you something to cry about."

Ranti sobbed that she did not want to die.

"Good," said Esho. "So here is the truth that will keep you alive and well. You are not a beautiful girl at all, and that is why I cut off your hair. You don't need it to distract you from your studies. I'm the only person in this world who cares about you and I'm giving you pearls here. Pearls that will keep you alive! You are not a beautiful girl at all, and if anyone tells you otherwise, know that they are murderers who want to kill you.

"Don't even stop to speak to them, because if you let them come close to you, they will try to touch your breasts and if they succeed in doing that, you are pregnant and that is it. Your life is over.

"Some men will try to force themselves on you when you are not watching, or when you are sleeping. That is what happened to me, many times. That is why I always carry a knife, and in the market today, I bought a knife for you; here, take it." She handed Ranti a knife similar to the one she carried in her headgear.

"If any man comes at you, stab him. There is no justice in this world and it is a wicked world, so you have to do what you have to do to protect yourself."

The following Monday when Ranti got to school with her hair all cut off, the boys started to laugh at her and to sing, *"feces has turned into a boy."*

A few weeks later Gboye invited Ranti to Sunday school telling her it was a lot of fun where they were told stories of the Bible and given snacks.

Ranti asked Esho's permission to go to Sunday school, and she received a beating for this. While she was crying, Esho started her lectures again. "There is no God anywhere, Iranti, don't start dreaming there is a God somewhere, because it is the kind of thinking that will get you into serious trouble. You are on your own.

"When the mad man that gave me Oshun first raped me, I was busy thinking of their Jesus and God and ghosts and trolls, and fairies and spirits and my dead mother, hoping they would come and take care of me. I was too distracted and wasn't paying attention. That is the kind of mindset religion gets you into such that you are not paying attention to important things.

"You have to protect yourself and take care of yourself. No one cares and definitely not the Christian God or the Muslim God and not even the indigenous gods like Ogun, or Oshun, or Oya. They don't give a damn about you or me, maybe they care about rich people, but about us, they don't give a damn. Your God is in your head. It is up to you what you do with it.

"If you allow men to ruin your life, then that is what you asked of your God, and if you focus on your studies in school, and go on to the university and get a good job, then that is what you have asked of your God. It is all up to you and your head.

"There is no Jesus Christ anywhere. And what are they going to tell you in their church? There is a hell and there is a heaven, or you will go to hell if you are bad, and go to heaven if you are good? *Panti,*" she hissed in disgust, "it's a load of crap. I was an innocent baby who had not even had a chance to sin, but my mother died, is that heaven? I was an obedient girl but my father raped me many times, is that the reward of heaven? I worked hard but a mad man gave me Oshun before I was ready, is that heaven?" She paused, as she looked distracted.

"You know, I never even saw his face, because everything happened in the dark. I wish I had seen the face of that mad man. Oh, the things I would have done to his face! If I could write I would have written 'rapist' on his face so when the people who found his body saw it, they would know why he died, sshh—," she hissed and spat on the concrete floor in their room. She cleaned it up immediately with the edge of her wrapper.

"No, Iranti, I have never been to heaven but I have been to hell, many times, and I didn't deserve any of it. I just came back not long ago but I tell you, if I deserved it, I will willingly go again, at least then I'm going for a reason I understand, like after I kill Akanbi, I won't mind going to hell again, but I won't choose that heaven of theirs which is a bunch of lies. Those people are fools and liars and I don't want you around them. You hear me?"

Ranti's changing body continued to give Esho a lot of sorrow especially that she looked exactly like Oshun at that age. She was becoming more and more voluptuous even though Esho knew she was not eating regularly. Her breasts were high and round, and so were her hips, and her skin looked and felt like velvet at the times she touched her to hit her.

Esho would stay up at night and watch her as she slept, and she looked vulnerable with an angelic face. "She is so innocent and needing of protection. But this is a cruel world," she would lament.

Men continued to stare at her and call her a lot of endearing names like rose, angel, and sweetheart. Esho knew Ranti was an obedient girl unlike her mother. She did not encourage the men. She stayed out of their way and was always running on the streets to avoid them.

Esho was convinced that if she did not do something, Ranti would end up like Oshun, dead. These men would kill her because Ranti was not feisty at all. Even Oshun who had been more belligerent and had been known to fight when it was called for; had been killed by men, so Ranti did not have a prayer of staying alive with the kind of body she had been given.

She knew Ranti would never use the knife she gave her to protect herself. It had even been difficult for her to kill the mice that ran around in their room sometimes. Each time they saw a mouse Ranti would become terrified and start to scream.

She also remembered the time she had the problems with the intestinal worms. Ranti would run out of the bathroom with the worms dangling from her behind, screaming as if the devil was pursuing her, instead of just reaching behind her and pulling the worms out of her. "If she can't deal with worms, most of which are dead, and small mice, how can she deal with a grown man with a knife if he comes at her?" Esho would agonize.

So for the first time in her life, she consulted the other mothers in the neighborhood. She asked them what she could do to protect Ranti from her sexuality and from men, and they told her.

"When you give birth to your daughter and you see that she is a feisty baby, you have to circumcise her right away. The tip of the clitoris is the fire between a woman's thighs, it is what makes them lose control and want sex all the time."

They told her that another reason to snip off the tip of the clitoris is because a baby should not be born to a woman who had not been circumcised. A baby's head must not touch the uncircumcised clitoris while it is coming out of the vagina. It is especially dangerous for baby boys. And boys that are born to uncircumcised mothers usually die before they reach maturity because it is like they have had sex with their mothers and it is a curse for a son to have sex with his mother.

Esho was stunned to hear this. She concluded that her father and the mad man that gave her Oshun must have smelt that she was not circumcised and so they had come after her.

Oshun did not have a chance of surviving either since she was not circumcised. It also explained to her why Lana died. It was like he had sex with his mother since his head must have touched Oshun's uncircumcised clitoris while he was being born. She lamented and stayed on her mat for a week, thinking about how her ignorance had killed Oshun and Lana, and this terrified Ranti, who thought she was becoming depressed again.

The following Saturday, Esho woke Ranti very early in the morning while it was still dark and they traveled on a lorry to a remote village. She did not tell her where they were going, and the second time she asked her, Esho's answer was to give her a hard slap across her face.

At the village they went to a hut. Esho asked Ranti to wait outside while she went in. She emerged a few moments later with a very old and dirty woman who took them to a shack and there were four men in the room. Ranti became terrified, but before she could run, the men grabbed her and knocked her to the ground. They spread her legs apart and held her down, each person holding a limb. The dirty woman had a knife with which she ripped off her underwear.

Ranti screamed for Esho to save her, but Esho had a blank look on her face, the same look she had on her face for months after Lana died, but Ranti continued to scream at her grandmother, hoping to bring her back from wherever she was disappearing to. Esho did not hear her. The dirty woman started to chant some incantations and to sprinkle some white substances on Ranti's genitals.

"Esho!" Ranti screamed, "These are men holding me down and doing things to me, haven't you always warned me to stay away from men, why did you bring me to men so they could ruin my life?" Ranti continued to scream at her grandmother.

She struggled with all her might but it was no use.

The old woman came at her with a knife held in her tremulous hand. She warned her to be still, otherwise her hand might slip and she might end up cutting other things she did not intend to cut.

Ranti continue to struggle. The woman started to cut her clitoris and the pain seared into her brain. She screamed in agony and with a sudden burst of energy jerked her pelvis, the woman's hand slipped and Ranti felt such unbearable pain as the knife cut deeper into her genitals and down into her left thigh.

She screamed again for Esho. One of the men let go of her as he hit her hard across the face. At that moment, Esho snapped out of her trance and lunged at the man who hit Ranti and started to tear at him. She extracted her knife from her headgear and was about to stab him when the other men grabbed her.

Ranti sprang up from the floor to run and she could see blood running down her thighs. She fainted.

When she came to, it was night and she was strapped onto Esho's back, the way she used to carry her when she was a little girl, and the way she had carried Lana's body the day he died.

Esho was chanting to herself. Ranti could not make out what she was saying but her left leg and genitals were throbbing with such unbelievable pain that each step jarred the pain into her brain. She kept going in and out of consciousness until they arrived at home.

The next day when she woke up, she was naked, her thigh was bound with a white bandage and there were some herbs on her genitals. Esho was sitting next to her looking at her with that trance-like expression. She helped Ranti sit up and the mat was wet with urine.

"Why, Esho? Why?" Ranti asked her. "Haven't I always been a good girl and tried to please you? I have never disobeyed you. I have always done whatever you asked of me. I have stayed away from men. I don't even talk to boys in my class, yet you broke your own rule and took me to some men to do this to me. Why?"

Esho's face was expressionless.

Ranti remained sick for about two months and she could not go to school. Gboye tried to see her but Esho would not let her into the room. Ranti heard her friend's voice outside of their door on many occasions. She too did not want Gboye to see her. She was embarrassed because she had started to leak urine.

Esho told her that the leakage would stop when she had healed, but after two months when most of the pain was gone, the leaking still continued. Ranti realized she would leak urine for the rest of her life.

Esho stopped hitting and cursing her, and for the most part became kinder toward her. One night, she tried to justify what she had done by explaining to Ranti that it was to protect her from men, so as to save her life and save her from her mother's fate, and even her own fate of having been raped many times. She said she was trying to be a good mother.

Ranti recovered but she had a big deep scar on her left thigh that ran from her groin to the side of her thigh from when the woman's hand slipped.

Her genitals healed as well but there was a big scar that formed on her labia majora and it started to grow bigger, growing into a keloid that covered her labia minora joining the two sides together. Sometimes it hurt her when she walked, and she could not run anymore because of the pain from the keloid. Esho had to get her bigger underwear.

When it was time for her to return to school, Esho made a pad of clothes from rags for her to line her underwear to soak up the constant leakage of urine. She advised her to go to the bathroom as often as she could to empty her bladder to limit the leakage.

Ranti became miserable and started to smell urine and feces on herself some of the time. Sometimes she would have sensations as if the worms were still dangling in her behind. She stopped going to the river to swim as she and her brother used to love to do, and as she had continued after his death. She continued to go to school and would go to the bookshop on Sundays, and it was a good place for her to disappear into the world of books. She also continued to do very well in school, coming top of her class, and even though she had missed about ten weeks, she was able to catch up pretty fast with Gboye's help.

She confided in Gboye about the mutilation and leaking urine, after she made her swear not to tell her secret to anyone. She would ask her if she could smell her. Gboye would tell her she did not smell of urine or feces, but she could smell the talcum powder she used to keep the pad of rags dry as much as it was possible, and to treat the excoriations on her thighs.

Ranti was surprised that Gboye could not smell her.

16

Mrs. Sanchez was very angry. She had tried several times to get Ranti to take a break from her typing. It was eleven o'clock at night and for the previous three hours she had camped in the kitchen, not going back to her cottage. The food she had prepared was cold on the dining table.

She came into the living room when she heard Ranti come in from the deck where she had been sitting and typing all day, except for the few bathroom breaks she took. She started to yell at her.

Ranti gave her a long look. "Aren't we forgetting ourselves? You are not Esho and I don't have to listen to you. Even then I stopped listening to Esho a long time ago," she said aloud.

She walked past the older woman and went into the refrigerator. She took a bag of the intravenous nutrition and bidding her good night, went to her room and closed the door behind her. She changed into her nightshirt and set the intravenous nutrition, as she lay on the bed with plans to go to sleep while the fluid emptied itself. She was very exhausted from sitting up for so long; her whole body ached but for some reason she felt light hearted, and it was a very good feeling.

She tried to find the words to describe her feelings but as usual she could not find any of her own, so she borrowed: *"What is astonishing about putting one's life into words, about telling a story, is that certain aspects of being are not only revealed but come to exist fully for the first time. Untold stories are like rooms without air."*

"These are stories I didn't even tell Dr. Obed. I've been meeting with him on and off for the past twelve years and I didn't tell him I had a brother. I didn't tell him that my mother was a prostitute and I didn't tell him Esho was a murderer. I told him about the mutilation and I told him I had to carry feces on my head for other people, but I did not tell him that I had a brother who died or that my mother Oshun was a prostitute. How could he have helped me? I didn't even give him a chance to know me.

"I didn't tell him about Lana because Esho forbade it. What an admonition! So many closed doors, so much of my life locked behind doors of secrets. No one has been shutting me out of places! That is what Dr. Obed has been trying to tell me these many years, he has been telling me that no one is shutting me out of places; rather, it is me who has been shutting me out of places with all these closed doors of secrets that are mine.

"Secret! That is what Lana became to us. He became a secret between Esho and I. We spoke of Oshun many times, but we never spoke about Lana. It was as if he never existed. But he did exist! He was my loving brother. He loved me so much and I loved him so much.

"What is that about secrets? *"When a secret is not told, grieving goes on anyway, and for life. The keeping of secret interferes with the natural self-healing hygiene of psyche and spirit. This is one more reason to say our secrets. Telling and grieving resurrect us from the dead zone. They allow us to leave the death cult of secrets behind. We can grieve and grieve hard, and come of it tear-stained, rather than shame-stained. We can come out deepened, fully acknowledged, and filled with new life.'*

"That's what it is. Shame! I am ashamed that my brother died. Why? What is there to be ashamed of? I wasn't ashamed that I carried feces on my head; I told people that. But that my brother died, I couldn't tell anyone.

"I can understand not telling anyone that my mother was a prostitute, or that Esho was a murderer, but that my brother died? That doesn't make any sense. I didn't tell Depo, whom I love so much, not Moradeke or Gboye, who are like sisters to me, and not Dr. Obed, one of the most benevolent souls I know.

"The secrets became painful boils under my armpits. They continue to hurt like hell. I remained in the land of the dead. That is why I risked losing my unborn babies again. I lost a baby before because of all these secrets and pain, all this unresolved grief. I don't want to lose my babies. I want birth and increase around me. I don't want to become Esho who lived in the land of the dead and whose touch was death itself.

"I'm feeling light hearted now because air is finally being let into the rooms in my mind where my stories have been stored, those stories I never forgot but that I never lived. Those wraiths that are dead but could not go away because there was no air let in for the wind to bear them off. I have to let in the air, that is the connecting of the prose and the passion, Boris' crossword puzzle.

"My brother's name was never mentioned between Esho and I again. There is no one alive who had known my brother so I could talk about him with them. Lana became a ghost locked away in a closet. I have the prose but could not find the passion because Esho forbade it.

Esho, who with hard-earned wisdom gave me the name "Memory," turned around and enforced amnesia on me in that critical area of my life that has to do with my only sibling.

"We will never mention his name again," Esho had said of the only member of the male species she was going to allow herself to love, the one man who was going to be her savior in a cruel world, the only man who could have cured her of her madness. He was going to use his penis to penetrate the world and open it up for us in a benevolent manner. He was not going to use his penis to rape women.

"But he was snatched away by poverty and tetanus; poverty because Esho could not afford to buy exploring children shoes, and tetanus because Lana never had the opportunity of getting the protective immunizations. How would Esho have known of a tetanus vaccine?

"I never said my brother's name aloud after that time he lay dying on the hospital bed. I was not allowed to mourn my brother's passing. I should have screamed his name. I should not have listened to Esho and I should have gone to the forest and the dumpsite and to the river, and the bookshop he loved so much and screamed his name aloud. Lana! Lana! Lana! Lana! I should have screamed. Now I have no one to talk to about my brother."

Ranti got out of bed and dragging the intravenous fluid pole along with her walked around the room and the tears came down as if a floodgate was finally let open.

"I am sorry Lana, I am so sorry. I found a man who loves me like I'm his sister. The same way you had loved me. I'm now carrying his children. You taught me about brotherly love and I found it in a man and in his boyfriend. You gave me my only doll that I loved so much and I named it Lana. I stopped playing with that doll after you died. I had to grow up in a minute.

"I also met an elderly man, he loves me like I'm his daughter, and he encouraged me to become a mother, his name is Boris. I found two women who love me like I'm their sister. You taught me about love, Lana, and I have been able to create a community of wonderful people for myself.

"Lana, I haven't been able to find a man to love me as a lover. You left before you taught me that. You left before you taught me that men could be brothers and lovers too. I couldn't learn by watching you with girls. I couldn't learn of the ways a lover should treat me. I didn't learn that a lover had to hold me in his mind and come after me if I am not there. I didn't learn that a lover should fight for me, and go in search of me if I'm missing. I didn't learn that a lover was not supposed to hit me or rape me. I didn't, because I didn't have the chance to watch you with girlfriends.

"I'm sorry I never talked to you. But I have accomplished a lot. I am a surgeon. I'm very good with a scalpel, though I almost killed a man once with a knife. So much has happened in my life that you might not know about.

"Esho, she went crazy after you died. You know she loved you so much. You were her world and she drew each breath for you. She went so crazy that she almost killed me. I didn't have you to protect me. I didn't have you there to make

Esho smile, so some of that kindness from her love for you would spill onto me. Oh so much Lana."

Ranti continued to walk around the room holding onto the pole as she continued to talk aloud to her brother and to cry. Her body was tired but her mind would not shut down. She told him of the genital mutilation, of the ostracism, and of Akanbi's cruelties.

"Esho why, why?" she cried into the darkness of the room. "Why couldn't you have just left me alone? I was on my way; I was doing well. I was taking good care of myself. I listened to you and stayed out of men's way and I didn't even talk to boys, I am still not talking to men. I still don't trust them.

"Why, Esho? You don't know what you robbed me of? You accused Akanbi of being a thief, but you did worse than he did. To kill the desire to have passion and joy in another human being is the ultimate sin, Esho, why did you do it? You know I read it in a book once, you know how I used to love to read books. I am still reading books because I want to know, I want to learn, and I want to heal. What you did is called Soul Murder.

"You didn't just kill your father when you stabbed him in the chest with the potsherd, you didn't just kill the mad man who gave you Oshun when you stabbed him several times with a knife, you murdered a lot of wonderful things in me too Esho. You murdered my ability to trust decent men, and the ability to see the truth of myself, that I am a worthy beautiful woman, a desirable woman.

"I leaked urine and became an outcast. I carried feces when you were sick after Lana died, but Esho, I continued to carry feces in secondary school because that became my punishment for not participating in sports, which I couldn't when you robbed me of my clitoris and gave me a painful keloid in its place.

"Today I continue to be an outcast. Good people, wonderful people invite me into their community but I panic and run. I run and I hide. I see doors that are shutting in my face whereas the doors are actually wide open and benevolent souls are beckoning to me. They see an accomplished beautiful woman, I see an ugly feces carrier, leaking urine and afflicted with intestinal worms.

"Esho, I am a brilliant surgeon today. You were there, you saw me win awards in residency training, but I don't believe I'm any good. I continue to think that people are making fun of me.

"Esho, I am a beautiful woman. I look in the mirror these days and a lovely face smiles back at me. It is my face, Esho, Iranti's face. For that moment I see it as a beautiful face but when I leave the mirror, I forget what I saw, and the next time someone calls me beautiful I become you, and I call him a pervert who wants to kill me.

"My lips are full and beautiful, my hair has grown back and it is kinky and beautiful. I am a beautiful woman, Esho. Why did you kill that in me? You stood me in front of a mirror when I was nine years old and you told me that I was ugly.

You cut off my hair and told me I didn't need it. You robbed me of what every girl needs to survive in this world.

"Esho I was a good girl. I didn't give you the troubles that Oshun gave you. I never raised my hands or my voice at you. I wanted to live but you almost killed me. In some ways you did kill me. I want a man to love me and make love to me Esho, I deserve that, but I can't seem to find such men. I am good at finding rapists."

The tears continued to run down her face. From time to time sobs racked her body and her head felt as if it would explode.

"Oshun, who were you? Where did you go when you left? Who with? Are you with them now? You left me when I was four days old and I didn't have the pleasure of suckling at a mother's breasts and gazing into her eyes to learn that people can hold me in their minds. You were not dead but I was a motherless baby. You nursed Lana but you deserted me. Was it because I was a girl? Were you afraid the curse would continue just as I am afraid to find out the sex of my babies now?

"I met you only once when you returned, before you left forever wrapped in a mat as your coffin. Even then, you didn't want to have anything to do with me.

"I was four years old and Esho told me when you arrived, "Your mother has come. That is your mother." She had been telling me I had a mother somewhere. I was happy when you came, I remember you. You were very beautiful. I wanted to be like you. I wanted you to hold me and hug me. I wanted you to tell me I was a pretty girl, just like you. Esho couldn't tell me that because she was terrified. I thought my mother would come and tell me.

"You see, Esho, she loved Lana so much, but she didn't care for me and I thought my mother would come and I would be first on her mind. Yet you came and you chased me out of the room. You gave me knocks on my head when I came near you. Then you left, and you never came back. Some men came and rolled you up in a mat and carried you away. Esho could not afford to buy a coffin for you to be buried in. They just rolled you in the mat you had slept on.

"You know, as I grew older, people said to me, 'You look just like Oshun. She was so beautiful, you could have been her twin sister,' and it gave Esho such grief and I suffered for it. At least if you had loved me and not abandoned me, I would have known that I suffered for something. I suffered for looking like my mother who did not abandon me.

"Was I repulsive? Was that why you could not wait to get away from me? Was that why you did not give me the benefit of a mother's milk? Or allow me to look into your eyes and see my eyes reflected in them, for me to acquire the knowledge that a mother holds you in her mind, and other people also could, and that good men could look at me and hold me in their minds?

"Esho used to say that she and I were motherless. She had to be fed goat milk so she would survive, but her mother died in childbirth. My mother did not die in childbirth, she ran away with a man. I wish I had known you. Maybe I would have been able to understand.

"I am forty years old and I am going to be a mother. I will not run away from my children. I will nurse my children at my breasts. I will hold my children's gaze. I will let them see their eyes reflected in mine. I will not yell at them or curse them out. I will not give them knocks on the head if they want to get to know me. If I have daughters, I will be very proud if they look like me.

"If I have sons, I will teach them that the world is full of kind and wonderful men, like their father, like Lana would have been if he had lived. He would have lived if you had stayed around to help Esho, if only he had at least a pair of plastic shoes.

"I think of you a lot Oshun. I know you were up against a lot. Your father was a rapist and a pedophile. Esho's father was a rapist and pedophile, and so you chose the same for the father of your children

"Your lover, my father, Akanbi, he was a thief, a cheat and a pedophile. He was a scum. He died you know, Esho killed him. She prayed for many years for smallpox to afflict him, I guess so she wouldn't have to do the horrible job of killing him, but smallpox did not afflict him because smallpox has been eradicated from the world.

"I don't yearn for him anymore. I was cured of him ten years ago and so I was able to pick a good man to be the father of my children. But of you I always wonder.

"Why? Was Esho so intolerable? She could be. I know because I lived with her till she died when I was thirty years old, but you had children.

"Did you go in search of your father? Were you hoping you would find him in the men? How did they treat you Oshun? Did they continue to molest you? Was that what you wanted? Was that all you wanted out of life? Or was that the most you thought you deserved?

"Not me, I deserve better. I have been working hard and I continue to work hard. I married a man but I left him because he was never gentle with me. He hurt me many times, he never came looking for me when I got angry and left. He never came after me.

"The books I read, they taught me that a man who cared for you would come looking for you to hold you. I left him. I am stronger than you. I am giving my children a good father. I wish I could do it in the context of a marriage but I still need to work harder for that, and I am working hard toward that. I will not run away from my children, I will stay alive to take care of them. That curse on Esho will end with me. I will not pass it on to my children.

"But Oshun I feel for you. Your father was a destroyer of hope. You were a product of violence visited on Esho. Wouldn't we be demanding sainthood of her to ask her to love you?

But it was not your fault. We do not decide these things. We do not decide into which homes we are born or whose genes parent us. Like Esho used to say, we do not decide by which vehicles we come to this earth. You were up against a lot, Oshun. A few years ago, in Rwanda, the citizens visited innumerable atrocities upon one another. Enemies raped women and they became pregnant and gave birth.

"Innocent children were born to these women fathered by sperms of rapists and murderers. What names did they give these children given to them in such violent manner of rape and murder? They named them—*"This is the curse from my enemy."* They named them, *"Look at the face of my violator."* They named them, *"This is the end to hope."* They named them, *Ha! "This is the gift of a demon."*

"A lot would be demanded of these women when we ask them to love these children. My heart went out to them when I read their stories in the newspaper and I could kind of relate. My mother was a product of rape too. So I understand, Oshun. You were up against too much."

Ranti paced the room all night holding onto the pole as she wept.

Mrs. Sanchez came in unusually early, at six in the morning. She angrily started to question Ranti who was standing by the window looking out at the ocean. Ranti slowly turned around and when Mrs. Sanchez saw her swollen face and red eyes, she stopped. They stared at one another for a long time.

Ranti's body was exhausted, but her mind would not shut down for her to rest. "I'm going for a swim in the ocean," she surprised herself because the words just tumbled out of her mouth. It was at that moment she realized she had not swum in over thirty-one years. She used to swim in the fast river by her childhood home every day, until she had the genital mutilation. She remembered the freedom of being in the water, swimming with the fast-flowing water that carries you with it, and sometimes swimming against it.

"That must be how birds feel when they fly, that is why penguins fly under water." She suddenly realized. "That's why I have always envied birds. Lana will approve. He had loved to swim. I should have continued to swim for the two of us," she said aloud to Mrs. Sanchez who still stood at the door with a worried expression.

She took out the intravenous cannula on her left arm because she did not want seawater getting into it. She put a band-aid over the site. She opened the dresser and brought out a thong, the only underwear she could wear since she became pregnant because she could not tolerate any kind of pressure on her abdomen. She maneuvered herself into the underwear and walked past Mrs. Sanchez who started to protest as she made for the ocean.

She arrived at the beach and tested the water with her toes. She slowly sank in up to her neck so the cold would not be too much of a shock to her, and the waves coming periodically and crashing into her face felt glorious.

She did not swim, but she moved around slowly for about twenty minutes. She felt very good as she remembered the joys of swimming in the river when she was a little girl. "That is a living thing I was forcing to become a ghost but it just refused to die."

She came out of the ocean and her nightshirt clung to her body. She started to walk toward the cottage but Mrs. Sanchez met her halfway and wrapped a big towel around her. Ranti smiled her thanks, but the older woman grabbed her in a tight hug. She held on to her and walked with her to the house where she helped her out of her wet nightshirt and into another one. She went to the kitchen and returned with a cup of coffee. Ranti nodded her thanks. She lay on the bed and Mrs. Sanchez pulled the blanket over her, pulled the blinds in the room shut and closing the door after her, left the room.

Ranti fell into a deep sleep and dreamt *she was in her childhood home where Esho rented one room. But this time all the walls separating the different rooms rented out to different families were gone. The house was just one big building with one huge room like a hall. Ranti was very happy. She started to run from one end of the house to the other. And her brother ran with her. She stopped to hug him and she held on to him as the two of them ran around in the big hall. First they ran straight across, then they ran diagonally, then they started to run by the walls, touching the walls and laughing aloud. She felt wonderful.*

Hunger pangs woke her at about six in the evening and she could not remember being that hungry in a long time. She went into the living room and both Mr. and Mrs. Sanchez were sitting on the sofa watching television. They looked relieved on seeing her. Mrs. Sanchez excitedly ushered her to the table on which there was food. She dug in and finished the plate of rice and chicken without pausing. She drank the cup of coffee Mrs. Sanchez later brought for her and she felt content.

She could not believe she finished the food when it hit her that the smell of urine and feces were gone! "I cannot believe this." She held her breath for a moment and slowly let it out. She sucked in a fresh breath. Nothing! No smell of feces and no smell of urine. For the first time she could actually smell the salty ocean air, and of food. It was as if she just discovered a new sense. She started to sniff the air.

Mrs. Sanchez, assuming she was coming down with a cold, ran to her room to get her jacket, and draped it over her shoulders.

Ranti smiled at her and patted her hand. She walked around the cottage sniffing everything. She went out onto the deck and stood there sniffing the salty air. She started to cry again. "Thank you, thank you, thank you!" she said aloud as she raised her arms to embrace the ocean.

She knew her brother had finally been borne away by the wind to his resting place, and he took the smell away with him. "He is no more a ghost, he was my brother and in my mind he will always be my brother. Now I can speak his name and he will always be with me, I don't have to listen to Esho anymore.

"The walls that I erected in my mind, the walls and barriers which had prevented me from connecting the passion with the prose are gone. I can move freely around in my mind and let the memories and the feelings that come with them have full reign, and because of that, the ghosts are being borne away to their resting places. I don't have to be afraid anymore."

She returned to her room and fell into a very deep sleep.

17

Early the next morning, Boris called Ranti for the first time since she had been on the island. She told him she had eaten a full meal the day before. He told her Jack was disappointed to learn she had gone to the island. Boris wanted to know if he could give him her number.

Ranti reminded herself who Jack was, "the dog walker; the man I hope will hold me and make me feel like silk." She gave Boris permission to give him her number.

Depo called a few minutes later. He was concerned because the Sanchezes called him the day before to tell him of her weird behavior, that she spent all day typing without eating or resting and spent all night crying; she went swimming in the ocean in her pajamas, and took out her intravenous line.

Ranti wondered how they were able to communicate so much to him because she knew Depo did not speak Spanish.

"What's going on, Ranti, why were you crying?" He demanded.

"Did the Sanchezes also tell you that I ate a full meal yesterday? Have they been calling you each time I laughed or smiled? What is wrong with me crying if there is something to cry about? They don't have a problem with me laughing or smiling at them, but I shed a little tear and they are on the phone calling you."

"No Ranti, it wasn't a little tear, she said you cried all night, that you didn't sleep for twenty-four hours. I'm coming down later today. Okay?"

"No, Depo, if you come I will be very angry with you. Don't come here and invade my privacy. I'm fine, I'm eating full meals, the smell is gone, the anxiety and the feelings of impending doom are gone, and do you know why? It is because

I had that good cry, so don't come and disturb me. Saturday is just tomorrow, don't come here today."

Depo was quiet for a long time. "I worry about you all the time, Ranti. I don't like it when you shut me out. That is all," he said in a conciliatory tone of voice.

"I know you do, Depo, and thank you. I will tell you everything when you get here tomorrow. I was just thinking of my deceased brother and that's why I was crying. But believe me, I have never felt better."

"What? You had a brother that died? When did this happen? Why don't I know about this?"

"Because Esho forbade me to ever mention his name again. His name was Lana, he died when I was six years old and yesterday for the first time, I mentioned his name aloud and that is why I was crying. I will fill you in when you get here tomorrow."

"I know your mother died and someone else but I always thought the person was Esho's child," Depo explained to her.

Ranti did not return to her laptop on Friday morning. She spent the day in celebration that the smell of feces and urine were gone, and enjoying the smell of the Island. She walked on the beach in the morning and in the early afternoon decided to go to the store, which was some thirty minutes walk from the cottage to purchase a swimming suit. She told Mrs. Sanchez who gestured to her, trying to tell her that her husband would take her to the store, but Ranti wanted to walk. She felt ready to explore the island.

As she was leaving the store after buying the swimsuit, a man who was coming in held the door for her. He smiled at her. She smiled her thanks and continued on her way. He ran after her.

"You're staying at the Sanchez's cottage right? I heard about you, that you are here to rest, and that you've been having a very difficult time with the pregnancy."

Ranti gave him a questioning look.

"It's a small island and people talk," he smiled apologetically.

Ranti nodded.

"Yes, I thought it was you, there aren't many beautiful pregnant women around. I watch you each time you walk on the beach and I finally saw you go into the ocean yesterday. I was wondering when that would happen." He kept smiling at her.

"Pervert!" She stared at him.

He stared back at her and catching himself offered his right hand as he introduced himself as Abe.

"Ranti,"

"Are you going back to the cottage? I just came to pick up a few things, I'll drive you back."

"No, thanks, I'll walk, it's good for me."

"Are you sure, it's some distance, and you walked here already."

"Thanks," Ranti nodded at him and started to walk away.

"Maybe, some evening we can get together and barbecue or just hang out." He suggested.

"Sure."

"Your husband comes in on weekends, right?" She caught him looking at her bare left hand.

She continued to stare into his face. "I don't have a husband and I don't have a boyfriend. I'm just pregnant."

Abe looked uncomfortable. "I'm sorry, didn't mean to pry. I just thought a man would be an idiot not to want to be with you, especially if you were carrying his baby."

"Babies," Ranti offered, not making it any easier for him.

"Oh, right. Anyway, I hope to see you around."

A few minutes later he drove up to her on the road and offered her the ride again, she waved him off and continued to walk home. She admonished herself after he drove off.

"He is not a rapist, he is not a thief, he is not Esho's father, he is not the mad man that gave Oshun to Esho before she was ready, he is not the cruel Akanbi, and he is not Brian. He might be a Depo or a Lana. Ranti stop! Stop casting angels in the role of demons. If he invites you to a barbecue, go and get to know him. Give him a chance, and stop calling him a pervert."

She spent the rest of the afternoon going in and out of the ocean, swimming for lengths of time as she used to do as a little girl. She felt very good with the smell gone and no nausea as earlier on in the pregnancy. She was also able to eat three meals that day which made Mrs. Sanchez very happy.

Later in the evening she continued her story. She felt excited about the project though she knew she would not offer it as a proposal for funding. If she did, they would just certify her as crazy, but it had opened some locked doors in her mind and she wanted to open more of them. Grant's suggestion that she present a paper on her work in Nigeria was not so scary anymore.

After dinner she sat on the sofa and continued where she left off.

18

When Ranti graduated from elementary school in 1976, she took the entrance examination to attend a private all girls secondary school, founded by the Anglican Church, St. Ann's School, that Esho had been told was a very good school where most of the women who had emerged as leaders in Nigeria were educated.

Each time they ran into girls from the school in their mauve dress school uniform, brown leather sandals and green beret, Esho would lecture Ranti for the next few days or until something else distracted her, impressing that she just had to go to the school if she wanted to make something of herself in this world, and not become an object men would use for their pleasure, or kill. Esho would get all worked up as she lectured her, and Ranti started to dread running into the girls from St. Ann's.

She too desperately wanted to attend the school. It was like if she did not, her life would be over. So she studied very hard and read almost all the books in the big bookstore, even books that were so advanced for her and did not understand what they were about.

Esho knew Ranti had the ability. She had continued to do very well in school and her teachers were very proud of her, for her intellect and for being a very responsible girl whom they could rely on. They constantly told her grandmother that she would grow up to be a great woman and a leader, as she had been in her school, where she was nominated as the president of the student body.

Ranti performed very well in the entrance examinations to St. Ann's School, achieving the best result of all the candidates, but Esho could not afford the tuition.

Gboye's mother told Ranti that her grandmother could ask the Anglican Diocese for a scholarship.

Gboye did not apply to the school because she was going to England to attend secondary school like her brothers. Ranti was very sad about this.

Esho dressed up in her best outfit, put on her only pair of plastic slippers worn only on special occasions and went with Ranti to the Anglican Diocese to request a scholarship. They were asked to fill out some application forms which Ranti did.

Two weeks later they were invited for an interview at the Anglican Diocese and at the end of the interview she was granted the scholarship. The diocese would pay the tuition directly to the school, but the money for Ranti's uniforms and books would be handed over to her father.

Esho told them Ranti did not have a father.

They informed her that on the application form they had a name, Akanbi, as Ranti's father.

Esho stared at Ranti for a long time, and for once in her life was lost for words. Ranti moved away from the reach of her hands to avoid her blows.

"Why did you write his name as your father?" Esho asked in exasperation.

"Because he is my father," Ranti asserted.

"No, Iranti, he is not your father. I have been telling you that you don't have a father, you are alone in this cruel world."

"But each time we see him, you say to him, 'Akanbi you wicked man, you have a daughter you won't even acknowledge, you will rot in this life and we will all see you brought to shame, you child of the devil, smallpox will afflict you and your ugly wife and other bastards," Ranti explained to her grandmother.

Esho continued to stare at Ranti in disbelief. "And, what is his response?" Esho asked. Ranti was quiet.

"What?" demanded Esho, "What is his response when I say that to him? What does he say?"

"He says he is not my father." Ranti answered in a subdued tone.

"Iranti, they won't give us the money because you wrote his name as your father, they will give him the money and you know what he will do with it. He will spend it on himself and his bastards. He won't use it to help us." Esho started to lament as she wrung her hands.

She tried to explain to the secretary at the diocese that Akanbi would not help them, but the secretary said that was their law, they would only give the money to the candidate's father.

Esho went to Akanbi later in the day and told him about the scholarship. He promised to go with her to collect the money and give it to her. Esho wanted to know when he would go with her. He said he was a very busy man, but he would try to make the time. Two weeks later, Esho learnt he collected the money the very day she went to him, but he did not turn it over to her.

"You just had to have a father, Iranti. Other children have fathers and you just had to have one too, didn't you? No matter how useless a man he is. A useless father is better than no father at all unh? You have just ruined your life.

"I told you that he is a cruel man, I told you, but do you ever listen to me? No, you don't. I have been telling you from the day you were born that you are alone in this world without a father, because *your* Akanbi, he is not a descendant of the Noah in the Christian Bible. He is a descendant of those people that Yahweh destroyed in the flood, and the likes of him were destroyed along with Sodom and Gomorrah. That is why he is such a cruel man. And that is the person you are calling your father?" Esho clapped her hands together in dismay with a look of disbelief on her face.

88   *Feasts of Phantoms*

"Now, here we are, you can't get an education because you had a choice. A father on the one hand, and going to secondary school on the other hand but you know what you did, you chose a father." She weighed her two hands against one another.

"A useless man for a father! A man, who won't even acknowledge you and abandons you over and over each time he sees you by saying you are not his daughter. A good for nothing man who will die a miserable death. If I ever come across him on a deserted path, the things I will do to him. It is because of the likes of him that I carry my knife with me all the time. Smallpox will afflict him and all of his bastards and ugly wife..." Esho cursed Akanbi for the rest of the day, and for the next three days did not get up from the mat to go to her job as a laborer.

Ranti became afraid that she was becoming depressed again. She apologized for naming Akanbi as her father and promised Esho that it would never happen again.

When the time came for her to start at the secondary school, she did not have her books and uniforms. Esho appealed to the diocese to help her, but the secretary accused her of deceit, and she in turn let the woman have the worst of her cursing tongue.

The secretary said that was the problem with poor people, they try to exploit the kindness of the church and lie repeatedly to get more money. She dismissed them and said they could not help them until the following school year.

"Iranti let me explain something to you. You are still a very young child and you don't understand a lot of things yet," Esho started in a calm tone of voice as they left the diocese. "The likes of Akanbi are very wicked men indeed, they are so wicked that it is unbelievable sometimes, and people like him do the most despicable things. Do you know why?"

Ranti stared at her.

"It is because they have no sense of shame. A person without a sense of shame will do anything, no matter how cruel or rotten or despicable it is. Nothing is beyond them. It is important to have a sense of shame, Iranti, because a person who does not have a sense of shame would think he is a god.

"He would demand more than his due, and you should never demand more than your due, because it is self-destruction, and such a person wouldn't know his limitations. I might not have gone to school or read books, but I have read my mind. I sit on my mat and I think, when I carry cement on my head at work, I think of life and I ponder. I continue to read my mind, Iranti. Having a sense of shame makes you humble and that is the most important thing you need in this world, humility that lets you know your limitations. Akanbi is behaving like he is a god, he is foolishly flaunting his shamelessness and he is heading for destruction.

"I will tell you a story. One day, the tortoise went to meet his friends at the bar. The friends started to complain about their wives one at a time. The first man said his wife was a prostitute. The second one said his wife was lazy. The third man said his wife steals and lies all the time, while the fourth friend said his wife was filthy. The tortoise kept quiet and didn't make any contribution to the conversation.

"The friends asked him, 'Is your wife perfect, tortoise? We complained about our wives and yet you didn't say anything about your wife.

'No, my wife is not perfect, her problem is that she doesn't have a sense of shame,' said the tortoise.

'No sense of shame?' The friends said. "You are a lucky man tortoise, didn't you hear our complaints about our wives? Having no sense of shame is not a problem at all, at least she doesn't steal, or lie, and she is not lazy or filthy and is not a prostitute."

The tortoise said to his friends, "Because she doesn't have a sense of shame, she is all those things your wives are."

"Iranti, your Akanbi is like the tortoise's wife and that is why he has never raised a finger to help you in your life and yet he stole your money. It is the most despicable thing I have encountered in my life," she spat on the ground in disgust. "It is worse than what my father did to me when he raped me, at least my father fed me, gave me shelter and he clothed me. This man knows we have nothing and this is your future, and he stole that from you, a man that each time he sees you deny being your father, yet he went to the diocese and told them he was your father, so they would give him your money! And we have never taken anything from this man. We don't owe him a thing! I have never encountered a thing like this in my life! I tell you, smallpox will wipe him and his family out. He is going to die a beggar. Mark my word."

For days following this, Esho had the trancelike look that used to scare Ranti. She started to go with Esho to her job as a day laborer, to carry mixed cement for people who were building homes. Two weeks later, as they were coming back from the day job, there was a car parked in front of their house. This was a rare sight and all the children were hovering around the car and touching it. Ranti was very curious as well. She started to walk towards the car, but Esho gave her such a look that she changed the directions of her feet. The neighbors pointed out Ranti and her grandmother to the elderly man sitting in the car, and he came toward them.

"What do you want with us?" was Esho's gruff reply to his greeting.

"I'm the chairman of the board of directors of St. Ann's school. Ranti had the best result on the examination for admission to the school. The principal told me of your plight, and how Ranti's father stole the money for her school uniforms and books. "We cannot allow the kind of brain Ranti has go to waste. The school will pay for her uniforms, books and the fees for her to live in the boarding house with the other girls. This will do her a lot of good. We have to nurture her talents. It will be a shame for this country and a sin to allow such an ability as hers to go to waste."

The chairman brought an envelope of money out of his pocket and gave it to Esho. "This is for you to buy her clothes and other things she will need for the dormitory. The school will make her books and writing materials available."

Esho shocked Ranti by going down on her knees in front of the chairman and embracing his feet. She was speechless and she had a look of wonder on her face.

Esho had never curtsied or knelt down in submission to anyone, and had taught her children the same, that no living person deserved that kind of adulation, and also that, while you were down there kneeling or prostrating to them, they would use the opportunity to kick you further down.

"Thank you for saving our lives, Sir," was all Ranti could say.

The chairman eyes glistened with tears as he went to his car.

Esho in a rare happy mood told Ranti the chairman's god must be special, because he was the first Yoruba man to ever do anything good for her. "He is a descendant of Noah in the Christian Bible. He is almost like the white nun who showed me a lot of kindness when I first ran away from home and lived in the convent. The chairman must have learnt the behavior from white people as he is very educated, and must have gone to white people's school."

She took her headgear and left the house. Ranti was very excited but she wondered where she was going because it was unusual for Esho to leave the house without telling Ranti, or at least one of the neighbors where she was going.

She had lectured Ranti, "always let people know where you are, and make sure you go to the place that you told people you were going. Don't tell people you were going to Mokola and then end up in Molete, because if a war broke out in Molete, people would say to themselves, thank goodness she went to Mokola, and they would not go to Molete to look for you or save your hide."

Ranti followed her out of curiosity but at a distance to avoid the usual punishments of being cursed out, or blows landing on her head and face.

Esho stood on the street in front of Akanbi's house. "Akanbi bring your cursed head out of that house, I have to talk to you, you bastard, rapist and thief, shameless scumbag. The neighbors should know what you did. Come out you coward!" She repeatedly yelled for him.

Some neighbors gathered around to watch, as they always found Esho cursing out Akanbi very entertaining. Ranti hid beside a building in embarrassment.

Isa, a vagrant psychotic who walked around the neighborhood with his rags and bags of junk, chanting to himself, *"If you want to marry me, bring an application, and I will give you a very good consideration,"* happened to arrive on the scene at about that time. He stopped next to Esho and listened to her.

Esho continued to call Akanbi to come out of his house and talk to her. Isa took up the chant for Esho and he would insert his own in between. It was as if he and Esho had choreographed it. Esho would shout, "Akanbi bring your cursed head out here, you thief, rapist and bastard." She would take a pause.

Isa will take over and say "Akanbi, bring your cursed head out here, you bastard, thief and rapist. *If you want to marry me, bring an application and I will give you a very good consideration."*

The neighbors laughed and clapped their hands at the performance. Someone chanted, "Isa, Esho will marry you, just look at her application and give her a very good consideration." They laughed again, and Ranti started to cry.

Akanbi eventually came out and stood on his balcony. Isa started to laugh as he pointed, "Akanbi came out," and he proceeded on his way chanting, *"If you want to marry me-------"*

"Ha!" shouted Esho, as she took off her headgear and tied it firmly around her waist. She held her knife in her left hand. She spat on the ground in disgust. "This is the face of a thief! This is the face of a rapist and a bastard. Akanbi you are not a descendant of Noah. The rest of your people were destroyed in the flood and in the Sodom and Gomorrah of your Bible. I know you know those stories because you go to church every Sunday.

"People of the neighborhood, let me tell you what he did in case you don't know, but I know that you know, because you have eyes to see and you have seen. He is old enough to have been my daughter's father but he got her pregnant three times, and he didn't raise a finger to help her.

"She was dying carrying his baby and he didn't help her. She died, and he didn't help me bury her. The first child my daughter had for him was dying and he didn't raise a finger to help me. He died and he didn't help me bury him. This is his face neighbors, take a good look at him and keep your daughters away from his door!

"Now my brilliant child Iranti got a scholarship to go to secondary school, but the idiots in our government will only give the money to the father. They gave him the money for my child Iranti to go to secondary school. Who does not want his or her child to go to secondary school? If you don't want your child to go to secondary school, raise your hand."

No hands went up.

"Good, so you can all appreciate what I'm talking about here. Akanbi the thief took the money and spent it, not on Iranti, but himself! Ask him to deny it if I'm lying against him. All of you are my witnesses. The very same Iranti that he refused to call his child, and each time I remind him that Iranti is his child he calls me a crazy witch, but he stole her money. He stole her mother and he stole her brother! Iranti does not owe you a thing, yet you continue to steal from her. But since there is a power greater than the power that a man who thinks he is rich today has, the school sent a man to my house today and he said to me, 'Iranti's destiny is not one in which she would carry cement on her head for the rest of her life.' He said that Iranti has a brain that it would be a sin before his God to let it go to waste. I have some respect for his God, though I don't care about any one's God but mine. He will help Iranti.

"My brilliant child, Iranti is going to secondary school and she will become a great person, while you Akanbi and all your bastards will rot in this life, and smallpox will afflict you and yours.

"Akanbi, you are not going to die in the midst of your loved ones. It is not a curse; it is the law that suspends this earth of ours, because as I have been telling you for years, you curse God with your behavior as you continue to flaunt your shamelessness in his face and there is no one who has cursed God and gotten away with it." She finished and started for home.

Ranti ran home so Esho would not know she had followed her.

19

Esho took Ranti to St. Ann's school the following Saturday that September in 1976.

Ranti had never been away from Esho in her life, and she was worried something would happen to her while she was in school, that she might not get up from her mat, not eat, and then she would die. She had even suggested she stayed at home and goes to school as a day student instead of living in the boarding house.

Esho had refused, "All I asked for was money for your tuition, books and uniforms, but we have been blessed by that man who wants you to live in the school. I want you to go and live there. Live with the white woman principal and learn her ways. You will be safe as there won't be men around. That is the best place for you now. I don't want you around in this neighborhood with the likes of Akanbi on the prowl. Do you understand? This is a blessing for us."

As Esho was leaving her in school to return home, Ranti braved her fears of being hit or cursed at, "Esho, will you be fine? You are not going to lie on the mat and not get up in the mornings, like you did that other --------time? I'm worried I won't be there to take care of you."

Esho stared at Ranti for a while, and her face softened. "No, Iranti, I will not lie on the mat and not get up in the mornings. I will get up every morning and go to my job. I will come and visit you every Saturday. Remember who we are. Don't follow the examples of other children or of wayward children. Remember why you are here. This is your hope to have a life that will be better than mine, or your mother's. This is your chance to be able to call the shots for yourself in this life. If you get this education for yourself, no man will be your boss. You will be the boss of your own head. Do you hear me?

"The first time my father raped me, I was your age. I was about eleven years old. See the difference? You are starting in secondary school and might become like that white woman principal one day, but when I was your age, my father was ruining my life, although yours tried too but there are powers greater than his in this world.

"You don't want to have a child at the age of thirteen or fourteen like I did or like your mother did. I want you to watch that white lady and become like her, maybe one day you will become the head of a school and ride in a big car like her."

Ranti nodded and Esho left without looking back, she wanted to touch her, but Esho only touched to hit.

Ranti returned to the room she had to share with nine other girls. She had to sleep on top of a bunk bed. Shara, the girl whose bed was at the bottom gave her a nasty look as she said to her, "I hope you are not a bed-wetter because if you rain pee on me I'll kill you."

Ranti was suddenly afraid, especially because she leaked urine. She instructed herself to double pack her underwear that night. She had never slept on a mattress before because Esho could not afford one, she would have preferred to sleep on the mat on the floor. Later that night, she could not sleep as the mattress was too soft and felt too lumpy for her. Shara started to complain that she was moving around too much and was disturbing her and she did not want to share the bunk with Ranti anymore.

On Sunday, they had an early breakfast and went to St. Ann's church for the morning service. They wore the school uniform of mauve dress, brown leather sandals with green berets perched on their heads. Ranti felt very proud. She wished Esho could see her in the school uniform. She could not believe she was a student of St. Ann's School.

In church she did not pray to the Christian God because Esho said he did not exist and the people calling on him were fools.

Shara continued to complain about Ranti, she called her 'ayo' at some point in front of the other girls and they laughed and looked down their noses at her. Ranti did not know what 'ayo' meant, but she realized she was being ostracized again. She was convinced they could smell her, even though Gboye had assured her that she did not smell. She wished Gboye had come to the school with her, but she had gone to England to go to school because her father was a rich man.

She reminded herself of Esho's many lectures she had been hearing all her life, more like short stories. Esho had told her when she brought her to school, "When you go to the market to buy, say an orange, you go directly to the stall of the person selling oranges and you ask how much she wants for it. If she told you the cost of the orange, you haggle with her so she can bring down the price. Always haggle because that is the only way you won't be cheated. While you are haggling with the orange seller, you look at her and pay attention to her. You do not allow yourself to be distracted by the person trying to buy mango from the mango seller next to the orange seller, because if you do, you will lose your focus and your goal, because you got distracted by listening to market noise and disaster is the only thing to come of that."

Ranti told herself Shara was 'market noise' and she would just ignore her and focus on her studies. She knew she would survive; everyone in her elementary school had ostracized her, except Gboye, and she had survived and done very well. The thought of Gboye cheered her. She had promised her they would be best friends forever and that she would come home for the holidays.

In the two weeks Ranti missed by not being able to come to school because Akanbi stole her money, Shara had established herself as a leader of some sort amongst her classmates. She told them who to talk to and who to ignore and the girls hung around her and on her every word. So by Monday, Ranti's first day of classes, other girls from the other dormitories knew there was an '*ayo*' girl joining them, and if you wanted to remain cool, you must not speak to her.

The teachers helped her catch up on the work she missed. By the end of her second week, she had caught up, and it was obvious she was a brilliant girl, because she got most of the teachers' questions right. Shara hated her more.

Three weeks after Ranti started in the school, she met Moradeke. She was from another dormitory and was in another arm of the class, 1A, while Ranti was in 1B. Every student in the school had chores she had to do in the morning before classes, and it was Moradeke's job to keep the front of the Principal's office which opened onto a courtyard clean.

The front lawn had coarse grass growing on it, but there was a patch devoid of grass due to the heavy traffic of feet walking on that patch. Not only was it dusty, it was also usually full of dirt as well because students dropped papers and other trash there. It was against school rule to drop trash on the grounds but the students did anyway.

The chores had to be completed by seven in the morning to give students time to shower, have breakfast and be ready in time for the eight o'clock morning assembly.

Ranti's morning chore was to clean her classroom. She finished her chore early because she was used to doing housework, unlike most of her classmates who were from affluent homes where they had servants to do the chores for them.

She was walking to her dormitory when she saw Moradeke crying because that morning was very windy, and as Moradeke swept the ground the wind blew around the dirt she just swept and gathered to throw into the garbage. The wind also blew dust into her face and she was spending a lot of time sneezing and struggling against the wind and the dust. She stopped to sneeze and wipe her nose at some point, and when she looked around her, the wind had blown the dirt around again. She continued to cry in frustration.

Ranti thought of going to help her but was afraid she would not want to speak to her like the other girls. She hesitated for a moment, but went over to her. She offered to sweep the courtyard for her. She got some water from the tap behind the building and sprayed it on the dusty ground. Most of the dirt stayed because they were now heavier, and the wind could not blow the wet soil. She took the broom from Moradeke and within three minutes the courtyard was clean.

Moradeke thanked her profusely. She said she had been afraid she would be late for school and miss breakfast, and get punished for being late. She took her broom from Ranti and hurried off to her dorm to get ready for the day.

Ranti saw her around school a few more times that week, but they did not speak because she was one of the cool girls who called themselves 'aso', unlike her who was un-cool and was an 'ayo.' Also, Moradeke was friends with Shara because they had attended the same elementary school in Lagos, and their mothers were both physicians and colleagues.

Two weeks later they had a mid-term examination and Ranti had the best result in her class. Her teachers were very proud of her as they asked the other girls to follow her example.

That night in the dorm, Shara, who though had continued to share the bunk with Ranti said to her, "So you are the smart one in our class *ehn*? We'll see. The likes of you don't belong in this school. This is a school with a tradition of being a family school. My mother and grandmother are alumni of this school and so are the mothers and grandmothers of most of the girls here, I don't know why they would allow you to come here. Your grandmother is a laborer. She wears rags when she comes to visit you, and she doesn't even have shoes. You are a disgrace and I'm going to get you out of this school because we don't want you to spoil the good name of St. Ann's school."

Ranti was used to being put down in this way. She too did not feel she belonged in the school because she had nothing in common with the girls most of whom had been to England for summer vacations and shopped in sophisticated stores.

She had seen them spend unbelievable amount of money at the school's tuck shop on candy and cookies. Most of them spent the same amount of money she and her grandmother lived on for a week, in just one afternoon. But she was determined to focus on her studies and not be distracted by 'market noise.' So she ignored Shara realizing she was jealous of her. She was grateful they did not know her secret of leaking urine and being afraid that she smelled of feces, but thankfully, no one has accused her of that yet. She climbed the bunk and went to sleep.

Two weeks later as she was coming back from evening study hall she noticed the girls in her dorm were looking at her in a strange way, and some of them were pointing at her. She walked to her room wondering what was cooking.

She started to get ready for bed when the dorm captain, a girl in the fifth year came to her room to ask her to come to the dining room. The whole dorm was there, about fifty girls from the first through the fifth year. She looked around and spotted Shara who smiled malevolently.

The dorm captain asked Ranti to stand in the center of the room. "We have reasons to believe you stole some of the other girls' food items and they are in your locker. What do you have to say for yourself? Are you going to confess or lie, because then we will know you are a liar and a thief?"

Shara and her group of 'cool' friends laughed.

"I didn't steal any food and I don't even have food in my locker. I didn't bring any snacks to school." Ranti explained.

"Is your locker locked?" The captain asked her.

"Yes it's locked."

"Why is it locked if you don't have any snacks in it?"

"Because that's the rule, we were told to always lock our lockers so my grandmother bought me a padlock."

"So you are telling me that if you opened your locker now, there wouldn't be any food in it since you didn't bring any with you to school."

Ranti nodded.

"When was the last time you visited your locker?"

"About a week ago."

"Why? If you didn't have any food in it, why visit it?"

"I couldn't finish my breakfast so I kept the rest there and I ate it later."

"Do you have the key to your locker with you?"

"It's in my room."

And so the interrogation continued. Ranti knew it was going to end badly for her. She thought of Esho and realized that she would definitely kill her this time, because if there was anything Esho despised more than men, it was a thief and a liar, like Akanbi. She decided she would run away because she would not stay around and let Esho kill her like she killed her father and the mad man who gave her Oshun before she was ready.

The dorm captain asked her for the key to her locker and when she opened it there were cartons of food in it. There were Kelloggs corn flakes, Weetabix, Cabin biscuits, tins of Bournvita and a bottle of orange squash. These were foods Ranti had never tasted in her life.

Ranti stood in front of her locker without any expression on her face and waited.

The whole dorm went "Ah!"

Some of the girls started to sing, "Ranti is a thief, look at her face; this is the face of a thief."

Ranti continued to stare at the food items in her locker, willing them to explain how they got there.

"Well, what do you have to say for yourself?" The captain demanded of her.

Some girls started to accuse her of stealing other properties that ranged from food to money to combs, shoes and underwear.

Ranti did not say a word.

"You know you will be expelled because this is a school with very high standard to maintain." The captain informed her. "In the morning I have to inform the principal."

Ranti did not sleep a wink that night. She buried her head in her pillow and wept all night. She wept for the opportunity that was going to be snatched away from her after all. First Akanbi tried to snatch it from her, but now some one else has succeeded. She knew it was Shara, but she did not have any proof except for the threat, and she knew she would not be believed. Shara was from a very important and rich family and all the women in her family were alumni of the school.

She finalized her plans to run away. After all Esho ran away at the age of eleven. She felt sad that she might never see Esho again. The thought of not seeing her grandmother again for the rest of her life scared her and made her cry even more.

In the morning she got up when the bell rang, did her chores and got ready for school. The girls continued to point at her and snicker behind her back.

She went to the assembly and looked around at the other girls and at the faculty. Some thoughts came to her that she did not belong amongst these girls and women. None of them leaked urine or smelled of feces.

She looked at Shara where she was pretending to close her eyes in prayer, and something gave inside of her. She wished she had a knife, "I will just settle this the 'Esho way," she muttered under her breath.

She remembered the hundreds of books she read at the big bookshop. The enduring messages from them were that a person should stand firm, fight for what is hers and not run away in fear. She quoted to herself, "*We only become what we are by the radical and deep-seated refusal of that which others have made of us.*

"In this school they want to make me into a thief and I'm not a thief. Just like in elementary school they tried to make me into a feces carrier and I'm not a feces carrier. I just had to do it at the time so we would have food and Esho would not die. It was an honest job. I didn't steal so we could eat. I didn't prostitute myself so we could eat. I did it and Esho didn't die. Esho should not be made into a cement carrier. She has been doing the job to take care of me.

"I will get this education, go on to the university and become a doctor and then Esho wouldn't have to carry cement on her head anymore, not for anyone. I will stay and fight because I am not a thief, and I am not a feces carrier. I'm the most brilliant girl in this class and I've never stolen anything in my life. I have gone hungry many times and I didn't steal to eat. I don't even like food, and yet I'm accused of stealing the things I don't like.

"I earned the scholarship to come to this school because I worked very hard in school and by reading those books in the bookshop. No one is going to take this away from me. Akanbi could not take this away from me and Shara will definitely not take this away from me! I will fight for what is mine! I'm going to fight to stay in this school! I earned the scholarship!" She affirmed.

At eleven o'clock she was invited to the principal's office and the white lady asked her if she stole the food items.

"No, Ma, I didn't. And that is the truth, I have never tasted any of those foods in my life and I wouldn't want to eat them, so why would I steal them. Ma, I don't even like food, you can ask my grandmother; she used to force-feed me when I was little so I could grow. Shara planted the food in my locker. She told me after mid-term exams that she would get me expelled from St. Ann's school because I didn't belong here. She said none of my ancestors are alumni, while her mother and grandmother are alumni.

"I have never stolen in my life. The chairman of the board has been to my house, you can ask him, he will tell you how poor we are. My grandmother and I have gone hungry many days when we didn't have food. In my family we don't take things that do not belong to us."

The dorm captain started to argue that she stole the food and that Shara saw her when she hid them in her locker.

Shara was called to the office and she told the principal a story of how she saw Ranti steal the food from her locker and some other girls' lockers. She said Ranti had a master key which can open most of the padlocks, and that she took the key from under her pillow where she had hidden it. She dug into her pocket, brought out a key and showed it to the principal.

At this point, the mathematics teacher brought Moradeke into the principal's office. She said Moradeke had something to say.

Moradeke narrated how Shara had been boasting that she had a plan to get Ranti expelled from school, and that she would plant the food in her locker. She named two girls who were present when Shara hatched her plan, and that Shara said Ranti was an embarrassment to the school and did not belong there because her grandmother was a very poor woman.

"Why didn't you tell us this before? The principal asked her.

Moradeke was quiet for a while. Finally, "I don't know Ma. I didn't know she would actually do it. I mean, lie against Ranti."

"Moradeke, I won't invite you to my house anymore and you won't be able to swim in our swimming pool. You are going to be sorry for this because I won't talk to you anymore and I will make sure the other girls don't talk to you too." Shara threatened.

The two girls who were present when Shara hatched her plan were brought to the office. They said Shara did not make any plans and Moradeke lied.

The principal looked very solemn and was quiet for a long time. "Shara, Moradeke, Bimbo, and Yemi," she called the four girls all of whom were very good friends and belonged to the 'cool' group.

"Ma," They answered her.

"Your grandmothers, mothers, sisters and aunts are alumni of this school. This is a great school that was established by the Anglican Church at the turn of the century. This school is seventy-seven years old. It has produced women leaders in this country. Professor Oyin Olurin is an alumnus of this school. She is the first woman ophthalmologist in this country. She was here on Friday to speak to the whole school. Do you think she achieved so much by lying and plotting against her classmates?

"Do you want me to name other women who have in the past graced the halls of this school with their presence, and continue to honor this school by what they continue to achieve out there? We have educated first women lawyers, doctors, commissioners, judges, engineers, scientists, and economists in this country. We have always welcomed intellect and talents and nurture them to great results. I want the four of you to think seriously about what is going on here today. I will give you until tomorrow to get your stories straight, and I shall inform your parents.

"We don't want girls whose intent in life is to victimize other people of lesser means than them. This is not what St. Ann's school is about. All of you students here are classless. You do not belong to any socio-economic group at this stage of your life because you have not started to work and earn money. When you get to the stage where you are working and earning money, then, you can lay claims to one socio-economic class or another. Your parents accomplishments are not your own. Each woman shall be judged by her own accomplishments, and not by the status of her parents.

"In this school every girl is as good and is equal to the next girl. So go away and I give you until tomorrow, and if you don't come back here to tell me the truth, I will get to the bottom of this in my own way and liars will be expelled."

"Ma, it's the truth, Shara planted the food in Ranti's locker to get her expelled from school, she said she hated her because she is very poor and her grandmother wears rags when she comes to visit her, and that she comes every Saturday to visit her, whereas her parents don't come that often to see her. Bimbo and Yemi are lying, Ma. I didn't know Shara would actually carry out her plans, if I had known I would have told the teacher. I told the moment I heard what happened in Ranti's dorm last night. I'm not in the same dorm with her Ma, so I didn't know until we were in Math' class today." Moradeke quickly explained to the principal.

"Bimbo, Yemi?" The principal looked to the other girls.

They shifted on their feet.

"Okay, you are dismissed. Remember liars will be expelled from the school."

"Ranti didn't steal the food. Shara put them in her locker. We were there when she did it." Bimbo blurted and Yemi nodded in agreement.

"Are you sure?" The principal asked and they both nodded.

Shara started to cry and to maintain that she did not do it and Ranti stole the food.

The principal said to her, "I will notify the police and they will take finger prints and we will know for sure who is the liar and such a person would be expelled from St. Ann's school and sent to jail."

Shara started to wail as confessed.

The principal apologized to Ranti. She commended Moradeke for coming forward and telling the truth.

The next morning at assembly, Shara, Yemi and Bimbo apologized to Ranti in front of the whole school for lying against her. They confessed that they planted the foods in her locker to get her in trouble.

Shara was suspended from school for two weeks while Yemi and Bimbo were suspended for one week. The principal continued to maintain that the school would not condone such behavior, and that she was not trying to educate liars and people who would victimize their fellow citizens, but she was trying to raise great leaders for the country.

Ranti did not report the incident to Esho, she was afraid that her grandmother would start to hit her and curse her out even though she was innocent, but she was happy she fought for what was hers. She was also happy she helped Moradeke earlier in the term and Moradeke came to her rescue by telling the truth.

That was another thing she learnt from the hundreds of books she read, that if you do good things for people, you will be rewarded. She knew Esho would not agree with her. Esho believed you should mind your own business and stay out of people's way. She told herself Esho did not know everything. She did not even know most of the things in the books she read.

Ranti continued to work hard on her studies and to spend most of her time in the library reading textbooks and the many novels and story books available there, and in that way was able to stay out of a lot of people's ways.

She and Moradeke started to wave to one another whenever they ran into each other, which was not often because they lived in separate dormitories and most of the time, Ranti would not make the effort to talk to Moradeke when she was with her 'cool' friends. Moradeke however would nod at her or wave to her whenever she saw her.

20

In late October each dormitory had to begin practice for inter-dormitory sports competition which would be held early in December. Ranti's dormitory had a dorm meeting in which the captain described for the benefit of the first year students who were the newest to the school, what the competition involved and that every girl had to participate. The only way a girl would be excused from participating was if she had a doctor's note.

Ranti became terrified because since the genital mutilation, she had not been able to run, even though she was a very fast runner before the incident. The keloid growing on her vagina rubbed against her thighs and hurts her, sometimes making it painful to walk. She was afraid that if she went to a doctor, then the whole school would know her secret. She panicked so much that she could not eat for many days.

They had to practice for the competition following afternoon study hall, when every girl was expected on the field in their dorm uniform that differentiated the girls into the different dormitories in the school.

Ranti wore her orange dress dorm uniform and went to the field with her classmates. Her room captain who was in the fourth year divided the ten girls into two groups to test their abilities at the different sports.

When she asked Ranti to run to the end of the field with four other girls, she asked to be excused. The captain told her every girl had to run so she could select the fastest runner to represent the dormitory.

Ranti said she had a medical problem that prevented her from running.

The captain wanted to know what the problem was.

Ranti stared at her. She did not want to tell her about her genitals but at the same time she did not want to lie.

The captain threatened her with punishment for defiance if she did not run with the other girls, and Ranti said she would take the punishment.

The captain stared at her. "You'd rather wash the stinking toilet than just run down the field?"

"Yes I will." Ranti asserted.

"Well, that's your choice. I will let the dorm captain know."

Later in the day the dorm captain told Ranti she had to wash the dorm toilets, used by the fifty girls in the dorm, everyday or until she decided to compete with the other girls.

In the first week of the preparation for the inter-dorm sports competition, the girls to represent the dormitory by competing in the different sports were selected, for the one hundred meter dash, the long distance run, high jump, relay races, long jump, shot put, javelin throwing as well as hurdles.

While her dorm mates were on the field practicing, Ranti spent the time washing toilets.

The second week after the athletes had been selected, the rest of the girls had to begin practice for the parade in their dorm uniforms and march to music from the marching band before the competition began. Ranti refused to march as well. She told the house captain it was because of her medical problem. The captain insisted she divulged this medical condition to her but Ranti refused.

As punishment for not participating in the practice for the parade, she had to wash the lunch dishes in her dorm, in addition to washing the toilets. Along with this, she still had her chore of cleaning her classroom.

One evening, a month after she started to do these chores, the captain invited her to her room. "Why are you such a stubborn girl?" she asked Ranti in a gentle tone of voice.

"I'm not stubborn, like I told you I have a medical condition that prevents me from participating in the sporting events."

"What is this mysterious medical problem? Asthma? Fainting spells? What? It has got to have a name."

Ranti kept quiet.

"Ranti you are a very strange girl. You don't interact with your classmates. You don't have any friends, yet you are very brilliant. I know you are from a very poor home. What are you afraid of? I know Shara has tried to make life difficult for you here but you can confide in me, I promise you I won't tell a soul anything you tell me in confidence and you won't have to wash the toilets and the dishes anymore."

Ranti kept quiet. She remembered when Shara accused her of stealing food, this same dorm captain had yelled at her and humiliated her in front of the whole dorm.

"Well Ranti that's your choice. I have to tell the principal what's going on here, and she'll get the truth out of you. You know that don't you?"

Ranti did the chores until the sporting events were held. This further distanced her from her classmates as a lot of socializing happened on the fields during the daily practice, with the girls in the different dorms getting to know more of one another.

The first term ended in December and the school was closed for three weeks Christmas vacation. The girls were very happy to be going home for the holiday and they excitedly talked about how the holiday was celebrated in their families, with family members coming from far and wide to visit. They discussed the foods that would be prepared and the gifts they hoped to receive, like new dresses and shoes.

Ranti could not share in the excitement, but she listened. It further alienated her from the rest of the world and made her feel more like an outcast. Esho did not believe in any religion, and even though they had neighbors, who were either Christians or Muslims, and who in spite of not having much money, celebrated their respective holidays. Esho forbade Ranti to join the neighbors who always invited them. So with her classmates excited about the holiday, Ranti threw herself more into her studies and into the books in the library so as not to be around to listen to them.

She went home to Esho that Christmas break and she felt strange in their one room accommodation, as it seemed very small to her. The neighbors were happy to see her and many of them commented that she was growing into a young woman. They congratulated her on the golden opportunity she had to attend the private secondary school, and many of them told their daughters to hang around her, so they could learn of ways to get into the school.

Esho was calmer and had stopped cursing her. Ranti was surprised that she did not yell at her at all in the three weeks she spent at home. On many occasions, she offered to go with Esho to her job of carrying cement for builders to double the income they would earn but Esho refused.

"That is not your lot in life Iranti. You are never going to carry cement on your head. You are going to become a great woman and other people will carry cement for you when you build your own home."

"Esho I will continue to work very hard and very soon, you won't have to do this job to take care of me anymore, I promise you." Ranti told her grandmother, who nodded and looked away.

Ranti returned to school in January of 1977 for her second term. Her first week back she missed Esho terribly, especially that Esho was kinder to her. She threw herself into her schoolwork as usual.

By her eighth month in the school, she had read all the books in the school library, and had started to read some of them over again. She wished she were a day student that went home after school so she could go to the big bookshop on Sundays and read the new books they always have imported from England and the United States of America.

One afternoon after study hall Ranti ran into Moradeke who was walking to her dormitory, she said hello to her, but Ranti checked to make sure none of her 'cool' friends was around to laugh at her, before she returned her greeting.

Moradeke wanted to know what she was reading as she checked her books. Ranti looked at her and thought she was the most beautiful girl she had ever seen, especially with her chocolate colored smooth skin. She suddenly became self-conscious that Moradeke might not want to talk to her.

"Peer Gynt? What is that?" Moradeke screwed up her nose in confusion. "What are you reading? You are always reading. I see you all the time, you always have your head buried in a book, no wonder you are so brilliant. The teachers like you a lot. They say you are a responsible girl who will be the head girl of the school when we get to the fifth year."

Ranti could not find her tongue. She felt overwhelmed that Moradeke was talking to her. None of the other girls ever talked to her. She wanted to say something so the moment would not end, but she did not know what to say. She wanted very much to have a friend in the school, someone she could confide in like she had Gboye.

"Thanks again for the other time. You saved my life when Shara lied against me. If I had been expelled from school, my grandmother would have killed me," she finally blurted out.

"Oh, that's okay, I'm sorry I didn't speak sooner, I didn't think she would do it, I thought she was just bragging. She's a spoilt brat who likes to have her way all the time and likes to be the boss of everyone. Are you still sharing the bunk with her?"

Ranti wished she was one of those people she read about in books who were very confident and always knew the right things to say in any situation. She looked at Moradeke again trying to find something to say to her.

"I like your hair, it's beautiful," she complimented her while running her right hand over her own head with her short hair that Esho had forbidden her to grow long.

"Thanks, I like my hair too, that's one thing I have that my sisters don't have. I have two older sisters, they are very pretty but I have the prettiest hair in the family. They hate me for it. Why don't you grow your hair? You are a very pretty girl you know, and if you grow your hair you will even be more beautiful."

Ranti was very happy. She smiled at Moradeke for the compliment. "I can't, my grandmother doesn't want me to; she said it would distract me from my studies. You know, if I spend a lot of time fixing my hair, time I should spend studying. I used to have very long hair until about a year ago." She stopped herself before she told her about Esho's fears and the reasons she cut off her hair.

"No it won't. You just spend an hour a week on your hair when you put it into braids or cornrow and that's not a lot of time. I could help you and then you could help me with mine, we'll be hair partners. Yemi used to be my partner but since she was suspended, she has stopped talking to me, so I haven't been able to find a regular partner. What do you say? It'll be so much fun and we could practice different hairstyles on each other, *Unh?*"

Ranti was excited, "I'll do your hair for you but I really can't do mine. Esho, my grandmother, she would go crazy if she saw my hair in braids."

"Tell her it's the school rule, you are the only girl with short hair in the school. Tell her the rule says every girl must braid her hair since we are not boys."

Ranti agreed as she gave Moradeke a grateful smile. "I have to tell her first before you do my hair. But I can help you with your hair on Sunday."

They parted after agreeing to a time to meet so Ranti can put Moradeke's hair in braids for her. Ranti was happy she would have a friend in the school after all. But she was worried about lying to Esho. She formulated what she would tell Esho in her mind for days. She wanted to get it over with as soon as possible because if Moradeke helped her with her hair too, then they would spend more time together. She wanted to be called beautiful by the other girls. Some girls already had the coveted title and the whole school seemed to have a different kind of respect for them. Moradeke had called her 'very pretty.' She went over the conversation several times in her mind.

She understood Esho's fears but knew they were unfounded. She had no plans of allowing any man near her to ruin her life. Esho had been worried that her long hair would be attractive to men, just like Oshun's beautiful hair had attracted men to her.

By Saturday, she had arrived at what she would tell her grandmother. Esho arrived promptly at four o'clock in the afternoon and Ranti was happy to see her as usual. She sat across from Esho who asked her about her schoolwork and teachers.

She answered all of her grandmother's questions as always, and told her she continued to do well in her studies and was staying out of trouble.

Esho looked her over. "Are you eating well?"

Ranti nodded. She was ashamed that she ate better in the school than at home where they could not afford three meals a day, even though the other girls complained all the time about the school food, calling it poor.

For the first time since Ranti started in the school, Esho brought her treats. She took down her headgear and inside were three oranges next to her knife. She gave the oranges to Ranti. "I was on my way when I remembered how much you love oranges, so I bought some." She looked into her granddaughter's eyes.

Ranti took them. She wanted to touch Esho. They sat across from one another and the big gulf was between them. "Are you well Esho?"

Esho nodded and looked distracted. They were both quiet for a long time.

Ranti realized that she and her grandmother did not really talk. They did not gossip about neighbors or anything like that. Most of the talking came from Esho yelling at her or giving her lectures on how not to ruin her life. She knew her grandmother so well, yet she did not know her at all. Ranti wondered what her desires are. Would she like to make friends with other women like she just made friends with Moradeke? Does she daydream about a different life or a better life?

"The gulf is always between us. I will like to touch Esho sometimes. I will like to hold Esho and have her hold me, but the gulf is always there, roaring with the force of the water inside of it. I learnt about gulf in geography, they are defined as a large area of sea or ocean partially enclosed by land, or a deep, a wide chasm, an abyss, and sometimes they suck things into them like a whirlpool. That's why it's so difficult to reach across and touch Esho. There is no connecting bridge. No one has ever tried to build a bridge in love and compassion to get to Esho, people have thrown ladders at her and they have hurt her so terribly. She loves the gulf, and she does not touch, she does not connect, except in violence."

"Esho," Ranti started suddenly. "There is something I need to discuss with you and I need to explain it to you so you won't be angry with me. It's not my fault, but in this school, they want the girls to braid their hair. If you notice the other girls, they have braided hair. I'm the only one in this school who wears her hair like a boys.' I don't have a problem with it because I understand that you don't want me distracted from my studies. But they told me during the week that I have to braid my hair. I told them I would speak with you first so I don't disobey you."

Esho's face clouded over the way it did when men looked at Ranti, but this time she did not explode like she used to do. She stared at her granddaughter for a long time. She looked around the big hall where other students were visiting with their family. She took in the students and their parents. She brought her gaze back to rest on Ranti, and continued to stare at her.

"I see that the girls have braided hair. Iranti, I am not a bad mother. I have always tried my best. It's my cursed head. If this school says it is okay for you to braid your hair and grow it so it is long, then that is okay with me. But remember why I cut off your hair in the first place. I didn't want you wasting too much time on your hair.

"I remember Oshun used to spend hours in front of the mirror fixing her hair, see where it landed her. There aren't men here. I give you permission but you must continue to have the best result in your class, the moment your grades start to slip, I am cutting off your hair, you hear me?"

Ranti nodded. "I have never disappointed you Esho, and I will not, I promise you."

And so Moradeke and Ranti became partners and did each others hair every Sunday and Ranti became happier in school. After a few weeks of becoming Moradeke's friend, some of the 'cool' girls who were Moradeke's friends started to speak to her, her loneliness started to ease off, and she started to relax in the company of the other girls.

She also started to watch these girls closely to learn their ways. Most of them had mothers who were professionals like doctors, lawyers, teachers and nurses. They would talk about their families with each other and Ranti wished she had a mother she could be close to, especially the way Moradeke was with her mother.

The girls also talked about their fathers, and at such times Ranti would almost cry. They would describe their close relationships with their fathers and how much they loved them. Shara especially was very close to her father. Her parents were divorced, so he would come visit her during the week, not just on Saturdays that was the official visiting day. Her mother came to visit her on some Saturdays.

Each time Shara saw her father's big car pull up from the class room window, she would start to jump up and down in her seat in her excitement, and if the teacher happened to be writing on the board, she would use the opportunity to bolt out of the classroom, run up to her father, who would pick her up and toss her in the air as if she was a little girl. They would both laugh hard and hug one another repeatedly.

Ranti along with the other girls would look out the window at them, and Shara who loved to show off, would put on a good show for her classmates. Her father always brought her food, snacks, pretty clothes and money.

Ranti would try to compare her classmates' families with hers and her loneliness would intensify. She would try to fantasize about Akanbi running towards her to pick her up, hug her and toss her in the air and catch her again, like Shara's father. She would become sadder because even in fantasy, she could not get it to happen.

So, she would daydream about meeting a man who would do that for her, "of course after I am a doctor, so such a man will not ruin my life, because then I will be his wife." Such fantasies she could get to fly.

Ranti returned home at the end of the first year to Esho for the eight weeks vacation. She insisted on going with her to her job of carrying cement for the builders. She and Esho had a big argument about this, with Esho insisting that her destiny was not one in which she would carry cement, but that she was going to become a great woman like her white principal.

"Esho, you are my grandmother and this is the work you do to take care of me. I'm a big girl now. I should be able to work with you. It doesn't mean I'm not in secondary school as well. I can't sit at home all day doing nothing while you work. Working with you will keep me busy and out of harm's way, I will be with you all the time."

Esho gave in and Ranti started to go with her to the construction site. They were able to make double the money that Esho alone would have made and for the first time in her life, Esho had some money left over that she was able to put in a savings account Ranti insisted she opened.

She had been thinking of how to get Esho employed in another profession so she would not have to do the hard manual labor. She thought that if they could save enough money, Esho could start some petty trading like a lot of the mothers in their neighborhood who sold some food items in front of their houses. So at the construction site she worked very hard.

Gboye was also home for vacation from England. They were very happy to see one another after that year of separation, and they had a lot to tell one another. Ranti shared her experience of her first year at St. Ann's school with Gboye, and Gboye told her about England where she was in school with white girls and boys. She was excited especially about the boys, which surprised Ranti because in elementary school Gboye did not like boys and was always fighting with them.

Ranti told Gboye about Moradeke, but Gboye reminded her of their promise to be best friends forever, and Ranti quickly reassured her that she remained her first best friend.

In her second year in secondary school, Ranti went through the same ordeal as the previous year when it was time to prepare for the sport competition, and she was punished again. Moradeke questioned her and Ranti confided in her after she made her promise to go to her grave with the secret.

Moradeke offered to get a doctor's note from her mother, but Ranti refused because she did not want more people knowing her secret, she felt that three people were enough. A week later Moradeke triumphantly handed her a note from her mother, excusing her from all sporting events.

"You told your mother? After you promised me you wouldn't tell a soul." Ranti yelled at her. "How could you Moradeke? Your mother and Shara's mother are friends and they work together. What if she told Shara's mother and she told Shara, the whole school would know and I would be finished here? I would have preferred to continue to wash the toilets and do the dishes." Ranti started to cry.

Moradeke started to cry too and to apologize. "I was just trying to help you Ranti, I don't think it's fair for you to have gone through that horrible experience, and you are still suffering, and then to be punished again. It's not fair. You are my friend and I wanted to help you. I'm sorry."

"You should have left me alone. I'm not from your world. In my world a lot of things are not fair, but I am making do. I'm taking care of myself. I don't expect fair and I don't look for fair. I have accepted my life as it is and I thought as my friend you would understand that." Ranti walked away from a tearful Moradeke, who repeatedly said she was sorry.

Ranti returned to her dorm and tore up the letter. True to her expectations, a week later Shara stood up in class one afternoon while they were between teachers and announced to the class, "I think I smell urine in this class, someone is smelling of urine." The other girls started to sniff the air. Some said they smelt urine too, while others said they did not.

Shara started to walk in between the rows of desks and chairs and to sniff each girl. She arrived where Ranti was and stopped. "It's in this general area." She announced. Ranti's neighbor started to protest that the smell was not from her.

Shara moved closer to Ranti and sniffed her. "It's Ranti. She smells of urine. "Do you know why?" She asked the class. "It's because she leaks urine. And do you know why she leaks urine? Because she got pregnant last year, and she went and committed an abortion and they injured her down there, so for the rest of her life she will leak urine. That's what happens to fast girls who start to have sex too early in their life. I know, my mother is a doctor, she explained everything to me."

The other girls went "Ha!" and they started to look at Ranti.

Ranti panicked because if Esho were to hear that she committed an abortion she would definitely kill her. Her heart started to race and she felt light headed.

The teacher arrived at that point and the girls took their seats.

By the end of the day, the whole school has heard that Ranti committed an abortion, her vagina was perforated, and she was leaking and smelling of urine. She started to receive the looks she received at the time Shara accused her of stealing food.

Ranti thought, "Life is not fair at all. I don't talk to men or boys and Esho cut me. I started to leak urine and I'm accused of committing an abortion."

She became ostracized again and the few girls who had started to talk to her after she became friends with Moradeke stopped talking to her. She had not spoken to Moradeke since they had the fight the week before. Moradeke got someone else to do her hair on Sunday, while Ranti had to do her hair by herself. It did not look as good as it would have had Moradeke helped her, but it was passable.

She knew she would not get into trouble with the principal on the accusation of having an abortion since her periods had not started, unlike most of her classmates who already had their periods. She knew that a girl could not get pregnant without having her periods because she read it in the third year biology book.

The rumor finally got to the teachers a few days later. Ranti was called to the staff room at lunchtime. The teachers asked her if she committed an abortion.

"No, I did not. I don't menstruate yet, so how can I become pregnant?" She snapped; sick of being made a scapegoat.

"I don't believe you, look at her breasts, she's at least a size 34D, don't tell me that with that body and that face, you don't have your periods yet. I have seen fathers on visiting day looking at you. You are from a very poor home and I'm sure you've caught on that with that face of yours and that body, you could make

110   *Feasts of Phantoms*

a lot of money. When do you do it? Do you sneak out of school at night? You are going to be expelled you know." One teacher started.

Ranti waited. The other teachers had a lot to say too.

"You had better not embark on that career for yourself because beauty fades."

"Keep committing the abortions and keep thinking you can get away with it, it's the likes of you who won't be able to have children later in life, and then you will wonder why God is punishing you."

"She has been punished enough. She is leaking urine already. I hope you've learnt your lesson."

"You are a very lucky girl, you have beauty and brains. God doesn't usually do things that way, he usually gives a girl either brain or beauty, but he gave you both. Don't ruin your life."

Ranti was quiet as the teachers pontificated. Suddenly a bolt of energy exploded in her brain, she wanted to laugh out loud. It dawned on her that Esho knew the truth. She would not believe she had an abortion because she was responsible for her leaking urine. "I am innocent, just like our last name, Jare, I am Iranti Jare—'Memory is Innocent.' I earned my scholarship to come to this school and I will graduate from this school with honors. I will go on to become a doctor. I have nothing to fear and it can't get worse than this. The secret is out, I leak urine, so what?" She smiled.

One teacher felt so strongly about the matter that she marched her to the principal's office immediately to inform the principal of the issue and prevent Ranti from corrupting the other girls.

"It's impossible for me to have gotten pregnant Ma, not only have I never had sex, I'm not even menstruating yet. My grandmother had me circumcised about three years ago. She thought it would keep me safe from men. I struggled when it was being done and the woman's hand slipped. She cut deeper than she meant to, that's why I leak urine. I've had this problem for the past three years. You can ask a doctor to examine me and they will tell you I have never had sex in my life and I have never been pregnant."

The principal looked at Ranti for a long time. "Is that why you don't participate in sports?"

Ranti nodded.

"How did this rumor start?

Ranti did not want to feed into Shara's sense of self-importance. "I don't know Ma, the girls were talking about me and today I was called to the staff room and it's obvious the teachers believed the rumor."

"That will be all Ms. Lawal," the principal dismissed the teacher. "Ranti didn't have an abortion, I believe her. She is a very responsible girl. Please make sure you tell the teachers and they should know better than harassing a girl the whole school has already made a scapegoat out of."

"Do you have any friends amongst the other girls Ranti?" the principal asked her.

"I did until this rumor started. Moradeke used to be my friend but we had an argument last week. She told her mother about my problem, she wanted to help me so I would be excused from sports. I think her mother must have told some other mothers, and they told their daughters and that is how the whole thing started. I know Moradeke did not mean any harm."

"You are going to be fine you know. If there is anything I can do to be of help, don't hesitate to let me know, okay. In fact I want you and Moradeke to clean my house. Usually girls in third year do that for me, but I want to be able to keep an eye on you, and I want you to feel comfortable to talk to me. I will talk to the prefect in charge of chores. Is that okay with you?"

Ranti nodded and felt honored that she and Moradeke would clean the principal's home on Saturdays. Usually it was a position given to very responsible girls.

The positive result from the rumor was Ranti did not have to serve the punishment for not participating in sports anymore.

Moradeke was relieved to see Ranti later in the day when she went to look for her. She hugged her as she apologized repeatedly.

21

Ranti and Moradeke started to clean the principal's house on Saturday mornings and house sit for her when she went out of town. This gave them more time together. They spent such times talking about their families and their hopes and dreams. Ranti introduced Moradeke to a lot of the books she had read, and Moradeke in turn introduced her to the world of romance novels, most of them from England, published by Mills and Boon.

Moradeke had hundreds of books because her sisters loved them and they would bring them to her when they came to visit. Many copies of the romance novels were in circulation in the school as many of the girls loved to read them too.

Ranti enjoyed them as much as the next girl and they increased her yearning to be normal, to be beautiful and desirable, and be someone that a man would fall in love with and vow to love for the rest of his life.

The novels provided much substrate for her daydreaming and she would vow to herself that she would achieve that, because she had as much right as any girl to that kind of life. She would repeatedly tell herself that Esho was wrong, that kind of life could be for them too. She would not allow the curse on Esho's head to continue with her. She would meet a man, who would fall in love with her, and she would fall in love with him, and he would love her very much and tell her she is beautiful, and he did not want to be with any other woman but her.

Ranti's menstrual period arrived towards the end of her third year after she turned thirteen. She had been afraid it might never come, and then she would not be able to have children. They had learnt about reproduction in biology and the teacher had advised any of them, whose periods had not arrived to ask their parents to take them to a doctors. Almost all the girls in her class were menstruating already.

Strangely for three months before her periods came, she had been experiencing severe abdominal pain that came on a monthly basis, similar to the menstrual cramps her classmates had accompanying their periods, but she did not have the periods, and the cramps had made her so sick once that she threw up many times and felt faint. She knew there was no way she was going to discuss it with Esho. Her grandmother would like it better if her periods never came.

Initially she was very happy the day she went to the bathroom to change her pads for soaking up urine and she saw the drops of very dark blood. The pain was there as well, along with the nausea that prevented her from eating. She shared the good news with Moradeke who insisted they celebrate. She told Ranti that when her periods came, her father killed a rooster for her and the family had a special dinner just for her, so she took Ranti to the tuck shop and bought her a pack of Goody-Goody caramel bars.

Two months later Ranti was not happy her periods started, as each month the cramps incapacitated her, and she bled just a few drops of very dark clotted blood, unlike with the other girls who bled more. She saw the used sanitary pads they did not dispose of the proper way, and were left all over the floor in the bathrooms.

She consulted Moradeke. Moradeke's mother suggested that Ranti sees a doctor because something might be wrong. Ranti did not ask Esho to take her to a doctor and did not tell her she was suffering. The cramps got worse each month and would arrive about three to five days before her periods and last for another week, such that two weeks out of a month she was in pain, and was so sick she would not be able to eat.

Very soon she learnt to manage the pain. Once it started, she would stop eating and eat once in three days sometimes, to keep the nausea down so she could continue to attend her classes. She started to lose a lot of weight and this worried Moradeke who told her mother, and the following Saturday when she came to visit, she asked Ranti a lot of questions and examined her abdomen, she gave her some painkillers to help with the pain. The medications helped a lot such that the pain and the nausea decreased significantly and she was able to eat more.

Ranti returned home at the end of her third year for the eight-week vacation before the fourth year. She went with Esho to the construction site during the day and she spent most of the evenings with Gboye who was home from England.

One day, returning from Gboye's house, she walked by the fast flowing river. She sat on the bank daydreaming about the kinds of lives she read about in the romance novels. She fantasized that Gboye's older brother, Goke would notice her. She was always excited to go to her friend's house with the hope that she would see him.

She suddenly realized she had a crush on him and she panicked wondering what Esho would do to her if she found out. She wondered if Oshun had a similar crush on Akanbi. She tried to imagine anyone having a crush on Akanbi and she was disgusted.

She thought of Goke and hoped he would see her as beautiful. Then she instructed herself to dismiss the idea from her mind immediately, because Goke in his school in England must be surrounded by prettier girls with lovelier dresses. She had just three dresses because that was all Esho could afford. She suddenly felt sad that Goke would never notice her, besides even if he did, it would go nowhere because of her problems of leaking urine.

She started to cry. "I will never have sex, not the kind Esho is afraid of, but the kind I could have had were I to get married. I will go to the university and become a doctor, I will buy a big car and live in a big house and have lots of books to read and lots of beautiful clothes, but I will never be able to get married and have children. Esho will not have to carry cement anymore and the two of us will continue to live together. I will be like the principal who has a big car and is well educated, but who doesn't have a husband and no children."

She cried for about ten minutes, then, she waded into the river, splashed some water on her face. She wiped her face with the skirt of her dress and continued on her way home.

She walked into the small forest where she and her brother used to play, and on to the dumpsite close to the forest where they used to explore for treasures. She tried not to think of her brother, but it dawned on her that she had not been back in the forest or the dumpsite since he died.

As she was emerging from the forest onto the dumpsite she saw big wooden crates hidden by some bushes close to the dumpsite. She went to investigate and there were five of them side by side, with most of them in the bushes where some weed had started to grow, thus concealing them more.

She walked around them and wondered what they were. She thought of going on home to avoid getting into trouble, but it felt as if the crates beckoned to her. She looked around to make sure no one was watching, then she went over

114 *Feasts of Phantoms*

to the first one, she tried to open it but it was nailed shut. She tried to open the others too with the same result. On the sides of the crates was written Toronto, Canada.

"I know where Canada is, we learnt about it in geography. This is a very poor neighborhood, I'm sure no one here has ever been to Canada. Someone is hiding something. I should call the police." She made more attempts to open the crates with no result. She convinced herself to mind her business and go on home.

The next day at the construction site, while Esho was busy, she sneaked over to the young carpenter who liked her and was always smiling at her each time their eyes met. Esho had noticed the carpenter's looks too, she had given Ranti one of her lectures, and warned the carpenter to stay away from her daughter and not ruin her life, because she was in secondary school and she would be going on to the university.

Ranti asked to borrow his hammer and pliers. She explained that there was a crate she needed to open and promised to return his tools to him the next day. He offered to help her as she might need some muscles to accomplish the task, but Ranti panicked and told him Esho would kill the two of them. He looked around for Esho as he gave Ranti the tools making her promise to return them the next day.

When they got home later in the afternoon, Ranti explained to Esho that she had to go and help Gboye with her hair as she ran out of the house. She had hidden the carpenter's tools at the back of the house since Esho would have noticed them in their one room accommodation.

She walked as fast as she could to the dumpsite and set to work with the pliers and the hammer to open the crate that was concealed the most by the bush, so she would not be seen in case someone came by. After about ten minutes of hammering and plying, it opened and inside was hundreds of books.

Ranti was stunned as books were the last things she expected to find in the crates. She stared at the books for a long time, "how did you get here?" she demanded.

The first one she picked up was rain-soaked and eaten by ants. There were about fifty books on the first layer that she threw out since most of them were destroyed. She felt very sad that someone would do this to books. "Books are full of treasures!" She exclaimed, "This is unforgivable."

Most of the books on the second layer were affected as well but she could make out some titles. She picked up a book that was mostly damaged. In the back flap was an envelope with "This is the Property of the Public Library of Toronto, Ontario Canada."

She became very excited. She had read about such public libraries that you could just walk into, sit down and read as many books as you wanted, or borrow the books to take home and no one would harass you. You don't have to hide or sneak in through the 'fetish room' on Sundays to read the books like she had been doing in the big bookshop.

Ranti could not believe her luck. She clapped her hands and jumped up and down. She continued to dig deeper into the crates and the books at the third level were fine. The damage had not gotten to them yet. They were books of fiction, history and biography. She picked up a book, and it was about Marie Curie who won the Nobel Prize on two occasions for her work on radiation. She opened the book to a middle page and a quotation by Marie Curie jumped at her: *"Nothing in life is to be feared. It is only to be understood."*

She started to dance with happiness. Then she wondered where she would keep the books. She was thankful the person from the local government offices who came periodically to burn the garbage at the dumpsite had not come before she discovered the books.

She remembered Lana telling her there were lots of treasures to be found in the dumpsite and they had found some treasures. There had been cans and boxes that were in fairly good condition and Lana made toy trucks out of them. Once they found a big carton and with empty cans of Bournvita as wheels, Lana made a truck and Ranti sat in the carton while Lana pulled her around. She told him she felt like the Cinderella he told her about from one of the books from the bookshop. Lana had laughed, he curtsied to her saying, "At your service Princess, I used to be a frog but I will be your coachman."

"You are not a frog, you are Lana," she had argued with him and he had tried to explain to her that the frog turned to a coachman and in another story the frog turned into a prince.

She remembered all the stories of princes and princesses he told her. She later read them in the bookshop. Her favorite was Sleeping Beauty. For some reason she felt a bond with that sleeping princess and constantly thought about her. She later concluded that it was because her prince came for her. Though a lot of princes tried to wake her from her slumber, when the time was right, the right prince woke her.

"The dumpsite is full of treasures after all. But it also killed my brother when he got injured here." Tears welled up in her eyes. She wiped them off and continued to look at the books.

"Some crazy person threw them away, but who would send books from Canada here? Why here? Was it meant for the school? But the school is very far away from here."

She opened all the crates so she could return the tools to the carpenter the next day and she took ten books home.

She practiced what she would tell her grandmother about the books. She knew how hungry Esho was for her to be educated. She convinced herself that Esho would agree she could keep the books. She warned herself to stand far away from

116   *Feasts of Phantoms*

her while she told her about the books to avoid her blows.

"Esho, you are not going to believe what I found by the forest today," she started when she arrived at home. "I found books, hundreds of them in crates, imagine if I read the books all the things I will learn from them, and they are from Canada. That is white people's land, and in places like that all the women are educated and they have good jobs.

"I will like to keep the books Esho, though I don't know who threw them away and why someone would throw such good books away and after I have read them, I will give them to the library in my school so other students can read them too." She breathlessly explained to her grandmother.

Esho was sitting on her mat. She leant against the wall as she listened to her small radio. The room was dark because she had turned down the kerosene lamp. She turned the lamp up and took a good look at Ranti as she stood in the doorway with the books in her arms.

"You can keep the books because that is the only thing you will ever get from Akanbi with the cursed head that smallpox will afflict, him and his bastards and ugly wife. That is the only inheritance you will ever get from him, so keep the books."

"Akanbi? The books belong to Akanbi? So what are they doing in the forest and why are they not in his house? I didn't know he likes books, so he knows people in Canada because that's where the books came from."

"I don't care who he knows. He is a useless man Iranti. That's what I keep telling you, he is a thief and he would steal from anyone, the man is scum." She started to spit on the floor in disgust as she did each time she spoke of Akanbi, but "Esho!" Ranti checked her.

She had explained to her grandmother that it was not healthy to spit on the floor in the room where they sleep and eat, after she learnt about tuberculosis in health science in her second year, and Esho had listened to her.

"Anyway, you know he is a school superintendent, it is his job to go round to schools to check on the teachers to make sure they are teaching the children well. He is also in charge of moving the teachers so if a school needs a teacher and another school has a lot of that kind of teacher, he should distribute them so they do there work well. He has not been doing any of that.

"If a teacher wasn't working well, instead of reporting such a teacher, he would start to harass the teacher and take bribes from them. If a teacher would like to move to a different school for any reason, they have to bribe him before he lets that happen.

"Some money from the government to buy chalk, duster and books for the schools, Akanbi has been eating, the same way he ate your money when the diocese gave you a scholarship, though he continues to deny that you are his daughter."

Ranti expected her to go crazy again as she had been each time the matter came up, but she did not.

"Do you want me to go on? You know I told you he is like the tortoise' wife without any sense of shame, shamelessness is the worst disease that can afflict a person in this world, I tell you. So about five months ago, you were in school and I didn't tell you so as not to distract you from your studies because he is not worth it. The police arrested him because he demanded a bribe from an undercover policewoman whom he thought was a teacher. She wanted to move to another school and she made the request but he told her the only condition was if she gave him money, and if she slept with him!"

She paused for a moment, "*Osshhiii*," she hissed in disgust. "She would pay him money and sleep with him too? I don't know why someone has not killed that scumbag! So the policewoman whom he thought was a teacher agreed, and he took her to his home." She paused again as had a look of wonder on her face.

"You know, Iranti, there is one thing I don't understand about these women who are married. It's as if marriage turns them into idiots. The things they accept from these men! *Unh!*" She snapped her fingers over her head in a gesture of warding off dirt. "*Lailai*, I can never take such things from any man. Anyway that's why I'm not married. I would have killed the man."

Ranti waited patiently through all the sidebars and for Esho to get to the connection between Akanbi and the books.

"A man is married to you and then he brings all kinds of women into the house to sleep with them while you are there! All sorts." She clapped her hands three times in dismay. "You know I mind my own business, I don't care about Akanbi with his bastards and his ugly wife, the only thing I care about is that justice be done on that man, and I know that it would be done.

"In this our lifetime, justice will be served, because the god of retribution of today is not as slow as the god of retribution of yesteryears. He moves with the new technologies available today. When I was a young girl he rode on donkeys to avenge wrong doings, and that is why my father got away with the evil he did to me until I took matters into my own hands and killed him, but today, the god of retribution flies in an airplane, so we will all see him punished. Smallpox will come into that house and afflict all of them and if he survives it, he would panhandle before he can eat at the dusk of his life.

"He thinks he's an important man now because he has a job with the government? At the twilight of his life all those things will be ancient history, unless smallpox has mercy on him and kill him off first.

"So, he took this woman home and his idiot wife was there, he asked her to get out of the room. Can you believe that, in my own home? I tell you, there would have been at least two corpses there on that day if I were stupid enough to marry anyone in the first place. Rivers of blood would have flown.

118   *Feasts of Phantoms*

"Anyway, to get to the question you asked me, Akanbi took off his clothes and he was naked, the woman blew a whistle and other policemen who had followed them secretly came out of nowhere and arrested him. They took him away for many days and that was when his idiot wife started to run around this neighborhood like *a chicken with its head cut off*, looking for some strong men to help her move some things out of the house.

"They moved those crates of books and hid them in the forest. They did it in secret but Oye down the street was one of the men who helped her, you know I buy kerosene from his mother. She told me that if the government had found the books in his house, as well as other things they had to get rid off quickly, they would have fired him from his job.

"The books came from across the seas. Some good people from the white people's land donated the books so our children here can have a chance to learn what their children know. Akanbi was supposed to give them to the schools so children like you could read them, but the useless man that he is, he doesn't care if children had books to read. The government paid him money, not as part of his salary, but more money to distribute the books to the schools because you know he bought that truck a few years ago. So he just brought the books to his house and left them there.

"I keep telling you, he is the kind of man who will steal breast milk from a baby's mouth. He is despicable." She hissed again. "If you want the books, take them, learn from them, but the problem is we have nowhere to keep them, this is a very small room." Esho finished her story.

"We can keep them at the back of the house. We can ask the landlord permission to keep them there. I will take some discarded iron sheets from the construction site tomorrow to put under the crate to keep them dry and I will get some to cover the crates. Thank you Esho and as I finish reading them, I will give them to the school."

"Iranti go and take the books because that is the only thing you will ever get from that shameless scumbag that smallpox will afflict. I don't know why they didn't lock him up forever. But I heard that he bribed the police and they let him go. He still has his job. You know I don't like to distract you with all his nonsense, but he got two girls pregnant last year. One of them tried to commit an abortion and she died. The other one had a child for him, but the same story, he wouldn't acknowledge the child. I'm glad you live in that school." She paused again as she had a far away look on her face.

"I could help his wife kill him you know, I would willingly do it. I have killed two men that were scumbags and pedophiles before, what is one more? The likes of him should not be walking the face of this earth with the rest of us. I don't believe in their Christian god because like I always tell you, your god is in your head, but I know the stories in their Bible. When I lived in that convent, I heard those stories everyday and like I keep telling you, Akanbi is not a descendant of

Noah. His ancestors must have found their way into that Ark when Noah was not looking because even going by their stories their god destroyed the likes of him.

"He did it twice. He did it in Sodom and Gomorrah and he did it when he flooded the world, but Akanbi's ancestors escaped. He is the cruelest man I know." She paused for a moment.

"I heard from Mama Oye when I went to buy kerosene the other day that he is sleeping with his *own* daughter. You know that one, the one that is about your age, the one whose eyes always looked to the north when she tries to look to the south. What is her name?" Esho snapped her fingers many times trying to jug her memory. "You know the one I'm talking about, she was in school with you when you were in primary school."

"Iyabo," Ranti volunteered.

"Yes, that's the one, the one with cross eyes. I heard that he's sleeping with her now. His own daughter! *Uhn! Hey, Hey.*" She clapped her hands in dismay. "Anyway, why am I even surprised? My father did it to me, and Oshun was a baby when he started to sleep with her, scumbag." She hissed again. "I hear all sorts on this radio and I believe them because most of them happen in this neighborhood. So go and bring the books and read them and become knowledgeable."

Ranti returned the tools to the carpenter the next day and she told him about the books. She asked him to help her construct a container made of iron sheets that would keep the books dry and away from ants and termites and he readily agreed.

The following weekend, the carpenter constructed a container out of the discarded iron sheets for Ranti. He also helped her move the books they could salvage into the container.

Ranti was in heaven as she dug into the books and was able to push the despondency that Goke would never notice her, or that she might never get married and have children anyway. She thought about Akanbi and the way some men treat their wives. She reassured herself that she did not want that kind of a life anyway.

22

On a Saturday afternoon toward the end of her fourth year Ranti and Moradeke house-sat for the principal who went to Lagos on a day trip. Ranti was lying on the couch in the living room because she was not feeling well as her cramps started again that morning, when the doorbell rang.

A tall bald man demanded to see the principal. He looked vaguely familiar to her, but she could not place his face. He came in a sports car. Ranti spoke to him through the window telling him the principal was not home. Moradeke who had been in the bathroom returned, but when she saw the man she hid in the kitchen.

The man demanded to be let into the house. Ranti apologized but refused.

He became very angry, "Do you know who I am?" he yelled at her.

"I'm sorry Sir, your face looks familiar but I can't place it."

"Really, you don't know who I am? What is your name? Answer me now?" he yelled again.

"Iranti Jare."

"Iranti Jare? Who are your parents?"

Ranti stared at him.

"Are you deaf as well? Who are your parents?"

"I don't have parents."

"You don't have parents? What do you mean, 'I don't have parents?" he mimicked her. "Everyone has parents. You didn't just drop from the sky did you?"

"No I didn't. My mother is dead and I don't know who my father is."

"Ah! You are a bastard. That's what you should have said. Who is your guardian? Where do you go on vacations, or do you live here with the principal?"

"I go home to my grandmother."

"Oh, you have a grandmother. What does she do for a living?"

"She's a laborer."

"I see, and how were you able to attend this school, if you are a bastard whose grandmother is a laborer?"

"The diocese gave me a scholarship."

"I see, so that tells me you are not a stupid girl, although you just behaved like an idiot by not knowing who I am. I will ask the diocese to withdraw the scholarship so you can join your grandmother in being a laborer. You are a disgrace to this school."

Ranti stared at him in shock.

"I want you to open the door this minute, or else, you wouldn't be the only one in trouble, your grandmother will be in serious trouble as well." He commanded her.

"I'm sorry Sir. The principal instructed me not to open the door for anyone. I can't disobey her."

"Okay, tell the principal I came to see her, Iranti Jare." He started toward his car.

"Sir, I don't know your name. I wouldn't know who to tell her came."

He turned around, "If you don't deliver the message, you and your laborer grandmother are in serious trouble." He got into his car and sped off.

Moradeke ran to hug Ranti who had started to cry. She wondered why her scholarship was always under so much threat. "Why wouldn't people just leave me alone so I can get my education?"

"He is the governor of the state, Ranti, didn't you recognize him? That's Brigadier Jamba." Moradeke informed her.

Ranti shook her head, "I thought he looked familiar, but I've never seen him when he wasn't in his military uniform, I didn't know he's bald since he always wore his cap in all his pictures. He has the power to take away my scholarship. As the governor of the state, people will listen to him."

Moradeke tried to reassure her that the principal would help her so she would not lose her scholarship but Ranti started to believe Esho. They were cursed and they were on their own. They were powerless and powerful people could abuse them and get away with it.

Moradeke was very angry that the governor called Ranti a bastard and she started to curse him out. Ranti just felt hopeless.

"Look Ranti, you know the principal is not a married woman. I heard rumors that she and the governor are having an affair. The governor is married, and of course that's why he would come visit her on a Saturday evening. He's doing something wrong and that's why he came down so hard on you. If he makes the diocese withdraw your scholarship, my sister is a journalist working for the Concord newspaper in Lagos, they're always looking for stories like this, I will tell my sister and they will publish the story, okay."

Ranti stared at Moradeke, convinced she had lost her mind. "And after you publish the story, he would then come after me and my grandmother and hurt us even more."

"Okay, this is what we will do, when the principal comes back, we will not tell her a thing. We will pretend as if he didn't come. It's his words against yours and the principal trusts you, but he's cheating on his wife already, so the principal knows he's a liar."

"But he's her boyfriend. Don't you think she trusts him?"

"He cheats Ranti, men who cheat are liars, you can't believe anything they tell you, the principal is not a fool, she knows that, maybe she's just lonely, you know, she is a white woman living in this country without her family, loneliness can make you do things you don't want to do. I like her, but her boyfriend is a liar and a cheat, even though he is the governor of this state, and my father said he is very corrupt too, steals money and all the rest of it."

Later that night when the principal returned, Ranti in spite of Moradeke's advice recounted the event in details. She apologized for not recognizing the governor explaining that she had seen him only in army uniform.

The principal reassured her that she would not lose her scholarship.

The following Monday, the principal sent for Ranti and when she arrived at her office, there was a soldier standing outside the door.

"Ranti come in, that's the governor's driver. He wants you to come to his office so he could talk to you. Don't be afraid, I told him you are the most brilliant student in the school and very responsible too, and you had never seen his picture without him in uniform. He'll like to apologize to you for threatening you and he wants to help you and your grandmother."

"I can't go Ma. I can't go to the governor's office. I can't go with his driver because my grandmother will kill me if she found out. I'm not even supposed to talk to any man. I accept the governor's apologies, but I can't go to his office. I'm sorry Ma." Ranti explained to the principal while shaking her head vigorously.

"Its okay, Ranti, he is the governor of the state and I'm your principal giving you permission, your grandmother will understand. This could be good for your family. He could help your grandmother find a better job. He was really impressed with how talented you are. Trust me, it's okay, the driver will take you and bring you back right away. He's a very busy man you don't expect him to come to your school to apologize to you, and he feels really bad."

Ranti thought of asking Moradeke to come with her but she did not want her to miss her classes. Esho's voice kept ringing in her ears, warning her not to go to any man.

"Come on Ranti, this is good for you, very soon you will be representing the school in debates and other functions. You will be the head of school next year and you will have to talk to important people like members of the alumni, and ministers, so this is good practice for you, don't be timid." The principal encouraged her.

Ranti checked her uniform to be sure it was clean and against her better judgment went with the governor's driver. She felt guilty that she was disobeying her grandmother, but she trusted the principal who had always been kind to her.

At the governor's office she was asked to sit in a room. The secretary offered her a soft drink but she declined, she was very anxious which did not help the cramps she had been having for the past four days. She was also nauseated and afraid she would throw up.

An hour later the governor came into the room. Ranti stood up.

"Good afternoon Sir, I'm sorry about Saturday, I didn't recognize you because in your pictures that I have seen, you always wore uniforms, like now. I recognize you now."

"That's okay, your principal explained everything to me, she told me you are a very brilliant girl and very responsible too. That is very good; you are the kind of student that makes me proud to be the governor of this state."

"Thank you Sir."

"But you are an arrogant young woman, aren't you?"

Ranti stared at him.

"You didn't kneel down in a gesture of respect to greet me, the governor of this state. Is it because you are brilliant and beautiful, you don't think you should respect anyone?"

"I'm sorry Sir, I don't mean any disrespect. My grandmother taught me never to kneel down to anyone. She said if I knelt down, while I am down there, they would kick me further down. She brought me up to be respectful and I'm not a rude person, Sir."

"I see, this grandmother, is that the one who is a laborer?"

"Yes Sir."

"What's her name?"

"Esho Jare."

"I see. Where do you and your grandmother live?"

"Bere."

"That's a very poor neighborhood."

"We are very poor Sir, and that's why this education is very important to me."

"What would you like to be when you grow up?"

"A doctor Sir."

"Do you think a doctor has ever come out of Bere?"

"I don't know Sir, but I will try my best."

"I'm sure you will. Let me tell you what it means to be the governor of this state," the governor started. "When the time comes for you to go to the university, even if you pass your examination, I can still prevent you from getting into a university. And not just in this state, but in this whole country. And I know that your laborer grandmother who lives in Bere doesn't have the money to send you abroad for university education.

"I have the money to send my children abroad to go to secondary schools and they are there and they will attend universities in England and America. That is the power that I have, Iranti Jare, the most brilliant girl in St. Ann's school whose laborer grandmother taught her not to kneel down to anyone. Do you understand?"

Ranti became terrified. She nodded.

"Speak! Or did your grandmother also teach you not to answer when spoken to?" He roared at her.

Ranti could hear Esho's voice warning her about being distracted, and that it is at such times that men would pounce on her. She looked around the room to see if there was a weapon handy. She would give him 'Esho treatment' she promised herself.

"Are you deaf?" He roared again.

"I, I understand Sir," she stammered.

"Good, I want you to go down on your knees, now."

Ranti stared at him, but she did not kneel down.

"Stubborn eh? Your principal didn't tell me that, she told me you were an obedient girl."

"I am Sir and I mean no disrespect."

"Really, but you just disobeyed me now."

"I don't want to disobey my grandmother."

"Oh it is a question of who to obey, the governor of a state or your laborer grandmother. So you chose your grandmother who is not here with us."

Ranti stared at him.

"Okay, don't kneel down. I want you to take off your clothes. I want to see if you are as beautiful without clothes as you look with clothes on you."

"I won't. I will not take off my clothes. I am sorry. I won't."

"It gets better, beautiful, brilliant, stubborn and a fiery temper. I like that in a woman. Do you have a boyfriend, say in Government College?"

"No, I don't."

"Are you telling me that those boys in Government College haven't been feeling you up when your two schools have dances?"

Ranti stared at him.

He came towards her. "Scream all you like, this room is soundproof, no one will hear you. This is where we have all the high level security meetings."

She backed away from him, but he kept coming at her, she scanned the room and there was no weapon handy, except the chairs. She thought of picking up a chair and crashing it on his head, but he was over a foot taller than her. He backed her into a corner, but she fixed her eyes on him.

"What a beautiful face but very sad eyes." He slapped her hard across her face and grabbing her dress by the neckline ripped it. The dress tore into her shoulders as the fabric gave way.

Ranti screamed and he slapped her again. Her lips started to bleed. She was in her petticoat. He tore at that too until she stood in her bra and underwear. She wrapped her arms across her chest and continued to cry. She pleaded with him to leave her alone.

"Go down on your knees!" He commanded again.

She stood up straight. He tried to hit her again but she evaded his blow. He grabbed her hair with his left hand to hold her head in place while he hit her across the face again with his right hand. He tore off her bra and moved away from her to have a good look.

Ranti cowered in the corner of the room and continued to cry.

He started to take off his uniform, he took off the shirt and his undershirt, and then he took off his pants, leaving his boots on.

He stood in his underwear and Ranti could see his erection. He came towards her and grabbing her hair, he moved her head towards him to kiss her, when all of a sudden she lost all muscle control as she became incontinent of urine and feces and she vomited at the same time. Her legs gave way and she fell to her knees. Most of the vomit ended up on him. He pushed her back in disgust.

"Jesus!" he yelled at her. "What kind of freak are you? What is the matter with you? Are you out of your mind? What do you think you are doing? You are going to clean that up, you pig."

He came towards her and Ranti backed more into the corner. She could not believe her eyes and was very embarrassed. She started to tremble as she cried.

He kicked her with his right foot and she removed her hands from her breasts to cover her face. He continued to kick her and she rolled herself into a ball, while cowering in the corner to reduce the impact of his kicks. She started to bleed from her face that she could feel swelling up, her arms and back hurt from his kicks.

After a while he got tired of kicking her. He stood still and stared at her for a moment. "Unbelievable! What did I expect from a girl from Bere, just because she has a beautiful body? You dog. You are not going to any university. You are going to end up a laborer like your grandmother. I would have given you such a good life, I would have taken you out of Bere, but you are a laborer. As long as I am alive, you are not going to any university, you are going to use all that brilliance to carry cement, mark my words."

He sat on the couch, he removed his undershirt and underwear, threw them into a corner and he put his uniform back on. He came over to where she was huddled in the corner and gave her one more kick before he left the room.

Ranti stayed in the corner and tried to get her mind to think straight. She kept thinking of Esho, she would never believe the governor did not rape her. "He did rape me," she corrected herself, "he just didn't use his penis. I can't go back to school looking like this."

The cramps had gotten worse. She stood up slowly and looked down at herself, she could see that feces, urine and blood were all mixed together and it made her woozy. She held on to the walls as she walked slowly to the bathroom next to the boardroom. She was thankful to find a shower there. She checked her face in the mirror. Her left eye was swollen shut. The many cuts on her face were oozing blood.

She took a shower in spite of the pain from the cuts all over her body, after which she ripped the towel into small strips, she made a diaper out of it and used the rest of it as a pad to soak the urine and the menstrual blood.

She wrapped a cotton dressing gown that was in one of the cabinets around herself, went back into the room and using her torn uniform and petticoat, she cleaned the room as much as she could. She cleaned her sandals of the feces and put them back on. She left the room and slowly walked out through the governors' secretary office. The people in the room silently stared at her.

She stood on the street and thought for a moment. It looked like it was about three o'clock in the afternoon because most of the people were leaving work to go home. She did not have money for transportation, so she started to walk slowly toward home.

She thought of Esho again, and was convinced she would kill her the way she killed her father and the mad man who gave her Oshun before she was ready, but at the same time she did not want to go back to school looking the way she looked. The girls would have a field day especially Shara who had remained her archenemy. She entertained the idea of running away but dismissed it immediately because she was in too much pain.

She arrived home at about eight o'clock, not that it was such a long distance, but she had to stop several times because of the cramps and her chest that hurt each time she breathed. She was thankful for the darkness that prevented her neighbors from seeing her.

When Esho opened the door, she stared at her blankly. Both of them stood across from each other staring at one another. Esho moved away from the door to let her in. Ranti looked at her grandmother and she burst into tears. Esho moved closer to her and raised her hand to hit her, but Ranti grabbed her raised hand, preventing the blow from landing on her.

She held on to Esho's raised hand and spoke very slowly, "Esho, you will not hit me anymore. You are my mother. If a lion is pursuing me on the streets I should be able to run to you for protection, not for you to become a hyena too. Don't you ever hit me again! I have always listened to you. I have been a very good girl, a very good girl Esho. I have always obeyed you. But with your constant cursing and hitting and cutting into me, you have made me into a punching bag for every fool walking on the street. Everyone now thinks they can take a swing at me because I have learnt not to defend myself.

"As my mother you are supposed to be my sanctuary. Are you going to chase me away the same way you chased Oshun away? Are you? If that is what you want, I will leave now and you will never see me for as long as you live. Speak now and I will listen to you and disappear, but you are never to hit me again."

Esho stared blankly at her.

"I live with normal girls. I hear the way they speak of their families. Their parents love them and protect them from harm. They don't beat them after they had been abused on the streets and ran home to their parents. They ask them what happened, and who did what to them. Those are the questions they ask their children. They don't compound their problems by beating them more."

Ranti walked into the room, she removed the sleeping mat from where it was folded and leant against the wall. She took it to her corner of the room, spread it on the floor and gently laid herself down on it. She faced the wall turning her back on her grandmother. Esho unfolded her mat, turned off the kerosene lamp and lay down.

An hour later, they heard knocks on the door. Esho got up and lit the lamp again. She answered the door ushering in Moradeke and the principal.

"Thank God you are here!" The principal exclaimed.

Ranti slowly turned around because of the pain all over her body and the principal and Moradeke both gasped at the same time when they saw her face. She sat up slowly. Moradeke covered her mouth with her right hand and started to cry.

The principal knelt down next to her. "I'm sorry Ranti, what happened? I thought the governor's driver would bring you back to school, I didn't know they would ask you to find your way; I would have asked my driver to take you and bring you back. Did armed robbers attack you? I was so worried when you didn't come back I went to look for Moradeke and she suggested we came here to check first."

"No, robbers didn't attack me, the governor did. He wanted to rape me and when I refused, he hit me on my face several times and when I fell he kicked me around. He did this, the governor of this state, brigadier Jamba did this to me. He is a rapist. He didn't want to apologize to me for anything. He asked you to send me to him so he could rape me. I walked home. It took me five hours. I couldn't come to school looking like this."

"I have to take you to the hospital. The police have to be notified. He can't be allowed to get away with this. Oh my God, and there I was thinking he is a decent man, I consider him to be one of my friends. Oh my God," the principal lamented.

Ranti refused to go to the hospital and she refused to have the police involved. "The law doesn't work for people like us, people like my grandmother and I. We have no rights as far as the law is concerned. We are the playthings of the rich. It will just make things worse for us. He threatened to harm my grandmother. I'll be fine. I'll stay at home till I'm feeling better and then I will return to school. I can't let people in school see me this way."

The principal appealed to Esho to make Ranti go to the hospital through Moradeke who acted as an interpreter, but Esho refused, and Ranti was surprised to hear her grandmother say, "If Iranti doesn't want to go, she is not going. She knows what she's doing. I trust her judgment."

The principal wanted her to come to school and stay in her house till she recovered but Ranti refused. "I will stay here with my grandmother."

The principal and Moradeke returned the next day with the chairman of the board who had come to Ranti and Esho four years before, to offer them money for Ranti's books and uniforms, as well as Moradeke's mother. The chairman interviewed her extensively. He asked her many questions for clarifications and wrote down everything she said.

Moradeke's mother examined her. She told the chairman that she had two broken ribs as well as contusions all over her body, along with the black eye.

Moradeke's mother was as upset as the other people. She insisted that Ranti comes with her to her clinic in Lagos, so she could better take care of her. Both Ranti and Esho refused. Ranti just wanted to be left alone with her grandmother. She did not want to go away with anyone, no matter how well meaning they were.

As they were leaving, Esho pulled at the chairman's clothes. He turned to her and she went down on her knees to appeal to him, "Please, we don't want any trouble. All I want is for Iranti to complete her education and go to the university. Please leave this man alone, he has not forced himself on her and she wouldn't get pregnant, I am thankful for that. He threatened her that he wouldn't allow her go to the university, maybe he will soon forget about us. We have no one to fight for us. It is just Iranti and me, and she is a good girl." Esho started to cry.

Ranti has never seen her grandmother cry before. Even when Oshun and Lana died, she shrieked and went crazy but she did not cry.

The chairman sat down again on the low stool. "Mama Ranti, we want our daughters to be safe when they go to school. When I came here four years ago, if I told you this would happen to Ranti, would you have sent her to our school? No, you wouldn't, because this is not what we want for our daughters.

"I am a father and I don't want this to be done to any of my children. He is the governor of the state for goodness sake, and he has to be held accountable. This is not the first time he has done this to secondary school girls. We've been hearing rumors. We can't allow this kind of behavior. We are going to take this from the top. We know the police won't arrest him; after all he is the governor of the state and he is their boss. Don't worry, you and Ranti will be safe, we won't let any harm come to you."

"She's a good girl, she listens to me. She's a good girl. She won't even hurt a fly. I know me, I could hurt people even if they had done me no harm but Iranti is not a girl like that. She is a good child." Esho continued to cry. They appealed to Esho again to let them take Ranti to the hospital but Esho was adamant as well. Moradeke's mother left a lot of medications for her while the principal offered Esho money, explaining that since she would not be able to go to her job while she was taking care of Ranti, the money would help.

Esho refused the money. She told the principal she had money saved up in bank for emergencies.

After they left, Esho moved the stool closer to Ranti's mat and sat on it. "Iranti, I know that I go crazy, I know I'm not like the other mothers, but you have to understand that I try my best. I never had a mother, so I didn't learn a lot of things and the few things I learnt, I learnt wrong. You are a child who has never raised her voice to me and you have never given me any trouble since the day you were born. You have remained in good health too. I am thankful for these things.

"Yesterday, when I saw you, I was afraid and when I'm afraid what I do is to strike out. I'm always afraid Iranti. I have never known a day without fear. I try to help myself and I say to myself that the worst has happened to me already in my life, what could be worse? All the people I ever loved have died. The people that I could call family, they rejected me, I have buried two children. What could be worse than that? I tell myself all the time that I have nothing more left in life to fear, nothing more to lose, but yesterday when I saw you at the door. You that you were supposed to be safe in school, safe from my nemesis, and you came to my door at night. I didn't know what to think, then, I realized there is still a lot I don't want to lose.

"I don't want to lose you Iranti because you are all I have. I know I never tell you that I am proud of you, but I am, I talk about you all the time at work. You fight in your own way. I fight to kill but you fight to win and you are wiser than your grandmother.

"You know, my mother, I don't know much about her because she died when I was being born, but the kind people who took me in when my father rejected me, they told me that she was the most beautiful woman in our village and that was why my father married her, because his father was the richest man in the village.

"Her name was Wura. It means Gold. My name means Treasure. Oshun was named after a goddess. Gold gave birth to Treasure and Treasure turned around and gave birth to a Goddess?" she grunted and shook her head. "It's all a joke! The gods are playing a joke on our line, they are laughing wherever it is they live. She was cursed too, that is my mother, Wura; her beauty was a curse. I look like her, which made my stepmother very angry.

"People continue to call me beautiful, I was cursed too, I gave birth to a beautiful child, Oshun and she was cursed too. The women in our family from generation to generation continue to look like one another and it is a curse. I know women who have used their beauty to marry Kings. Our beauty continues to kill us in this family." She shook her head in sorrow.

"I don't know much Iranti, I sit here and listen to the radio and I hear a lot, the world is full of wonders and I realize that I don't know a thing. You are growing up, you read all those books at the back of the house and I know they teach you a lot and I am happy.

"There are some women born into the kind of world that you and I were born into, and they are told they are toys for men. They accept and they become prostitutes. You and I know a lot of them in this neighborhood. Your mother accepted that she was a toy for men and it killed her. I refused to be a toy for men and I killed.

"You in your own way, you are refusing to be a toy for men too. I am glad you stood up to that useless man that smallpox is going to wipe him and his family off the face of the earth. You didn't bow to him at all. He is not a descendant of Noah. You and I are in this together and I will continue to try my best to take care of you."

Ranti was shocked again to see this side of her grandmother. She thought, "It's all those romance novels I have been reading. That's why I lost my focus because they distracted me. Esho warned me, she told me that fantasizing about her dead mother, ghosts, fairies and trolls distracted her at the time the mad man who gave her Oshun raped her. She warned me, what was I thinking? I wanted to be like the other girls? Esho and I are not like the other girls, we are either toys for men or we are without any man to love us or protect us and we will continue to live in fear. The next time any man comes near me, I will not be distracted and I will give him 'Esho treatment.'

"It is such an irony. *'It is as if that thing you are most afraid of keeps pursuing you.'* She wondered if she read that in a book, she was not sure. "But it is true of our life. See how much Esho is afraid of men, yet she was repeatedly raped by men. Oshun died because of men. I have never had sex in my life and I was mutilated because of Esho's fears and striking back, since that is what she does when she is afraid. I don't talk to men, not even boys and I was accused of committing an abortion. I still avoided men and a man with power raped me, not with his penis, but with his tongue, fists and booted feet. That which we are afraid of continues to pursue us and scare us. Esho is always afraid and so am I.

"I am going to the university so that I will be able to take care of myself and no man will ever threaten me again. I will not get married nor have children if this is the kind of life they would be born into. The curse ends here, with me."

Ranti remained at home for two months as she healed. The school board protested to the federal government requesting that the governor be removed from his position and punished. Moradeke's father who was an economic adviser to the president put a lot of pressure on the military government, and ten weeks after the incident, the governor was removed from his position as the governor of the state, but he was promoted to the rank of major general and given another position in Lagos.

The principal who had been planning to retire in two years decided to take an early retirement. She continued to apologize to Ranti that she exposed her to danger by insisting she went to the governor when she did not want to go. She was full of remorse which Moradeke interpreted to mean she was sorrier to have been having an affair with the 'asshole governor.'

Ranti returned to school six weeks before the year ended. After the fifth year students took their final examinations, and graduated from the school, she was elected the head of the student body, while, Moradeke became her deputy, for the following school year.

She continued to work very hard especially that the final year was very decisive for her with regards to passing her examinations and getting into the university. She took her responsibility as the head-girl of the school very seriously and did her job as responsibly as she had always done.

She, Moradeke and two other girls were also the debating team, and on most Saturdays, they went to several debating competitions to represent the school.

It was a very good year for Ranti because she, Moradeke and Gboye sat for the admission examination to the university, and were accepted into the preliminary program for medicine.

23

Ranti wrote until four Saturday morning. She woke up at noon feeling very refreshed. She stayed in bed for another hour thinking of the part of her life she wrote the previous day. "So many rooms in my mind without air, so much unresolved grief; no wonder I was feeling so depressed."

When she came out of the bedroom Mrs. Sanchez was in the living room watching television. Ranti knew she took the job of taking care of her very seriously and she felt guilty for making her worry. She resolved to speak with her about giving her some privacy. If she wanted to sleep until the evening, she should be allowed to do so without her standing vigil by her door.

"I have to get some lock on that door. What if I had a man over?" She smiled at the thoughts. She had not had a man over anywhere in twelve years.

Mrs. Sanchez fussed over her in her usual manner as Ranti nodded and sat down to eat the late breakfast. Later in the afternoon she went to the beach. She swam in the cool water not venturing too far away. When she came out of the water and was going to get her towel, her neighbor, Abe, came towards her holding the towel in his hand. He smiled as he offered it to her.

Ranti took it from him, and initially wanted to scowl at him for taking her towel, but she smiled as she wiped her face. He looked her up and down. She was wearing a lime green bikini, and her pregnant abdomen protruded massively in

132   *Feasts of Phantoms*

front of her. His eyes traveled down her body and they rested on the big scar on her left thigh for a moment.

Her heart skipped a beat.

"I saw you and came to say hi. I said to myself, I better keep an eye on her. We don't want her swimming too far into the ocean. You look great, pregnancy becomes you." He smiled again.

"Thanks," Ranti answered.

"I'm having a barbecue tonight and was wondering if you would like to join me."

"Oh, I'm sorry, I can't, not tonight. My friend is coming in from New York and I'm not sure when he's getting here."

He looked disappointed.

"Please ask me again." She quickly added, afraid he would not invite her again.

"You bet I will. How long are you staying on the Island?"

"Another six or seven weeks, I still have about fifteen weeks to go with the pregnancy but my doctor wants me back in New York by the time I'm thirty weeks pregnant. I belong to the high risk category."

"Good, we still have time. I'll be here for the next five or six weeks as well. Then I'm off to God knows where, so I will ask you again."

Depo arrived at about eight that evening without Grant who was too busy at work to take the weekend off. Ranti was happy to see him especially for the distraction from her reminiscence. She wanted to talk to someone familiar.

He was glad to see her without the intravenous line she had for weeks and that she had more fullness to her, having gained some weight. He kissed her and held on to her for a long time. He bent down to caress and kiss her abdomen.

"Your daddy is here, kids, say hi to him. Kick his hand so he can feel you." Ranti said to the babies.

"What the hell is going on Ranti?" he demanded.

"First of all, I want to know how the Sanchezes were able to communicate so well with you."

"Mr. Sanchez' cousin is one of our secretaries. She translates."

"That explains a lot. Depo," she started with a lot of excitement, "I have never felt this good in my life. It's great. This is what happened. I tried to write the proposal like Grant has been urging me to do and for almost three days, nothing. I could not write a thing! I started to panic. I thought I was becoming brain dead. Then it dawned on me that I was blocked because of the way I was feeling, trying to keep a lot of pain away, so I couldn't write the proposal and that is why I had been so sick, and the smell, the vagina pain and all the rest of it.

"You know this is a thing I've read in a lot of books. You know, something terrible happens to a person, something very painful, they don't want to think about it and they block it. But then, that's not the only thing that gets blocked, the whole of their personality becomes blocked, it's like they are in a prison, on lockdown.

"And it affects every aspect of their life, just because they are trying not to go to just one place in their mind, everywhere is on lockdown as well; even the places they would like to go. You know what I'm talking about. And yet they continue to feel the pain they are trying to avoid anyway, that kind of thing.

"So I decided I would write about myself as Dr O. has been suggesting to me for the longest time, and maybe that will help unfreeze me, and my brain would work again. I tell you, I started Depo, and I couldn't stop. It was as if my hands developed a will of their own independent of my brain. And I just kept writing and writing and writing, I mean typing. But then I couldn't sleep because I started to think about what I had written, and then the floodgate just opened, and then I started to cry about my brother and my mother and Esho. But the next morning I went to swim in the ocean,"

"But you don't swim," he interrupted her.

"Ah! I used to love to swim Depo. I used to love it a lot, but then my brother died, and I still swam after that, and then the genital mutilation happened and I stopped. But then I swam and I felt so free Depo, it was such an unbelievable feeling. I felt like a bird soaring and soaring and soaring. Have you ever seen an eagle soar? It is so majestic, that is how I felt. Then I slept and woke up and ate a full meal in how long and then I realized that the smell was gone. Gone! That is what happened to me Depo, I'm not going crazy."

"Wow, I didn't know you could swim, and I thought I knew you so well, and I've never heard about this brother. I'm sorry Ranti. I wish you had told me about him. You do keep a lot of secrets and it's not good for you or our relationship. It will be difficult to show you I love you if you keep a huge part of yourself locked away from me. How can I be there for you when you do that? This is a big one; that you had a brother that I never heard about. What happened to him?"

"You think it will be difficult for you to love me if I keep a big part of me from you? What about me loving myself? That is the madness Depo, what I have been doing to myself. I understand it's just crazy all around, I can't love myself and good people can't love me. I was killing myself." She paused.

"You know what? You are the father of my children and you are my best friend. I won't keep anything from you ever again. We are going to raise these children with full knowledge of whom we are. You are probably the only person who will read it, so," she got up and retrieved her laptop. She turned it on to her story and handed it over to him. "Knock yourself out. It's all there so far. You know most of the rest."

They had dinner and Depo started to read her story while she cuddled in front of the television. At about eleven o'clock after he had been reading for an hour she went to bed.

She woke up in the middle of the night to use the bathroom and Depo was in bed with her. In the morning when she awoke, he was staring at her. "Oh spooky," she told him.

He grabbed her and hugged her and there were tears in his eyes. "Oh Ranti, I'm so sorry. I had no idea you went through so much. You kept so much from me. I now understand a lot of your fears, especially about the smell and feeling that you are not welcomed in certain places and that doors would be shut in your face.

"But you know what, like your principal said when that girl Shara accused you of stealing food? 'Each woman shall be judged by her accomplishments and not the accomplishments of her parents.' Sweetheart, you have overcome a lot. Those are your accomplishments and they define you. That must have been what I saw in you the first time I saw you at the university and do you remember my first words to you?"

"I want you to be the mother of my children." Ranti quoted him.

"Yeah I want my children to have the fighting spirit I could sense in you, even though I didn't know it as such, or maybe it was me who needed that fighting spirit. You remember I was living a life of so many lies at the time too. I was doing what was expected of me. I'm sure that's what I saw in you and I fell in love with you. You fight to win like Esho said of you.

"I never told you this, but you encouraged me to come out with my sexual orientation. I remember when you came back from England after the surgery and I came to the airport to get you. The woman who stepped off that plane was a beautiful confident woman who just glowed and you bounced when you walked. I remember thinking, 'she has reclaimed herself'. And I wanted to reclaim myself too. You encouraged me to be honest with myself and I started to tell myself I could do it. I could drop out of medical school and pursue my dream career and I could be honest with myself about being gay.

"That very night, I sent my application to the architectural school in France and the next weekend I told my mother. Your love at the time and your fighting to be educated inspired me, Ranti. This is who you are, a woman who has accomplished so much, a fine surgeon and a finer human being. And I'm positive the rest will fall into place for you, because you are a fighter and that is all you need in this world; that's what I've come to learn.

"Ranti, you are not the only one who had to fight for life or for happiness. It's a battle that I continue to fight everyday, you know, you have some idea of what it could mean to be gay in this world. You used to worry about me and for good reasons too. That's what life is Ranti. It's an illusion that it's easy for anyone, anyone who would be honest will tell you that life is not easy to live, you have to fight for it everyday. It's like you have to win your freedom every blessed day. Didn't you quote that to me a while ago? Didn't you tell me, *"He who wins his freedom must conquer it anew each day?"*

"It doesn't matter what you are given or not given, what matters is how much of a fight you are willing to put up for what you desire and for your right to exist in joy as much as it is possible, and that is Freedom. And you are a General in the army of fighting for what she wants. That's why I am the luckiest man alive that you are my best friend and the mother of my children.

"The only battle left General," he gave her a mock salute, "is not that you should find a man who will make love to you in a way that will make you feel like silk, that's not it at all. There are lots of men out there who would do that. The only battle left is for you to see yourself as you truly are. Once that is accomplished, the war is won.

"You are always quoting all those great books you read to me. I have some quotations for you too. *Identity depends on achievement* and *Identity is the grandeur of man.* That is you are what you fought to achieve for yourself and not what you were given. It is something that I tell myself often. And you have achieved a lot."

Ranti moved into his arms. "I'm getting there, Depo, writing these things down and having the dialogue with myself, I'm getting there. I'm practicing at it. I can silence Esho's voices of fear that are inside my head more and more now, as well as her admonishments that were unfounded.

"She forbade me to ever speak of my brother and for thirty-three years I obeyed her and it has cost me too much. It has caused more deaths, because children continue to die, my unborn child died twelve years ago and I was risking losing my unborn children now, but I'm silencing her voices in my head more and more. I'm practicing it and it is getting easier."

"What became of that girl Shara?" Depo wanted to know.

"I don't know. When we graduated from secondary school, I remember she went for her Advanced level in England. Moradeke will know. Her mother and Shara's mother are friends. Interestingly she's never spoken about her. I'll ask her next time I see her."

They spent the Sunday swimming in the ocean and Depo took her to the only restaurant in town for an early dinner. Early on Monday morning, he returned to New York City.

24

The first words Depo did say to Ranti that September of 1981 was "I want you to be the mother of my children." Ranti had thought, "And you are lucky Esho is not around to hear you."

She speechlessly stared at him because she was stunned. She had read in hundreds of those romance novels about love at first sight and there and then looking at Depo, she believed it was possible. Her heart started to race. Her hands shook so she held on tighter to her folder.

"I can see those boys are bothering you, stick with me and I'll take care of the situation." And he had done so.

It was her first week at the university. Ranti had been in line for four hours to receive the matriculation number that would identify her as a student, but many people had been coming, and on seeing their friends or acquaintances in line would pretend they were saying hello, only to cut in line. She was frustrated and had yelled at a few of them for cheating her in this way. The line jumpers had laughed, or snickered and the boys had thrown some sexist comments at her. Three boys tried to cut in line right in front of her. They were not friends with the person ahead of her but just pushed their way in.

"You can't do that," she said to them. "I've been in line for the past four hours, this is not fair. I have things to do as well; you should learn to wait your turn."

"Why are you in such a hurry? You should learn some patience. Or do you have a hot date?" One of the boys said to her.

"Yes, she has the hot date with me," another one said.

"I saw her first and suggested we come to her, I wanted to ask her out," said the third boy as he snatched her purse from her.

"Hey, give me back my purse this minute. What do you think you are doing?" Ranti yelled.

"Come on, lighten up, just trying to be friendly, if you want your purse, you have to agree to go out with me, otherwise I'm not giving it back to you."

Ranti stared at them and wondered what she was up against. She had heard of girls being harassed in this way by boys who just take liberty with them. "Do I have to fight all the time here too? I just want to study to become a doctor, why won't people leave me alone?"

"Give me my purse now otherwise you will be sorry," she warned the boy.

"Give me my purse now otherwise you will be sorry," he mimicked her.

He started to walk away with her purse and Ranti panicked because all the money she had for food for the month, as well as for her books for the year was in the purse. The diocese had continued to give her scholarship and she barely had enough for food, accommodations and books. If this boy stole her money she would be in serious trouble as she would not be able to buy her books and go hungry for the month. She ran after him demanding her purse.

The boy's friends started to laugh at her and that was when she saw Depo following her and the boy making away with her purse. He charged at him in a threatening manner and demanded the purse from him. "You are stealing from her. You are a thief." Depo was much taller than the boy and he quickly gave him the purse.

Depo handed the purse to her as he said, "I want you to be the mother of my children," with a smile of recognition as if he just ran into a dear friend he had not seen in a long time.

Ranti stared at him and wondered what Esho would have said about everything. The purse-snatcher threatened her that if she did not go out with him, he would not give her back her purse and money, and this handsome rescuer actually wanted to ruin her life.

"Thank you," she said to Depo as she returned to her place in line. The three boys did not come back. Depo stood next to her on the line and promised to prevent other people from harassing her. He continued to give her that smile of recognition.

Ranti did not know what to think, but she liked him a lot. There was something very comforting about him and he was very tall and handsome. He reminded her of the men in the romance novels; the only difference was those men were Caucasians. She stopped reading the novels after the governor assaulted her and she had stopped daydreaming about a romantic life for herself. She stole a sideways glance at him. She could not believe he had come to talk to her, though he too wanted to ruin her life by asking her to be the mother of his children.

"Maybe he wants to marry me?" She wondered. "He had said, 'mother of my children,' but he didn't say I want you to be my wife and the mother of my children. That is the kind of thing a man who is already married might say to a woman he wants to have children by. Maybe his wife could not have children like the men that came to Oshun's shrine after Esho first had Oshun. That means he still sees me as a toy. He should go to hell and stay there. But he's too young to be married. He's probably only a little older than me." She argued with herself.

He caught her looking at him and he smiled again. He looked like he was very happy to see her.

"I like him," she said to herself. "I can't believe such a handsome man would talk to me. I just have to be very careful around him," she advised herself.

After she got her matriculation number, she thanked him for staying in line with her and told him she was returning to her hostel.

"I'll walk with you to keep predators away," he smiled. "My name is Depo Jacobs."

"Ranti Jare."

"Nice to meet you Ranti, that's a pretty name. I'm in first year of medical school and I see you are new to the university."

Ranti nodded. "I'm in the preliminary year. I'm in for medicine as well."

"So you want to be a doctor? I don't want to be a doctor. But my father will only pay my tuition if I study medicine. I want to be an architect and design buildings. It's the most exciting profession in the world, so I'm studying medicine for now, to please my father. After that I'll go to France to study architecture."

Ranti was very happy that he was talking to her.

"I've always wanted to be a doctor as far back as I can remember. I want to be a gynecologist and take care of women."

"You are lucky." Depo told her as he flashed her that smile again. He offered to hold her folder for her and she gave it to him.

When they arrived at the hostel, he asked her if he could visit her the next day and she nodded.

Ranti ran to the room she shared with Gboye and Moradeke. She excitedly told them about her meeting with Depo at the same time describing him.

Moradeke was equally excited for her and she started to tease her, "Hi Mrs. Depo, or Mrs. Jacobs, no, Dr. Mrs. Jacobs."

"Is he Efunwunmi Jacobs' son?" Gboye wanted to know.

"I don't know. Who is Efunwunmi Jacobs?" Ranti asked.

"I'm sure he's her son. You don't know Efunwunmi Jacobs?" Moradeke was surprised.

"She's an anchor on national television, the most beautiful woman in this country, though she is getting old. Her husband is richer than sin. She has just one child. Good for you, Ranti, you picked a good one," Gboye told her.

"We don't have a television set," Ranti volunteered.

'As rich as sin,' that's the saying; 'As rich as sin.' Moradeke corrected Gboye. "She is still very beautiful. I saw her on television on Sunday before I came to school. I heard that her husband married another woman, so she left him. I wouldn't put up with that nonsense either. Can you imagine that, to be married to such a beautiful woman and leave her for another woman? I can't stand polygamy and that's what men do when they become rich like Depo's father. They think they can oppress women with their wealth. My sister said he divorced her because she couldn't have more children, you know my sister Funmi, the journalist; so that's why he married another woman, to give him more children. He's such an asshole." Moradeke hissed in disgust.

"I would kill the man first. I would refuse to divorce him and I would still kill him," Gboye informed her friends.

"That's what my grandmother would do." Ranti joined in.

"Men are disgusting sometimes. I'm sure Depo is Efunwunmi Jacobs' son. Funmi said she's a really nice woman. I'll like to meet her, I just love her clothes," Moradeke concluded.

The next day, when Depo came at about five in the evening to visit Ranti as he promised, both Moradeke and Gboye were there to assess him. Ranti introduced her friends to him and he smiled at them as he said hello.

"So how is your mom? She is Efunwunmi Jacobs, right?" Gboye asked without preamble.

"She's fine," Depo nodded

"I love your mom. She's such a beautiful woman. She's so classy and so light skinned. Can you introduce me to her the next time she comes to visit you?" Moradeke could not control herself.

"Sure, no problem, I will." Depo looked at Ranti and gave her that smile again.

The four of them were quiet. After a while, Depo invited them to the student union building for drinks and *Suya,* "my treat," he offered.

And so Ranti and Depo became friends. He took his classes in another part of the campus from where she took her classes, but almost every evening he would walk to her hostel to visit her or take her out. They usually ended up in the student union building where a lot of the students hung out.

They talked about their families with Ranti telling Depo that it was just her and her grandmother, but, "I can't introduce you to her, not until I'm a doctor, she would kill me if she found out that I'm even speaking to a boy. I'm supposed to be concentrating on my studies and not hanging out with boys."

"Why?"

"She's afraid boys will ruin my life, by getting me pregnant."

"Maybe some boys, but I won't ruin your life. I want you to have a good life. I want you to become a doctor because I know it's very important to you. I don't want to have children yet either. I'm too young and after I finish here in medical school, I still have like four or five years ahead of me to study architecture. So it's going to be a while.

"I'll like you to meet my mom though, you will like her a lot, she is very nice and she will like you too. You remind me of her. The first time I saw you, it was like I was looking at a younger version of her. She's very beautiful too, like you. The next time she comes to visit me, I'll introduce you."

Ranti smiled. "Okay, I'd like to meet your mother, I like meeting mothers, like Moradeke and Gboye's mothers. They are very nice women. Is it true your father left her? Moradeke said he did."

Depo nodded. "The whole country knows, thanks to the tabloid since my mother is an anchor for NTA. He said she couldn't have more children, so he married a woman who is just a little bit older than me. What can I say?" he shrugged.

"I'm sorry. It must have been very painful for your mother."

"Yes, she was very hurt, especially the way she heard about it. She along with the rest of the country read about it in the newspaper. But she's doing fine now. She's a very strong woman."

A week later, Depo was standing by a big car outside of Ranti's physics class when her lecture ended. His mother was sitting in the car. Efunwunmi Jacobs came out of the car and Ranti stared at the most beautiful woman she had ever seen. She smiled as she stood in front of her, but the older woman took her in her arms as she gave her a big hug, similar to Gboye's mother's hugs, just that she was a much slimmer woman.

"She smells so sweet." Ranti smiled.

Efunwunmi caressed her face. "Depo told me you are a very beautiful girl. He said you remind him of me and looking at you I must say that is a huge compliment. I'm pleased to meet you." She gave her that smile of Depo's she had come to love so much. A smile that seemed to say, 'It is so good to see you again.'

"We're going to lunch at Premier Hotel, will you come with us?" Efunwunmi invited Ranti, but she declined shaking her head.

"Mom, don't listen to her, she is coming with us. She is shy." Depo insisted.

At that moment, Moradeke and Gboye came out of the class and came to join them. Moradeke was beside herself with excitement.

"It's so good to meet you, Ma. I can't believe I'm talking to Efunwunmi Jacobs. I'm a big fan of yours. I love your clothes and the way you read the news. I'm friends with Depo and Ranti, my name is Moradeke Ayodele." She offered her hand and Efunwunmi took her hand and shook it formally.

"I know your father. He's the economic adviser to the President, right?" She asked Moradeke who smiled and eagerly nodded her head.

"My name is Gboye, and I'm friends with Ranti and Depo too." Gboye said to Efunwunmi as she offered her hand.

"Well then let's go and eat," Efunwunmi announced.

25

Ranti's problem with the cramps continued and kept her in pain two weeks out of a month, and she missed lots of classes because she just could not get out of bed. Her friends suggested she go to the university health center, but she refused. She did not want a doctor examining her and finding the damage done to her genitals because the doctor might tell everyone and she would be an outcast again. She was grateful the university was big with lots of students unlike St. Ann's School.

After she had been at the university for six months, Depo finally demanded an explanation from her. The cramps seemed to be getting worse each month and she was missing more days of classes.

Ranti told him about the genital mutilation and that she was convinced it was responsible for her cramps, since her menstrual blood did not flow as the other girls' did. He became horrified as she described the circumcision to him so she stopped and did not tell him she leaked urine. She was grateful he had not tried to make out with her like a lot of her friends' boyfriends did.

Gboye had asked her if she and Depo made out and when she told her they did not, she pronounced that something was wrong with him.

Ranti had taken offense. "Just because he respects me and doesn't want to ruin my life doesn't mean something is wrong with him. I like it that way. If he were to make out with me and he smelled me, don't you think it would be the end of the relationship?"

"No, it wouldn't if he really cared about you. And I have been telling you for years, get it into that thick head of yours, you do not smell. No one can smell you. You are a beautiful girl, Ranti. Lots of boys want to go out with you. Some of them have asked me if you and Depo are really serious or if you are just casual friends. So what are you? Are you really serious or casual friends? I need to know."

Ranti had ignored her.

The following month, Depo insisted that she sees a doctor because she had not been able to get out of bed for a week. "You are never going to become a doctor if you are sick half of the year. Look, Ranti, I'll take you to my mother's doctor in Lagos. That's far away from here and he is really good. I'll call my mother and she will send her driver."

"No Depo, don't call your mother, please don't. I can't go to Lagos. I've never been out of Ibadan and my grandmother will kill me. I'm going to be fine and I will catch up on what I have missed."

"No Ranti, you are not going to be fine. Even if you passed the examinations, they won't promote you to the first year. You are in university now and attendance

142   *Feasts of Phantoms*

is a big part of your grades. The lecturers will assume you are not serious and just blowing off classes. Your grandmother doesn't have to know. She comes to visit you on Sundays. Today is Tuesday. We will be back long before then. Please," he appealed to her.

Moradeke and Gboye joined him in appealing to her.

Ranti wanted relief from the pain. It was getting worse each month and she was getting too thin from not eating. She was afraid she might have to drop out of medical school if she became really sick, so she agreed to go to Depo's mother's doctor in Lagos.

Even though she trusted Depo, he was still a man and she remembered going with the governor's driver without asking Moradeke to come with her, so this time she asked Moradeke and Gboye to come with her.

Efunwunmi took them to her gynecologist at his clinic on Victoria Island. Ranti asked her to stay in the room with her as the doctor examined her. Even though she was embarrassed to have to tell the doctor her history in front of the beautiful and poised Efunwunmi, she feared being alone with the doctor more.

The doctor listened attentively without interrupting her. His face did not show any expression. Efunwunmi started to cry after she described the mutilation.

The doctor examined her and it was very painful for her even though he tried to be gentle. After, he sat down next to the examining table. He took a piece of paper on which he started to draw the female reproductive organ. "Let me explain to you what's going on here, Ranti," he started. "When you were circumcised and the woman's hand slipped, the knife cut into your bladder," he showed her the relationship of the bladder to the vagina in his drawing.

"And that's why you have been leaking urine. Luckily, surgery can correct it, though in future when you are ready to have babies, they have to be delivered by caesarian section, because having a baby through the vagina could damage your bladder and urethra again." He paused and looked at her.

Ranti nodded.

"The reason you continue to have the cramps is that your menstrual blood is backed up. You are right that your blood doesn't flow as it should, and it's because the scar on your labia goes deeper into the vagina vault, and it is blocking the flow of the blood, so all these years since your periods started, most of it has been backing up; some has been reabsorbed by the body, but not fast enough and that is why the cramps are getting worse each month.

"You are going to need surgery to clean out your womb and remove the keloid. It's going to be an extensive surgery. And it will take you about six weeks to recover, especially for the fistula to heal, because you are going to have a catheter draining your bladder for that long."

He looked at her and Ranti nodded again.

"How soon can she have the surgery?" Efunwunmi asked the doctor.

"Efunwunmi, for her to get the best care possible, I would suggest England, especially for the fistula repair. She is such a beautiful girl. She should have the best care available. I know an expert."

"England? I can't go to England, we can't afford it." Ranti started to cry. "I'm doomed, I'll never become a doctor because these cramps won't leave me alone and I can't afford to have the surgery."

"Okay, I'll arrange everything. Will you give us a referral?" She heard Efunwunmi say to the doctor. "Don't worry Ranti. I'll take care of you. You mean the world to my son and any friend of my son is my child. It's not your fault that this happened to you, it's because your grandmother is an illiterate and didn't know any better. Don't worry about money. I'll take care of everything. I know how important becoming a doctor is to you and you will become a doctor. We won't let this stop you."

Ranti continued to cry. She could not speak but she kept shaking her head trying to tell Depo's mother that she did not have to pay for the surgery. She felt overwhelmed and her heart started to race. She would have to drop out of medical school and return home to Esho, and even then she would be too sick to work with Esho carrying cement. Her future would be bleak. She might eventually die from the menstrual blood backing up. She would die like Oshun and Lana and that would just kill Esho. But if she had the surgery, she would be able to pursue her education and go on to a bright future, and Depo's mother was willing to pay for everything; she had told her not to worry about anything.

She resolved that she would pay Efunwunmi back every cent and more, and for the rest of her life she would be grateful for these angels that had been sent into her life in the forms of Depo and his mother.

Later in the day, Ranti went home to Esho. Esho looked scared when she saw her, because it was unusual for her to come home during the week, but Ranti quickly reassured her that she was fine. She and her friends had formulated the story she would tell her grandmother so she could go to England for eight weeks.

"Esho, I have to go to Abeokuta for two months. It's part of the training to become a doctor. From time to time they send us to places like Oyo, Ogbomoso and Igbo-Ora for rotations. They will take us there on a bus and bring us back, but if we decide to come home before the end of the rotation, we would be responsible for our transportation. I don't think I will come home at all, because it would be too much money, but I will write to you, and Moradeke or Gboye who are not going yet will bring the letters to you and read them to you."

Esho stared at Ranti for a long time. "Why are they not going? Aren't they in your class?"

"They divide us into groups, even though we are in the same class. I'm not in their groups. They use our last names to put us in the groups, so the three of us are in different groups. They will be going later."

Esho was quiet. Ranti realized that the most she had been separated from Esho was one week, as her grandmother had always come to visit her in school every week, and had continued to do so since she started at the university. She wondered how the two of them would survive the separation. It dawned on her that Esho with her non-demonstration of affection loved her in her own way, because her friends' parents did not visit them that often, and tears sprang from her eyes.

Esho continued to look at her. "Iranti, I know the time will come that you will go away on your own, I just didn't know it would be so soon. Write to me, I will be very happy to receive letters from you. I have never received a letter from anyone in my life."

Ranti was tempted to tell her the truth, but was afraid Esho would go crazy. "Esho, I'll never leave you. Wherever I go after I become a doctor, we will go together. You are my only family, Esho, and we belong together."

"There is no reason to cry, Iranti. It will all be well," her grandmother reassured her, still standing across from her.

Ranti wanted to hug her, the way her friends' mothers hugged her, but Esho did not touch.

She spent the night with her grandmother and in the morning when she was leaving, Esho surprised her by hugging her. "I will miss you Iranti, but I will be very happy to receive those letters from you and if your friends bring them to me, I will reply, they can help me write back to you. I can't come to Abeokuta to visit you, because it would be too expensive. I hope you understand."

"I understand Esho and you are my world." Ranti tearfully seized the opportunity to hug her grandmother again.

Three days later Efunwunmi and Ranti left for England. Depo wanted to go with them but his mother insisted he stayed in school. "There is no point for both of you to miss classes. Ranti will be fine. I'll stay with her until after the surgery and your aunt will take care of her till she is ready to return to school," she assured her son.

Ranti had continued to cry. She was overwhelmed by Efunwunmi's kindness and generosity, as well as by the fact that she had lied to Esho. She felt so guilty that her heart started to race. She had lied to Esho only one other time in her life, in secondary school when she wanted to grow her hair.

She wondered what it would be like for Esho if she never returned. What if she died on the operating table, or in a plane crash? What would her friends tell Esho? She panicked so much that she had to go to the bathroom to throw up. The thoughts of never seeing Esho again frightened her so much that she almost changed her mind about the surgery. She wanted to ask Efunwunmi to tell the pilot to turn the plane around, that she had made a mistake.

Efunwunmi assuming her tears were because of the cramps comforted her by repeatedly telling her the suffering would be behind her soon.

In London they spent the first night with Efunwunmi's sister, and very early the next day the two women took her to the hospital where she was admitted in preparation for the surgery. Everyone was very kind to her as they reassured her that she would be fine.

The surgeon visited her and brought with him a plastic model of the female genitalia. "I was told I'll be treating a very beautiful and brilliant medical student from Nigeria." He smiled at her and most of Ranti's fears abated on seeing his reassuring face.

She nodded.

He took her right hand in his, "Mr. Edwards at your service Ma'am. I'm a Uro-gynecologist and genital mutilation is my area of specialty. What are your plans for after medical school?"

"I plan to specialize in gynecology and help other women with similar problems."

"Okay then, we had better start your education now. With this model I'm going to explain to you what happened and how we intend to correct it. Feel free to ask me any questions. You and I are going to be in this together for the next six weeks, we are partners." He smiled at her again.

Ranti had the surgery three days later and two days after that Efunwunmi returned to Nigeria because of her job.

Ranti stayed in the hospital for six weeks as she recuperated from the fistula repair and the evacuation of the menoschesis in her uterus. She had been writing letters to her grandmother addressed to Moradeke and Gboye on a weekly basis and had been receiving replies from Esho who thought she was in Abeokuta.

Her grandmother wrote that she missed her very much and it had been hard separating from her, but she knew that good things did not come easily. A person has got to make a lot of sacrifices, and not seeing her for eight weeks was too small a sacrifice for what they would achieve in the end. She had continued to give her the usual lectures about not losing focus, concentrating on her studies and staying away from men.

Each time she received Esho's letter, she would cry.

Depo wrote to her often, telling her how much he missed her and he would have loved to visit her but his mother forbade it, and he still would have come but he did not have enough money for the plane ticket.

Moradeke and Gboye wrote as well, bringing her up to date about the happenings on the campus and that they were keeping good notes in class, so it would not be too hard for her to catch up when she returned.

Three days before she was discharged from the hospital, when Mr. Edwards removed the catheter which had been draining her bladder for the previous six weeks to keep it dry and allow the fistula to heal, Ranti held her breath as she hoped she was dry, but at the same time was afraid the hole might still be there.

It took a while for her bladder to get used to holding volumes of urine again. But by the second day, when she had trained herself not to run to the bathroom every five minutes, she was dry.

She could not believe the miracle given to her by these people her grandmother would have called "Descendants of Noah." She shed tears of joy as she continued to go to the bathroom to check her dry underwear that was without a pad all day long.

"Esho, there are good people in this world, there are kind people. Efunwunmi and Depo are kind and so is Mr. Edwards. The world is not full of the likes of your father or the mad man that gave you Oshun, or Akanbi, or Jamba. There are lots of wonderful people in the world," she cried, talking to her grandmother in her mind.

Ranti was discharged to the care of Efunwunmi's sister, who took her home and fussed over her for the two weeks that she remained in England, for two follow-up appointments before she returned to Nigeria.

She was very appreciative of the opportunity she had been given. It was like a new lease on life, a life free of cramps and of leaking urine, or of the keloid in her vagina. She felt free, as if a heavy load had been lifted off her shoulders. She wanted to sing and run through the streets of London in jubilation, telling everyone she met her story. She felt that she looked different and she could feel herself laughing and smiling more.

She was convinced that she had been chosen for something special and even though she did not believe in God because of her grandmother's teachings, she promised whoever or whatever it was that arranged and organized these things that she would be worthy of this opportunity for a healthy life.

She was able to appreciate the difference between the likes of Esho's father, the mad man that gave Oshun to Esho before she was ready, Akanbi, and Jamba on the one hand, and the likes of the Anglican diocese, the chairman of the board of directors of St. Ann's school, Efunwunmi, Depo, Gboye, Moradeke and Mr. Edwards on the other hand. "Esho would agree. The latter group is made of descendants of Noah in the Christian Bible," she said aloud to herself.

She felt lucky that she did not step on a broken bottle and die like her brother, or that she did not become disobedient and not listen to Esho like Oshun had. She had a chance of going to school as well as the opportunity to read all those books at the big bookshop and from Akanbi's irresponsibility, and they had taught her a lot. They had taught her what Esho could not teach her.

"I am a very lucky girl, a very lucky girl. I am the luckiest girl alive." She repeated to herself throughout the flight home.

Her friends were at the airport to meet her. There were tearful reunions, and

Depo especially could not stop his tears as he hugged her repeatedly.

"You are stunning," he said to her. "Your eyes are sparkling and you have put on some needed weight. You look free, like someone who had been enslaved and who just won her freedom."

"I eat every day. I don't have to be afraid to eat anymore. No more cramps. I can't remember a time without the cramps," she beamingly told him.

Ranti returned to Ibadan and went to see her grandmother immediately. Esho wept as she hugged her granddaughter to her. "Iranti, this is your face. I am so happy to see your face. I have missed you so much. I didn't think I would survive this but I did. Iranti, this is your face." She held on to Ranti and repeatedly caressed her face.

Ranti started to cry from the relief of seeing her grandmother. She was happy she had survived the surgery and came back home. She wanted to tell Esho the truth, but she was afraid she might go crazy and would not hug or touch her anymore.

Acquaintances and friends started to tell her she was blooming more. They told her that before she went away, she was very beautiful and she returned a much more beautiful girl, she had outdone herself. More boys in her class continued to ask her out on dates.

She spent the rest of the year catching up on her schoolwork, and two months after she returned from England she sat for her examinations. She passed very well but unlike her usual record, she came twentieth out of the two hundred and ten students in her class, but she was not upset because she got something bigger.

26

Over the vacation period following the end of her first year in medical school, Ranti returned home to Esho. She insisted, in spite of Esho's refusal again, on going with her to the construction site to work, and so double the amount of money they would earn for those two months.

They had saved money over the years and along with the spending money from the scholarship, most of which Ranti saved, they had enough so Esho could start to sell cooked food at the building sites for the workers instead of carrying cement. Ranti felt that Esho was getting too old at the age of forty-six for the job of carrying heavy cement on her head.

She explained her plans to Esho who agreed with her and in the second month of her vacation, Esho started to cook food to sell to the workers, while Ranti continued to carry cement. When she returned to school in September of 1982, Esho did not have to carry cement anymore.

Ranti concentrated on her studies as usual, as well as continuing her relationship with Depo. She saw him only once over the break, because he, like her two friends, went to England for vacation, but when he returned she went to the campus to spend the day with him.

She had started to think a lot about sex. Gboye was already sexually active and had told her friends it was the most wonderful feeling in the world. Moradeke had not become sexually active, but she had been making out with the boys she dated.

In Ranti's experience, sex was a destroyer of life. It had killed her mother and turned Esho into a very bitter woman who was ready to kill any man, who made advances to her, and she had destroyed her genitals because of sex, and also Jamba had almost killed her because of sex.

But Mr. Edwards had told her after the surgery that she could begin to have sex without worrying about harm to her. He had actually encouraged it in that it would keep her vagina open and prevent the backing up of her menstrual flow. He gave her some of the dilators he used to dilate her vagina shortly after the surgery and encouraged her to do it frequently.

He had noticed her discomfort while he was having this conversation with her and had returned later to talk to her when a nurse was not present. He explained to her that it was perfectly normal to have sex or even masturbate, and she should not allow the trauma of the mutilation to rob her more than it should. He also recommended she use tampons instead of sanitary towels for the same reason.

Ranti had continued to use sanitary towels. She was reluctant to stick anything up her vagina and in some ways the tampons reminded her of the worms that came out of her when she was a little girl.

She had hoped that Depo would make sexual advances to her and she had told herself she would accept. They would just have to use condoms so she would not get pregnant. She loved him so much and he had a wonderful mother. But Depo did not make any sexual advances to her, not even to make out. She started to worry that her vagina would close again.

She thought of using the dilators, but could not, each time she tried when she was alone, she imagined Esho giving her disapproving looks and she would start to hear her lectures in her head.

She confided in Moradeke because she did not like Gboye's attitude toward Depo, especially where sex was concerned. Gboye had continued to say there was something weird about Depo and that he should be having sex with Ranti after a year of dating. Once when Depo came to their room, Gboye was half naked and she did not make any effort to put on some clothes as she stared at Depo. She later reported to her friends that he was impotent, because he did not even have an erection on seeing her naked breasts.

Moradeke suggested she use the dilators to masturbate. Ranti shocked her by saying she had never masturbated in her life. "It's as if Esho would catch me and I'd be in serious trouble, Moradeke. I have thought about it a lot, but I just get so scared that I drive the thoughts out of my mind."

"Okay, Ranti, think of it as a medicine that you have to take to prevent your vagina from closing again. Just pass the dilators in and out about ten times a day. It's medication, not masturbation," Moradeke insisted.

"I can't. I can't put anything in there, Moradeke, not even tampons. I start to feel sick and the crawling sensations return as if there were worms coming out of my behind again. I've tried but I can't," Ranti lamented.

Moradeke thought for a while. "This is what we will do. There are lots of boys in our class who like you. I see them drool over you, why don't you pick one of them, the one you like the most, like that guy Bambo, he's always following you with his eyes, and he's good looking too and a gentleman and he can have sex with you."

"I can't, Moradeke, I love Depo. I don't want someone else to touch me. I'll feel cheap. I've really convinced myself that if it were Depo having sex with me, then he's not ruining my life; after all he and his mother just saved my life. I wouldn't feel that way about any other boy."

"Okay this is what we will do. You are going to tell Depo everything. You will then ask him to do it for you, to keep your vagina from closing again. If he refuses which I doubt that he would, then I'll do it for you. It might sound like lesbian sex but that vagina is not closing again, Ranti, because those years of menstrual cramps were hard on me too."

Two days later, Ranti found the courage to speak to Depo. They were alone in her room. She simply brought out the dilator and showed it to him. She explained what it was for and asked him to help her with it.

He took it from her and looked at it for a long time. "Is it clean?"

She nodded.

"Okay, what do I do? I don't want those cramps to come back."

Ranti explained to him what he had to do for her. She took off her dress and underwear and lay on her bed. Depo moved over to her and sitting between her spread-out legs inserted the dilator into her vagina; he kept checking if she was okay, and was he hurting her?

She reassured him that she was fine. He passed the dilator in and out about ten times and stopped. She felt very excited especially that Depo was touching her. She covered her face with her right arm to hide a smile. She told herself that it was only a question of seconds before he took off his pants and had sex with her, but he did not.

150 *Feasts of Phantoms*

He pulled the dilator out of her and though disappointed, she sat up and pulled her underwear back on. She looked at him and he averted his gaze.

"You have to help me every day Depo. Moradeke volunteered but it feels weird because she is a girl like me. You know what I mean."

"I do, Ranti. I'll help you as long as I'm around."

"What do you mean as long as you are around?" Ranti asked him.

"That's one thing I've wanted to talk to you about. I'm dropping out. I don't want to continue with medicine. This is not what I want to do with my life. I'm leaving at the end of the month; there is no point waiting till the end of the year. I'll be going to France. I've been accepted into an architectural school there. My father is very angry with me, but my mother is more understanding. She's disappointed I won't become a doctor, but she said my happiness is more important. It's going to be rough for me there, because my father is refusing to pay my tuition. My mother will help but she can't foot the whole bill so I'll have to get a part-time job."

Ranti panicked as Lana's dead body on Esho's back flashed into her mind. "You mean you are going to leave the university and go to France? I won't see you again?"

"Of course you will see me again. I love you, Ranti. I'll come home on vacations, though it might not be often since money is going to be tight, but I'll write to you all the time."

"Depo, please make love to me, have sex with me, please I'm begging you. Don't go away without giving me that one thing. I love you Depo, I want to be the mother of your children though I don't want to get pregnant now, we are not ready, and I want to marry you."

He looked at her for a while. Then he looked away. "I can't marry you Ranti, I'm sorry. I can't marry you."

"Why? Is it because I used to smell of urine and feces, because of the mutilation and because my grandmother is a very poor woman? Is that why Depo? I know it's too good to be true; I have always known I'm not good enough for you, I got carried away again." She started to cry.

"No, no Ranti, stop. Stop it. You know that's not true and that is crazy talk. If that were the case, then I'm the one who is not good enough for you. I love you, Ranti. Stop thinking that way. I'm so sorry. I'm going away anyway, what's the point of talking about sex and marriage and children when we might not even see one another for the next few years. You might meet someone else and soon forget about me."

"Forget about you? Depo, maybe you are the one who has met someone else and wants to forget about me. I can never forget you for as long as I live. You saved my life for goodness sake. I have loved you from the first day I saw you, when you rescued me from those boys. Depo it was love at first sight and I will always love you. If you have met someone else, I'll understand but I'll always love you."

"Ranti, I wish to God I could marry you. There is nothing that would give me more pleasure and because it is not so, I am suffering here. Look at you. You are a very beautiful girl, and I know a lot of guys envy me because you are my best friend and we are together all the time, but I can't. I know you want me to make love to you but I can't. It has got absolutely nothing to do with you, it's all me.

"Ranti, I need you on my side. I need you to promise me that though I'm breaking your heart here, and you might want to kill me for what I am about to say to you, that you will not share it with a soul. Not even Moradeke and Gboye. Please, Ranti, I need you, otherwise I'm totally alone and I'm scared as it is."

Ranti sobbed. She nodded at him through her tears and her heart started to race. She moved over to him and held him in her arms because she could see he was really scared.

"Depo, what is it, please tell me, you know you are safe with me. I worship you Depo. That is how much I love you. I'll never do anything to hurt you or betray you. You can count on me."

He held on to her too. "Ranti, I'm not like the other boys, I don't want to be with a girl, not just you, but I don't want to be with any girl at all. I'm attracted to men and I want to have sex with men. I'm sorry Ranti, but I love you very much, and I have prayed I could make love to you like I know you want, and I'm sorry I can't."

"Gboye got it!" Ranti said to herself. "Gboye has known for the past year."

Ranti had read some books where the protagonist was gay. Life is very hard for them. People are very cruel to them. She understood from reading the books that it is the way they were made. It is not any fault of theirs because it is their biology, but the world has continued to blame them and harass them and even kill them. She sobbed aloud at the thought that someone might attack Depo if they found out.

She looked at him and he was in tears too. "Depo, I'm sorry. Will you be safe, someone wouldn't attack you and hurt you; please be careful, I don't want to lose you, you mean the world to me. Will you be safe? Please don't tell anyone you are that way, they might hurt you, please. I can't lose you. People can be so mean. If I lose you, I'll just die, please Depo. Promise me."

"I haven't told a soul and I will not. My mother knows and you know. She loves me and she is worried about me, just like you are. But she is a great person who has always been there for me. She told me that all she has ever wanted for me was my happiness. I'm lucky, Ranti. I have two great women in my corner. I'll be fine. I was afraid you would be horrified and not want to have anything to do with me ever again."

"How can I be horrified? How can someone as kind and wonderful as you have been to me be horrifying? If you are that way Depo and you are you, it is not a horrible thing at all. I'm angry that the dream I had is not real. I'm very angry about that. I'm going to miss you like crazy and I'm going to cry for a long time but you are here." She touched her chest. "Forever and ever, you are here."

He looked at her and kissed her on the lips. "I'll help you with the treatment. Let Moradeke help you when I'm gone. It's okay. I like her; she is kind. I'm sure Gboye is kind too but she can be too much and she scares me, but since she is your friend some things must be good about her."

Ranti smiled through her tears, "Gboye scares a lot of people, but she is my protector."

She did not tell her friends about Depo's sexual orientation. She threw herself into her studies to distract herself so she would not have to think about him. For weeks after he left, she could not eat and each time she forced herself to eat she would become nauseated. She told herself she had to stop dreaming of a romantic life with any man. Esho had told her repeatedly that in their line with the curse on their heads, they were just playthings for men.

Twice she had given herself over to the fantasies and both times she had been burnt. She had fallen hopelessly in love with a man who could never love her back in that way or make love to her like in those romance novels.

She told herself she should concentrate on becoming a doctor and not think about Depo or sex anymore. She started to make herself pass the dilator into her vagina everyday to keep it open.

Her friends began to worry since she was losing weight again, but she assured them she was fine, she just missed Depo. They were sympathetic and Gboye told her the best way to get over a failed love affair was to get into another one right away and not waste time pinning away, and that this time she should pick a more aggressive man and not someone who was just too passive like Depo and could not bring himself to make love to her.

Depo on his part wrote to her regularly as he had promised, and she wrote back to him, trying to sound more cheerful than she felt. She continued to warn him to be careful around people who were homophobic.

Eight months after Depo left, as Ranti was giving herself the daily dilation treatment, she started to feel some stirring in her vagina that felt very exciting and she wanted more of it. She continued to pass the dilator in and out of her vagina and the good feeling intensified. She smiled to herself and her naked butt on the bed felt good too. She wished Depo was there to rub his hands on them. She eventually climaxed and realized she had just masturbated. She was very happy. She started to cry out of sheer relief. "I am normal after all," she told herself, "not everything was damaged."

She was still crying when Gboye busted into the room. Ranti tried to quickly dry the tears. "Why are you crying? Still crying over Depo?" She demanded in her usual abrupt manner.

Ranti smiled because though she still missed Depo, the pain in her heart had eased off significantly. "No, Gboye my sister, I just masturbated and it felt like heaven. I am a normal woman after all."

"You just masturbated?" Gboye gave her a disgusted look. "You mean you have never masturbated in your life? What? You need a boyfriend that will have real sex with you. I love Depo, but there is something wrong with that boy and he wasn't all that good for you. Of course you are a normal woman, all that mutilation business is behind you, Ranti, this is the best time of your life, this is the time that you can have casual sex with anyone, don't waste it, because once you are married, that is it.

"I am sure Depo is getting it up in France, you know what they say about that country or at least about Paris, it's the city of love. Well it's a good thing you started with that. You are claiming your body as yours. Masturbating and trying out different things is the way for you to know what you want sexually and what you don't want. You are taking charge of your body."

Ranti smiled as she shook her head at her.

She started to masturbate each time she gave herself the dilator treatment and she loved it. She told herself she did not need any man. She could do it for herself while still imagining that it was Depo making love to her.

27

In their third year of medical school, Moradeke started to go steady with one of their classmates, Bode. She even began to talk of marriage. Ranti liked Bode for her friend. He was gentle and handsome, about five feet eleven inches in height and slim in stature. He and Moradeke looked beautiful together with him complementing her dark chocolate complexion with his own light skin. He was also from a similar background as Moradeke. His mother was a lawyer in Lagos while his father was a surgeon.

Ranti started to despair that she would ever be good enough for anyone to want to be with her in a loving manner and not just as a plaything. Even Depo had wanted her for his selfish reasons. He did not want to marry a woman but he wanted children. She wondered what it was about her that told men she was a toy.

She watched Moradeke and Bode together and she wanted what they had. Bode was always coming to look for Moradeke and whenever they had a fight and

Moradeke started to give him the silent treatment, he would apologize repeatedly and ask her friends to appeal to her on his behalf. He would buy her gifts to let her know he was sorry and he would run errands for her. Ranti did not believe anyone would ever want to take care of her in that way.

A lot of the young men in her class had continued to ask her out but she was afraid that it would be a repetition of her experience with Depo, so she kept declining. She concentrated on her studies and she continued to do very well as was typical for her.

Gboye in her own way was 'whipping it up' with the boys. She was having a ball as she kept telling her friends and was always going on dates with one boy or the other. Most of the boys she dated wanted more out of the relationship, but Gboye would let them know she was not interested. In this way she broke many boys' hearts, as they would try to pursue her by coming repeatedly to the room she shared with Ranti and Moradeke. In Ranti's opinion, she treated them poorly.

With Moradeke going steady and Gboye never being in short supply of willing men who treated her well, Ranti started to have some stirrings in her heart as well. She told herself she was giving up on men too early. She had two bad experiences and that was not enough reason to make all the men in the world her enemy as her grandmother had done.

She acknowledged that with the governor, she had been totally powerless, but she had herself to blame for walking with her own two feet into his office, in spite of her grandmother's warnings. With Depo, his heart was in the right place, it was just his sexual orientation that was somewhere else and besides he had given her the greatest gift anyone could ever give her.

She remembered the many books she read and how the authors' recurring messages were that one should never give up after trying once or twice or even three times. That a person should learn from each experience and strive to do better next time. She reminded herself that she was not someone who gave up on life. If she were; she would either have died, or would have lost her scholarship one way or the other. She had had to fight for the kind of life she wanted and she had been blessed that great people had come her way to lend helping hands like her two girl friends that were more like sisters to her, and Depo and his mother. Even the Anglican Diocese had been a great blessing to her though she and her grandmother did not believe in their God, and did not go to their church.

She remembered reading in the mythology book, *The Hero with a Thousand Faces*, "You should start working on the path you believe is yours, work hard, do not be afraid and do not refuse challenges and helpers will come, they will just appear and work with you," or something like that. It was a long passage in which the author explained this in mythological terms and it had made such an impression on her that she copied it in the journal where she kept quotations.

She went to her closet to retrieve the journal and she read it aloud to herself, trying to get it to stick in her head, and to remember it as a reassurance. *"[On the Hero who has not refused the call to adventure]: The helpful crone and fairy tale godmother is a familiar feature of European fairy lore; in Christian saints' legends the role is commonly played by the Virgin. The Virgin by her intercession can win the mercy of the Father. Spider woman with her web can control the movement of the sun (American Indian mythology). The hero who has come under the protection of the Cosmic Mother cannot be harmed. The thread of Ariadne brought Thesus safely through the adventure of the labyrinth. This is the guiding power that runs through the work of Dante in the female figures of Beatrice and the Virgin, and appears in Goethe's Faust successively as Gretchen, Helen of Troy, and the Virgin...*

"What such a figure represents is the benign, protecting power of destiny. The fantasy is a reassurance—a promise that the peace of Paradise, which was known first within the mother's womb, is not to be lost; that it supports the present and stands in the future as well as in the past (is omega as well as alpha); that though omnipotence may seem to be endangered by the threshold passages and life awakenings, protective power is always and ever present within the sanctuary of the heart and even immanent within, or just behind, the unfamiliar features of the world. One has only to know and trust, and the ageless guardians will appear. Having responded to his own call, and continuing to follow courageously as the consequences unfold, the hero finds all the forces of the unconscious at his side. Mother nature herself supports the mighty task. And in so far as the hero's act coincides with that for which his society itself is ready, he seems to ride on the great rhythm of the historical process."

She decided that if any of the boys she liked asked her out on a date, she would go.

A few days later, while they were on rounds in the surgical ward, Tolu whispered into her ear, "Ranti, you just glow and you are distracting everyone; even the residents are looking at you." Ranti smiled at him and nodded her thanks.

Later in the day he invited her to lunch.

Ranti liked him and had always exchanged a few words with him over the years. He was a very exciting person who had lots of friends and a very busy social life. And he always had jokes to tell his classmates. He was from Lagos and always went home on weekends.

She went to lunch with him and he later invited her to lunch again the next day. They started to hang out and some evenings he would visit Ranti in her room. Her friends approved of him.

Moradeke, who had known him in Lagos, told Ranti he had two older sisters who were married, and a brother that died two years before in a motor vehicle accident. Ranti did not know this about him. She instantly felt a bond with him in that she had lost a brother too and she resolved to ask him about it.

Tolu however did not want to talk about his brother, who had been three years older than him. "What's done is done. I don't think about him or talk about him anymore. I even stopped talking to his friends, many of whom wanted to become my friend and kind of look out for me. They said that's what my brother would have wanted.

"I made it clear to them that I don't need any charity or anyone looking out for me. I have enough friends of my own and I can take care of myself. What's the point on dwelling on what has happened?"

Ranti did not agree with him. She wished she had someone to talk to about Lana. Someone who had known him and had loved him as Tolu's brother's friends must have loved him that they wanted to take care of his brother. Lana did not appear to have had friends even though he died when he was nine years old. No one from his class had come to her to talk about him.

"Lana had friends," she remembered. Then it dawned on her that his friends had been too young. They probably did not know what to do and they must have been too scared.

"I think it's great that your brother's friends want to look out for you. Your brother must have been a wonderful friend to them. That's a gift he gave you, I mean your brother. You can never have too many friends, Tolu. Friends are a blessing in one's life."

"I don't want to talk about it Ranti, I mean it. So don't bring it up again," he warned her.

Ranti wanted to know about his family, she would ask him about his parents and sisters, but Tolu was guarded about this as well. Very soon she learnt not to ask him so many questions because he would become quiet and start to sulk.

Three weeks later, he came to visit her one afternoon while she was alone in the room. They sat on the bed next to one another and at some point he moved over to her and started to kiss her. The warning bells went off in her head. She could hear Esho shrieking at her to be careful. She tried to concentrate on the kiss and shut out Esho's voice.

Tolu pulled up her top and started to touch her breasts and Ranti calmed herself so she could enjoy his touch. She told herself that it was better than masturbating. Something about the masturbation with the dilator had started to leave her sad.

Tolu pulled at her underwear but she stopped him.

"I will be gentle with you, I promise." He tried to reassure her.

"I don't want to get pregnant. I don't want to ruin my life."

"Oh come on, you won't get pregnant, you don't get pregnant by doing it just once. You'll see."

Ranti pushed him away from her. "Are you stupid? Where have you been? You're a medical student and you are talking as if you're an illiterate. Of course I can get pregnant by having sex just once or even half of once."

"I can't get you pregnant Ranti, I just can't."

"What do you mean? Are you sterile? Did you have mumps when you were a little boy?"

"I've had sex with lots of girls and none of them has become pregnant."

"That doesn't mean a thing. The only way we can know for sure is if you had your sperm tested and you don't have any. Have you had them tested?"

He shook his head.

"Then I'm not having sex with you, and besides these many girls. I don't want to have sex with someone who is sleeping with every girl he meets."

"Oh come on Ranti, I'm not seeing anyone now except you. That was before now. I just want to be with you. I promise. Even when I go to Lagos on weekends, I don't see anyone. It's the truth."

"I will have sex with you only with condoms, okay, I don't want to get pregnant and I don't want to catch a disease."

"Are you saying I have a disease?" He became angry. "If you don't want to have sex with me that's your problem, but don't ever say I have a disease."

"I'm not saying you have a disease. You just said it yourself that you've been with a lot of girls and sometimes these diseases are silent and you might not know you have them. I'd like to have sex with you Tolu but I'm not going to ruin my life or risk my health."

"Okay, I'll go and get some condoms and will be right back." He left in a hurry.

When he returned fifteen minutes later, Moradeke, Bode and Gboye were in the room. Ranti could read frustration in his face. She gave him an apologetic smile.

The following day in class, he invited her to his room telling her his roommate was gone.

Ranti went with him and they had sex. She was disappointed. He was not gentle with her. He held her too tightly and sucked on her nipples so hard that for days, they were sore.

Three days later he invited her again but she declined. He angrily wanted to know why not. She lied that she had to go visit her grandmother.

She avoided him for the rest of the week and he finally demanded an explanation from her the following week after he returned from Lagos. She told him that he was too rough with her.

She was also afraid that if he continued to have sex with her in that way, her repaired fistula might rip apart again. She did not tell him this, because somehow she knew he would not understand what she went through and might tell his friends.

He promised to be gentle, saying he was rough because he had been too excited.

Ranti decided to give him another chance, and he did make the effort to be gentle with her, but from time to time he would get carried away and pinch her. Ranti would tell him he was hurting her and then he would catch himself.

He later explained to her that it would take some time for them to learn what the other person wanted and he was learning how to please her.

He continued to go to Lagos on weekends to hang out with his friends in their homes or dorms at the University of Lagos. Most of his friends were from rich homes and he loved to tell Ranti about their glamorous lives.

One Thursday Ranti asked Tolu to hang out with her instead of going to Lagos for the weekend. He refused. She asked him a few more times and he continued to refuse.

Seven months later, Moradeke returned to school from a visit home. She told Ranti that she saw Tolu at the University of Lagos with another girl and they were making out in public.

Ranti was devastated. Her friends consoled her that it was better she found out then rather than later.

When he returned to school the following Monday and Ranti confronted him, he denied the accusation saying Moradeke must have been mistaken.

Moradeke found out more information about the girl from some of her friends in Lagos and she told Ranti that Tolu had been seeing her for months.

Later, Ranti told Tolu she did not want to continue the relationship with him unless he stopped going to Lagos on weekends and spent more time with her. He did not go to Lagos for the rest of the month.

A month later he just disappeared. Ranti was worried. Gboye and Moradeke were not. They both told her to forget him, that he was a cheat. Two weeks later on a Friday, he reappeared and came to Ranti's room in the middle of the night. Ranti went out to meet him in the hallway so as not to disturb her friends who were asleep. "Where have you been? I have been so worried about you."

"I had to take care of some business in Lagos. I didn't know I would be gone for so long."

"Tolu, I don't get you. You left without saying a word to me, what was I supposed to think? If you really cared you would have let me know what was going on. You can't just disappear and then just reappear. You don't have any respect for my feelings; otherwise you wouldn't have behaved that way."

"Okay, I'm sorry, it won't happen again, I'm back now, do you want to come to my room, I miss you and my roommate is away."

"No, I will not come to your room. Who do you think you are? You think I'm your toy? Just go and come as you please and then at the snap of your fingers I will run to you. Go to hell Tolu."

"Ranti, let me tell you what your problem is. You are too full of yourself. And I don't know what it's based on. Yes, you are a beautiful girl but there are lots of beautiful girls around. You are not the only one, and you know what, most of them have rich parents too. You wear clothes that are not in fashion and I have been doing you a favor by going out with you. I have been trying to give you some class here. You go to hell."

"I'm poor Tolu, but I have never tried to be someone else. My grandmother works very hard to give me what I have, but do you know the difference between you and I? I'm not ashamed of me, while you are ashamed of your family and you'd rather hang out with your rich friends and go to their homes with them. You are a fake, while I'm real. You are a lousy lover too; you continue to hurt me and you keep saying 'I will be gentle next time' but you never are. It's like you are raping me. Those other girls can have you. It's you who is creating a hell for yourself and you are going to be very happy there."

"No, I'm a good lover. Those other girls you are so jealous of tell me all the time. And I go to them because you are so cold. They are easier to sleep with than you are with all your rules and always complaining that I'm hurting you. You are the one who is frigid and so dry. Having sex with you is like sleeping with a log," he yelled at her.

Ranti went back into her room and cried till morning. She ignored him in class and three days later she saw him making out with a girl in the second year.

She was very sad, not so much because the relationship with Tolu ended, but because she felt hopeless about ever finding a man to love her and cherish her, especially the way Bode cherished Moradeke. She concluded that it was because of her grandmother's social class, that boys want to go out with girls from rich homes.

Her friends encouraged her to date other boys.

28

Receiving an education for most young women was twice the ordeal because they had to expend a lot of energy fighting sexism, and they had to contend with sexual harassment from some male faculty, who felt entitled to have sex with them. Ranti had her share of the harassment as well with some of the men who knew she was from a poor home promising her money. She tried her best to avoid them.

One evening, as she was leaving the classroom where she and a few of her classmates had been studying, a gynecologist who had been harassing her for a while came out of his office as she walked by his door. He pulled her into the office before she could react in any way and roughly pushing her against the wall, he started to kiss her.

Ranti struggled to free herself as he kept pushing his tongue into her mouth. She started to gag and before she could warn him, she felt vomit rise up into her throat. She was able to push him off in time to throw up.

He was bewildered as he yelled at her because some of the vomit splashed on his shirt. He commanded her to clean it up. Ranti picked up her bag of books from where it had fallen, "I cleaned up the governor's office that time because I was a naïve girl. I'm not anymore. You clean it up." She told him as she walked out of his office.

"I'm going to make sure you fail Obstetric and Gynecology, you silly girl," he shouted after her.

A few weeks later, she took a test in surgery and the lecturer who had been sexually harassing her refused to return her graded paper to her, even though he gave the rest of the class their papers. He invited her to his office to review the test with her.

Ranti went to his office and he started to force himself on her. She thought of throwing up to keep him away, but she was not nauseated. So, she just let go of her bladder and urinated in his office.

He could not believe his eyes and he too started to yell at her. She told him she had a bladder problem and she loses control when she becomes excited.

"Good luck to your boyfriends then, you freak," he yelled at her as she left his office.

Following these two incidences no lecturer made a pass at her, though some of them started to call her a freak or a weirdo. She told herself she could live with the names as long as they left her alone.

Six months after she ended the relationship with Tolu, she agreed to go out with one of Bode's friends Jide, who Moradeke had been telling her liked her a lot. He was three years ahead of them and was an intern.

They went out as a foursome. Ranti had a good time and she agreed to see him again. He told her the first time he noticed her was the year before. They had been in the elevator together and he had stood behind her admiring her fine figure and had been sorry when she got off the elevator on the third floor. He had wanted to ask her out but could not get up the courage until he became friends with Bode and realized Moradeke was her friend.

Ranti liked him, especially because he was admiring of her.

One month later she agreed to have sex with him. She insisted on condoms. He did not want to use condoms. He, like Tolu, promised not to get her pregnant.

Ranti could not comprehend their logic. "How will you not get me pregnant when we are not using condoms or any other contraceptives?" She asked him, thinking something must be wrong with these men who were doctors but decided to forget their medical knowledge and put her at risk.

"I don't believe in contraceptives," was his shocking reply.

"You don't believe in contraceptives? Do you know what they call people who do not believe in contraceptives?"

He stared at her.

"Parents! That's the name for people who do not believe in contraceptives. And I am not ready to become a parent at this time. I have to become a doctor first."

She kept hearing Esho's voice telling her that men are just interested in one thing and one thing only, ruining her life. She started to believe Esho and wondered why she was trying so hard to be in a relationship with the hope that it would be different.

Moradeke and Gboye had both told her they always used condoms. Moradeke said that though she trusted Bode, you can never know another human being fully and she was not putting herself at risk of catching a disease. She was not too worried about getting pregnant. If she got pregnant, she and Bode would marry. Gboye on her part had a lot of partners and told her friends she had to keep herself safe from diseases.

Jide reluctantly agreed to condoms, though each time Ranti had to put up a battle with him. Finally she told him it was not worth it for her to have to fight with him all the time and she did not want to have sex with him anymore.

He finally agreed to use condoms without the usual arguments and fights, but like Tolu he was too rough with her. His hugs were too tight, his kisses were too biting and her nipples would hurt for days. He would promise to be gentle with her but he never was.

Ranti confided in her friends and they advised her to stop sleeping with him because he was not making love to her, he was raping her; their boyfriends were gentler. She took their advice and told Jide she did not want to continue the relationship with him. She felt more hopeless. There did not seem to be a shortage of gentle men around, Gboye who was sleeping with three or four boys a year seemed to always find them. She wondered why she just could not find one. She resolved that she was done with sex. Esho was right; they had a curse on their heads that attracted rapists.

Jide became mean to her when she ended the relationship and each time he ran into her in the hospital, he would call her a bitch or a whore. She tried to avoid him when she could.

At about eleven o'clock on a Saturday night two weeks later, he came to her room and just walked in without knocking. It was obvious he had been drinking. Gboye and Moradeke had gone to a party. Ranti was studying at her desk.

She asked him to leave.

"I'm not leaving, you cunt, you owe me a fuck and I'm getting it tonight and you know what, your majesty, I'm not using a condom, and you know one more thing I'm going to do to you, I am going to give it to you up your anus. I heard girls like that. Girls like guys who are rough with them and not nice guys.

"I've been very nice to you but you have no respect for me. You go around teasing guys. A lot of people hate your guts. You know what they call you? A whore! You go around tantalizing people with your swaying hips and swinging breasts. You arrogant bitch, simply because you are smart and beautiful, that doesn't give you the right to go around teasing men. I'm going to teach you a lesson you won't forget for the rest of your life." He lunged at her and slapped her hard across her face with the back of his right hand.

Ranti was stunned as Jamba flashed into her mind. She reared back in the small room and picking up her chair said, "I'm going to kill you Jide! I swear I'll kill you."

He lunged at her again as he grabbed the chair from her. He threw it across the room and it landed on Gboye's bed. He grabbed her by her left arm and tried to throw her onto her bed face down, but he missed, slamming her face against the wall. Pain shot into her brain and she felt herself slipping into unconsciousness. She wanted to scream but her throat seemed to have closed in on her. She bit hard into her lower lip drawing blood, so the pain would keep her alert. She repeated to herself, "He is not raping me. I am not giving in to him."

He pushed her onto her bed face down and dug her face into the mattress, but she continued to struggle with him. She started to move her hand around looking for something, anything. Her hand rested on a pair of tweezers under the mattress. She gripped it and managed to flex her hand and stabbed him in the face

He yelled and let go of her as he held on to his right cheek. She sprung up from the bed and ran toward the kitchenette. She grabbed a knife and showed it to him. "I am going to kill you, Jide! I promise I will kill you and I won't be sorry at all."

His face was bleeding and he gave her a look of wonder. He started to walk purposefully toward her and in order for him to know she was serious, Ranti moved purposefully toward him too, with the knife held high in her right hand ready to stab him. He stopped in front of her as the knife touched his chest.

She warned him, "Walk out of my room. Don't make any sudden moves otherwise this knife is going into your chest, and since you are a doctor, and I hope your knowledge of anatomy is better than your knowledge of fertility, so you know which organs are in there. I will kill you and dump your body on the street. I swear I will kill you because no one is hurting me ever again!"

He looked at her for a moment and Ranti locked gaze with him. He slowly moved away from the knife and walked out of the room.

Moradeke suggested reporting Jide to the police but Gboye did not believe the police would arrest him and it would only traumatize Ranti more. "Forget him, Ranti, he's garbage. There are nicer men around. No one has ever pulled that crap with me and it's because I'm bigger than most of them. A lot of men will try to take advantage of you if they know they can overpower you. That's why I'm thankful I'm big. I know they call me Amazon and Joe Louis. But they know not to mess with me."

The following Saturday Gboye returned to the room in torn clothes, covered in blood. Her friends became alarmed, but she assured them she was fine, as she said to Ranti, "Jide won't be bothering you anymore. And neither will any other boy around here. I just gave him a lesson he will never forget. He's in the emergency room where they are stitching his face together."

"Gboye, what did you do?" Moradeke demanded.

Ranti started to clean Gboye's face with a wet towel.

"I hate it when people take advantage of other people. It just eats at me. Since he attacked you, Ranti, I have not been able to sleep or eat."

Moradeke and Ranti exchanged looks wondering what she was talking about, because Gboye had a very big appetite and she had been eating very well and had been snoring every night, as was her style.

She saw the looks and explained to them. "I know I have been eating, but I haven't been enjoying my food. You know I love food, but I haven't had the appetite; I eat because I need to keep up my strength. If I behave like you do, Ranti, going off food and eating once a day or once in two days, I will lose weight and people will start beating me up on the streets. I can't let that happen. When I walk into a room everyone knows I'm in the room and they know not to mess with me, and I like it that way. That is why no boy will dare raise his hands at me and I keep telling you, eat more, gain some weight, people will have more respect for you.

"I know I have been sleeping but it hasn't been the deep sleep in which I pass out. I kept dreaming of that asshole attacking you and I'm sorry I wasn't here. I was with that Chuks who was a total waste of my time. So tonight, I decided to take care of the situation and I went to Jide's room in the house officers' resident.

"He was surprised to see me but I didn't give him a chance to speak. I just started to hit him. I split his lips and his upper cheek and broke his left arm. The other interns tried to stop me so I asked him to tell them what he did and that as soon as he told them I would leave him alone.

"He finally did when I showed him a knife and told him I was going to carve 'rapist' on his face. He's not going to be raping any girl any time soon and by tomorrow the whole college would have heard, and no one will bother you ever again Ranti."

Tears sprang from Ranti's eyes as she embraced Gboye. "Thank you Gboye, thank you, I love you, thank you. That's what I wished I had done to him, but I don't have your size or strength. Thanks for looking out for me again."

"Gboye, I'm glad you are my friend," Moradeke started. "I have a few people on my list too. Professor Ojoge wants to sleep with me and I refused, so he's been tormenting Bode. He always picks on him and only asks him questions in class. Any time Bode gets the answer wrong, he says to him, 'I'm sure your parents didn't send you to school because of girls. If you will leave girls alone you will do better in class. I'm going to make sure you fail this class.' It's not fair. You know in England and America, what these professors do to us is a crime. It's called sexual harassment, just because they have the power and we don't."

"Trust me, Moradeke there are lots of them I would like to beat up, but at the same time I want to become a doctor. If I beat up a lecturer, I would be dismissed from the university. The other day when that fat fool Lado, who has been hitting on me, finally got me to his office, he started to talk about how much he loves me; and crap like that. I stood there and pretended to listen.

"Then he wanted to kiss me. Have you seen his teeth? Ugh," she shuddered in disgust. "There is some greenish-bluish stuff on his bottom gum, Jesus! As he came toward me, I moved my hand and it 'accidentally' hit him on the face. I said I was sorry, that it's because I'm much taller than him.

"The fool said it was okay and asked me to sit on his lap. Can you imagine me sitting on anyone's lap? I weigh over two hundred pounds for goodness sake. So I said okay and I stepped on his right foot and leant all of my weight on it. I pretended I didn't know what I was doing. He tried not to show that he was in pain, but after a while he said I was leaning on his foot. I quickly moved and apologized. I said it might not be a good idea for me to sit on his lap since I'm such a big girl.

"I turned around and 'accidentally' hit him again with my left hand across his face. His glasses flew off and landed by the door. I apologized and told him I've always been clumsy and my mother won't even let me touch her china. I went to retrieve his glasses. I picked them up and then opened the door. He came behind me and as I gave him the glasses with my right hand, I hit him with the door with my left hand. I apologized again and pretended that I was really sorry.

"I said I'm afraid because I'm so clumsy I won't be able to train as a neonatologist, and that, I love children so much. Of course I don't want to be a pediatrician. I want to be an orthopedic surgeon. I told him it was best if I left before I broke more things in his office and he readily agreed. I did the same thing to Ngadi in pathology. No lecturer has bothered me since then."

Ranti reminded them, "Since I peed in Ake's office leaving that mark I heard is still on his carpet, and vomited in Kereke's office, no lecturer has bothered me. They call me a freak or weirdo, but you know what? That's okay; I can live with the names."

"I need to do something so they will leave me alone. I heard Moji Ajayi started to wail when that dermatologist invited her to his office and made a pass at her. She sobbed so loudly and she told him, 'What you just said is spiritually disturbing to me, since I am a born-again Christian.' Everyone on the floor knew what was going on." Moradeke said.

"It's sad that we have to resort to these tactics. It's hard enough being in medical school. It's like double the stress for us because we spend as much time and energy on our studies as we spend warding these married men off. It's not fair." Ranti said.

"Well, women don't have any power in this country," said Gboye, "so we have to take care of ourselves whichever way we can. It's useless reporting them to the authority because if you do, you still get blamed. Remember that undergraduate student that was gang-raped a few months ago; the judge threw the case out. He said the girl had been dressing provocatively and that by dressing in that manner she invited the boys to rape her. I'm sure I will be accused of dressing provocatively because I love to wear tight and short skirts and low-cut tops.

"I wear them because I know I look very good in them. I like to look good, it's my business if I like my body and try to show it off, that doesn't give any boy I have not invited to touch me the license to rape me. That is why, girls, I make sure I eat to keep up my strength to defend myself and Ranti take my advice, stop skipping meals, you will be stronger. And you know what? You would have been able to pluck out one of Jide's eyes when you stabbed him with the tweezers."

"I know what I'll do so these men will leave me alone. I will tell my father, he is a powerful man in the government and I'll give him their names and if they continue, I'll ask Funmi to write about the 'Traumatic Effects of Sexual Harassment on Undergraduate Female Students in our Universities' in her newspaper. I will ask her to mention a few names. You know the really bad ones, that way their wives will read the newspaper and they would be in serious trouble. They won't be able to connect it to me because Funmi has a different last name since she got married," Moradeke decided.

Her friends agreed with her though they doubted it would stop the harassers as most of them abused their wives at home anyway, but the newspaper article would cause some embarrassment for them.

The story of Gboye beating up Jide did go around the campus and girls started to call him rapist. When Ranti ran into him in the hospital a few weeks later, his left arm was in a cast and the scars were still fresh on his face. He pretended as if he did not see her and she pretended as if she did not see him as well.

Following this, Ranti decided to forget about men.

29

On a Sunday afternoon at the beginning of her fourth year, Ranti went home to visit Esho. When she walked into the hallway of the eight-room-building that they shared with seven other families, a nasty stench hit her.

There was something familiar about the smell. Her mind immediately went to the time she was in plastic surgery rotation and they had lots of patients who were victims of burns and of tropical ulcers that would not heal. She wondered why there would be such a smell in her house.

Even though the house was mostly congested with the other families of four or even up to six to a room, they had always kept it clean.

As Ranti sat in the room with Esho, the smell continued to bother her. She could not eat the meal that Esho had prepared in anticipation of her visit, but at the same time she did not want to offend Esho by not eating.

"What is that smell?" she finally blurted out when she could not take it anymore.

Esho looked at her for a moment. "I'm used to it now. At first it used to bother me such that I couldn't eat, but this is my house, what would I do? We wouldn't cut off his leg, would we?" She said in resignation.

"Cut off whose leg?" Ranti demanded, "Esho, whose leg?"

"The smell is from Oke's leg. He arrived from Lagos five days ago. He sustained the wound when he fell off a bus over a year ago and it wouldn't heal. He has been to a lot of doctors and even to *babalawo*, but the leg continues to get worse. He is not able to work because of the pain, so they fired him from his job and he came back home to his parents. Isn't that sad? For a grown man to have to come back home to his parents and for them to have to take care of him, and they don't have much either.

"They think his wife cursed him with black magic and that is why the leg won't heal. Mama Oye said she knows a very powerful *babalawo* and she promised to take them to see him so he can remove the curse on the leg," Esho explained to Ranti as she shook her head in sorrow.

"His parents are such good people, we've been living together now for fifteen years and they have never done anything to offend me. But I mind my own business. I don't believe in all that black magic and *juju* nonsense, I'm too practical for that. But that's their belief. So they are not taking him to the hospital anymore."

Ranti stood up from the low stool on which she had been sitting. "Esho, I'll take him to my medical school, they'll take care of the wound for him. I've seen a lot of wounds that wouldn't heal. They are called tropical ulcers. Sometimes they need surgery and a lot of caring but they heal eventually. I'll go and have a look at his leg."

"No, Iranti, don't go, it's none of your business. I stay out of people's way and they stay out of mine. Don't interfere in other people's problem," Esho warned her.

"No Esho, it is okay to help people. I'm in medical school and I know a little about these things. I can take him to some of my lecturers and they will help him. Esho, that is why we have neighbors, to help one another; just like you said, his parents have always been good to you, so why won't you be good to them in return? You never know, you or me, we might need their help one day."

"No one helped me when I needed help, Iranti. They all stood by and watched until my child died when he sustained a cut on his foot. Don't go to them. I mind my own business in this house and that is why it has been peaceful for me to live here."

When Oke's mother opened the door for Ranti, the stench from the room blasted her in the face and she reeled back to catch her breath. The elderly woman gave her an apologetic smile. "*Sisi College*," she greeted Ranti, addressing her with the respectful title the neighbors gave her since she matriculated at the university.

"Mama Oke, Esho told me Oke was home and that he injured his leg in Lagos. I wanted to say hello to him."

Oke's mother looked embarrassed as she slowly moved out of the way. Oke was lying on the mat on the floor. His father sat on a chair by the wall. The room was dark because the windows were shut and the blinds were closed. The smell made Ranti sick to her stomach but she did not allow any emotion to register on her face.

She and Oke were not friends. He was some six years older than her and since he was a man and because of Esho's warnings, she had exchanged very few words with him in all the years they had been neighbors, mostly staying out of his way. She knelt down beside him on the mat and asked if she could look at his leg. He looked ashamed as he cringed into himself, as if hoping to disappear into the floor.

"Oke, I'm a medical student. We see a lot of problems like this at the hospital and doctors are able to help the patients. I'll just have a look at it," she tried to reassure him.

He looked up at his parents and they exchanged anxious looks with one another. Ranti stood up while they decided whether to let her examine Oke's leg. She could read indecision and fear on their faces.

"Why don't we start by opening these windows so light and fresh air can come in?" Ranti moved closer to the windows to open them.

168   *Feasts of Phantoms*

Oke's father started to protest. "The neighbors will be angry with us because of the smell. It is best if we keep them locked and stay to ourselves."

"No, that won't be the best thing at all, and the neighbors will not die," Ranti told him as she pulled the blinds and opened the windows. "It's not Oke's fault that he has this wound. Fresh air will help everyone. The smell is coming from the bacteria growing on the wound. The name of the bacteria is pseudomonas and medications will get rid of them." Ranti knelt down next to Oke and looked at the leg.

The festering wound that it was must have started on a spot on his left shin, but it had extended about ten inches in diameter around his leg. Many pockets containing pus were weeping, and the areas without pus were bluish-green. The stench was terrible.

"Oke, I will come back tomorrow morning and take you to the hospital with me. The doctors can help you. It's going to be painful because they might have to do surgery and they might have to take fresh skin from other parts of your body to cover the wound so it will heal better, so it's going to be a pretty rough ride to recovery, but you will recover and be able to return to your job in Lagos and you won't lose your leg." She paused and looked intently at him.

"But if you do nothing and just lie here in your parents' room," she gave him that intense look again, "you might end up losing your leg, or the bacteria from the leg might go into your blood and that could kill you. It doesn't have to get to that, there is help available Oke." Ranti finished and waited for his response.

Oke stared silently ahead of him. Ranti looked at his parents and they both averted their gaze. "I will be here at seven in the morning, please be ready." She instructed them.

"I don't like that Iranti. I don't like it at all. I mind my business in this house and I want you to do the same. Did they come to you for advice? Did they say to you, 'Iranti, we do not know our way to the hospital, please show us the way?' Did they? I want you to mind your own business. Don't come back to take him to the hospital, let them find their way. Okay?" Esho was very angry.

"No, Esho. That is not how life works. People help people. If you have knowledge of something and other people don't, you help them. You point them in the right direction. That's why life is tolerable for all of us. I'm a medical student and I just can't sit back and watch him die or lose his leg. I can't, Esho, and I'm helping them unless they tell me to mind my own business. But as long as they haven't said so, I'm helping them." She paused for a moment.

"At the time of your child, Esho," she was afraid to mention his name since Esho had forbidden her ever to mention it. "Maybe they didn't know and that doesn't make them bad people..."

"Iranti, we are not talking about that, I am warning you." Esho yelled at her, so she kept quiet.

When Ranti arrived at the house at about six thirty the next morning in a hired taxi, Oke and his parents were ready and waiting for her. While the driver helped Oke into the taxi, Ranti went to knock on her grandmother's door, even though she knew she would have left the house to go to her job. As she expected, Esho was not there.

A surgeon admitted Oke into the hospital and with Ranti's help explained to him and his parents the treatment regimen. He was started on intravenous antibiotics and nutrition to help build his immunity and the following day he was taken into the operating room for extensive debridement of the wound.

When Ranti visited him later in the day, he was in tears and in a lot of pain and he told her the pain medications were not working at all. He wanted to be discharged home, because the doctor told him they might have to debride the wound at least three more times to remove all the dead tissue. He was convinced the pain of the treatment would kill him. He wept as he told Ranti that the pain from the leg before the debridement was more tolerable.

Ranti appealed to him to stay and follow the doctor's plan. "Oke, you are still a very young man with a bright future. You have elderly parents; it's not their job to bury you if you were to die and you will die if you don't take care of this leg. That will be terrible for them. I know. Remember Esho lost two children. She went to hell after. The sight of a parent losing a child is not a thing I want to witness again for as long as I live, so please, for the sake of your parents, agree to this treatment.

"It is more pain now, I agree with you. The medications are not working as well as they should because there is still a lot of infected tissue on your leg but with the second treatment, the pain will get less and the medication will work better.

"It's like a lot of pain now, so you can have a life free of pain in the future, as opposed to a life of chronic and sustained pain for a very long time and that might eventually make you lose your leg or even kill you." Ranti weighed her two hands against one another, "Pain now, your leg back in working condition and your health and life back later, or pain now and forever, losing your leg and life eventually. Which will it be, Oke?"

The following week after he had the second debridement, he and Ranti had the same conversation again, with Oke convinced that the pain of the treatment would kill him first. He repeatedly threatened the nurses and Ranti that he would discharge himself against medical advice.

The surgeon maximized his pain medication and warned him that if he gave him more, he would be overdosing him, but two days following the second treatment when Ranti visited him, he told her that even though he remained in a lot of pain, it was much less than it was after the first treatment.

"And after the third treatment, it will even be less. You are on your way to a life free of pain, Oke, and that's because you are bearing the pain now, and allowing the doctors to get rid of the dead tissue in your wound, the dead tissues that have no business in a living body in the first place, and that could kill you or make you into an invalid because they have been allowing deadly bacteria to grow in them. You are slowly saying good-bye to a life of pain and hopelessness," Ranti assured him.

Ten days later he was in tears from the severe pain after the third treatment. But this time he did not threaten to leave the hospital.

"And tomorrow it will be much less, Oke," Ranti smiled at him.

When she visited him the following evening, Oke was not on his bed as was usual for him. She found him on the balcony hanging out with some patients and laughing with them. He leant against the wall supporting himself with a pair of crutches.

Ranti smiled at him, "When was the last time you stood up, Oke?"

He returned her smile. "Ten months, two weeks and three days ago. I calculated it this morning. On a scale of one to ten with ten being the worst and one being the least, the pain is a five. For the past eight months, the pain had been at least an eleven. Thank you Ranti, thank you very much."

One week later he had the skin transplant taken from his thigh onto the wound and the following month he was discharged from the hospital. He could walk again, though with the help of crutches and he told Ranti that the pain was eighty percent less than what it had been for the previous year.

He and his parents were very grateful to Ranti and as Esho later told her, they thanked her each time they saw her.

The neighbors were equally grateful to her for saving them from the stench from Oke's rotting leg. The landlord said to her, "Now that we have a doctor in the house, no one needs to die a useless death anymore."

Four months later, Oke was able to return to his job in Lagos. Ranti was happy she had helped Oke save his leg. She remembered how Efunwunmi, Depo, Moradeke and Gboye saved her life too by insisting that she receive treatment to correct her mutilated genitals and Efunwunmi paid for it. "It's the least I should do to help Oke. He doesn't have to die like my brother died. No one should die in that wasteful manner anymore."

30

Brian O'Connor had always paid Ranti lots of attention since their first year in medical school, but toward the end of their fourth year he became more aggressive in the ways he pursued her. He came to her one day in the library and asked her to help him study for pathology examination since she was the most brilliant student in the class.

Ranti had always thought he was a handsome man, with his height of about five feet ten inches, medium body build with a head full of thick black hair, full round lips, very dark chocolate complexion and beautiful white teeth.

She agreed to study with him and so every night they met in the library.

Gboye and Moradeke were happy she was spending a lot of time with Brian, though Gboye maintained that he was ashamed of himself.

Her friends asked her what she meant by that, "It has to do with his name, why would a Yoruba boy, born and raised in Ibadan, have Irish first and last names? Something is not right." She explained to them.

Moradeke gave her a look that said she was crazy. "That's not his fault. He didn't name himself, his parents gave him the names, they are the ones to blame or accuse of being ashamed, and besides there are lots of Nigerians with English names. Lagos is full of them. Depo's last name is Jacobs."

"I know that, Moradeke," Gboye said with lots of irritation, "the families in Lagos with English last names have histories that we all know. Their ancestors were the enslaved people who returned when slavery ended in the Americas. What is Brian's story? I'm happy you are talking to another boy Ranti but I just had to say what I think."

"I'm not marrying him, we just study together. I agreed to study with him so if we are together a lot, those lecturers who always verbally harass me would be reluctant to talk to me if they see me with him. I'm tired of fighting them off," Ranti told her friends.

"Don't marry him, but at least have sex with him; have sex once in a while, it's good for you," Gboye advised her. "And besides he is the kind of man you like to sleep with anyway, I know your taste in men now. You like medium built, dark-complexioned men with thick hair and good teeth. And that's describing Tolu, Jide and Brian."

"Depo doesn't look like them though and that is her first love and the deepest, the real thing. Depo is very light skinned and much taller, so you can't say the others are her taste in men. Depo has the best smile of them though, very genuine and sweet. He is the best one for you Ranti," Moradeke added.

"Whatever." Ranti rolled her eyes at her friends.

She gradually grew to like Brian and to entertain the idea of making out with him and even having sex with him. She tried fantasizing making love to him but Depo's face kept intruding, as it did when she was with Jide and Tolu.

A month later, she received one of the usual bimonthly letters from Depo. She ran to her room to enjoy it in quiet. Depo told her about his life as always and that he met someone who meant the world to him and they had been in a steady relationship for the previous month. His name was Dave. He was from England and was studying music in Paris. He wrote that he had never been happier.

Ranti tore up the letter before her friends returned because she had not shared the information about Depo's sexual orientation with them, and she did not want them to read this letter as they had read some of his other letters.

She became depressed again. Somehow, Depo meeting a man and being in a relationship with him concretely told her he would never love her, as she desired. She cried herself to sleep that night.

Two days later when Brian invited her to his room she went with him. He started to make out with her and she did not stop him. He proceeded to have sex with her and she just asked him to use a condom.

They had sex but she did not feel a thing. She did not have any of the wonderful feelings she used to have when she masturbated while thinking of Depo. Brian was not gentle with her at all. He was as rough as Jide and Tolu had been. His touches were too intense.

She stopped masturbating and threw the dilators away. She told herself she was looking for a dream that did not exist and had been too sensitive because of her previous trauma, which explained why she was experiencing normal sex as painful. Her fantasizing about Depo all the time was keeping her from living in the real world of relationships.

She acknowledged that she could not learn about sex from anyone. Esho never had sex after the mad man that gave her Oshun raped her the second time, so maybe her expectations were unrealistic. She wondered if she had been too hard on Jide and provoked him into assaulting her.

She told herself to be grateful that a boy still wanted to be with her. So she continued to have sex with Brian as often as he asked her even though for the most part it was painful for her.

Four months later, he took her home to meet his mother and aunts. An aunt told him he had done well in finding for himself a beautiful girl, although his mother's older sister was offended that Ranti did not curtsy to greet her.

Ranti quickly apologized and knelt down. She told herself she would do everything in her power to belong to that family and would stop thinking about Depo.

Ranti sat for the board- examination that would give her the opportunity of residency training in the United States of America in her fifth year of medical school. She wanted to train to be a gynecologist but knew she would not be admitted into the residency training at her university because of the way she treated the many lecturers who had sexually harassed her.

She passed the examination scoring in the ninety-seventh percentile and she applied to many residency-training programs, grateful that America was a big country with lots of programs.

A few weeks later she received several letters of invitations for interviews. She wrote to the programs that she was in Nigeria and would not be available for interviews until after she graduated in June of 1987, but a program from the University College of New Jersey was willing to interview her over the phone, after which she was accepted.

Built into the medical school program in the fifth year was an opportunity to go abroad to England or the USA, for a six weeks rotation in the specialty the student hoped to pursue.

Ranti, Gboye and Moradeke already had hospitals that invited them for the rotations in England, with Ranti going to rotate with Mr. Edwards who had repaired her genitals five years before.

Ranti had been saving money for this trip for the past five years.

At that time in the country, in an attempt to curb corruption, there was a government restriction on the amount of foreign currency that you could purchase if you wanted to travel abroad to five hundred dollars a year. If you needed more money, you had to get a special permit from the necessary ministry.

Ranti needed fifteen hundred dollars for her six weeks stay in England, so like her classmates she applied to the Ministry of Education for permission to purchase more money, but she was invited for an interview with the minister of education.

She and her friends were surprised because all their classmates were granted permission to buy more foreign currency without having to appear for interviews. Moradeke volunteered to ask her father who was a friend of the Minister of Education. She left immediately to go to the hall warden's office to make a phone call to her father.

She returned half an hour later and announced, "We have to start listening to news instead of always playing pop music on the stereo. And we need to either start buying newspapers every day, or put money together and buy a television set. We are living in the dark here, girls, it's as if we were not in Nigeria at all." She paused, "I'm sorry, Ranti, Professor Ade is not the minister of education anymore. He was transferred to another ministry. The current minister is," she hesitated, "I'm sorry, it's Major General Jamba."

Ranti developed a panic attack. "I will never become a doctor. He promised me that as long as he was alive, I would not become a doctor. Oh my gosh! If he is

174   *Feasts of Phantoms*

the minister of education, he could get the university to fail me. Oh my gosh, oh my gosh." She could not breathe and she started to sweat. She sat on her bed.

Her friends ran to her and Moradeke started to fan her face with a flat book while Gboye started to take off her blouse to unhook her bra.

"I know General Jamba. I was in school with two of his daughters in England; really ugly girls! What happened? What's going on?" Gboye was confused.

Moradeke told her that when they were in secondary school, Jamba tried to rape Ranti and he beat her up pretty badly, breaking her ribs. He also told her that as long as he was alive, she would never become a doctor. "He has the power now because the university is under his ministry."

"What?" Gboye was stunned. "Why didn't you tell me this? He can't do anything to you; trust me, he can't. His son, who is the same age as my brother Goke, is a drug dealer. He sells cocaine in England. If this man tries anything to prevent you from becoming a doctor, his son is going to prison for a long time. When I get to England next month, I will casually walk to the police station and let them know."

"No, No, No, No, we can't do that." Said Ranti as she took in big gulps of air, "That's too risky and too dangerous. I will simply not go for the interview and quietly stay here and finish my medical education. We have only four months, girls. In four months we are doctors. I don't want to rock the boat. I will just lay low and four months will pass quickly."

"It's a good idea. I'm sorry you can't come to England with us, Ranti. It would have been so much fun. Don't go for the interview and he will just forget about you. He is a busy man who has the ministry for the whole country to run." Moradeke hoped.

"I don't like the idea at all." Gboye fumed. "It's not fair. He shouldn't be allowed to get away with things like this. It is not fair. Ranti works hard. Ranti you have always worked hard since I have known you. If anyone deserves this opportunity, it is you. You should go for the interview, I will come with you, let's see what he would dare do."

"Gboye, fair has never worked for people like me and my grandmother. It works in your world. We are different. You guys don't even have to worry about buying the foreign currency. Your parents are giving you checks to their foreign accounts. I appreciate your love and concern but I think I will go with Moradeke on this and just play ostrich. Giving up going for the rotation is a small sacrifice. After all, I already have the residency spot in the USA and it is just four months." Ranti explained to her friends.

In March, Moradeke and Gboye left for England for the six weeks rotation, and Ranti wrote a letter of apology to Mr. Edwards that she was unable to come due to lack of funds.

A month before their final examinations in early May, a messenger from the dean came for Ranti. Her two friends went with her. They sat in the waiting room while she went in alone.

"Ms. Jare, you are to report to the Ministry of Education in Lagos immediately. I have a letter in my hand from the office of the minister that you were asked to report to the ministry three months ago but you refused. You are being investigated on charges of examination fraud. Do you care to tell me what the heck is going on?" Professor Cole demanded of her.

"Ranti, you will have to fight to the end," she told herself. "You started this fight to get an education right from elementary school. You and Lana fought hard and it cost him his life. This education is too precious because your brother sacrificed his life for it, when he injured his foot as the two of you ran away from the bookshop where you used to read books without paying for them. This education is too dear for you to give up now, so you will have to fight to the end. This is exactly what Esho has been telling you all your life. You have no one. You have to fight for yourself."

The dean looked expectantly at her.

"Sir, I'm as surprised as you are." Ranti started. "You are the dean of the medical school, have I ever been accused of examination fraud? Wouldn't you be the first to know, Sir, before the ministry in Lagos?"

He looked at her for a long time. "Ms. Jare, I don't know what's going on here, but I don't like the smell of it. You are a very brilliant young woman and have always had the best results in your class. I know you have been up against a lot in this college. Your female lecturers fight for you to be given honors in your classes, especially in obstetrics and gynecology and pediatrics, but the male lecturers refuse to award you the honors.

"Personally I am of the opinion that you deserve these honors in all your classes. The American Medical board even agreed with me; you had one of the highest scores in their board examinations that were not graded by us here.

"I know why the men are against you. It might seem as if I'm locked away in this office removed from everything, but I know what is going on in the college. Why the minister would concern himself with what should be a local matter is beyond me. This is a very corrupt country, Ms. Jare, and this man could prevent you from becoming a doctor which would be a tragedy not just for you but for this country."

Ranti started to cry. She could hear the chairman of the board of directors of her secondary school again, when he came to her and Esho to give her money so she could attend St. Ann's school after Akanbi stole her money. He had said exactly the same thing.

"Ms. Jare, what is your relationship with the minister?" He offered her a chair.

Ranti sat down and started her story while Professor Cole sat across from her, offered her a handkerchief and listened without interrupting her.

"The bastard! I did hear your story when he was governor of the state, but I didn't know the name of the student. The likes of him should be behind bars but this is Nigeria. It's very unfortunate. I wish you had come to me when you wanted to go for the rotation in England. The college would have helped you.

"His accusation is a very serious one though, and it could be very hard to prove that he is lying. He could intimidate a lot of your lecturers into accusing you of the same thing.

"Ms. Jare, we are up against a big problem here but I will try my best to help you. I want you to be assured of that. Stop crying. Keep studying for your examination and I will see what I can do. You have a month to go and you will become a doctor. I'll be honored to graduate you from this medical school."

Ranti nodded as she tearfully left his office.

"His only son is going to prison." Gboye said of Jamba as they left the dean's office, "We will go to the warden's office now, so I can call my brother in England and he will call the police on his son. Goke has a lot of information on him, including credit card fraud. I'm sure he's involved in credit card fraud as well."

Moradeke suddenly screamed, "I've got it!"

Ranti and Gboye looked at her.

"This is what we will do." Moradeke started, "We will go back to Professor Cole and tell him about Jamba's son in England. We will send an anonymous letter to Jamba with a warning that if he doesn't leave Ranti alone and if he does anything to jeopardize her ever becoming a doctor, his son would end up in prison in England.

"He will probably ask his son to come home immediately, but even then we can still tell the police in England, and Scotland Yard can still pick him up here in Nigeria. They've been known to do things like that and Funmi will publish the story in the newspaper and Jamba would lose his job."

"I like the idea, dirty for dirty, I like it very much." Gboye said. "I don't know if Funmi publishing the story in her newspaper will make the government fire him though. The people in our government have no sense of shame otherwise he wouldn't have been promoted after he tried to rape Ranti and he had raped other girls. But the blackmail could work and after you graduate in one month, Ranti, and you leave for the US like you planned, then we will report the son to the police in England. They are not finding credit card fraud funny at all."

Ranti was scared. But she realized she did not have a choice. This man was determined to ruin her life. He could even jeopardize her future in the US, though she already had the residency spot in New Jersey. She remembered Esho telling her after Jamba attacked her that she fought to win and it is a better way than fighting to kill.

She had been having anxiety attacks for the past three months, but she resolved that she would fight this time too and win. She agreed with Moradeke's plan and they returned to Professor Cole's office immediately.

He looked at them for a long time. "You girls do know how to take care of yourselves, don't you? I wish more girls would know they don't have to be victims. It's the only way we can fight him, in his own dirty way. And we have to act fast. I don't want him telling more people that you cheated on your examinations, Ranti. Clearing your name would be more difficult then. Who is going to write the letter? I will have it in his office first thing in the morning."

Gboye volunteered since she knew the details of his son's activities, which she included in the letter with specifics. She asked him to withdraw the accusation against Ranti by writing to the Dean that it had been a mistake and another student from another college committed the examination fraud, and that he should write a letter of apology to Ranti for making the mistake. Both letters were to be addressed to the Dean as his first letter had been and copies sent to Ranti.

The Dean reviewed the letter, made some corrections and had his secretary type it. He promised to get it to Jamba the next day.

Three days later the Dean called Ranti to his office again. Both letters arrived from Jamba and they followed Gboye's instructions.

Professor Cole was so happy that he hugged her. "Congratulations, in three weeks I will not address you as Ms. Jare anymore but as Dr. Jare."

Three weeks later when Ranti's result was released on a Wednesday afternoon and she passed her final examinations, she ran home to inform her grandmother that the struggle was over. She was a doctor.

Esho held her face in her hands the same way she did when she returned from England, five years before. "This is my child, Iranti. She is a doctor! My child is a doctor. Me, Esho, the daughter of Wura who died in childbirth because there was no doctor present and as such she could not raise her child. Me, who had to run away from rapists. Me, who carried cement on my head so that we wouldn't starve to death. Me, who has buried two children because I didn't have money for a doctor, or know any doctor to come to my rescue and save me.

"My child is a doctor today. Iranti, this is your face, I am holding Iranti's face in my hands. Thank you Iranti, thank you, I have triumphed. I have triumphed over my enemies. We did it, Iranti. We did it.

"Look at Akanbi, he lost his big job with the government and his children are school dropouts. Not one of them graduated from secondary school. Iranti thank you. You have made all my toil and hard work worthwhile; thank you for not bringing me to shame. Thank you my daughter."

Ranti wept as she clung to her grandmother. "I owe it all to you, Esho, I owe everything to you. It is your honor that I'm a doctor today."

Esho went out of their room and she called to her neighbors, most of whom had been living there since Ranti was born. "Our daughter, Iranti Jare, my child that all of you helped me raise became a doctor today. I want to thank you for your love and support. We have produced a doctor in this house. She is going to the white man's country next month to learn more about being a doctor."

The neighbors embraced Ranti and Esho as they congratulated them. They told Ranti they remembered when she was born. They touched her face the way Esho had touched her earlier and they were happy to be included in the success.

Esho took her headgear. As she started to wrap it around her head, she walked out of the house. Ranti noticed she did not have the knife in it. She did not tell Ranti where she was going, but Ranti knew she was going to Akanbi to gloat.

She smiled, "Esho deserves the triumph." She followed her at a distance, as she had that time eleven years before after Akanbi stole her money. She too wanted to see Akanbi's face when he received the news that she was a doctor.

Esho stood in front of Akanbi's house. She called out to him in her usual manner. The neighbors knew there was going to be a show so they stopped what they were doing and watched. Isa, the vagrant psychotic who wandered around the neighborhood, was not around this time and Ranti was thankful for that.

"Akanbi, bring your cursed head out of the house, I know you are there. Your car is out here. You son of the devil that should have been destroyed in Sodom and Gomorrah, or washed away in that flood in the Bible that I know you read. You are not a descendant of Noah. Akanbi bring your cursed head that smallpox will afflict out of your house." She yelled several times and after a while he came out and stood on his balcony.

"What is it this time you crazy witch?" He asked Esho, "What do you want from me?"

Esho gave a derisive laugh, "Want from you? Want from you? How dare you ask me a question like that? It's not as if you have ever done anything for me, or my child, rather you have been stealing from us. I don't want anything from you and I will never want anything from you, you thief, you lowlife scumbag, pedophile, rapist, armed robber." She spat on the ground in disgust.

"Me and mine will never want anything from you ever again for the rest of our lives. Rather, we will ignore you when at the dusk of your life you begin to panhandle on the streets before you are able to eat, or when no one wants you around them anymore because smallpox has begun to eat your body. I will live to see that day.

"I have triumphed Akanbi, I have triumphed. Iranti, the daughter of Oshun, the baby that you snatched from my breasts and got pregnant, not once, not twice but three times and each time you denied that you were the father of her children? *Paga!*" She hissed and spat on the ground again; still not able to believe that a person could be that wicked even after all the years.

"Iranti, whose money you stole eleven years ago even though you continue to deny her as your child and you never helped her, yet you went to the diocese and told them she was your child so you could steal her money? Agh! Wickedness!" this time she cocked her right index finger in her mouth in a gesture of stark raving disbelief at the cruelty, then she spat on the ground one more time.

"Iranti is a doctor today! Did you hear me? SHE IS A DOCTOR!" She shrieked at him while clawing her fingers toward him.

"Helpers came to me when I had no one and they helped my daughter and me, and she is a doctor today. We will never suffer again. I have triumphed. I am the mother of a doctor!" She proudly slapped her right palm on her chest. "From this day on, nobody should call me Esho anymore, all of you neighbors, do you hear me? As from this moment on, my name is Mama Doctor because I am the proud mother of a doctor.

"That's all I have to say to you, Akanbi. I advise you, pray for smallpox to come and take you out of your misery very soon, because the misery coming to you will be worse than the kind that was visited on that man Job in the Christian Bible. I'm sure you know the story of Job since you go to church every Sunday. But unlike Job whom God saved because he realized that the errors of his way was in his arrogance in calling himself a pious man, he became humble even though he was already a good man and God saved him and blessed him abundantly. For you, Akanbi, there will be no redemption because you have been flaunting your shamelessness in the face of God; you've been behaving as if you are a God yourself.

"You are going to suffer in vain, because like I have been telling you since the day you first came to steal milk from my children's mouths, you are cursing your god with your behavior!" She spat on the ground one more time, turned around and made for home.

The neighbors hugged Esho, congratulating her. They accepted her instructions and started to address her as "Mama Doctor." They hugged Ranti as well and some of them said they would send their sons and daughters to her, so she could advise them on ways to get into the university.

Ranti watched Akanbi. His face was expressionless but he held her gaze, and she locked gaze with him as well. She felt some stirrings in her heart, but it was not of triumph like Esho felt; she could not describe the feelings, but it was very uncomfortable, of fear? Or pity? She was not sure. She broke his gaze and followed her grandmother home.

She returned to the university later in the day to phone Efunwunmi Jacobs inviting her to the graduation ceremony. She had maintained contact with her over the years and Efunwunmi had traveled to Ibadan once to see her in her third year. Efunwunmi was happy that Ranti thought so well of her to invite her to the ceremony.

"Mrs. Jacobs, there is no way I would have become a doctor without you. You

180   *Feasts of Phantoms*

saved me from becoming an invalid. You saved my life. Every day I have sent a prayer of thanks to you. I wouldn't have become a doctor without you."

Ranti had continued to thank Efunwunmi and Depo in her mind all through her medical education, especially when she rotated in obstetrics and gynecology, and saw many women who had fistulae, though it had been mostly from obstructed labor in unattended childbirth.

Most of them were outcasts because they constantly smelt of urine and feces. They had malnutrition and a host of other medical problems. She had watched as doctors tried to repair these women's fistulae and some of the time the surgery had failed, throwing such women into severe depression. Each time she saw a patient like this, she appreciated all over again the gift that Efunwunmi Jacobs gave her and she had grown to adore the woman.

The next morning, as Ranti, Gboye, Moradeke, Bode, Brian, as well as their classmates who passed their examinations were sworn in as doctors by Professor Cole, Esho beamed from ear to ear as she sat next to Efunwunmi.

The following day, Gboye made the call to Scotland Yard in England to inform them of drug trafficking and credit card fraud perpetrated by General Jamba's son, and a few days later she received a call from her brother in England that he had been arrested.

31

Ranti wrote until about five in the morning. At noon, knockings on the door woke her. She pulled on her nightshirt and opened the blind to check through the window. Abe was standing on the deck and when he saw her he waved. She let him in through the back door.

"You must forgive me. I didn't mean to interrupt your sleep. I came to check to be sure you were fine when I didn't see you on the beach today. You usually swim or walk in the mornings."

"Please come in, it's okay. I didn't go to bed until five; I was working on some things. It's time I woke up anyway." She stood away from the door to let him in.

"I was wondering if you would have that barbecue with me today, and I wanted to go swimming, so maybe we could swim together."

"Sure, give me about thirty minutes, I have to eat first." She said to him as she turned back to go to her room.

Ranti joined him about twenty minutes later. She was so excited she ate in a hurry. She kept telling herself to take it easy; he was interested in her, that was why he came to look for her and he was not going away. They spent the afternoon together swimming and sitting under his umbrella.

"So, where is this 'goodness knows where' you are off to in about five weeks?" She asked casually as she plopped down next to him on the mat.

"Afghanistan or Iraq, I don't know yet. I'm a freelance photographer. I sell my pictures to magazines and newspapers. I've been working on a picture book about the horrors of war. Those places are pretty hopeless these days. You just have to be thankful for what you have."

"Isn't it dangerous to go into Iraq at this time?"

He shrugged, "That's what I do. Every job is dangerous. What do you do when you are not waiting for the babies to be born?"

"I'm a gynecologist. I work in Nigeria. So I'm on an extended vacation for now, till the babies are born and till I raise enough money to go back." She explained the details of her work to him.

"Uhn, 'Hope out of Despair.' I'll like to photograph those women before, and after you return their hope to them. That is really remarkable. I have good contacts at the New York Times and Newsweek magazine. They could do an article on you and your work to attract more funding. I'm sure lots of westerners will sympathize. How did you get interested in this kind of work?"

Ranti did not want to tell him she was the one searching for 'Hope out of Despair,' at least not on a first date. "Let's just say it's something very close to home for me. These are my people doing this to our daughters. You know what I read in a book once? *'Everything I have written is most minutely connected with what I have lived through, if not personally experienced; every new work has had for me the object of serving as a process of spiritual liberation and catharsis; for every man shares the responsibility and the guilt of the society to which he belongs. That was why I once inscribed in a copy of one of my books the following dedicatory lines: To live is to war with trolls in heart and soul, To write is to sit in judgment on oneself.'*

"He is right you know, especially about sharing in the guilt and the responsibility of the society to which we belong, so this is my way of attempting to liberate myself. I wish I could do more though, especially in the area of preventive education. It's so easy to destroy something but yet so difficult to build anything." She looked pensively at the ocean.

"Each time I call my mother, she says to me, 'Abe, I hope you find what you seek.' I don't know what I seek, but it's like I need to keep moving. I'm forty-five years old and it's only in the past couple of years that I realized I needed time to unwind, and I've been coming here once a year for six to eight weeks. Before then, I just moved from one disaster to another.

"Coming here gives me time to think. The ocean, it is calming, but then I start to get itchy and I can't wait to be off to the next chaos. Bosnia, Typhoon, Rwanda, Darfur, I have been there. It's like these places beckon to me. I think my mother is right, but the truth is, I don't know what it is that I seek.

"Okay, we're going too deep here." He smiled at her. "You know I'm going to ask the pertinent questions. Why are you doing this all by yourself, I mean the pregnancy and that man who was here over the weekend, who is he?"

Ranti looked at him. "He's my best friend and the father of my children." She caressed her naked abdomen.

"I saw the two of you a lot over the weekend, mostly here at the beach. I wanted to say hello but I didn't want to intrude. I saw you at the restaurant as well. He loves you very much," he paused for a moment, "He's gay, isn't he?"

Ranti gave him a sharp look.

"You don't have to be Einstein to figure that one out. You told me you are not married and you don't have a boyfriend; you are just pregnant, and here is this devoted man who is your best friend and the father of the babies."

"I suppose so," Ranti nodded as she looked away.

"He is a lucky guy."

"No, I'm the lucky one. He has been a blessing in my life. He is very dear to me. So what about you, any wife tucked away somewhere or a sweetheart, children?"

He shook his head, "No, I haven't been that lucky. I tried marriage once, a while ago. I was married for about five years but whatever it is that I'm seeking interfered. I'm not good at long-term relationships, but the short flings leave a bitter taste in my mouth too.

"I envy those guys who are able to settle down, go to a job every day and return to their homes in the suburbs, to their children and wives. I'm a nomad. I worry that I'll wake up one day and I'll be a lonely old man. But at the same time, it's like, if I don't go to all the boiling places in the world to put the catastrophes on record, I'll die. Does that make sense?"

Ranti nodded. "It's the same for me too. I work in Nigeria, and compared to my peers I'm a pauper because I work for free, and I have nothing to my name, not a dime; the only things I can call mine in this world are these babies.

"I could be practicing in America and taking home over three hundred thousand dollars a year, but when I see the faces of the women after their surgery and they are dry, not draining urine or leaking feces, the gratitude which they are not able to express in words, but that you could read in their faces? It is worth more than a billion dollars and no matter what the hardship or the risks involved, I'm ready to go on. For me too, it is like do this work or die.

"And it is like going to the boiling places in the world because for some bizarre reasons, these women's communities don't want them helped in this way. Twice, my patients have been killed. They were teenagers, because once they are free of the burden of leaking urine and feces, they bloom, and become the beautiful women they are, and they begin to exercise their sexual rights, and then they are accused of prostitution and killed. I can't go back now. I have to find a way to get to these women. These are things I will worry about after I have the babies."

"We are in similar professions, exposing the horrors of the world. Maybe you are seeking something too, and I hope you find it," Abe said to her as he caressed her left hand.

"Thank you. May we both find what we seek so in our old age we will not be alone," Ranti said to him.

He nodded. "Does it mean your work has prevented someone from marrying you?"

"I was married once, but I left. He didn't treat me well."

"I'm sorry," he said, and she nodded.

Later in the evening, when Ranti told Mrs. Sanchez she was going to Abe's cottage for dinner, the older woman nodded saying "Mr. Abe, okay."

He kissed her as he let her in. "You look great, though I prefer you in the bikini. You shouldn't wear clothes at all."

"Sure, and the police would have locked me away in some nudist prison, and we wouldn't have met."

He offered her a soft drink, reminding himself she should not drink alcohol in her condition, as he sat her down in his living room. He continued to go out to the deck to check on his barbecue. After a while, Ranti followed him out on to the deck overlooking the ocean, just like the deck in her cottage.

After they had eaten and were sitting on the couch talking, Abe moved closer to her and asked her if he could kiss her. She nodded. He took her in his arms and kissed her softly on the lips.

He moved closer still, and in a protective manner gathered her in his arms. He kissed her again on the lips and Ranti wanted to dissolve into his arms so she could enjoy his kisses. It was at that moment she realized how much she missed being held and kissed by a man. She wanted more, but at the same time she was afraid.

She wanted so much for him to make love to her but then she remembered the last time anyone had sex with her. That was her ex-husband raping her and she aborted her unborn baby that night.

She reminded herself that just like Esho had repeatedly warned her, and as she had come to find out for herself, sex is a destroyer of life. In her history, it had led to too many deaths.

But she wondered, "How could something that is supposed to bring people together in love be so deadly? Without sex there would be no procreation and humanity might come to an end, except for the rare cases like mine where people get pregnant through expensive medical technology.

Feasts of Phantoms

"Sexual intercourse," she thought, "is that indispensable temporary merging of human beings. It is the tapping into that fountain of regeneration, of bounty and creativity that keeps us sane and alive, the fountain that keeps us human, the must-have fountain of all-giving and all-knowing, that primal place we must visit often to be able to continue in this demanding world.

"I have suffered too much in this pregnancy to lose these babies now. These are very expensive babies in every way. Medical bills alone are over a hundred thousand dollars and there will be more to come, and I know Depo is not complaining, but then the emotional cost of the two failed conceptions, as well as the morning sickness everyone suffered through, not just me, but Depo, Grant, my girlfriends and even Boris. I am over forty years old and this might be my last chance of being a mother. I don't want to waste it over the desire for a one-night stand. I have waited twelve years without sex. Why not wait another six months?"

She instructed herself to get up and leave Abe's cottage. She did not want to lose the babies because she was tired of all the deaths, but at the same time she wanted Abe to hold her and love her.

"I want to be held in love by a man. I want to connect with another human being because that is what sex is about; it is about connection, feeling human and being held by another human being. I know that it has been perverted by many because of pain and trauma. In my family, we have only known about the perversion of sex, but in my head I know it is a wonderful thing. Look at Depo and Grant. Look at Moradeke and Bode. It is a wonderful thing and though I have known only the perversion of it, I want to experience the wonder of it too. I want to feel like silk.

"I want to leave this desert that has been my habitat, a place where I cannot find the source of life-giving water. I want to move to a fertile land, a land dripping with milk and honey, a land of rain, mist, dew and of fertility, survival and wholesomeness. Like the poem, *The Waste Land*:

> Here is no water but only rock
>
> Rock and no water and the sandy road
>
> The road winding above among the mountains
>
> Which are mountains of rock without water
>
> If there were water we should stop and drink
>
> Amongst the rock one cannot stop or think
>
> Sweat is dry and feet are in the sand
>
> If there were only water amongst the rock
>
> Dead mountain mouth of carious teeth that cannot spit
>
> Here one can neither stand nor lie nor sit
>
> There is not even silence in the mountains

But dry and sterile thunder without rain.

There is not even solitude in the mountains

But red sullen faces sneer and snarl

From doors of mudcracked houses.

"I came to the ocean for this and I want to take the fullness and the solitude and the freedom of the flying singing birds into my heart, into my mind. I want to know a fertile land. Iranti," she encouraged herself, "Abe is not Brian. He is a gentleman. He is not a rapist. Take the frightening leap and give him a chance."

"Ranti, I want to make love to you. I have wanted to make love to you since the first time I saw you at the store, when you wouldn't let me give you a ride home. Can I make love to you?" He interrupted her thoughts.

She hesitated for a moment but she nodded.

"Is it okay with the pregnancy?"

She nodded again as she told herself that he understood. "He is aware that I'm in a vulnerable position because of the pregnancy. He will be gentle with me."

He took her to his bedroom, he sat on the bed and as she stood in front of him, he gently helped her out of her loose voile pant and shirt.

"Gosh! What a beautiful body!" He exclaimed. "It's just perfect."

He kissed her bulging abdomen and gently untied her thong. He caressed her butt and she closed her eyes. He pulled her toward him as he helped her lie next to him.

She was both excited and scared, but she repeatedly reassured herself, "This is perfectly natural and this is the way it's supposed to be. He is none of the men who had hurt me in the past. I should give him a chance."

Abe was a very gentle lover. He kept asking her if she was okay and he told her where he wanted to touch her. It was as if he could sense her previous trauma and after a while she was able to banish her fears and relax in his arms.

She did not close her eyes. She kept them open and looked deeply into his eyes and he maintained eye contact with her. She read acceptance in his eyes. He stayed with her. He was not somewhere else and his eyes did not inform her that he wanted to be somewhere else.

She felt like silk; his touches were soft like whispers and her heart almost stopped. As he climaxed, tears sprang from his eyes such that he looked like an angel to her.

She removed her right hand from his back where she had been holding on to him and caressed his face. She used her right thumb to wipe some of his tears and she licked it. He smiled at her through his tears. She bent toward him and kissed him on the lips and on his eyes. He held on to her without saying a word.

Ranti could not believe the gift she was just given. She did not have an orgasm, but she felt wonderful. "Someone finally made love to me. This is what it feels like to be made love to," she told herself repeatedly.

In the morning, when she awoke, he was still asleep as he tightly held on to her. She kissed his face and he awoke. He gave her a big smile and returned her kiss. He started to kiss her all over her body and Ranti leant back into the pillow and gave in to him.

He touched her in his whispering way again, and tears came to her eyes because it was as if he were reading her a poem of hope, and not the poem of wasteland that was stuck in her head. He kissed her eyes and asked her if she was okay. She nodded. "It's so beautiful, it's like art," she told him.

He kissed her again as he continued to love her, and for the first time in her life she had an orgasm while in a man's arms. She lay in his arms as tears of gratitude streamed down her face. She wanted to say thank you to him, but she did not have the words. The tears continued down her face. Abe looked at her and he seemed to understand. He took a tissue and wiped at her face.

Later, they went swimming in the ocean and Ranti could not believe that the height of good feeling was possible. It was as if she kept outdoing herself in that area. She had thought she felt her best when the smell disappeared, or each day, after she had written more of her life story and was able to release the ghosts to the wind to bear them away, but after being held and loved by Abe, she told herself she had climbed to the highest mountain in the world.

She stole a glance at him as he swam away from her. She warned herself to hold on firmly and not allow herself to slip. She should not go falling in love with him because of his gentleness and sweetness, and because he was the first man to make love to her. His gentleness and probably because he was a "seeker" too, which must be responsible for his sensitivity, made it possible.

She warned herself not to lose focus because he had made it clear that he was a nomad, and she had learnt to leave unwilling men alone and not go pursuing them. She told herself she had to learn to separate gratitude from love.

32

As Ranti walked into her cottage at about ten in the morning, she could smell Mrs. Sanchez cooking and she felt hungry enough to eat an elephant.

The phone rang. "Hello, this is Jack calling from New York. Can I speak to Ranti please?"

"The dog walker," she smiled to herself. "Hello, how are you? This is Ranti."

"It's so great to hear your voice. This is the third time I've called. There is no voice mail to leave a message. How are you? How are the babies? I was disappointed when I didn't see you at the diner three days in a row. Initially I thought I was just missing you, but then I asked Boris, and he told me you haven't been feeling well and you went to the island. I hope you are feeling better."

"Thanks, much better. And thanks for calling. Sorry I missed your calls. I've been spending a lot of time on the beach. How is it going with you? How are the dogs?"

He chuckled, "They are fine. So when are you coming back to the city, you still owe me a dinner date, remember?"

"I do, in another four or five weeks, I think."

"That long? I don't think I can survive that long without seeing you, remember I was seeing you almost every day for six months. I had kind of gotten used to seeing you at Boris', I told him the place is not the same without you. He misses you too."

"I know. I miss him too, a lot. But coming here has been very good for me and the babies. I was running the risk of losing them because I was so sick. But I'm feeling much better now and the babies are kicking like crazy these days."

"The ocean air will do that for you. I love the ocean too. I'm glad you and the babies are doing fine. It's so good to hear your voice. Can I call you again sometime?"

She giggled to herself as she hung up and went to take a shower.

She spent the rest of the week with Abe who came to her cottage in the evenings, sometimes bringing food or eating Mrs. Sanchez' dinner, and then he would spend the night with her talking or watching movies. In the morning they would go to the ocean to swim. Ranti did not return to her writing.

On Thursday morning Depo called to tell her he would not be able to come for the weekend, as he had deadlines at work. Ranti was not too disappointed because it afforded her more time with Abe.

Jack called her later on Friday as he had promised and tried to convince her to come back sooner to New York City. She assured him that she would have dinner with him like she promised, before the babies are born.

Spending time with Abe and enjoying the way he was treating her made her begin to think a lot about her failed marriage and ex-husband. She could not believe that a partner could treat her in such a decent manner.

She acknowledged that the relationship was new, barely a week old and people put forth their best foot early in relationships, but she remembered clearly that none of the men she dated in medical school even bothered to do that in the first weeks with her.

They had been too demanding and too demeaning of her, as if they were doing her a huge favor by going out with her, and she had felt that they were doing her a huge favor. Those were times she felt worthless about herself, with all the trauma of genital mutilation, and she believed she smelt of urine and feces. She realized that she had somehow invited them to treat her in that way. On Friday morning, she returned to her laptop and continued her story where she had left off.

Ranti returned home to Esho for the two weeks before she left for America that June of 1987, while Moradeke and Brian started their internship. Gboye planned to leave for the US in August. She had asked Ranti if she could live with her while she studied for the board examinations, and Ranti had happily agreed.

Moradeke on her part did not want to leave Nigeria because of Bode who was interning in Lagos, although they both planned to move to the US later for residency training as well.

Four days after their graduation, Brian asked Ranti to marry him. She was ecstatic that someone chose her. She had been afraid that she was so worthless that no one would ever pick her to be his wife, "He wants a life with me; he does not see me as a toy after all," she told herself.

She accepted his proposal, but did not want to get married right away, as he wanted. Brian insisted that if they were married, then he could accompany her to the US as her spouse, traveling on her visa, but if they did not get married, he might not be able to join her.

Ranti asked for time to think. She was afraid to tell her grandmother she wanted to get married, because Esho was anti-marriage and she had been particularly happy since Ranti became a doctor and had continued to sing to herself that she triumphed over her enemies. Ranti did not know how to tell her she was bringing an "enemy" home.

Brian continued to pressure her to marry him before she left, and said that if they did not get married he might meet someone else. Ranti did not like the pressure, so she confided in her friends.

"He wants to use you to go to America, Ranti. If he really loves you and wants to marry you, he can wait a year. He can work hard and pass his own examinations and then follow you, going on his own visa. Don't give in to his pressures," Gboye advised her.

Ranti did not want to give in to the pressure, but at the same time she was afraid he might lose interest in her and pursue another girl, a girl more beautiful and more desirable than her, and there were lots of such girls around.

Moradeke response to her fears was, "Then you don't want to be with a person like that. It really means he wants to use you. Tell him to study for his examination, and if he really wants you that badly then he should come after you, he should fight for you in that way. Look, he's a jerk and wants to exploit you Ranti. You know how difficult it is to get a visa to the US. I don't think you should marry him. What do you think, Gboye?"

"Forget him," was Gboye's curt reply. "The asshole is trying to use you. Don't marry him. There are plenty of good men who would marry you, Ranti."

"Not in my world; no there aren't good men, the only good one happens to be gay," she said to herself.

A few days later, while she and Brian were in bed, she suddenly asked him, "Why do you want to marry me, Brian?"

He looked at her for a while, "What kind of question is that?"

Ranti gave him an intense look.

"Because you are a doctor," he hesitated, "you have a bright future."

"What? You want to marry me because I'm a doctor? There were forty girls in our class who are now doctors, and there are hundreds of girls in training to become doctors. Why don't you go marry one of them? You are an asshole Brian, oh my gosh!"

She got out of bed and started to put on her clothes.

"Come on, Ranti, that's not the only reason. I love you. You are a very beautiful girl."

"Really Brian, I'm a beautiful girl? How come you've never told me that before? You always criticize my clothes and hair style; you've never paid me compliments!"

"You are beautiful, but not all that beautiful, don't let it go to your head. My mom still takes the crown, and I know a lot of girls more beautiful, but I picked you. I want you to be my wife. I chose you, Ranti, I didn't want all those other more beautiful girls," he explained to her as he pulled her toward him.

Ranti got back into bed with him. She told herself that he picked her over all those other more beautiful girls with solid homes who never smelled of urine or feces. "And of course he is right. I know I'm not a beautiful girl, I'm not delusional."

Depo thought she was beautiful but he chose to have sex with men and not her. She convinced herself to be grateful to have Brian. He was handsome and her children would be beautiful after all. He would save her from lots of humiliation and shame.

A week later Brian took her home to visit his mother and aunts, and the women kept dropping hints about the two of them getting married before Ranti left for America. One of the aunts suggested that Ranti should not go without Brian if she really cared about him.

Ranti affirmatively told her she was going.

"You could lose him, you know. There are lots of girls who would give their right arm to marry a doctor, especially one as handsome as my nephew," she said, and Ranti panicked because she believed she was not good enough for his family.

"It's not good for a young woman to go abroad by herself. I hear all kinds of stories about what our girls get up to abroad; they go into prostitution and fight over men and it's because they are so lonely being so far away from home," the aunt continued.

"I'm a doctor. I don't have to become a prostitute. I'll be making enough money to take care of myself," Ranti asserted again.

"Ha, Brian, are you sure you want to marry a doctor? Women doctors are so arrogant. The way they look down on other people, it's as if they were too good for anyone. They don't make obedient wives. As a nurse working in the hospital, I see a lot of them that are divorced within two years of marriage because they refuse to listen to any man. Ranti is already arrogant as you can see, telling me she can take care of herself. If you can take care of yourself why don't you marry your money then? Let me tell you, '*pride goes before fall*' young woman. Who do you think you are?" The aunt responded, giving her a very dirty look.

Ranti kept hearing her friends' advice that she should not marry Brian. She realized she was going to have problems with his aunts, especially as Brian just sat there, not defending her.

But she desperately needed to get married. It was an urgent feeling for her, as if, if she did not marry someone, then it would be confirmed, she was worthless. And she did not want to be worthless. It would mean she was only good as a toy for men and not good enough for normal people to want her in their families, and she wanted to belong to a family of mothers and fathers and aunts, uncles and cousins.

"Ranti, apologize to Brian's aunt. You are going to be a wife in this family; you have to learn to be respectful and not answer back when spoken to. We all know you are brilliant and beautiful, but those are not assets that will help you stay married. Humility is the most important attribute that will help you stay married. Your in-laws have a lot of power over you; they can tell your husband what to do, whether to care for you or not, and even if he should marry a second wife. If you want to stay married and not be replaced by another woman, you have to be humble," Brian's mother advised her.

Ranti imagined what Esho would do to her if she caught her with these women listening to their stupid talks. But she did not want to end up like Esho, alone, lonely and bitter. She told herself that it must be the prize you pay to belong.

"She is not even all that beautiful, she is too short," the aunt continued to talk about her as if she were not in the room. "It's women like her who get fat once they have given birth to one or two children and then it will be obvious to their husbands that he married an illusion. And that is when men start running the streets looking for truly beautiful women."

Ranti looked to Brian to defend her but he did not; he pretended as if he was not there.

"I'm sorry, I mean no disrespect," she apologized to Brian's aunt.

"You can't kneel down, oh, now that you are a doctor, you are too big to kneel down to anyone," the aunt asked, still determined to torment her.

"I was brought up not to kneel down to anyone but I mean no disrespect," she tried to explain to the woman. Some part of her was determined to fight back. She cursed herself for kneeling down to them five months before.

"Mama Brian," the aunt turned to Brian's mother, "good luck with this one. If you want my advice, Brian should not marry her; she is going to be trouble because she is too arrogant."

Ranti wanted to cry. Her life in elementary school flashed before her eyes, when shortly after her brother died, she had to do the work of emptying feces and the neighborhood kids and her classmates ostracized her, and started to make fun of her each time they saw her.

She stood up and told Brian she would like to leave.

"I'm not ready to leave, I'll see you later." He said to her.

"But you brought me here in your car."

"Take a taxi since you are in such a hurry."

The aunt was not done with her. "Tell me Ranti, who is your father? Who are the Jare's? Where are you from? I don't know any family with that name."

Ranti remembered the governor calling her a bastard when she told him she did not have a father. If she told Brian's family her family history, they would ridicule her.

"We are from Ibadan," she answered the aunt.

"I don't know any family with that name and I know every family worth knowing in this city. What does your father do for a living?"

"He is dead. He died when I was four years old and my mother died when she was pregnant with a baby a few months later. My grandmother raised me."

"What did he do before he died, this father of yours."

"I don't know."

"You don't know? I knew it! She is from a broken home. Maybe the woman you call your grandmother is your mother who got pregnant out of wedlock. Brian, you can't marry her. Her mother is a prostitute. What does she do for a living, this grandmother of yours? Where does she live? Where is your home? We will come to your home, you know, at least to ask the head of your family for your hand in marriage. You didn't think of that when you started lying, trying to seduce Brian here. You saw a handsome doctor from a well-to-do Ibadan family, and you thought you could just marry him to give you a good name. It isn't going to happen because we have to do a thorough investigation of your family and background."

Ranti panicked. She started to smell urine and feces and to feel the genital pain she had before the surgery. Her palms broke out in sweat and she repeated to herself, "We are not like other women, we are playthings for men; no one will marry us and make us their wives or the mother of their children."

She looked around the room and everyone stared at her, including Brian. She kept thinking, "He is not even defending me. He has thrown me to the hyenas." She wished her girlfriends were with her, especially Gboye. She slowly picked up her purse and walked out of the house. Brian did not stop her and he did not come after her.

She was too ashamed to tell her girlfriends what she had endured. They had told her to forget about Brian and of course she could not tell Esho either. But she was full of despair.

Later that night while they were getting ready to turn in for the night, Esho who was still in a celebratory mood said, "You know what I would love more than anything in this world, Iranti?"

Ranti turned around to look at her.

"I would love to go to my village, where I was born. I will like to take you there and show you off to all the people who shunned me and wanted to make me their foot mat.

"I know my father is dead but if he were still alive, I want him to see you and to know that I raised a doctor. I want my stepmother to see you. I'm sure they have not produced a doctor in that village."

Ranti was quiet for a long time. She sat down heavily on the mat. "What is the name of your village, Esho? What was your father's name?"

"Alebido Ekiti. It's near Ikole. My father's name was Ojo."

"Do you want to go Esho? We can go before I leave for the US. I will come with you," Ranti offered. She wanted to go more to have a sense of having some roots and of belonging to a place where the family name was old. To be able to prove to Brian's aunt that she had family too, family that extended to more than just her grandmother, but Esho made it clear they were not going for a family reunion.

"Oh, Iranti, if there is anything I love in this world, it is revenge. I will prance and show off, I will gloat. I bet none of my half brothers' and half sisters' children amounted to much, like Akanbi's children. I want to gloat, Iranti, because I worked hard for this. I want to enjoy it."

Ranti looked at her grandmother and something scared her about her thirst for revenge. A picture of Esho behind bars flashed through her mind, if while she was in the US, Esho took matters into her hands as far as Akanbi was concerned and she assaulted him.

"Esho, come with me to America. I'm going because of your hard work. There is no one who deserves this more than you do. It is a faraway place and I might not see you for a whole year. Come with me, please, you are all the family I have; we shouldn't be separated, there is no need for it."

Esho was taken aback. "I can't go to white man's land. What will I do there? Who will I know there? I hear it's very cold. No I'm staying here with my own kind."

"Esho, you will know me there and I will know you there. You have been working all your life and you need a rest. I am a doctor Esho. I will be earning enough money that the two of us won't be able to finish spending. This is your victory, you are all I have," Ranti appealed to her.

Esho thought for a moment. "That means your answer is no. You won't go with me to my village so I can show you off."

"Esho, I read in a book that sometimes a victory is won that no one else knows about, but for the person who won it, and it is not less sweet. You have triumphed. Let's leave it at that."

Esho was quiet for about five minutes. Ranti lay on the mat and turned toward her.

"I have been thinking of you in the white man's land. I have been thinking that I will miss you. You are all I have, Iranti, and if you say you want me to come with you, I will come with you."

"Thank you Esho, thank you," Ranti ran to hug her. "But I'll have to go first since we have money for just my ticket. But as soon as I get there, and find a place and work to earn some money I will send for you, in August. That's in two months, and that is when Gboye plans to come and the two of you could come together. It would be easier that way."

Esho nodded. "So we shouldn't waste money going to Alebido Ekiti."

A week later Ranti left for the US without seeing Brian. He did not know where she lived, because she had never brought him home with her, and she did not go to look for him. But she knew if he really wanted to see her, he would have gone through either Moradeke or Gboye.

Gboye drove her to the international airport in Lagos. Moradeke, and Esho who had never been to Lagos, came along. Efunwunmi met them at the airport as she had promised Ranti when she came for her graduation two weeks before.

Ranti looked at the four women who were very dear to her and she started to cry. Esho appealed to her not to cry since she would see her in less than two months. Her friends promised to take care of Esho and help her with travel plans.

She arrived in the US on the 20th of June 1987, ten days before her residency training was to begin. She took a taxi to the hospital in New Jersey as she was advised, and the chief resident of her program took her to a furnished apartment close to the hospital, where she could stay up to six months. She unpacked her one suitcase and ate the Chinese food he got for her; then she called Depo as she promised him she would. When he answered the phone, he asked her for her number so he could call her right back.

"I don't want you piling up your bill, as you must be on limited funds for now," he explained to her when he called back within minutes.

Ranti was so happy to hear his voice that she started to cry. "I'm homesick, Depo, I miss home so much. I wish I hadn't come here at all. I'm so alone. I have never been alone, Depo. Esho was always there in our one room, and then I always had you, Moradeke and Gboye. This apartment is too big."

"Honey, you still have us. It's so good to hear your voice. We have not spoken to one another in four years. I wish I could touch you and hug you. I miss you Ranti. I'm coming over as soon as my classes are over at the end of the month, like I promised, so don't worry, I will see you in less than two weeks."

Ranti continued to cry. "Thanks Depo, thank you so much. You are a lifesaver as always. I saw your mom, she is fine and she came to see me off at the airport."

"I love you Ranti, very much. So don't cry, you will be fine, it's overwhelming when you are in a foreign country and do not know anyone. You know what? I have a cousin in Philadelphia, I'll give him your number so he can call you and if there is any problem, you can call him, okay?" He reassured her some more before he hung up.

Ranti called Moradeke to let her know she had arrived in the US safely and to let Gboye and Esho know.

She spent the following week in orientation into the program and getting all the necessary documents such that by June 29th when Depo arrived, she was happy she had the last day of the month off.

He came to the apartment by taxi from the airport and when she opened the door for him, she jumped on him and held on tightly to him like she would never let go. She started to cry. He hugged her too, and when he was finally able to pry himself from her, he had tears in his eyes as well.

Ranti looked at him and she had never seen anyone more beautiful in her life. She hugged him and kissed him again. "Depo, you are just the most beautiful man I know. I love you so much and I have missed you so much. Oh my gosh!"

"You are even more beautiful than I remember, and a doctor who is going to start her training as a gynecologist! I am so proud of you. You are amazing, Ranti, do you know that now, do you know that you are amazing? Just look at you." He kissed her again.

She settled him into the second room and they had dinner. They kept looking at one another, laughing, hugging and kissing. They spent the next day in New York City, sightseeing and just walking around and trying to catch up on their respective lives.

The following day, Ranti started her residency training. Depo stayed for a month although she saw him about three nights a week and one day on weekends, as she was in the hospital the rest of the time. He spent the time looking at firms that could hire him in New York City, so he could start the interviewing process while completing his final year of architectural training in France.

Ranti felt welcomed in her program by the other residents who were intrigued that she was from Nigeria, and she was impressed by the respect awarded to the residents by the faculty, and the fact that no one was sexually harassing anyone. For the first time in her life, she felt that lecturers were interested in her mind and not in just getting her into bed. She was relieved that she would not have to use her weapons of urinating or throwing up in someone's office in America.

On the last day of July she received her first salary, and they had time to go out for an expensive dinner. She paid her rent and necessary bills and had just a little left over. In mid- August when she received the first of her bimonthly paycheck, she was able to buy Esho's ticket.

Gboye and Esho arrived at the end of August and Ranti felt more at ease to have her grandmother to take good care of her.

Gboye started to study for the board exam and provided good company for Esho while Ranti was at work. Esho was overwhelmed in the foreign land whose language she did not speak.

Two weeks after they arrived, Gboye suggested they enroll Esho in a literacy program so she could learn English. In that way she would get more out of living in the US, because she would understand a lot of the programs on the television and radio. Ranti explained this to Esho in detail and she agreed, so she was enrolled in a program that was locally available.

Three months later when Gboye sat for her examinations she passed and started to apply to programs for residency training, and by February was accepted into a preliminary surgical program in the Boston area.

Moradeke and Bode were married in April of 1988. Ranti, Gboye and Esho returned to Nigeria for the wedding, as well as Depo.

Esho was happy to return to the only home she ever had—the one-room rented in Bere, and where her neighbors were happy to welcome her back. Ranti had agreed to keep the room. When they arrived this time, she suggested they buy beds, which they could afford, instead of continuing to sleep on mats on the floor, and Esho who after some initial discomfort of sleeping on a bed when she first arrived in the US, agreed to the purchase.

Brian was at the wedding and Ranti who was one of the bridesmaids tried to avoid speaking with him, but he came over to her at the reception.

"I've missed you, Ranti, I was a fool. I was angry with you when you left my mother's house that time and I expected you would apologize. You know you were rude to my aunt, and she is a very nice woman. The problem with you is that you are constantly up in arms, because you anticipate that someone would do something to abuse or insult you. She did not mean any harm. She was just trying to explain some things about our culture to you. God! You look great. I couldn't take my eyes off you through the church service. I don't want to lose you again."

Ranti looked at him, and she had missed him too. She had thrown herself into her busy first year of residency, but had continued to wish they did not break up. In her free moments she had continue to wonder if she would ever be good enough for any man to choose her. Even though her friends had continued to tell her there were plenty of good men in the world, and she would eventually meet someone decent, it had not happened for her. Moradeke married her sweetheart, and Gboye had continued her career in dating a lot of men, even when she got to the US; she found her way into the Nigerian community and had dated a lot of the single men there.

Ranti did not believe anyone would ever want her to be his wife. It was the curse on Esho's line. Even amongst her colleagues in the hospital, she had been asked out on dates, but they just wanted to sleep with her. She did not want to pursue a relationship just for sex; she wanted more.

"It's good to see you too, Brian." She started, "You know, the least you could have done on that day when your 'nice' aunt was abusing me was to have defended me a little. You threw me to the hyenas. I wouldn't have done that to you, and I don't want to be with a man I can't trust to take care of me. She wasn't teaching me about our culture! Remember, I am a Yoruba girl too, even more so than you are with your Irish names. She was abusing me and you just sat there as if you were dumb."

"Ranti, I'm sorry, she scares me too. I didn't know that's what you wanted. If you had told me that's what you wanted I would have stopped her."

"What? Come on Brian, you are not stupid. I needed to scream at you, 'Brian save me,' before you would come to my aid? I don't believe you, and even for the next few days it did not occur to you to come looking for me." She started to walk away from him.

He followed her. "Look Ranti, I'm sorry, I've really missed you. I didn't know I would miss you as much as I did. Give me a second chance, please. Let's start all over again. I love you and I want to marry you. I realized after you left that you are the only girl for me. I did go out with two girls and I tell you, I missed you terribly, I feel empty without you."

Ranti looked at him for a while. "No wonder you kept writing to me all the time, to let me know how much you missed me…"

"Oh come on, Ranti, give me a break, I didn't have your address in the US. I would have written to you."

"And I'm sure when you asked my best friend, Moradeke, whom you work with, and whom I know you talk to because she invited you to her wedding; she refused to give it to you, right?"

"Look Ranti, I say I'm sorry, I've been a fool, I really missed you. Give me a second chance and I'll prove to you how much I care about you. See, you are not even in Nigeria anymore, and you don't have to see my aunts or my mother. This is between the two of us. We are the ones who care about each other, not them. I was a fool and I lost sight of what's important."

Ranti hung out with him for the rest of the week before she returned to the US. She decided to give him a second chance because he looked contrite to her. When they had sex, he tried to be very gentle with her but Ranti, who was used to his way of making love, convinced herself that it was how it felt to be made love to by a man. She told herself she was the one who was too sensitive to pain because of her trauma of genital mutilation.

Gboye stayed back in Nigeria to take care of her visa and other necessary documents before her residency training began. Esho stayed as well so she could spend some time with her neighbors whom she had missed a lot in the eight months she was in the US. She assured Ranti that she would return with Gboye in June.

Ranti continued to be afraid to leave Esho alone. She was afraid she would get into trouble by assaulting Akanbi, whom she had continued to hate as vehemently as ever. So she had a serious discussion with her before she left.

"Esho, remember what I told you about victory that you achieved, that even if other people do not know about it, deep in your heart you know you have triumphed?"

Esho nodded.

"Please, Esho, I am begging you, leave Akanbi alone. It's okay to curse at him from a distance, but don't go near him at all, even if he provokes you in any way. Look at the condition of his life now. He is pathetic. He lost his job and his house that once used to be the most beautiful in the neighborhood is in ruins. We have more money than he does now, Esho, he can't hurt us. No one can hurt us in that way anymore.

"Esho, we won! You have been to America. No one in this area has ever been to America. Akanbi is already being punished for his evil ways. None of his children has amounted to anything, whereas your child, due to your hard work, has achieved a lot. Esho, please leave Akanbi alone. The gods are rewarding him already." Ranti paused for a while. "Don't go to your village either. Think of me, do you promise?"

Esho looked at Ranti for a long time and she reluctantly nodded her head in consent.

33

A week after Moradeke's wedding Ranti and Depo left Nigeria on Air France.

"Depo, I need to tell you something." She started when they had been airborne for a while. He gave her his full attention.

"I'm thinking of getting married to Brian. He asked me for the second time, and I said yes."

Depo stared at her in shock. "Why?"

"What? What do you mean why?"

"Why did he ask you to marry him?"

Ranti started to get angry, "Maybe, because he finds me desirable. Maybe, because he has been having sex with me, and he likes to have sex with me. Maybe, because he loves me, what do you mean why did he ask me to marry him? Some men find me desirable, you know."

"Ranti, please don't go there. You know that's not what I'm talking about." He pleaded with her.

"Please tell me what you are talking about then. You are my friend and I'm trying to talk to you and you are putting me down." Ranti knew she was being unreasonable, but she could not stop herself. She continued to be angry with Depo for not returning her affection. She tried to tell herself that he loved her as much as he possibly could, and that he could not help his sexual orientation but she just could not get a grip on her anger.

Depo continued to give her a tender look, and she burst into tears. He moved over to her and took her in his arms.

"Depo I want to be someone's wife. I want someone to want me and make me his wife. I don't want to be worthless, because that is how I feel, worthless. I love you, Depo but you can't love me the way I want to be loved. I want to have sex with my husband, and have children with him, raise the children in a normal home without fears. I want that and I refuse to accept that I can't have it."

"I know, Ranti, and no one deserves it more than you do. I'm sorry, I love you and I will continue to love you for the rest of my life. I'm sorry I'm not the man you want me to be. But I'm also protective of you. I don't know much about Brian but the little I know of him; he is not good enough for you. I was his roommate's friend before I dropped out of medical school and he is a user. He is superficial and flaky. It's like, if you are of no use to him, you are not on his radar."

"Maybe he's different now, Depo; he was young then, we were all young then. What did we know? He loves me, he told me that many times. I was seeing him before I went to the US. I've been seeing him since the fourth year but then we had a fight just before I left, and I think it was a way for us not to miss each other. You know how people would rather fight with you than say they would miss you. But when I saw him again, I realized how much I love him. He had never used me."

"People don't change, Ranti. We, you and I, have said good-byes to each other many times. We didn't fight. We told one another how much we would miss each other. We shed a few tears, and we were fine. That is how people who love one another behave. I don't think he has changed and I don't want him to hurt you."

"Depo, you are like a brother to me, and I want to marry him. I need your support. I need to know you will be there for me. Esho is going to give me a hard time about this, not because she doesn't like him, but you know Esho is against marriage or even a man and a woman talking to one another. So I'm going to have to fight her on this. I need you on my side."

Depo was quiet as he held on to her. After a while, "Ranti, I am on your side, and I always will be. But can I ask you to do just one thing? Can you give yourself time before you marry this guy? Just one year. You might meet someone else. You are a beautiful girl and very kind too, people will see that and want to marry you. You can do much better than this guy. That is all I ask of you, but if you decide to marry Brian, I will be there for you."

"I may be a beautiful girl to you, Depo, but I am not to a lot of people. No one is asking me to marry him. People who are in committed relationships are asking me to sleep with them. Gboye has a lot of friends in the Nigerian community in New York and New Jersey. I have attended a few parties with her, and married men hit on me, Depo. They know; they can smell it on me. Esho told me many times that the women in our line, that is what we are good for. Toys for men! I refuse to be a toy for men. This is the only man who asked me to marry him and I am marrying him."

Depo held on to her till they landed in Paris where he bade her goodbye until the summer when he would be moving to the US to begin work for a firm in New York City.

Brian started to write to Ranti and to call her on a regular basis as he continued to profess his love to her, and it helped her, such that she was not as lonely without her friends or Esho.

Esho and Gboye arrived in June, and Gboye left immediately for Boston in preparation for her residency training.

Esho continued with her literacy classes and study of English, and very soon was able to enjoy programs on television, with her favorite ones being violent movies of revenge. Whenever Ranti was available, she would invite her to watch the movies with her, and Esho would get all worked up as she sided with the underdog, and would begin to curse out the villains, yelling that they are not descendants of Noah and predicting that smallpox would afflict them.

Ranti was tempted on several occasions to tell her, "Thankfully, smallpox has been eradicated from the world." She realized that Esho had found her Akanbi in these American movies.

Before Depo arrived to begin his job in New York City in July, Ranti prepared Esho for his arrival since he would be staying with them until he found an apartment.

"Esho, there is something I need to discuss with you, and it is very important," she started one Saturday night after they returned from the movies.

Esho had seen the commercial for one of the movies she loved so much and she asked Ranti to go with her. She had enjoyed herself tremendously as the bad guy was fatally punished for his crime against the weak who were not able to defend themselves. She had talked about the movie all the way home, and how there is justice in this world after all, that it might take time but justice will still be served to the deserving. "If smallpox doesn't get them first, other good people with power would, and like they showed in the movie, and as I have always known, the god of retribution of today is not as slow as the god of retribution of yesteryears. Today, he flies in an airplane to mete out justice," she had concluded.

Ranti wanted to ask her what "smallpox" meant to her. She realized that her grandmother might have a totally different disease in mind, but she felt that a man coming to live with them was more important than debating smallpox as a lethal weapon.

"Esho, you know how over the years as you struggled to raise me and get me a very good education in spite of the unfavorable conditions of our lives, helpers have come to us. You remember the chairman of the board of directors at St. Ann's school?"

Esho nodded. "If there are angels in this world, he is one of them, and providence will continue to smile on him."

Ranti smiled because it was rare for Esho to pray for anyone. "When I went away to school, I met a lot of people like him. They were kind to me. Like Moradeke and Gboye have always been kind to me. They helped me and protected me from harm in many ways. I became very good friends with them. Do you remember the woman that came to my graduation, Efunwunmi? She was also at the airport to see me off when I was coming to America? You remember I told you that her son was friends with Moradeke, Gboye and I, and that he helped us a lot when we first started at the university especially when boys tried to harass us?"

Esho nodded. "And you told me that her son was in school overseas. That he changed from your university."

"That's the one, his name is Depo. He's a very good person, very kind and gentle, like the chairman."

Esho stared at Ranti.

Ranti continued, "He helped me a lot when I needed help and he has never asked anything in return." She wished she could tell Esho that he lifted off the curse Esho put on her head when his mother took her to England for the corrective surgery.

"He is coming to America. He's like Gboye was last year, trying to find his way here. He has a job in New York City, but he doesn't have a place to live yet and he needs to work for some time to save up so he can get his own place. I told him he could live with us for now. Esho, he is a good man and you will like him. He doesn't want to ruin my life and he has never done anything to make me think he has that intention."

Esho was quiet for about five minutes and Ranti patiently waited. She realized that Esho had never lived with a man before. Not since she was eleven years old when she ran away from home. The only other male she had lived with was Lana who died at the age of nine.

"Iranti, you are a woman now, a woman who is taking care of herself. You have your job, you have money, you have your own car, and you just bought a house. My child bought a whole house. Me who rented one room from someone all of my life, I couldn't even rent a big room. Me, who carried cement on my head so other people's homes could be built. I see the way people talk to you, with a lot of respect. They look up to you and admire you. They are impressed when they realize you are a doctor. I don't think any man can ruin your life now.

"Over the years you have taken care of yourself the way I could not. I remember when that 'calamity of a man' that smallpox is going to destroy, Jamba, tried to ruin you. You fought, Iranti, and you made me so proud. That is when I started to trust your judgment the way I could never trust your mother. I see your friends, and they are good people. Their parents are good people. If you say this Depo is a good man, and you want to help him as he helped you in the past, it is okay if he comes here to live with us. I will take care of you as I have been taking care of you. It is okay, Iranti."

Ranti hugged her grandmother. "You will like him, Esho. You will like him a lot because he is a good man."

Ranti continued to agonize over how she would present Brian to Esho. She was relieved about the way she accepted the idea of Depo and it gave her some hope that when she raised the issue of marriage, Esho would be accepting of it as well.

Depo arrived a few weeks later and he moved into the spare bedroom in her new three- bedroom house. Esho welcomed him and made him comfortable; she cooked for him and offered to wash his clothes. Ranti was very happy for his company, though they rarely saw one another as she was on call almost every other day.

A month after he arrived, on a rare free Sunday for her, he took her to New York City to show her the project his team was building. They had lunch and as they were walking around the city, he asked her if she was still going ahead with the marriage to Brian.

202   *Feasts of Phantoms*

She told him she was and he would like to get married by December.

He wanted to know if she had told Esho, and she said she had not.

"Ranti, that's a sign. You are having second thoughts too. You told her about me when I was coming, didn't you?"

Ranti started to get angry again. "You know something, Depo? It is not your place to tell me how to run my love life. Since you have removed yourself from that position, it is none of your business."

"That's not fair, Ranti. You know that is not fair."

"Isn't it? Isn't it? What am I to do?" She yelled at him in exasperation. Her eyes were blazing with anger. "Continue to pine for a man who can never make love to me? I love you Depo. Jeez, I love you more than you could ever imagine. I used to masturbate to the thoughts of you. And there I was, me, a person who doesn't have a clitoris, I used to come like crazy; I used to have such powerful orgasms and without a clitoris. That is how much I love you and wished you were this Brian or any other man for that matter.

"Do you know the last time I masturbated, the last time I had an orgasm? It was in my fourth year of medical school, when you wrote to me that you met that English boy, Dave. I stopped then and I have not touched myself since. I started having sex with Brian, and I haven't had an orgasm since then. It was an illusion, Depo, masturbating to you, because I am never going to have that. Brian is real and I want to live in the real world, even though it might not be all that pleasurable.

"I have not told Esho because she is anti-marriage, but she is getting more and more open minded since she has learnt to speak English and has been watching programs on television. She is learning a lot. I will speak with her when the time is right. This is the reality of my world, Depo. I'm not like other girls. I don't have the luxury of picking and choosing. I am not Cinderella whose prince is waiting in the wings for her."

"But you are *Sleeping Beauty* who is just in a hurry and can't wait for the right Prince to wake her, and so you are settling for less." Depo interrupted her. "You are wrong. You have a choice of picking and choosing. You are the one who sees yourself as someone who doesn't have a choice, and in that way you limit your choices. You are a very beautiful woman, Ranti. I'm not the only one who has ever told you that, in case you think since I'm not heterosexual I might not know what is beautiful in a woman.

"You are gorgeous, and you have the personality to go with it, but you continue to sell yourself short. You could be more, and you could go far. You are the kind of woman men marry to be their queens, and that is the least you deserve but you don't see that at all.

"You continue to see the scared little girl a lot of trauma was visited upon. And you make choices like you were still that powerless little girl, and that is why you are settling for this Brian. He is using you. He is using you to come to America. You have your own home, you are doing well in your program, you are taking good care of your grandmother, you don't need…"

"And I need a man to hold me at night, Depo." Ranti cut him off. "I want the whole package. I'm not stopping at just achieving success in my career. I want the whole package, wife, lover, mother and gynecologist."

"Ranti, listen to me," Depo persuasively started. "You are jumping steps. What you are doing is short-circuiting what can never be short-circuited; you are trying to cut corners here and doing such things usually ends in tragedy. I know you feel that because you had the genital mutilation you are worthless, and that if you marry this Brian, then it would mean that you are not worthless, so you can't wait for a good man and you are jumping into this marriage. But you are not worthless, Ranti."

She gave him a nasty look.

"Let me finish here," said Depo. "Do you know how many times I have wanted to propose to you, to ask you to marry me, or even try to have sex with you? Because if that could be so, it would appear to make life easy, but then we would both end up miserable.

"I am a gay man in a heterosexual world that is mostly homophobic, and I have to deal with it and go on with my life, I have to accept the fact that I wasn't born a straight man, and I have to live this life I have been given. I did a lot of work Ranti to come to that realization.

"What you are trying to do by marrying this Brian is trying to avoid the pain and the sadness that come with your history. You are trying to cover it over and make it not be so, you are trying to make all those trauma of genital mutilation and Esho's pain and trauma disappear and pretend as if they never happened. You are trying to rewrite your history. But they did happen.

"It isn't any different from an alcoholic or a drug addict who covers his or her pain with alcohol and drugs. They make the addiction their lives so they don't have to deal with the real pain; they use the addiction to block it, and you know how such people's lives turn out.

"I could cover the fact that I'm homosexual by marrying you, Ranti, and I would be behaving like an alcoholic or a drug addict. That is what you are doing, rushing into this marriage with Brian so you don't have to feel the pain. But it's an illusion and I'm afraid that it's going to end in tragedy because Brian will abuse you and repeat the trauma that you are trying to wipe out. It will be a repetition of your past history and not a new life, and a new life is what you need. That's all I have to say, Ranti."

Early in September, Ranti told Esho about Brian. "Esho," she started that Sunday afternoon while they were in the kitchen, being as careful of the way she presented the matter to her as she had always been. "I have some important news to tell you. There is a man who was my classmate in medical school; he's my friend and he's a good man. When we went for Moradeke's wedding, we met each other. He asked me to marry him and I have agreed."

Esho stood there in shock with the kitchen towel in her hand as she stared at Ranti. "I thought you would marry Depo. Who is this man and why don't I know about him?"

"Because I never told you about him, I don't want to marry Depo and Depo doesn't want to marry me. Depo has no intention of marrying ever. I do want to get married Esho, and I want children. It will be good for you to have grandchildren to care for. I want to be a mother."

"What is wrong with Depo, why doesn't he want to get married? He loves you. I see the way he looks at you, and he is a very good man. He is caring, he respects me and he is good company for me. There are not a lot of men like him around, you know. Why will you not convince him to marry you and why will you marry someone else?"

Ranti thought, "Esho, I am seven years ahead of you in that same thought, but it's not going to happen." She looked at her grandmother and did not know what to say. From the conversations with her lately, she realized that Esho had begun to appreciate that men and women could have sex without it being traumatic for the woman. She got that much from the movies and the talk shows. But she did not think Esho could wrap her head around the fact that some people are born homosexual. It was not on her horizon, and her head might just explode, so Ranti shamefully took the easy way out.

"Esho, don't ever say anything about this to anyone for as long as you live. You have to take what I am about to tell you to your grave." Ranti gave her an earnest look. "Depo cannot have sex. I don't know the details, but he had an accident when he was a little boy. So he can't give me children and I want children."

Esho was stunned, and she looked scared. She sat down on a chair close by and continued to stare at Ranti. Her hands shook.

Ranti was shocked at her reaction, but then it later dawned on her that Esho had wished that calamity on a lot of men, and it scared her that it could actually happen, especially to a man she had come to like a lot. Neither of them said anything about the matter again until the following week when Esho brought it up.

"What is the name of this man who wants to marry you?" Esho surprised Ranti by asking her suddenly one morning as she was hurrying off to work.

"Brian."

"Brian? What kind of name is that? Is he a white man? You cannot marry a white man. They are different from us, and the children you want so much will not look like you." Esho looked disgusted.

"He's a Yoruba man, he just has white names," Ranti snapped at her.

"Why? What's wrong with his people, they were too ashamed of being Yoruba that they gave him a white name?"

"Unbelievable," thought Ranti, "Esho is using her newly acquired literacy and understanding of English to participate in prejudice." She rolled her eyes. "I don't have time for this discussion now, I will see you tomorrow and then we can talk about it, and I will tell you why he has white names."

Esho did not bring up the subject again until the following Monday evening when Ranti returned from work. "Iranti, you know, sex is actually overrated," she started.

Ranti gave her a strange look.

"There is more to a marriage than sex," said Esho. "The fact that Depo cannot have sex should not stop you from marrying him."

"Of course you are a good authority on that, Esho, since you have tried marriage with sex and marriage without sex." Ranti said to herself.

Esho continued, "I asked Depo if he knew this Brian and he said he knows him. I asked him if he thinks he will make a good husband for you and he said that he trusted your judgment. He said you are good at taking care of yourself and he will look out for you and make sure you are fine." She paused and looked distracted.

"There is so much misery in this world, Iranti. Now that I watch television and understand what they talk about and I read Depo's newspaper, I see there is so much misery in this world." She paused for a moment. "Do you know that during Hitler's war, I remember Hitler's war, I was a little girl at the time; it was then that my father raped me, so I remember Hitler's war very well." She paused again. "But what I did not know is that he killed a lot of people because he did not think they were good enough. They didn't do anything to him, they didn't offend him in any way, but he just killed them. I saw it on television. Did you know this, Iranti?"

"Yes, Esho, I read it in one of my books when I was a little girl. He did it because he was an evil man. He didn't like anyone who didn't look like him, and even the people he killed were white like him."

"Ha!" Esho clapped her hands three times in dismay. She clasped her folded hands over her breasts. "I thought I've heard it all! You know, I used to think I was the only one in the world with bad luck, with a cursed head. But I'm not alone. Even the people with our color who live in this country, I was surprised when I got here and I saw a lot of black people like us; I thought everyone would be white. But Gboye told me their forefathers were enslaved and brought here hundreds of years ago. I watch television and they are still very angry about it, they still suffer from it. Uhn!" she exclaimed again. "Slavery!" she grunted and kept quiet for a while.

"I was never enslaved by anyone the way the ancestors of the black people in this country were enslaved, but I know about slavery, Iranti. I know about slavery because if you are not the master of your own head, you are in slavery. That is why I want so much for you. That is why I want you to be the boss of your own head. It is not just about being poor or not poor, Iranti. It is more. Do you know that you can be a millionaire and still not be the master of your own head? Do you know that, Iranti?" Esho gave her an intense look.

Ranti stared at her.

"I don't know how to explain it," Esho went on. "You know, because you have been such a good child and you listened to me and worked hard in school and you are a doctor today, you have pulled us out of poverty. We will never be poor again. Look at me, I don't even work anymore and I don't have to worry about money or where our next meal is coming from. But you know Iranti I am not the boss of my own head. There are feelings and thoughts that come over me and take possession of me, and I wish I had better control. I can't explain it, but I want you to have control of your emotions. Having a good job is just one part of it, I don't want you to be a slave to anyone, not like having a master the way black people in this country had masters, and not in your head too." She paused again and looked distracted as she stared out of the window.

"On television, they talk about fathers sleeping with daughters and having children by them, and some of the daughters are happy with it! I hear some things and I develop headaches for the rest of the day."

"Esho, if the programs upset you that much don't watch them. I know a lot of people who don't watch a lot of the programs, they call them trash."

"But I want to know! It's as if I have lived in darkness all these years, always thinking of what I will do to Akanbi since I took care of the mad man that gave me Oshun before I was ready, and I took care of my own father, but Akanbi got away. It continues to break my heart. That man, smallpox will afflict him and his bastards and ugly wife. He will panhandle at the dusk of his life. The calamities visited on Job will be child's play compared to the disasters that will happen to him…" She spent the next few moments cursing Akanbi.

She returned her attention to Ranti. "Anyway, this man who wants to marry you, what does he do for a living?"

"He's a doctor like me. He was in my class in medical school."

"Where is he now?"

"He's still in Nigeria, but he wants to come here and live with us and start to study more like I'm doing and like Gboye is doing."

"Why did you not tell me about him?"

"I didn't want to upset you, Esho. I didn't want you to think I was putting myself in danger of having my life ruined."

"Is he a good man, Iranti? Is he a good man like Depo? If there are angels, may they smile on Depo because that is a good man if there is a good man anywhere. It is the likes of Akanbi who deserve to have an accident such that they won't be able to have sex with a woman, since they use their penis to destroy and kill women. But there is nothing fair in this world. That is a lesson I have learnt. I have a question though, why does this man have a white name?"

"When he was a little boy, his parents got divorced. Then his mother couldn't take care of him and his older sister and younger brother, so she sent him to go and live with some white people, the kind of people you lived with when you ran away from home. It was a Catholic mission, but for men. They changed his name."

"They changed his name?" Esho yelled in shock. "And his parents stood for that nonsense? Where were their heads? And the mother gave up her children? I was not a good mother but I never gave up any of my children. Even when I had to tie a shawl tightly around my abdomen to stop hunger because I didn't have any food to eat, I never gave up my children. The white people like to do crazy things like that, they wanted to take Oshun from me too, and put her in a home for children without mothers, but you know what I did? I ran away while I was still pregnant with her. I might not have liked the way I got Oshun, but she was my child and no one was taking her from me. I never ran away from children. I know what it feels like not to have a mother, and I never did that to my children. What is wrong with this Brian's mother? I don't like them."

"Esho, I'm not marrying his mother. I'm marrying him, and it's not his fault if he was sent away. Have some sympathy. You had to run away too. He has done well for himself in spite of it; he's a doctor today."

"Are his parents poor, like we were?"

"No they are actually well to do."

"So they don't have any excuses. Oh, they are those rich people who never have time for their children?"

"Esho, I don't know. All I know is that I love this man and I want to marry him and I need your blessing. I want to have children."

"Okay, Iranti, I don't know much, but I trust you. I trust your friends too, Gboye and Moradeke. What do they say about this man?"

"Esho, they are not the ones marrying him, I am. I don't care what they have to say. Do I have your blessing or not?" Ranti was getting angrier by the minute.

"Well, with your tone of voice, even if I say no, you will still do what you want. I just thought that your friends look out for you and it's good to listen to them that's all. Okay, marry him if you want. I will be here to keep my eyes on you, and Depo promised me the same."

Ranti hugged her. "Yes, Esho, you will be here to keep your eyes on me and take care of me."

In the fall of 1989, Bode and Moradeke arrived in the US. Bode had passed his board examinations in Nigeria, and had received several invitations for interviews for residency positions. They moved in with Ranti, Esho and Depo.

208   *Feasts of Phantoms*

A week after they arrived, Gboye took the weekend off and traveled to New Jersey to visit Moradeke. Ranti was happy to have all the people she loved so much with her under one roof, and Esho was thrilled as she played hostess and doting mother to them.

Ranti was on call on Friday, but when she arrived home on Saturday afternoon in time to join them at lunch, Esho started with a speech.

"I am very happy that all of Iranti's friends are here now. Gboye, you have been taking care of my child for me from elementary school, and I am very happy that you have continued to be friends with her. Moradeke, you became her friend in secondary school and I know you were a big help to her. She told me about you, Depo, and how you were a blessing in her life at the university and for the past few months that you've been living here with us, everything she said of you is the truth. I'm very happy that Iranti has created a family for herself.

"She told me she wants to marry a man named Brian. I do not know this man because she never brought him home to me. I asked her why she didn't introduce this man to me before and she said she was afraid of my reaction. She's right about that. I did not want any man to ruin her life when she was in school. But she's a doctor now. She's doing well and taking care of herself and of me. No man has the power to ruin her life unless she allows him.

"It would have made me very happy if it is Depo that Iranti wants to marry but she told me she does not love Depo in that way. Depo, it breaks my heart, because I know you love my daughter very much. She warned me not to speak about this with you and I can see she's giving me dirty looks, but I'm an old woman and I have a right to my opinions. I don't know this Brian yet, but I don't like him. I don't like the sound of him, Iranti I want you to marry Depo,"

Ranti yelled at her grandmother. "How can I marry someone who has not asked me to marry him? How Esho? Am I going to put a gun to his head and force him? What are you talking about? You have to watch your tongue. You may think your age gives you the license to say anything, but it is not so. You have to respect other people's feelings."

"Okay, I'm sorry if I misspoke. Depo I see the way you look at my daughter and I know you love her very much and she loves you too. And you are a very kind man. I know I don't understand a lot of things in this world but I just have to voice my opinion. You are her friends and I hope you all know this man. What do you honestly think of her marrying him?"

Gboye and Moradeke looked at Ranti, but she avoided looking at them.

"Esho, this is my business and you just embarrassed me in front of my friends. What more do you want from me? I have always done what you wanted of me. For the first time in my life I'm trying to do something more, be more for myself and you have a problem with it. What do you want from me? Not to ever marry and be childless?

"I want more Esho. I want to be a wife to someone. I want to be mother to some children. You are a mother, am I not entitled to at least that much? You and I spoke in private and now you are putting my business on the streets, you have to learn to respect me okay?" She was so angry that she left her food untouched and went to her room in tears.

Depo, Moradeke and Gboye joined her a few minutes later.

"Ranti, if you want to marry Brian we will support you and be there for you, but you have to protect yourself. You should have a prenuptial agreement. We talked about this yesterday and we agreed," Moradeke told her.

"You did what? I can't believe this! So all of you think it is your job to run my life now. My friends got together with my grandmother behind my back, to decide the best thing for me, since I can't take care of myself. Unbelievable!"

"Yes, Ranti, we decided 'behind your back' because we love you, said Depo. "We don't think Brian is good enough for you, and we are being honest here. But if this is what you decide to do, as your friends we will look out for you. We are not going to turn our backs on you. Brian is a user, so that's why it's best if you contract a prenuptial agreement with him, and we are not going to apologize for that."

Ranti's eyes were blazing with anger as she turned on him. "Depo, you have a month to get out of my house. One month; that is all you have. If you had never come into my life, I would have been fine. Did you tell my friends, when you were getting cozy with them yesterday behind my back, discussing my future, did you tell them why I'm in this predicament? Did you?"

She gave both Moradeke and Gboye a questioning look. "Did he tell you what's going on with him? Why the only man I am hopelessly in love with can never love me back? Did you tell them?" She demanded of Depo.

He nodded as he continued to look at her. "I told them yesterday."

Ranti suddenly felt deflated as she continued to cry. "I love him, he has had my heart since I was fifteen years old, and I can't stop loving him. I need to marry Brian to cure me of Depo. He has become a disease to me. He is the perfect man, yes, like Esho said, but the problem is the perfect man for me does not want to have sex with me."

Moradeke started to cry as she went to lay next to Ranti on the bed, hugging her.

Gboye sat on the chair and there were tears in her eyes as well.

"I'm sorry, Ranti, I am very sorry but I love you and I will always love you. I will move out as soon as I can, but you are getting a prenuptial agreement before you marry Brian. That, I am not sorry for and I'm not going to let you make yourself vulnerable to an exploiter more than you need to."

"Get out, get out of my room. Get out now. I hate you, I hate you, and I curse the day I met you. Get out." She yelled at Depo as she threw a pillow at him.

"We are sorry, Ranti, he told us last night. We love him too, and it doesn't make him less of a wonderful person. But I'm disappointed too because I had hoped the two of you would get married. But he loves you dearly, Depo does," Moradeke consoled Ranti.

"It just breaks my heart. What a waste of a good-looking sexy man. What a goddamn waste? I won't forgive him though. I love him too and he is a wonderful person but I won't forgive him for going around taunting women and not delivering. It's just a big waste," Gboye announced.

"But we insist on the prenuptial," Moradeke informed Ranti.

"Yes, you are getting one even if I have to beat you up." Gboye asserted. "I don't care how much you love Brian, you are getting one, to protect you now, and the future earnings that you will have. You are going to be an obstetrician and a gynecologist in this country. You are going to become a very rich woman. You need to protect yourself and your future earnings. So you are getting a prenuptial, end of story."

Ranti was quiet for a while. "Girls, I need to marry Brian. I need to get Depo out of my head. I love Brian and he wants me, but I love Depo also. I can't continue to live like this, you are my sisters not just my friends, and I need you to understand this and be in it with me.

"You can't know what it feels like to be me. You can't know what it is like to have leaked and smelled of urine and to continue to smell feces on myself. I'm very insecure about myself as a desirable woman. No man has ever come after me saying they wanted me. Men have always left me or deny that I am theirs. And on top of it all, I went and gave my heart to a man who can never return my affection the way I want. Like Esho always said, 'the gods are laughing at us.' I need to do this, girls, and I need you with me. Please." She pleaded with them.

Moradeke hugged her again. "We understand, Ranti. We do. We are on your side and we will support you and take care of you, and that is what we are doing by insisting on the prenuptial agreement. Depo understands too. He does, and Ranti, he loves you, he has always loved you."

"I hope Esho doesn't know he is gay, it will just blow her mind." Ranti said to her friends.

"No she doesn't, she thinks he can't have sex because of an accident he had as a little boy. We didn't tell her otherwise," Moradeke assured her.

"I need to go to Depo and apologize for yelling at him. I love having him here but then it's hard on me," Ranti explained to her friends as she dried her eyes and went in search of Depo.

He was in the living room watching a game on television with Bode, while Esho was cleaning the kitchen.

"Depo may I speak with you, please?" She said to him and he followed her out on to the deck. She jumped up and swung her arms around his neck, she kissed him on the lips. "I love you, Depo, I'm sorry I yelled at you, I'm just frustrated about this whole thing. You don't have to leave because I love having you here. Please stay for as long as you wish."

"I know you love me Ranti, you and my mother are the two dearest people I have in this world. I understand about your need to get into this marriage, more than you can believe. I will be behind you the whole time, watching out for you and supporting you. Maybe there is something there and I'm just judgmental, only time will tell. I have no plans of moving out at the end of the month because my loft will not be ready then. It will be ready in two months and that is when I will move out, when I am good and ready." He smiled at her.

She kissed him again, "Thank you for being in my life. Thanks a lot."

"The pleasure is mine and thanks for telling Esho that I had an unfortunate accident as a kid that left me unable to have sex. I'm a virile man for your information."

"I know, I don't think she can wrap homosexuality around her head just yet. She is just getting used to the idea that there can be healthy sex between a man and a woman and not just rape. Give her time. Maybe she will learn about it on Oprah first."

They returned to the living room to join the other people. Ranti went to sit next to her grandmother. She hugged her and said to her, "Esho, thank you, I will be fine, my friends are with me."

Esho looked around the room at Ranti's friends and they all nodded to her, assuring her that Ranti would be fine.

Two weeks later, she mailed the prenuptial contract to Brian, with a letter explaining that she would like him to enter into the agreement with her, as a way for her to really believe he was marrying her out of love. She reminded him that shortly after they graduated from medical school, she asked him why he wanted to marry her, and he said because she was a doctor. Even though he tried to take his words back at the time, she would feel more secure in his love, if she knew he was not marrying her just because of that one factor.

She impressed on him that the only condition by which she would marry him was if he signed the papers and returned them to her. As soon as she received the papers, she would begin to make travel arrangements to come to Nigeria so they could have the wedding, after which he could be given a visa as her spouse.

She was very anxious after she sent the documents to him by courier as she waited for his phone call. It came three days later in the middle of the night. He was as angry as she expected.

"Ranti, you have just insulted me and my family. I'm not signing that stupid document. Who do you think you are?"

"I'm the woman you said you wanted to marry because you loved. Look Brian, people are saying the only reason you want to marry me is to use me to get a visa to come to the US, and based on your reaction now, they are right. And you said it before. You told me the reason you wanted to marry me was because I'm a doctor with a bright future. Well, the only way I will marry you is if you sign those documents and return them to me. I need to be sure that you truly love me Brian."

"My mother and aunts said I shouldn't sign the papers. They think I should marry someone else. They don't like you."

"Good luck to you then, Brian." She told him and hung up the phone. She plopped back onto the pillow and started to weep. She did not sleep for the rest of the night.

Four days later Brian returned the signed and notarized copies of the prenuptial agreement with a letter of apology. He said his mother and aunts put a lot of pressure on him, but he loved her and would like to marry her.

The following week, Ranti bought a ticket to Nigeria to bring him back with her. Esho wanted to go with her but she refused since she would be gone for just one week. Depo insisted on going with her so he and his mother could be her family at the ceremony. Initially she refused but with pressure from Esho and her friends, she gave in and he traveled with her.

Ranti was grateful to have Depo and his mother in her life. The traditional wedding ceremony involves the families of the bride and the groom, and Efunwanmi was there for her and also brought a lot of her very rich family and friends from Lagos.

She also hired a caterer for the wedding. She saved Ranti from a lot of humiliation and elevated her status, because Brian's family were very impressed that she knew *the* Efunwunmi Jacobs, the most beautiful woman in Nigeria and a famous anchor on national television.

34

Ranti, Depo and Brian returned to the US a few days after the wedding in December of 1989. The following week, Depo moved to his loft in New York City, taking Moradeke and Bode who did not have a place of their own with him. They explained to Ranti that they wanted to give her and Brian some privacy since they were newly married, but Ranti knew they did not want to be around Brian.

Within the first month, Brian started to complain about Esho living with them, that she was always watching him and she disapproved of him. He wanted Ranti to send her back to Nigeria.

"This is Esho's home, and I'm all she has. You have always known that fact, I've always told you that Esho stays with me."

"She is always around, I try to study and she is in the kitchen banging about. She hogs the television and she just gets on my nerves. At least I didn't bring my mother here to live with us."

"Brian, go to the library. It will be quieter there. That's what Gboye did when she stayed with me while she was studying, and Esho was here all the time too."

"This is my home too, I'm your husband, I should feel free in my own home, I should be free to stay and study here if I want. We never have any private time together, between you always going on calls, and the free time you have, Depo, Moradeke, Bode and Gboye are here. I haven't had a full week with you alone, and it's frustrating. And why do you have to go on so many calls? Are you the only resident in that place? You are on call every other day. I don't believe you go on calls all the time. Maybe you are seeing someone behind my back."

Ranti stared at him, unable to believe her ears. "I'm seeing someone behind your back? Is that what you said to me Brian? Are you accusing me of having an affair? I go to work to earn the money we all depend on and you are accusing me of having an affair. Aren't you a doctor? Didn't you start residency training in Nigeria? How many times were you on call in a week?" Ranti demanded of him.

He did not answer her.

"I need an answer Brian because I've never been this insulted in my life. I don't understand you at all. Since we got married, each time I go to work you complain. Do you want me to stay at home and for the two of us to stare at each other all day? Then what is the point of our coming to America? We should have stayed in Nigeria and your rich parents could have supported us then."

"If you want me to trust you that you are not having an affair, then don't go on calls so often, go once or at the most twice a week. Then I will know for sure you are not seeing someone. I mentioned all these calls of yours to my mother and she too thinks you are seeing someone. She said if you truly love me, you wouldn't go on so many calls."

"Brian, I do not make the schedule. I am a resident in obstetrics and gynecology, and this is it! These calls are mandatory. Even if your mother doesn't know that because she is not a doctor, you should know I have no control over my schedule."

"The problem with you Ranti is that you are spoilt. You can't survive without your mother around you. Some of us grew up without a mother fussing over us all the time, and we were fine. Esho should let you grow up too instead of always hanging around and fussing over you all the time."

"Esho is my grandmother, my mother died when I was four years old."

"What's the difference? At least you always had her. She is your mother. I was sent away to live with the reverend fathers when I was five. It was hard but I dealt with it. I didn't have a mother or a grandmother constantly asking me if I had eaten or what I would like to eat like Esho is always doing with you."

They started to have these arguments on a regular basis, and Ranti continued to tell Brian that Esho would live with her as long as she was alive. The arguments continued each time she had to go to work as well. Brian would start to sulk early in the mornings. He would complain that she disturbed his sleep when she tried to get ready. At some point he suggested she use the bathroom at the other end of the house instead of using the master bathroom.

He would insist she cooked for him because he did not want to eat Esho's food. "My wife should cook for me and not another woman. You are my wife and you have never even cooked for me, not once. You are always giving the excuse that you are busy with your job. There are millions of women in the world who go to jobs every day, Ranti, and still respect their husbands by cooking for them."

After a while he refused to eat Esho's food, because he was afraid she might poison him since she did not like him.

"Esho settles her scores explicitly with a knife, and not poison," Ranti thought. She tried to reassure Brian that Esho would never poison him.

One evening, when she returned home after a call and was tired because she had not slept in almost two days, Brian met her at the door with a bowl of food that he thrust into her face.

"See, I told you your grandmother is a witch. She doesn't want our marriage to succeed and she tried to kill me," he yelled at her.

Ranti pushed her way into the kitchen so she could close the kitchen door against the February cold. She scanned the living room for Esho. She did not want her to hear Brian calling her a witch.

"Brian please, can I come in first? I haven't sat down since yesterday morning. I'm tired and I don't need this from you now," she appealed to him.

"You don't need this from me? So it's okay for your grandmother to kill me? Is that it? Well it isn't going to happen because I'm not going to stand for it. Look at the so called food she prepared for me. I was suspicious when she had been civil to me all day.

"Usually, she ignores me, but today she asked me how my studies were going and if I was worried about my exams. She said she remembered Gboye was worried she wouldn't pass when she was studying for the exams, but she passed. Then she told me she was going to boil some yam and make some egg stew, that it's one of your favorite meals, she wanted to know if I would like some and I said okay.

"Look at what she is calling egg stew. Look at the maggots she cooked and gave to me. Look. These are maggots! Even a blind person can see that. I'm calling the police on her. You never believed me but this is evidence." He was yelling and his eyes were bloodshot.

Ranti for a moment wondered if she had married a mad man. "Jesus, Brian, you are paranoid. These are not maggots. This is the white of the egg. Maggots would be thicker and longer for goodness sakes." She scooped up a spoonful of the egg stew and ate it.

"See, I just ate it. In fact I'm eating everything because I'm starving, and you can make yourself a sandwich."

Ranti dropped her purse on the dining table and took the bowl from him. She went to the stove and opening the pot of yam, served herself some and got more egg stew from the second pot on the stove. She sat down at the table and started to eat.

"Is that what you are going to say? You are not going to cook something else for me? I am your husband and it is your job to take care of me."

"Yes, Brian, and it is your job to take care of me too, because I am your wife. I have been on my feet since yesterday morning. I'm not cooking tonight. It's either you eat this food that Esho prepared or you make yourself a sandwich."

He left the kitchen and a few minutes later he returned dressed up, and snatching her car keys from the kitchen table he left the house.

Brian continued in these ways to torment her. She tried her best to placate him quickly and quietly so Esho would not hear them. Each time they had a fight, he would call his mother in Nigeria and she would tell him what to do, which he would then try to impose on Ranti.

Sometimes his mother would lecture her on the best ways to take care of Brian if she would like to remain married. She would threaten her that if she did not start doing what Brian wanted he might be forced to marry another woman. After a while, Ranti refused to take her calls.

"Brian, your mother can't be ruling our marital home from Nigeria, this is between the two of us," she would tell him. "Why do you have to discuss everything with her and get permission from her before you do anything or even speak in a civil manner to me here?"

"I will keep calling my mother, every day, as long as Esho is living here with us, because Esho has been telling you not to take care of me," he would respond to her.

Shortly after he accused Esho of trying to kill him by feeding him maggots, he stopped eating in the house and each night, when Ranti returned from work, he would take the car and go to his friend's house in Teaneck.

Four months after they were married, he took the car to go out late one Wednesday night, but he did not return in time for her to go to work the next morning. She had to call a cab.

They had a fight about this and he shocked her by telling her that he would drive her to work and bring her back home so as to prevent her from going to see her boyfriends, since he did not believe she went to work all the time.

216   *Feasts of Phantoms*

"You are a doctor Brian, why are you talking as if you don't have a brain?" Ranti demanded of him.

"I need a car all the time too. If you need a car to visit your boyfriends, buy another one."

"You know we can't afford a second car at this time since you are not working yet," she tried to reason with him.

"Then ask your boyfriends to buy you a car."

Ranti shook her head in disbelief.

"If you let me manage your money, the way it's supposed to be since I'm your husband, you will see that we can afford a second car," he told her.

Ranti gave in to him and he started to take her to work in the mornings and pick her up. On many occasions, she had to get rides from her colleagues when Brian would not show up two to three hours after her shift. At other times, she would take a cab home.

A month later, frustrated, she went to her bank and took out a home equity loan to buy a used Honda Civic, so Brian could have the newer Honda Accord car to himself. He was enraged when he saw the car. He said she bought the car without consulting him, as he would have forbidden it, and she wanted to have her freedom to be able to visit her boyfriends.

"You know what you are Ranti, you are a whore. That is what you are. And I'm going to smash the car."

"If you smash the car, you are going back to Nigeria tonight, because I will call the police on you and withdraw your visa, she warned him, and his response was to slap her hard across the face.

Ranti backed down and kept quiet.

Six months after they got married, Ranti was able to get a week off work and they drove to Niagara Falls for honeymoon. Brian was calm for about a week after the honeymoon and did not bring up the usual arguments. But two weeks later, he asked Ranti to give him access to her checking account so he could withdraw money to spend instead of having to wait for her to give him money.

Ranti explained to him that there was no money left in her account after she paid the mortgage, insurance, loan for the car and other bills, and after they bought groceries, because she had been giving him half of what was left and keeping the remaining half for emergencies. "You have more spending money than I do, Brian."

He accused her of lying and that she was hiding the rest of the money. Ranti brought out her checkbook as well as the stubs of her paycheck to show him that there was no money for her to hide anywhere.

"Ranti, the problem with you is that you don't know how to manage money. Elvis P,"

"Elvis P? Who is that? What are you talking about, Brian?"

"Stop giving me those looks as if I'm crazy. That was his nickname. He was in your clinical group, Sola Alao."

"Oh, I didn't know that was his nickname."

"You mean to tell me you never noticed he had Elvis Presley's hair style? Anyway, he's in his third year of residency training in Ohio. He told me that he has been able to save a hundred thousand dollars since he started working in America, just three years ago like you, yet you are always complaining about money. See how wasteful you've been."

Ranti looked at him for a long time and wondered if he was an idiot. "Brian, it is not possible for your friend Elvis or whatever you call him to have saved a hundred thousand dollars from his salary as a resident. Even if he never spent a dime of it, he couldn't have made a hundred thousand dollars yet in income, because the average salary for a resident is twenty seven thousand dollars a year, so he hasn't even earned ninety thousand dollars yet. He is either lying to you, or he is trafficking cocaine into America like some Nigerians are doing now. Maybe that's what he's doing and he's not being honest with you."

"I knew that's what you would say. He is just more careful with his money while you are wasteful. I can help you with your money if you will just trust me a little and not listen to Esho all the time. You could get more money back from the income tax you pay. If you withdraw that prenuptial nonsense you made me sign, I will help you. For example, my niece, Pelumi, she's an American citizen, but she's living in Nigeria with her parents until she is eighteen when my sister plans to send her here for college. We can claim her as a dependent. We just need her social security number and you will get more money back. See, that's one way I can be of help to you."

"Brian, who are you?" Ranti asked in shock. "I am not committing tax fraud. I am not cheating the government and I don't want to have this discussion ever again."

"If you really want me to believe you, and you want to prove to me that you love me, you will hand over your pay check to me when you get it. And as your husband, I will be in charge of the accounts in this house. That's what my mother told me."

"No, Brian, I don't need any help with the accounts. I'm not handing it over to you. I'm giving you a lot of money as it is; money I really can't afford to give you. You've been buying clothes every month since you arrived. I haven't bought so many clothes since I've been living here. I wear scrubs most of the time. You buy expensive shoes and shirts, things we can't afford. Even Depo and Bode who work and earn money don't spend so much on clothes and shoes, and you haven't even started to work yet."

"Don't you ever compare me to another man as long as you live, Ranti. If your

Depo is such a prince why didn't he marry you? I'm sick of the man being around all the time."

A few weeks after this argument about money, he informed Ranti that his aunt Vicky was relocating to America and would be staying with them until she found a job.

"Your aunt Vicky cannot stay in my house, Brian, no way. That woman hates my guts, and has used every opportunity since you and I started dating to make my life a misery, and you have not attempted to protect me."

"What do you mean, 'no way' I have a say too, this is my house as well, and I'm your husband. If Esho can stay here, then Aunt Vicky can stay too, and she is arriving in two days."

"Brian, your aunt is not staying in my house. Your mom, maybe, and that's because she's your mother, but not any of your aunts. She called me a bastard and she called my grandmother a prostitute and you sat there as if you were a log of wood. This is payback. Do her a favor and tell her she is not welcome here. If she comes here, I will call the police on her. Remember this is not Nigeria where the husband's family can abuse the wife and get away with it. This is America and this is my house; I pay the mortgage here."

"I knew it, I knew you would go there, just because I haven't passed my exams yet and you are the one bringing home the bacon, I knew you would rub it in my face. You know what; I think I made a mistake marrying you. They warned me that you were arrogant and full of yourself. My aunts warned me especially about signing that prenuptial thing. They were right. My aunt is coming here and if you don't let her stay in this house Ranti, you will be sorry."

The following day, Ranti told Esho that Brian wanted his aunt to live with them, but she had refused. She asked Esho to call her at work the moment the woman arrived, and that she would call the cops on her, because she was mean to her in Nigeria.

Esho, who loved revenge more than anything in the world, called Ranti the moment Brian, who went to get his aunt from the airport arrived with her. Ranti told Esho to get her coat and go to the library that was walking distance from the house.

As Ranti walked in through the kitchen door, the aunt looked her up and down and ignoring her, turned her back, and started to speak to Brian.

"No, not in my house," Ranti said to herself, "You are not treating me like shit in my own house."

"Vicky," she called her, dropping the respectful title of 'aunt.' "You can't stay in my house. You are not welcome here. I explained that to Brian already. Please leave."

Vicky could not believe her ears. "What? This is Brian's house too. I am his aunt, how dare you speak to me like that? I warned you Brian, she is arrogant."

"Brian doesn't have a house yet, at least not in this country. He might own the whole of Ibadan City, since you are a prominent Ibadan family who knows everybody, but he does not have a house here. This is my house and I'll say who comes in here and who doesn't. So please leave, or I'll ask the police to help you."

Vicky demanded of Brian. "Are you going to stand there and let her speak to me in this manner?"

"Are you out of your mind, Ranti? This is my mother's older sister. If Esho can stay here and Gboye can spend weekends with you, then my aunt is staying here too."

He continued to take his aunt's luggage upstairs to the guest room. Vicky followed him, shaking her head in disbelief and hissing in disgust.

Ranti called the police and asked them to help her eject an intruder who had refused to leave her house. Ten minutes later, when two police officers arrived, Ranti let them in and pointed toward the guest room. They went upstairs and escorted Vicky out of the house, and Brian went with them.

Brian returned home three days later and he did not speak to Ranti. She ignored him as well and they did not speak to one another for weeks.

On a Saturday evening three weeks later, a couple of Brian's friends that Ranti had never met came to visit him. They stayed in the living room watching a game and drinking beer. Brian who was a social drinker and drank beer about once a month was having too much to drink, and as the evening wore on he and his friends became louder. The friends eventually left and Ranti went to bed. Brian joined her about an hour later.

"I want to have sex tonight, Ranti," he announced.

"That's very romantic Brian. I'm not having sex with you. You've been drinking beer and I can't stand the smell as you know."

He got out of bed and walked to her side of the bed. "You are my wife and I'm having sex with you tonight. You can't deny me that. If you try, I will force you and you can't call the cops on me this time."

"If you force yourself on me Brian, it is called rape. Are you a rapist?"

He hit her hard across the face, and before she could react pounced on her and ripped her nightgown off her. He bit into her neck as he dug his nails into her sides. His kisses were very brutal. She tried to push him off but she could not.

Early the next morning, she left for a call and did not return home until Monday evening. She wore a turtleneck under her surgical scrubs.

Two weeks later, he forced himself on her again, and Ranti gave in without fighting him to prevent his bites and pinches.

One year after he arrived in America, Brian sat for his examinations and when he received the results two months later, he had failed. The tension continued to mount at home and Esho stayed out of his way too. Ranti's friends stopped coming around as much as they used to.

Brian sat for the examination again six months later and he failed again. He became meaner, and once while he was in the kitchen and Esho came in to get some water, he yelled at her without any provocation.

Esho gave him a long look. "Let me explain something to you, Brian," she started. "I warned my child not to marry you because I knew even without having met you that you are a loser. I asked Iranti a few questions about you, just a few questions and I knew. You have been living in this house for the past two years and I have stayed out of your way. I know all the things you do to my daughter, don't think because she pretends and puts up a brave front I don't know. But do not mess with me.

"Iranti will tell you, I have taken down men who were ten times the man you are. I have killed two men who messed with me before. Did you hear me? I killed them and escorted them to the gates of hell, because that is where they went, and I will take you down. I could make life impossible for you in this house if I so choose. So, stay out of my way and I will stay out of your way.

"It is Iranti who thinks that a useless husband is better than no husband at all, just like she thought that a useless father was better than no father at all. You have been warned."

Following this, Brian renewed his argument about Esho going back to Nigeria.

He started to prepare for the examination again after Ranti convinced him to enroll in Kaplan school that had been known to help other candidates. He sat for the examinations the third time six months later and passed.

His moods lifted and he became more tolerable to live with. Six months later he started his residency training in family practice as Ranti was rounding up the final year of her training, that year in 1991.

A few months later, Moradeke who was in her second year of residency training gave birth to a baby boy and both Gboye and Ranti were very thrilled to become aunties. Esho offered to help with the baby and Moradeke gratefully accepted.

Esho would leave for New York City on Sunday nights to return to Ranti on Friday nights, as Moradeke or Bode always ensured they were home on weekends to spend time with the baby.

Brian was happy that Esho was not around so much and he became nicer to Ranti. He started to talk about them having a baby too, and he would try to be gentle with her when they had sex. Ranti wanted desperately to become a mother too, especially with Moradeke looking more and more beautiful as she basked in the joys of motherhood.

Eight months later when she did not become pregnant Brian suggested they consult one of her colleagues. Ranti was worried that the genital mutilation, and the menoschesis she had for many years might have damaged her uterus.

She went with Brian to consult a specialist. She told the doctor her story, which Brian heard for the first time.

He became mean to her again, and he started to accuse her of trapping him into the marriage when she knew she could not bear children. The verbal abuse increased. Ranti tried to convince him that she was sure she could have a baby, and they needed to keep working at it. She reminded him that all the tests she had came back negative, and there was no reason for her not to become pregnant.

A few weeks later, he brought out his most cruel weapon. Ranti was ovulating as she had started to monitor her cycles, so she suggested they had sex.

"You want to have sex?" he asked her and she nodded.

"Go take a shower first before I have sex with you."

"Why do I have to take a shower first, I took a shower this morning."

"Ranti, you can't blame a man for trying here. In case you don't know, you do smell. It's just not nice to say things like that to people. You've always had this whiff of urine and feces about you, but I didn't get it until you told me about the genital cutting Esho did on you. I know you make an effort to cover the smell with perfumes, only it still comes through, but it disappears for a while after you take a shower."

Ranti panicked and started to weep. She ran into the shower, staying longer than usual to wash off the feces and urine on her. When she came out of the bathroom, Brian told her he was not in the mood for sex anymore.

She appealed to him that if they did not have sex then, they would lose a month in their eagerness to have a baby.

"I just can't get over the smell tonight Ranti, sorry," he said as he turned his back on her.

She cried all night and did not sleep a wink. She too started to smell the feces and urine on herself and to feel the genital pain again, as well as the crawling sensations in her anus. She stopped eating and started to lose weight.

Brian continued to reject her in this way each time she asked him to have sex so they could try to have a baby, and at times he would sleep in the guest room. He would tell her the smell was overpowering and it was probably because she was on her mid-cycle, but other times he would rape her.

She did not tell her friends what was going on in her marriage. She did not want to admit to them that they had been right. Her feelings of worthlessness intensified.

In June of 1992, Ranti graduated from her residency training. She received awards for outstanding performance and the faculty had great things to say about her. They were happy she was staying on at the hospital for fellowship training in reconstructive genital surgery.

222 *Feasts of Phantoms*

Even though she would have loved to go to England to train under Mr. Edwards who repaired her genitals when she was fifteen, and who was one of the world's specialists in the reconstruction of the kind of genital mutilation she had experienced, she decided to stay to work on her marriage.

Later in the year, Efunwunmi came to New York and Ranti who just adored the woman went to visit her. Over the years, she had managed to save fifteen thousand dollars that she offered to Efunwunmi, as part of the payment for her surgery she had paid for eleven years before. "Mrs. Jacobs, without you, I wouldn't be where I am today, I would probably be dead. I owe you more than I could ever repay with money, but I want to pay back the cost of the surgery and my plane ticket to England. I know it cost you twenty six thousand pounds, here is fifteen thousand dollars; I will pay the rest as soon as I'm able to. Once again, thank you."

"First of all, call me mother, don't call me Mrs. Jacobs; you are my daughter Ranti. And secondly, are you out of your mind?" Efunwunmi yelled at her.

"I told you at the time that you meant the world to my son, and any friend of my son is my child too. I can't accept the money from you. Wait until I tell Depo, he's going to be so angry with you, you are insulting me."

"I'm sorry I didn't mean to insult you. It's just that it's a lot of money and I promised myself I would repay you. And it cost you and Depo a lot, because when he was in school in France, and his father refused to help him, if you had this money then, it would have made life easier for him but you didn't have it because you spent it on me," Ranti quickly apologized

"And Depo was fine," said Efunwunmi. "He paid for his own education and I'm sure he respects himself as a man more because of that. He worked hard to earn what he wanted. You have repaid me enough by becoming a doctor and a gynecologist, and I know you chose the specialty so you could help women in similar predicaments. And besides, Mr. Jacobs paid for the surgery. That's about the only good thing he ever did with his wealth. I went to him at the time, though we were divorced, and I knew he felt guilty about the way he had treated me. I told him your story and he gave me the money." She paused for a moment.

"But what you may do is try to get a day off work and take me out to lunch and shopping. A woman likes to shop with her daughter once in a while."

Ranti readily agreed.

35

Two months before their third wedding anniversary, Ranti missed her period. She was happy but anxious. She waited three days before she took a home pregnancy test and it was positive. She warily put a conference call to her girlfriends. Gboye and Moradeke were not happy, though, and they let her know it.

"Ranti, I know you want very much to become a mother but I'm sorry, I'm just worried, Brian is a jerk and I don't want you to have children with him," Gboye said.

Ranti was hurt that her friends could not share in her excitement. Moradeke started to speak but she hung up on them. She went to the bathroom to weep.

She was afraid to call her grandmother who was with Moradeke to tell her the news. Brian was on call and he would not be home until the following day. She felt totally alone.

Depo called her later in the day saying he heard from Moradeke that she had missed her period.

Ranti kept quiet. She expected he would react the same way as her girlfriends.

"Ranti, please don't hang up on me. You know I love you. I'm not happy about your marriage and I wish you would leave Brian. We know about the beatings; we see scratch marks on you all the time. Wearing a turtleneck in summer is not exactly in fashion and it's not comfortable, so we know. You are pregnant and I'll be here for you. I don't like Brian but I will love your child the same way I love you. I'm begging you, leave Brian. File for a divorce from him and move to England. No one should be beating you and raping you. I'm worried more now that you are pregnant because men who abuse their wives abuse them more when they are pregnant, so you are not safe with him. Even if you don't want to go to England to train under Mr. Edwards now, you can move in with me. Please Ranti I'm begging you, I don't want this man to kill you."

"Are you done Depo? I know you've never liked Brian and you never gave him a chance. You don't want me, and you don't want anyone else to have me. You just can't be happy for me. People do change, Depo. When he realizes he's going to be a father he might change." She hung up.

As she was dozing off at about midnight the doorbell rang. She wondered who could be coming to see them that late. She got out of bed and into her dressing gown and slowly climbed down the stairs. She did not turn on any light in the house as she peeped to check who was at the door. It was Depo.

She let him in and stood away from him with her hands folded on her chest.

Depo moved toward her but stopped himself. They stared at one another.

"I love you, Ranti. I just came to say congratulations on the pregnancy. I know how much you wanted a child, and to tell you that I'm here for you."

She burst into tears and ran into his arms.

The following day when she told Brian she was pregnant he stared at her for a moment and asked her if she was sure. She nodded.

"I wanted us to really plan the pregnancy so we'd have a boy. I wanted us to have sex around the time you ovulate. That way we would have been certain of having a son. I'm sure you are pregnant with a girl which is disappointing." He walked away from her.

Ranti went to lie on Esho's bed.

An hour later, he came looking for her. "What are you doing here? You miss your mother so you came to lie on her bed. You are pathetic. I have a question though, how could you have become pregnant when you and I never had sex at the times you were ovulating? I explained to you that your body emanates an odor that is just terrible and that I can't tolerate at those times, so the baby can't be mine. It must be one of your boyfriends', so don't pass it off as my child, okay? I could have named Depo but he is a girl like you, since he likes to pee sitting down."

As he turned around to leave the room, that thing that used to snap inside of Ranti at the moments when injustice was being done to her, and which had not stirred in a while, snapped. "You are a bastard, Brian. Everyone has been telling me that you are a sick bastard and a loser, but I have been defending you. You are going to die a miserable death. Fuck you. You don't want this child? Fine! Then it's not yours. You probably knew all along you could not get a woman pregnant, impotent rapist that you are. Go to hell."

Brian was shocked as he stared at her. He slowly retraced his steps out of the room.

The next morning as she was leaving for work, he said to her, "Ranti I'm glad you are pregnant. I know how much you wanted this. I don't know what came over me yesterday. Maybe it was the shock of the news. Are you okay?"

She gave him a dirty look as she picked up her purse and walked out of the house.

Ranti was happy she was pregnant; because it meant the mutilation did not damage her beyond repair; she was still a woman. She wished her friends were on board with her, but she realized that they had never been able to understand what it was like to be her. They always had good lives. Moradeke got pregnant within a month when she made up her mind to get pregnant, while it took her over a year.

When Esho arrived for the weekend and Ranti told her the news, Esho looked at her for a long time. Ranti burst into tears and Esho took her in her arms.

"Iranti, you are a very strong person. You have always been stronger than me and wiser too. You will be fine. What do I know? I am the one who should know about these things and point you in the right direction but what do I know? You are wading into unknown territory here, unknown because no one in our line has ever done this before, but you did not let that scare you. You are taking the risks that I was too afraid to take.

"Iranti, you and I are in this together. Having a child is a good thing. Children give us hope and they cure us of madness. There is nothing to cry about. Look at you, Akanbi is your father but you have turned out much better than I could have imagined possible and I'm very proud of you. This child is a blessing and it is welcome," Esho reassured her.

Later that day, Esho asked Ranti if she wanted her to stay during the week instead of going to Moradeke's, but Ranti told her that Moradeke needed her more than she did.

When Moradeke came for Esho on Sunday, Gboye was with her. They took turns to hug her. "Ranti, we are very sorry about our reactions when you told us the news. There is no excuse for it. We behaved like jerks. It isn't our place to tell you who to marry or have children with. And we know how important this is to you, we are very sorry." Moradeke apologized and Gboye consented.

Ranti returned their hugs, "I need you now more than I have ever needed you. Please don't turn your backs on me. I know that Brian is a jerk, but I can't just leave him. Don't you guys understand? It's not that easy for me. I'm staying out of his way, and I'm being very careful, but this is not a time for you guys to abandon me."

Gboye hugged her again. "We know. We are here for you. But if he ever touches you again, please Ranti, I am begging you, call me. Do you promise me that you will call me? I mean it Ranti, and you know that I love you, but if I see a scratch on you, because I know you might start to protect him, I will kill him! I'm not kidding. Wife beaters get worse when their wives are pregnant. That's why we are all so worried. We don't want to lose you. Okay?"

"I hear you, and I'm not going to let him kill me. I moved out of the bedroom already, and if he comes at me I will kill him first. I don't want to die girls."

Brian returned to being himself a week after Ranti announced her pregnancy, with his constant paranoia and demands. She stayed out of his way as much as it was possible and tried not to fuel his irrationality. She continued to sleep in Esho's room because she did not want him raping and biting her.

Six weeks into the pregnancy, the morning sickness started and by the following week she could not go to work. The sicker she got the more demanding Brian became, constantly asking her for one thing or the other like, "Ranti, I can't find my socks." Or, "where did you put my toothbrush?" "You haven't cooked anything in this house in weeks, and when are you going to move back to the

226   *Feasts of Phantoms*

bedroom?" "If I get a girlfriend, then you have yourself to blame because you have been depriving me of sex." "I know a lot of pregnant women who still work, take care of small children and their homes and husbands." On and on he would continue, constantly nagging her.

Ten weeks into the pregnancy, Ranti woke up one Thursday morning and there was blood on the bed. Brian had been on call the day before. She called him.

"I can't come home now, I have to work. Call a cab," he said to her and hung up.

Ranti was shocked. She called him back. "Brian, I'm bleeding, you have to come home and get me."

"Why? I'm not an obstetrician, what will I do? Call a cab, or better still, call 911. I have to go. I have to finish my rounds." Brian said and hung up on her again.

Ranti started to cry. She did not know what to do and was afraid she would lose the baby. She lay on the bed for a while and then it suddenly occurred to her that her placenta might have separated, which could be dangerous for her. She grabbed the phone and quickly called for an ambulance.

While she was waiting, she called Depo to tell him she was bleeding and had called the ambulance. He promised to meet her at the hospital.

Her obstetrician was able to reassure her that the placenta was not separating and the fetus was fine. But he confined her to absolute bed rest. Esho returned home to take care of Ranti and Moradeke had to fly in her mother-in-law from Nigeria on a short notice to help with her infant son.

Ranti was in the hospital for three weeks, and she did not see Brian at all for that period of time. Esho faithfully came to the hospital in the mornings, arriving as early as eight o'clock, and she would remain with her till seven o'clock at night. It was on the third day that Ranti discovered that Esho was walking the five miles each way to and from the hospital. Ranti yelled at her grandmother for not taking a cab.

Depo came every day from New York to see her, sometimes arriving as late as ten at night.

Moradeke came in every other day to see her and sometimes Bode would come too. Gboye came down three times in the three weeks from Boston and called three or four times a day. Yet Brian did not show up, not once, and he did not phone her.

Ranti called him a few times to ask when he would come visit her. He told her he was busy with work and he was studying for his licensing examination.

She was more embarrassed than hurt because her friends could see her humiliation, the friends who had warned her on many occasions not to marry Brian. But they were kind enough not to mention him at all.

Esho told her he would only come home early in the morning to get ready for work.

When Ranti returned home from the hospital and confronted him about his abandonment of her, he told her he was too busy to visit her.

Fifteen weeks into the pregnancy, Ranti was able to return to work. She did not move back into the master bedroom with Brian who continued his behavior of being demanding of her and accusing her of all manner of ills from prostitution to stealing and lying. She ignored him and stayed out of his way.

Two weeks later, Brian returned home at about one o'clock on a Saturday morning, drunk, and went into the guest room where Ranti was. She woke up when she heard him at the door fumbling for the light switch. She sat up and turned on the bedside lamp.

"You are my wife and I am having sex with you tonight," he announced to her.

Ranti started to panic. She quickly got out of bed, and grabbing the telephone, ran to the other end of the room as far away from him as possible.

"Who are you calling? Depo the queer to come and save you, your queer in shining armor?" He laughed in a sadistic manner. "We haven't had sex in five months and I have needs Ranti. I am exercising my rights as your husband tonight." He lunged at her from across the bed.

Ranti cowered in the corner and tried to call 911, but he jumped at her from across the bed, knocking the phone from her hand. He pulled her up and threw her on to the bed. She landed on her back.

"Brian please, please, I'm pregnant. Please, don't do this, please, I'm begging you please." She pleaded with him quietly so Esho would not hear them. She was afraid that if Esho heard them and found him raping her, she would stab him to death.

Brian slapped her hard on the face and tried to rip her nightshirt off. Ranti stopped struggling with him, so he would not keep hitting her. She did not want to lose the baby, so she lay as still as she possibly could, as he raped her. He was as brutal as ever. When he was done, he climbed off her and left the room.

She lay on the bed in tears, and was not surprised when an hour later her abdomen cramped in an unbearable manner. She went to the bathroom to check herself, and she had started to bleed again. She walked slowly down the hall to wake Esho.

She delivered the dead male fetus twelve hours later. And when she was discharged from the hospital the following day, Depo took her and Esho with him to his home in New York City. She felt numb.

Her friends and grandmother appealed to her to file for divorce, and she told them she would give it some serious thought.

Esho insisted she file right away, threatening that she would not return to New Jersey as long as Brian was there because if she saw him she would kill him. "Iranti, you continue to surprise me. This is not the child I raised. This is not the child that fought the governor when she was just fourteen years old. Where are you Iranti? You have always been able to fight to take care of yourself. I know the answer to life is not to go around killing people the way I used to do, but at least leave this man. You are a doctor. You are earning good money with which you have been taking care of him and me and yourself. This is not worth it Iranti. He continues to abuse you, cheat on you and he just killed your baby. He just killed my grandchild. Where is your head? I know you didn't have the cursed head that I had and that your mother had, but you are behaving in a way that is making me very afraid," Esho pleaded with her.

Ranti believed Esho that she would kill Brian if she saw him, so she asked Moradeke to take her home with her. She promised her friends and grandmother that she would think seriously about leaving Brian, but in her mind she believed she could appeal to him, and if she were able to get across to him he would change.

She just found it difficult to believe that a person could be that cruel, and also she did not want to have failed in the marriage. She believed that if she gave up on the marriage, then it would be confirmed that she was worthless, and she did not want to be that.

Three weeks after Ranti lost the baby, Brian's mother arrived on a visit from Nigeria. Brian tried to be civil to Ranti before his mother's arrival, and he politely asked her to prepare dinner.

At dinner, Brian's mother suddenly asked, "Ranti, are you barren?"

Ranti was shocked at her insensitivity and stared at her, unable to speak.

Brian answered his mother by narrating the whole of Ranti's traumatic history of genital mutilation in an equally crude manner. He laughed as he told his mother that he did not want to have any children with her, since she smelled of urine and feces, and he did not think she could carry a pregnancy to term, as she just lost a baby that it took her over a year to conceive.

Ranti was stunned.

His mother, who had not forgiven her for having her sister arrested and deported back to Nigeria two years before, said to Brian, "We warned you not to marry her, but you were desperate to come to America and you felt she was your passport. The person who helped Vicky buy her visa was going to help you, but you remember what you said to me, 'Mom, this girl is actually begging me to marry her, she is desperate and I don't have to spend any money, she will get me a legal and free visa and will support me until I'm on my feet. It's a free ride and after I finish my residency, I will just divorce her.' How much longer do you have? You can divorce her now; you are earning your own money, and please marry a woman who can bear children. I am eager for grandchildren."

Ranti started to feel dizzy. She convinced herself that she was having a nightmare. It was at that moment she finally heard her friends' and grandmother's warnings and concerns. It was as if she had been asleep for the previous four years, and suddenly she just woke up!

She got up from the table, took her purse and coat and left the house. She went to her office in the hospital where she put a conference call to her friends.

"Don't go back to the house. I'm on my way. I'll be there in an hour Ranti. I'll come get you. Stay in the hospital and wait for me. It's a good thing Esho is not there," Depo instructed her, and both Moradeke and Gboye agreed with him.

She hung up the phone and that thing that used to snap in her at times she experienced injustice, snapped inside her again. She felt as if she were not herself, that her body was not hers, and like she could observe what she was doing.

She felt as if the person that used to be her, and whom she was observing, was on automatic pilot. She reminded this person she did not think was her anymore that Depo had asked her to stay in her office in the hospital and not go back home, and he would be there as soon as he could.

But then she told this other person who was not her anymore that the house belonged to her. She had worked hard for that house. She and Esho toiled and labored and endured a lot of hardship to get that house, and her brother paid with his life for her to get an education. She reminded her that, as a child at seven, she had carried other people's feces on her head so she and her grandmother would survive. She reminded this other person that Brian never loved her. He used her. He had been using her and raping her.

She heard Esho's voice echoing in her ears, "We are not like other women Iranti, we are toys for men, and that is why we are always afraid."

She had refused to die like her great-grandmother, or kill men like her grandmother or become a prostitute like her mother, but she had been raped many times, and she crowned it by marrying a rapist and an exploiter, even though her friends who had eyes to see such things had warned her.

But she had wanted to change destiny and re-write history. She wanted to prove Esho that they could be worthy women, that men would want to be their wives and mothers of their children, but she ended up marrying a rapist.

"That is my house, I worked hard for it and I'm not giving it to him. I am going to do what I should have done to him a long time ago. Esho taught me what to do to men like him and she bought me a knife but I wanted to be a lady. I am going to give Brian 'Esho's treatment' tonight, for his cruelty and for raping me. This is payback," she calmly explained to this part of her she had dissociated from, as she got into her car and drove back to her house.

She parked in the garage next to Brian's new BMW and walked into the house. It was about nine o'clock at night and the living room was empty. She went to the kitchen and picked the biggest knife. She hid it behind her as she walked to their room. Brian was brushing his teeth in the bathroom.

She stood by the door and said to him, "I want you to leave my house this minute, you and your mother."

"*Your* house? I'm not going anywhere and don't you dare pull that stunt you pulled on my aunt again. You got away with it because I was new to this country then and I didn't understand how the system worked, plus Aunt Vicky did not help her case by buying a visa that was not authentic. My mother is asleep, she hasn't recovered from jet lag yet so don't start any nonsense tonight." He brushed past her, and started to climb into bed.

"Brian, get your mother and leave my house, now," she warned him again.

He took a good look at her. "Are you drunk? You have a spaced-out look about you. That would be something. I have never seen you drunk. Guess what, I'll be merciful tonight, I'm feeling generous, so let's make love, come here, and you don't even have to take a shower before I touch you today, come on," he patted the bed.

"I said, take your mother and get out of my house. I'm warning you, if you don't, you are both going to be very sorry."

"And I say, take off your clothes and get into bed now! I want to have sex with you. Don't you want a kid anymore; though I'm sure you are as barren as the Sahara desert; even in the Sahara it rains sometimes. Come on, before I change my mind."

"Get out, and take your mother with you, this is your last warning," she shrieked.

"My last warning? Who do you think you are? Let me tell you something, you do not threaten me, you hag. I will take you when I want you okay? I did you a favor by marrying you. I know what you and your grandmother had to do to feed yourselves when you were little. You used to empty other people's buckets of shit. 'Feces carrier' is what you are. Just because you happened to win a scholarship, now you think you are somebody.

"I know all about you Ranti, you lying bitch. Your father, the one that is 'dead,' Akanbi, he told my mother everything about you and your precious Esho, that crazy witch with her knives.

"My mother has been giving your father money so he wouldn't starve to death. He went to her because you wouldn't send him money, and after all the man did to help you and your prostitute of a mother, and how he tried to save your brother when Esho cut off his foot. I know all your secrets Ranti. Akanbi has been visiting my mother on a regular basis for the past two years. My mother even helped him find some jobs to do, '*Feces carrier!*'" He hissed in disgust.

Ranti started to pant. "Get out now!" she shrieked at him. "Get out or I'll kill you."

He came toward her and hit her hard across the face. She fell against the wall and the knife clattered off. He ran for the knife and picking it up came back to her before she could pick herself up from the floor. He held her right hand in a vice-like grip.

"You want to stab me, is that it? You want to do to me what Esho had trained you to do to men. Guess what? I will mutilate you again since I'm done with you and no man will ever want the feces that you are. I could cut into your pretty face but there is plastic surgery these days, so I will just cut your vagina again. That, no amount of plastic surgery could repair and you will continue to be as frigid as the North Pole, and smell of feces and urine, because I will make sure you start to leak again."

He pushed her onto the bed and ripped her dress off. She screamed and he hit her across the mouth again. Her lips started to bleed. He tried to take off her underwear but Ranti fought him with all her strength.

She struggled with him and sustained many cuts on her legs, abdomen and arms. He cut off her underwear with the knife, and while pinning her down by sitting astride her, he poked her vagina with his fingers spreading it apart.

She continued to struggle but Brian had her pinned down. She dug into his back with her nails and scratched him. She tried to sit up so she could bite into his back. She started to whip her feet up and down as she continued to struggle to prevent him from cutting her, when she felt a searing pain from her vagina. With a sudden burst of energy, she bolted upright and sunk her teeth into his back, determined to extract a pound of flesh. He loosened his grip on her and she was able to break free.

She sprang up and picking the bedside lamp, crashed it on his head. It gave her time to run out of the room. She ran downstairs to the kitchen and he ran after her. In the kitchen, quickly opening a cabinet she retrieved the three knives there. She held them ready and waited for him. She was naked except for her bra and she could feel blood running down her thighs.

As he came at her, she expertly threw one of the knives at him, as if it was a dart. It lodged into the right side of his chest. He stared at her in disbelief. He could not speak, but continued to walk purposefully toward her, so she threw the second knife. It lodged below the first knife.

"One more?" she asked him, "you want one more? I'm good as you can see, and I'm aiming for your heart this time." She aimed, but he stopped walking as he slowly sank back and fell heavily on his back.

Ranti stood where she was, and she could hear the phone ringing. She went to the wall to answer it, and it was Depo. He was at the hospital. He reminded her that he had asked her to wait for him.

"I think I just killed him, Depo. I stabbed him twice, he's on the kitchen floor and he's not moving."

"Ranti, don't move, don't do anything, don't touch him, I'll call the police and I'll be there as soon as I can. I'm just ten minutes away." He tried to transmit some calmness to her.

When the ambulance and the police arrived, Ranti was still standing in the kitchen, not moving as Depo instructed her, naked except for her bra, as the blood continued to run down her legs. She still held on to the third knife.

A police officer came to her and took the knife from her. He informed her that she was bleeding.

"He cut my vagina. That's why I'm bleeding." She calmly told the officer as she pointed to Brian who was unconscious on the floor, with the two knives sticking from his chest.

The officer led her to sit on the couch in the living room as he covered her with her coat. He was talking but she did not hear him. Two paramedics came in to the kitchen. As they started to take Brian away on a stretcher, Depo arrived.

"I'm a friend; she called me when he started to beat her. I made the call. I was coming to get her but she was not at the hospital where I asked her to go. She is a doctor, they are both doctors," Depo explained to the officer.

"Depo, he cut me again, he cut my vagina again."

"Jesus, that fucking bastard, I'm going to kill him."

He made to go at Brian as he was being wheeled out of the kitchen, "Easy there, cowboy, don't make this worse than it is," the officer stopped him.

"His mother is upstairs, I think she's asleep; you know, jet lag." She announced to the room. "Please don't take me to Metro hospital, I work there," she pleaded with the officer.

Ranti was discharged from the hospital the following day and Depo took her back with him to New York City. She was told that the injury to her vagina would heal without any complications, as it was no more than a tear, similar to episiotomies given to some women during childbirth.

Depo told her the police boarded up her house. Brian's mother was sent to a women's shelter. Brian was in critical but stable condition because the knives cracked some of his ribs, punctured the upper lobe of his right lung, and tore into his liver and part of his stomach. "The asshole is going to live, so don't worry about that."

Moradeke brought Esho to Depo's loft the next day and the two of them told her what had happened between Ranti and Brian. Esho looked at Ranti for a long time and she started to cry. "It's my fault, Iranti, it is my fault. I'm the one who couldn't give you a normal family or a sense of belonging in the normal world, and you started to crave it. I remember when you were a little girl, each time you saw a family with mother, father and their children, you would stare at them with such longings. It is my fault, you wanted it so much and you worked hard for it. I am sorry Iranti, I am very sorry."

"Esho, how can it be your fault? How can it be your fault when Brian used his own hands? I married him. I went into the marriage with my eyes wide open, Esho. There is nothing he did to me in the marriage that he did not do to me before the marriage. I have been lying in this bed since yesterday thinking about the whole mess. Everything he did to me after I married him, he had done to me before I married him. He gave me a preview of the coming attractions but I refused to see them. I kept telling myself I was in love.

"Is it that he called me ugly? He did it before. Or that he accused me of prostitution? He did that before I married him, when I spoke to other boys in our class.

"I married a wicked man with my eyes wide open. My friends warned me, many times. You, Esho, you warned me, but I was like *'the hunter's dog that was determined to get lost. No matter how much the hunter blew his whistle to call it back, it would not hear.'* That's me! Gosh, I must really detest myself to believe this is what I deserved.

"It's all my doing, *Eyitemi,* this one is all mine. But I get it now. I finally heard you. I will get my head out of the clouds and start living in the real world. You are right Esho, you have always been right, these things are not for the women in your line, your mother Wura, you Esho, my mother Oshun and me Iranti, we are not like other women. We are playthings for men and the gods continue to have a good laugh over our plights and my attempts to change destiny."

Esho and Moradeke looked at Ranti with tears in their eyes as she spoke.

"Please don't speak like that Ranti, don't," pleaded Moradeke. "A lot of women make mistakes with their first marriages, but then they are able to make a better choice next time. You are still very young. You are just twenty-seven years old. You remember my sister Funmi, the journalist in Lagos; her first marriage lasted just one year, because her husband started to use cocaine. She left him immediately and she has been happily married to her second husband for almost ten years now. Don't sound so defeated Ranti, of course you deserve a good husband, and to be married. This is just an opportunity to learn a good lesson from all these."

Esho continued to weep.

Ranti started to stay in bed like Esho did during her own periods of depression. She felt heavy like she weighed a million tons and everything was an effort for her. She stopped eating and taking showers. Trying to do the sitz bath she had been instructed to do by her doctor, so her vagina tear would heal, was like climbing Mount Everest.

Depo became worried about her, and he was afraid to leave her at home alone while he went to work. She would lie in bed and stare at the ceiling for hours on end, but her mind was blank. Finally, he brought Esho back from Moradeke's house to care for her.

234   *Feasts of Phantoms*

Esho would appeal to Ranti to eat and she would just stare at her grandmother. Esho started to feed her, and even then she would eat only a few bites.

When Depo came home from work, the two of them would get her into the shower, and later she would refuse to come out of the shower. She would tell them she needed to stay longer to get rid of the smell of urine and feces, as well as the worms crawling in her anus.

Esho would leave the bathroom to go and weep.

Depo tried to convince her that she did not smell and there were no worms, but she could feel them and sometimes she saw them on the bed with her, crawling all over her.

Her girlfriends took time off work on several occasions to join Esho and Depo in caring for her, as well as convincing her that she did not smell, and there were no worms anywhere. Finally, Depo hauled her off to a psychiatrist, physically picking her up to carry her into a cab.

He told the psychiatrist, Dr. Obed, her story, while she and the psychiatrist listened to him. Dr. Obed explained a lot of things to her and Depo, but she did not hear most of it because she was concentrating on not gagging from the overwhelming smell coming from her. She was embarrassed, certain that the psychiatrist could smell her and would probably start to laugh at her and point to her.

He continued to speak and she kept staring at his mouth. At some point she heard him say to her, "You want to be a normal girl, no way, you smell. You don't belong in my posh office on Park Avenue. Get out of here, *feces*."

She marshaled the little strength she had and stood up.

Depo looked at her, "Where are you going honey?"

"He asked me get out of his clean office Depo. I don't want him mad at me. I'm leaving." She turned to the doctor, "I'm sorry to bring this filthy body of mine into your office. I apologize. If you want I will clean everything so they don't smell anymore."

Depo started to cry. He stood up and put his arms around her. "Please Ranti, please sit down. You trust me honey and you know I'll never lie to you, I have never in my life lied to you Ranti, remember that. The doctor did not say anything like that. It is safe here Ranti. You trust me don't you?"

She looked at Dr. Obed and he gave her a gentle look. She moved over to Depo, "Hold me Depo, hold me in your arms so people wouldn't smell me, but they will smell your nice aftershave and cologne. Hold me in your arms please."

He held her in his arms and she clung to him.

Dr. Obed prescribed some medication and gave the script to Depo, with a lot of instructions.

They left his office and Ranti continued to cling to Depo, wanting to disappear inside him and not be seen by people, some of whom were pointing at her and laughing. She was relieved when they returned to his loft and she could go and hide in her bed again.

With the medication she was finally able to sleep. She had a dream that *she was in the hospital giving birth. Depo was very happy and he came to the hospital with a bouquet of roses for her. The baby came out of her and she looked at it but it was an alien baby. Its head was octagonal and very huge as were its eyes; it stared at her with huge eyes that wanted to eat. It started to make a sucking noise. She was horrified but Depo was happy. He said the baby was beautiful.*

Depo took her back to the Doctor in his sophisticated Park Avenue office a week later. He appeared kinder to her this time. She did not hear him say that she smelled. He told her she looked more rested.

She told him that she had slept a lot.

He asked her if she wanted to tell him something, "anything?"

She told him she had a dream in which she had an alien baby. She thought it horrifying but Depo was very happy and said the baby was very beautiful. She looked at Depo, and he smiled at her.

Dr. Obed smiled at her too. He reassured her that it probably meant she was at the beginning of a transformation of herself. She could be the baby in the dream, something not formed yet, trying to heal and become whole. That Depo saw it as beautiful meant that he saw the potential in the baby, the potential in her.

"Oh, that's a relief. I thought it was the curse on my ancestors continuing, and that if I gave birth to a baby, she would be an alien."

Dr. Obed said to her, "Being an alien may also mean that it is a new beginning, unlike the old that we know. You mentioned a curse on your line of ancestors. The alien baby could mean that it would not have that curse. It would be different from its ancestors and in that way it is a dream of hope, that with psychological hard work, the curse could be lifted. That the past would become the past and would not continue to impose itself on the present."

"No, doctor, I'm not going there anymore. Each time I hoped to be different, I paid dearly for it. I'm not even going to have children. The curse ends here, and dies with me. And no man is molesting me again. I will not put myself in that position to begin with, and if it happens, like I'm assaulted, then you guys would be visiting me in prison, because the next man who messes with me, I'm killing him."

"I'm glad your fighting spirit is coming back. Anger is a good thing. It helps organize the energy you need to fight this depression. Dreams are good too, even when they appear scary. They will help you understand yourself a lot. But this is a dream of hope and I'm happy you had it; it speaks to a good prognosis," Dr. Obed explained to her and Depo.

When they left the psychiatrist's office, Depo took her to his lawyer friend to begin steps toward her divorce.

Ranti continued to see the psychiatrist on a weekly basis, and she started to have repeated dreams of being locked out of many places. She seemed to have at least one variety of the dream each week.

The first time, she dreamt *that Gboye was getting married but she was not invited to the wedding. She learnt of the wedding from a stranger and she was shocked that her best and oldest friend for so many years would not invite her to her wedding. She complained to Moradeke who said they did not want her at the wedding because she smelled of feces.*

Two days later, she dreamt *that she went to Dr. Obed's office for her appointment but the doorman would not let her in. He also accused her of smelling, and warned her that she must never be seen anywhere on the island of Manhattan again.*

She continued to tell Dr. Obed these dreams and he would say to her, "It's a good thing you are having them, Ranti. This is how you feel about yourself now, this is how you see yourself but there is no reality to it. It's the past that keeps imposing itself on the present and preventing you from having a good future. You are a brilliant and an accomplished doctor, and a good human being, and you would be welcome in all the quality places of the world.

"I know that once in your life your classmates ostracized you because you had to empty other people's feces to earn money to feed yourself and your grandmother, but that is not now. After all, Gboye was the only one who spoke to you at that time when no one else would. So the dream is not based on reality. And you are a colleague of mine, though you are my patient and you are always welcome here in my office."

Eight weeks later she withdrew from her fellowship program.

36

"Iranti, may I speak with you?" Esho asked as she helped her out of the shower three months later. She handed her a towel, and helped her rub the water off her back. Ranti was naked as she sat on the bed to begin to dress. She looked at her grandmother.

"I notice that you are not leaking urine anymore, I am very happy. Iranti, you have been a wonderful child. A mother could not have asked for better. I spent my life cursing the mad man who gave me Oshun, but Oshun gave you to me. I look back on your life as you were growing up. I should have been very happy, but I was too bitter to enjoy it, and I hurt you too much.

"Do you remember what you said to me the day the governor attacked you, when you came home and I went crazy and wanted to attack you too? You said I had made you into a punching bag and that everyone took swings at you, because you had learnt not to defend yourself.

"When I asked for your forgiveness after Brian did this to you, you said I wasn't to blame, but you see, I am. It's my fault for cutting your vagina when you were nine years old, because you were raped that day when four men held you down. I told you on that day that it was okay, that men could rape you. That is the message I gave to you. And that is why you married Brian.

"That was the message I gave Oshun when she was a young girl too. I told her all she was good for was to be raped, I told her that her father was a rapist and that was the best she deserved in life, and Oshun, being who she was, plunged head on into that life.

"I gave you the same message, but in your own fighting way, and maybe it is because of all those books you read, you knew you had to fight me. You fought the destiny I was trying to impose on you. But you couldn't fight all the way. It's like you were torn in two directions. And that is why you went to the governor's office but when you got there, you fought.

"If I did not give you the message that you were worthless and all you were good for was to be raped, you wouldn't have listened to your principal and you wouldn't have gone to that man's office at all. It's that same confusion that made you marry Brian and put up with his nonsense, but your fighting spirit made you stab him. I wished you had killed him.

"I watch television now. I watch movies. I am learning. This is my own school. I heard it explained on television, that, we, the parents, tell our children what they will be in the world, what they should expect from the world and let the world do to them.

"I heard that and I pondered on it for a long time. Parents are *the* gods. We, the Yorubas have always known this with that saying, '*There is no god like mother.*' There is no god anywhere like most of the religions would have you believe. God is in your house with you in the form of your parents. Whatever message they give to their children, it becomes written in stone.

"Like the proverb, '*In our interactions with the world, we bring treasures from home.*' It's my name, Esho. What treasures did I give my children? I gave Oshun despair and hopelessness and it killed her. I tried to do the same with you, but you fought me. Thank you for fighting me, Iranti.

"I remember when you were a child. I was so worried about you because you were unfolding like a rose out of its bud. I would watch you as you slept. You looked so peaceful, like a vulnerable angel. You loved the world so much, oh, how you loved life. I remember you running down the streets when you went to school, or came home or ran errands. You were so full of life and vitality.

"You would laugh with the other children and your voice would ring in my ears for a long time. You would read books and come home to tell me what you had read or learnt in school and you would be so excited, and your face would just glow with happiness at discovering the world. You would tell me stories while you jumped up and down, and dance as you sang songs that came with the stories. The world was a beautiful place to you.

"Little things would fascinate you so, puddles of water running down the gutter, they enthralled you, and you would stand there and stare at them and laugh. You would watch grasshoppers as they went about their business, and your face would be filled with wonder. You came home with flowers in your hair.

"You brought home strange insects and asked me about them, but I knew nothing, and I would yell at you because of my ignorance, but the next day you would bring another one home. You were trying to teach me about beauty, but I was a shade, I was dead.

"You would help the older people carry their heavy bags, Iranti, that is beauty. It does not get better than that. That is God. That is perfection.

"But did I appreciate the angel that was sent into my life to heal me of so much trauma and pain? No, I did not. I focused on the vehicles that brought you to me in the form of the mad man that gave me Oshun, and in the form of Akanbi. I hated the vehicles by which you came to be born, because that is all they were, just vehicles. They could have been more, but they chose not to be. I focused on genetics, and I tried to stop God from coming into my life to cure me of madness through you.

"I told you that you were not beautiful because I believed it would protect you from harm, from men. You are not beautiful Iranti. You are more than beautiful because you are a wonder. You tried to make a beautiful song of God out of my trauma. You took all of us, Wura, Esho and Oshun. You combined Gold, Treasure and a Goddess into Memory, and it became a wonderful transformation in you. Thank you for being my child and my companion all these years." Esho held Ranti's face in her hands.

"I gave up on life at the age of fourteen. I died then and because of that everything I touched died, but you refused to die, and you fought me. You knew you had to fight me, how could you have known?

"You never called me Mama. Oshun called me Mama. My other child, he called me Mama, but you did not, you started to speak and you did not follow their examples. You started to dance to the drum in your head, and you started to call me Esho. I thought it was strange at the time, but something made me respect that, and I let you call me Esho.

"The spirit to fight is in you, Iranti. Please don't give it up. Keep fighting. Don't give up on men. Fight for a husband. Fight for a good man to be the father of your children. Your friends are surrounded by good men. I've been living with Moradeke now for eighteen months, taking care of Ayo. Bode is a good man. I didn't know there were such men in this world. Olu that is courting Gboye, he is a good man too.

"Depo is a good man. Forget all I ever taught you about men and look to the future, it is all yours. I died at the age of fourteen, but you are not dead. Iranti my life, my love, do you hear me?" Esho held on to her face and stared into her eyes as she spoke.

Ranti nodded with tears streaming down her face. "Depo is a wonderful man Esho. He saved me. When I went to the university, I was sick most of the time because of the circumcision, and leaking of urine, and the cramps that I used to have then, and each month, they got worse. They became so bad that I couldn't go for my classes two weeks out of every month.

"He told his mother and she took me to England. I had the surgery then. That was the first time I went away. I told you I was going to Abeokuta, but I lied to you. I'm sorry.

"Efunwunmi took me to England and paid a fantastic amount of money for the surgery. Without their help, I wouldn't have become a doctor. They lifted the curse, Esho."

"I didn't know," said Esho. "I knew the problem went away when you went to the university but I thought it just healed. I am ashamed of myself. I have been since the day I took you to that woman. Oh, Iranti. I died at the age of fourteen and the person that has been around is a ghost, a ghost destroying everything she touched. I don't like it at all.

"I hold Moradeke's baby in my arms now, and I see life, and my heart jumps with joy. Babies cure us of madness. They are balm for aching hearts. Efunwunmi and Depo? Providence will continue to smile on them. I've always said it, long before I knew they gave me this gift of life.

"I know Depo can't have sex. But he can still be the father of your children. I want him to be the father of my great-grandchildren. I hear on the television that they can do things like that now. They can get his sperm into you and you could become pregnant. I'm sure you know of such things."

Ranti looked at Esho and smiled through her tears. "I know of such things Esho, but I can't think about children now. I'm just too tired."

"I know. You are just coming back from hell. I've been there a few times myself. It is very tiring, but it will get better. Once you quoted one of your books to me, you told me you read in a book that a Native American father was talking to his young son after he became a man. You told me that he said to his son:

As you go the way of life,
You will see a great chasm.

240 *Feasts of Phantoms*

Jump.

It is not as wide as you think.'

"Did you not tell me that? I'm now giving that advice back to you Iranti. Jump again and again and again if you have to, and you will get it right. You were on your way but I messed things up for you. You were right before I interfered, forget my interference, please."

Ranti nodded, as she thought, "If only Esho had an education, she would have been much more. She might have been healed of her bitterness and hatred. She is getting so much from reading and watching television now, even though she learnt English so late in her life. If only she had an education."

A month later on a Saturday when Gboye was visiting, Ranti decided to get her house ready for the market by removing her belongings as well as Esho's, and putting Brian's property in storage. Moradeke and Gboye went with her.

Depo was out of town on a conference. He wanted them to wait for him but Gboye had to return to Boston the next day, so he made them promise to inform the local police that they were going to the house, even though the case had been closed, as neither Ranti nor Brian had been prosecuted.

The officer at the police station wanted to know if they expected trouble but Ranti told him she did not think there would be trouble, because her husband was in Florida with some family members, where he was recuperating from his injury, and he had been told he could not return to the house, as that would be trespassing.

But when they arrived at the house at about eleven o'clock, it was obvious that Brian was there. Ranti's car was in the driveway, which meant he had been driving it. She was surprised because Depo had changed the locks.

Moradeke suggested they call the police immediately but Gboye refused. "If Irish has the audacity to come back to this house, I am going to teach him a lesson he will never forget," she said as she parked her car. She went into the trunk to get a baseball bat she had obviously brought with her for such a purpose, since she did not play baseball.

"Gboye, please, I don't want any trouble. They are not prosecuting me for hurting him because he hurt me too, but they could prosecute you. Please, he is not worth it, let's just call the police and they will get him out of here."

"Just get him out of here?" said Gboye, with a look that seemed to ask Ranti, "are you an idiot?"

"Don't you get it Ranti?" She continued. "He won't leave you alone. He will begin to stalk you and make your life a misery. That's what men like him do. He is a bully. You don't treat bullies peacefully. You beat them up and let them know not to mess with you. That is the only language they understand. Wife beaters don't leave their wives alone because of the police or restraining orders. Most of them don't stop until they kill the women, but that's not happening to you because I'm going to kill him today."

Moradeke screamed as she bolted out of the car and started to run across the street. She shouted that she was going to ask Ranti's neighbor to call the police. She knew there was no reasoning with Gboye when she got that way.

Gboye kicked down the kitchen door. She ran through the house, calling out, "Irish, bring your raping ass out here. Where are you?"

Ranti ran after her, begging her to calm down.

Brian came out of the master bedroom ensuite with a towel around his waist. He was shaving. A young woman lay half naked on the bed. Ranti stopped at the door to stare at the woman. The woman stared back at them in shock.

Gboye did not break her stride. She lunged at Brian and started to pummel him with the baseball bat. His towel fell as he tried to stop the blows and cover his face. He kept yelling at Gboye, threatening that he would kill her if she did not stop hitting him.

Gboye was like a woman possessed as she continued to hit him. When she saw his penis, she said between blows, "So this is the puny thing you've been raping my friend with. Jeez, I have never seen one this small and I have seen a lot. Ranti, get a pair of scissors, let's do the women of the world a huge favor by cutting it off."

The woman on the bed started to shriek hysterically, and Gboye yelled at her, "If I were you, peroxide bitch, I would pick up my clothes and disappear, because I'm coming at you next."

The woman scrambled out of bed and picking up her clothes ran out the door.

Ranti started to pull at Gboye as they could hear a police siren. Gboye would not stop. Brian was in a pool of blood on the floor and he was hardly moving. Ranti knew the police would arrest Gboye, because Brian was still married to her, so Gboye would be the trespasser.

She kicked Gboye hard with her boots to get her attention and wrestled the bat from her hands as two police officers ran upstairs toward them. When they came in, Ranti was holding the bloodied baseball bat.

"Put down the bat, lady, put it down, now!" One of the officers yelled at her.

Ranti dropped the bat at the same time frantically yelling at the policeman, "He started to attack my friend with the bat and I tried to protect her. I was afraid he would hurt her like he hurt me before. I had to protect my friends and myself."

The officer came toward her. He yanked her arms roughly behind her back and handcuffed her. "Are you okay, Ma'am?" He asked Gboye.

The second officer went over to Brian where he was on the floor writhing around in pain. He spoke into his phone, calling for an ambulance.

242   *Feasts of Phantoms*

The first officer took Ranti downstairs. Another police car arrived, as well as the ambulance. A second police officer took Ranti from the first officer and escorted her into the back of his car.

Three hours later, she was released to Gboye and Moradeke. The detective who handled the earlier domestic violence case told them that Brian would be prosecuted for trespassing, and it was a good thing they had reported to the police earlier in the day before they went to the house.

"You had no choice Doc, I'm glad you protected yourself this time, and you took your friends with you. Otherwise he would have assaulted you again. Unfortunately, men like him don't stop, but I think he will have a lot of respect for you now," he said to Ranti as he continued to give Gboye a knowing look.

"Thanks Ranti, thank you for thinking fast and saving my hide. I don't think the officer believed you did the beating though. He kept looking at me, and once when he was taking our statements; he winked and nodded knowingly at me. How does it feel to be in jail? I always wondered what it's like behind those bars," Gboye said to her as they walked out of the police station.

"It's actually not too bad. There were two women in there with me. They asked me if I was arrested for turning tricks. I said no, that I beat up my husband with a baseball bat because I caught him in bed with a woman. They were really happy to hear that, they looked at me with lots of respect," Ranti laughed. "But, thank you Gboye. I'm glad you gave the jerk the beating of his life. Did you see the woman?"

"I saw her, she's not a woman. She's a girl. She's probably sixteen years old, she ran down the street as I was coming back from your neighbor's house. He must have been cheating on you for a while, the asshole." Moradeke hissed in disgust, as she patted Ranti on the back. "But all that is history. He is history to us now. We will go back to the house, get your things and Esho's things and ask the Salvation Army to take his stuff."

"Brian is *the tortoise's wife without a sense of shame*, and that is why he would add cheating to his list of shameless behavior," Ranti thought, remembering Esho's story.

Ranti was not sorry as the Salvation Army men took away Brian's expensive clothes, shoes, and ties as well as his other toys, like his stereo system, video camera and computer. She reminded herself that she had paid for most of them anyway, because, even after he started to work, he had continued to spend her money, shopping in expensive stores as if he was a model for the cover of GQ magazine, buying shoes that went for four hundred and even six hundred dollars a pair, and he had bought himself an expensive BMW car. Gboye had said he was dead inside, like a corpse, and that is why he needed to dress up like that all the time, to make people think he was a real human being.

On their way out of the house, Gboye slashed the tires of his car and poured a bag of salt into his gas tank.

The house sold three weeks later while Brian was still in the hospital recovering from the broken nose, ribs and from the old injury to his liver and lungs from when Ranti stabbed him that ripped open again with the beating.

One month later, she went to court with Depo as her divorce was finalized. Brian did not appear in court.

37

Six months after her divorce Ranti left for England to begin her training with Mr. Edwards. Esho remained in New York helping Moradeke with her son and Ranti returned periodically to visit her and her friends, and also in 1993 when Gboye got married, and again in 1994 when Moradeke had her second child and Gboye had her first son.

She did not date. She focused on the training and on a future of returning to Nigeria to work with victims of genital mutilation. She was able to learn a lot about reconstructive surgery from Mr. Edwards who had a lot of patients from the Arab countries and North Africa, where the severe forms of mutilation were still practiced.

She completed her training in late 1994 and returned to New York City. Depo at the time was in a relationship with another architect and Ranti was happy to find that she was not jealous of the man. She actually liked him when Depo introduced them.

She realized she had come to accept Depo for who he was and let him love her in his way. She also wondered if she had given her heart to him, knowing he was gay, as a safety net for her so she would not have to deal with men and sex, because at that time she had been truly afraid of men and sex, and it is not possible to love the things you are afraid of. But she had stopped being afraid of men after she stabbed Brian.

She started to work at a free clinic in Brooklyn while she sent out proposals for grants, to give her the funding to go back to northern Nigeria to begin work with women with genital mutilation. In early 1995 a women's group in California awarded her twenty thousand dollars grant.

While in England, she met a surgeon who worked in a small hospital in a village in the northern part of Nigeria, and he had been happy to learn of her plans to work with victims of genital mutilation. He invited her to his hospital with a promise to support her.

Ranti contacted him after she received the grant. She wanted to know what equipment he had in his hospital so she would know what to shop for. He gave her a list of needed equipment and by the time she finished shopping the twenty thousand dollars was gone.

Depo bought her plane ticket and asked her to leave her passports and other important documents with his mother in Lagos before she traveled to the village, for safekeeping.

The surgeon welcomed her happily; especially the much needed surgical equipment, and the following day she began to work as he had rounded up a lot of women in the area who needed the surgery.

It was re-traumatization for her as she interviewed the women and listened to their stories. Most of their stories were just like hers, generational perpetuation of trauma, both knowingly and unknowingly on the part of their communities, families and parents but mostly their mothers.

As a borrower of words to describe her emotions, she remembered, *"Even if a feeling has been made secret, even if it has vanished from memory, can it have disappeared altogether? A weapon is lifted with the force of a forgotten memory. The memory has no words, only the insistence of a pain that has turned into fury. A body; tender in its childhood or its nakedness, lies under this weapon. And this body takes up the rage, the pain, the disowned memory with each blow."*

Some of the women developed the fistulae from obstructed labor. The head of the baby becomes impacted in the birth canal, where it traps the urethral between it and the pubic bone, and the rectum between it and the sacral bone. This causes the necrosis of the tissue and they later slough off causing the holes and the eventual leaking of urine and feces.

Most of these women with fistulae from childbirth had no business having children at that stage in their lives because they were children too. They were twelve, thirteen or fourteen years old. At that age they were still growing and their pelvises were not big enough to allow a baby's head to pass through.

The women who were very sick from malnutrition became outcasts, and attracted more abuse from a community that tried to make them the containers of all they hated about themselves, and thus targeted these defenseless victims.

Ranti heard horror stories of what life could mean for a woman with uncorrected genital mutilation and fistulae, of the kind she had had. Most of them were given in marriage by the ages of twelve, thirteen or fourteen. She realized, at that age she was having her genitals repaired due to Efunwunmi's kindness, these women were experiencing unbearably painful intercourse with their husbands.

They told her stories of genitals being torn apart again.

They told her stories of beatings when they refuse to have intercourse with their husbands because of the terrible pain.

They told her stories of being divorced and becoming marked women in a society that rejects divorced women.

They told her they had to panhandle on the streets before they could eat.

They told her of being sold into slavery in a country where slavery was illegal to repay the bridal price when they were divorced, and the abuse a slave had to endure, which ranged from physical and emotional abuse to sexual abuse.

They told her stories of being raped anally and orally since their assaulters could not rape them in their scarred or torn vaginas.

Shakespeare's *Titus Adronicus* tormented Ranti while she was awake, and terrified her in her sleep.

A lot of the women were not candidates for surgery because of kidney failure or severe malnutrition and anemia. They would not have survived the surgery. Ranti wept to have to tell these women she could not help them at all, or that she could not help them until much later, when they had built up enough immunity to endure the stress of surgery.

She did not have enough money to house and feed them, but she tried her best. She employed them as cleaners and cooks to ensure they had at least one good meal a day.

This was dehumanization at its worst, not that any form of dehumanization is acceptable. She wondered, what were these women's hopes and dreams, their aspirations? What were their reveries? They did not want much. They did not ask much of the world. They just wanted to be continent. They just wanted to be able to hold on when they needed to hold on, and to let go when they wanted to let go. They just wanted to be able to contain their bodily drainages. They just wanted to be the owners of their bodies, and as such of their minds. They just wanted to be human beings.

Just like her, they just wanted to matter and be necessary in the world. Yet they were traumatized at such a tender age. They were like rose buds forced to open prematurely. What happens to such a bud? It dies, and it never blooms into the beautiful flower it should have been.

She wept because this was not necessary. This was not necessary at all. Oh this was so preventable.

She was grateful for her own training in the smell of urine and feces that came to visit her in moments of despondency. Because of it she was able to sit with these women who smelled so pungently. She did not gag, and was able to hold their hands in compassion and weep with them.

She knew they appreciated and adored her. They were grateful that one person was able to tolerate their smell and sit with them for an hour without covering her nose or spitting in disgust. Oh they were so grateful.

246   *Feasts of Phantoms*

She cried herself to sleep on many nights and realized that surgical correction of these women's problems was just the tip of the iceberg of what they needed. "More needs to be done, more has to be done. They have to be helped to know they are worthy human beings who have a right to life and continence, and not victims. They have to be empowered to become financially viable. They need a lot more than surgery."

Her favorite fairy tale "Sleeping Beauty" came to her mind many times. She realized why she felt such a bond with the princess of that tale. "That princess was prematurely raped too, in symbolic terms, long before she pricked her finger with the needle in the spindle.

"The good fairies who bestowed blessings on her were her ancestors, the women in her family who gave her all her feminine attributes. They blessed her into womanhood. They gave her a beautiful body and hoped she would use it to perpetuate future generations. For her to know that she held the future of the human race in her womb. For her to know that she was a desirable woman, a very beautiful woman, because she was herself.

"And the crone that put the curse on her, that is like Esho mutilating me, and the women who mutilated their daughters—my patients, because of cultural proscriptions.

"Sleeping Beauty was raped for the first time when she was a baby with that curse from the ugly crone. She was raped at a tender age and she closed off. That was why she slept for a hundred years. But time is a generous healer. Time healed her. It repaired her trauma and she was able to respond to a prince who arrived at the right time. She was able to open up again because of the luxury of time.

"That is my story too. That is my mother's story, and my grandmother's story as well as my great-grandmother's story. It is a story of mothers, a story of every woman.

"How old was Wura when she gave birth to Esho and her placenta did not separate? Maybe Wura was just thirteen years old too and had no business giving birth to a baby at that stage in her life. Maybe that was why her placenta did not separate.

"Esho was repeatedly raped at a tender age, and her rose bud never opened again, but the thorns survived because the root of the stalk remained in the soil. She became a dead rose bud with the thorns all around it. The thorns pricked everything to death, just as the princes that tried to wake Sleeping Beauty before she was fully recovered were pricked to death in the hedges around her palace.

"What nature of soil nurtures that rose stalk with the dead bud but intact thorns? It is a desert soil, the soil in a wasteland. It is not a fertile soil but a hostile soil, one of violence, revenge and of pain and sorrow, and the likes of Akanbi continue to give it water.

"Esho is a Sleeping Beauty. But she probably would not wake up again, not even after a hundred years. The soil is not a fertile one and as such Esho cannot forgive, and she would not heal, because Esho was cast out on the day of her birth. She too had a wicked fairy godmother who cursed her. Her mother's death because the placenta did not separate was Esho's first curse. She is like Ishmael who was cast out, but Ishmael had Hagar with him, but Esho could not even take Wura with her.

"The placenta that did not separate started a series of deaths. It could not be buried so Esho would know that that particular point on this earth where she stood was the center of the world, and she had her own source of life-giving waters. Her dead mother, like a desert, took her placenta with her, leaving Esho to make do without life-giving waters, and Esho's alienation led to despair. What do we do with despair? Violence! That is what we do with despair.

"Her rose stalk with the dead bud but living thorns is like those carnivorous plants that eat insects and small animals. She continued to kill off prospective princes.

"Oshun, that was her fate too, but Oshun died with her rose bud, just as Wura, the gold of Alebido Ekiti village, died in childbirth. When their rose buds that were forced to open prematurely closed and shriveled, they died, all in all, thorns, stalks and buds, taking Wura and Oshun with them.

"Oshun's stalk did not survive with the thorns in place to protect her. She did not know that she needed the protective thorns, like the shrubs and the hedges around Sleeping Beauty's palace.

"My shrubs and hedges are in place. Oh they are very much in place. I have not dated a man in almost four years and I have no desire to let a man touch me. I hope my hundred years of healing slumber will not be forever. I hope my stalk will remain alive and I will allow the descendants of Noah in my life to continue to fertilize it for me, because so far in this journey of my life I have come to appreciate that the world is not all malevolent; it is balanced equally by benevolent forces too.

"Depo is right. I tried to short-circuit something that cannot be short-circuited. I tried to re-write history. But I want to heal. I will take my time to heal this time. I will take my time to accept the story of my ancestors as my own and mourn it and move on. I am grateful for the luxury of time, but I pray that my hundred years will be up soon so that like Sleeping Beauty I will wake up to my prince at the right time. I want my stalk to survive so my bud can flower again. I want a second chance.

"These patients of mine, what will become of them? Will they ever wake up again? Will they at least develop some thorns to protect their lives for now? I want to help them develop some thorns, at least until their hundred years are up, so they can take care of themselves and know they don't have to be slaves or outcasts. I want them at least to be able to protect themselves so they will not be raped orally and anally.

"Their buds have been prematurely killed off but they still need the thorns. Maybe, oh maybe, as I hope for myself in the near future, I will be given a second chance of flowering again, and they too will have a second chance. Oh so much needs to be done."

Ranti stayed in Nigeria for three months on her first trip. She operated on about fifty women, and by the time she left over ninety percent of the surgery was successful.

She returned to the US empowered to solicit more funds. She remembered the looks on the faces of the women when they became dry for the first time in years. She remembered how she had wanted to run through the streets of London, announcing that she was dry to everyone she saw in jubilation when she had her own surgery.

Her patients had hugged her and cried.

They had been speechless. The words they wanted to say, to convey their feelings of gratitude to her were of feelings that came from the part of mind where speech has not yet penetrated.

They had offered her earrings and head ties or shawls, as thanks. Those articles had been the most they possessed, and she had told them that she understood what they were trying to say to her, that her gift to them was priceless.

She told them she understood more than they would ever know, and that she was the lucky one who was in a position to dispense such pearls, and they were healing her, even though they were the identified patients.

She was able to return to Nigeria six weeks later with more equipment and surgical materials that were donated by the hospital where she trained, and this time she had over twenty thousand dollars in cash to purchase more materials.

She stayed for three months again and returned to New York for two weeks, for Esho who was happy to be helping Moradeke with her children.

36

Two years after Ranti began working in this hospital she was invited to the World Health Organization in Geneva in response to a proposal for funding.

She had written a comprehensive proposal incorporating steps to rehabilitate these women, as well as much-needed preventive measures so more girls would not be subjected to the trauma. After a two-day interview at the World Health Organization, she was offered a million dollars to work on the project.

Ranti was shocked. She had asked for half of a million dollars but the field officer explained that she had underestimated the cost of the project, which in his experience usually cost much more.

But the condition was that funding of such magnitude had to go through universities or the government. So, her fund was sent to the government of Nigeria, but with stipulations that it be spent on her project. She was still hopeful especially since the minister of health for the country was a woman known to favor women and children in her policies.

Ranti went to New York to share the good news with her grandmother and friends, and Esho said, "You have got to places I never imagined possible for a human being, more so someone from my line."

Ranti went to the Ministry of Health in Abuja to ask for the money, and she was frustrated for months, as it was tied up in bureaucracy. She was asked to make trip upon trip to the capital city, and this cut into the time she could have been taking care of her patients so much that she wondered if it had made sense for her to have written the proposal in the first place.

One Monday morning, six months later, she read in the newspaper that there had been another cabinet reshuffle by Abacha, the dictator who had installed himself as the president of the country two years before; and as such there was a new minister of health, General Jamba.

Ranti stared at the newspaper unable to believe her eyes. "He is my Nemesis. He keeps coming back into my life at critical times," she said aloud to herself.

Over the years, he had remained in the government of the country as he had been shuffled from one ministry to another. "What do you expect when we are being ruled by psychopaths who keep playing musical chairs with the fate of the country? The World Health Organization thought they were helping disenfranchised Nigerian women, but what they have actually done is to make the despots ruling us richer by a million dollars, isn't that ironic?" She knew Jamba would steal the money if it had not been stolen yet.

She called Moradeke to tell her that Jamba had been appointed the new minister of health. She wanted her sister, Funmi, who was a journalist with the Concord newspaper in Lagos to print an article on her work in the northern part of the country, saying that the World Health Organization gave her a grant that the government would not release.

Moradeke was happy she finally had an opportunity to use the weapon that her friends had always teased her about, "The pen is mightier than the sword." Each time the three of them had to find a solution to problems of lecturers sexually harassing them when they were in school; Moradeke always offered her journalist sister's services in printing an article on the situation. So, this time she gladly called Funmi.

The following day, Funmi, who had become an editor for the newspaper sent

250   *Feasts of Phantoms*

some of her staff to interview Ranti in her village, and a week later an extensive article appeared in the Concord newspaper on genital mutilation and its adverse effect on the victims. There were photographs of the women who consented to their pictures being taken, with their stories.

The nurses and other staff who worked with Ranti were interviewed as well, and the article concluded that "The World Health Organization was so impressed with the work that Dr. Iranti Jare had been doing in the village that they awarded her a grant of a million dollars so she could better serve the women, but the money has been tied up in bureaucracy for the previous six months, and has not been released to her and her staff so it could be used for the women who desperately need the help."

Ranti spoke with two more news magazines that wanted more details on the grant, and in the following days more newspapers and magazines carried the news, urging the dictator government to release the money so it could be used for the people.

One month later the World Health Organization wrote to Ranti that they would be sending auditors to her village, to assess her project to see if she needed more assistance, because it was a project they wanted to continue to use to address the problems of genital mutilation.

Ranti wrote back that the money had never come to her. The federal government refused to give her the money, so the auditors need not come to her village except to see the huge need for her services, but for auditing purposes they should go to the Ministry of Health in Abuja.

Two weeks later, she was invited to Abuja by the minister of health, General Jamba to discuss her project.

Ranti ignored the invitation.

Another week passed and she received another letter personally from General Jamba, in which he wrote:

Iranti Jare,

Like I told you many years ago, I will have a say in your life and career. You blackmailed me at the time you were about to graduate from medical school. I fulfilled my end, but you failed to honor your end of the deal when you ratted my son out to the police in England and my son, who is innocent of any crime, is languishing in prison in England for the crimes he did not commit. Yet you think you will go on with your life and be rewarded.

I invited you to my office to discuss the funding from the World Health Organization for the projects you lied to them about, but you did not have the courtesy to honor the invitation from the government of your country. That action confirms your lies.

The money will not be released to you either now or in the future. I have sent it to my account abroad to await the release of my son from his unfortunate incarceration.

Your money will be used for his rehabilitation into society because he has lost ten years of his life due to your lies.

Yours truly,

He signed his name,

General B.O. O. Jamba.

The Honorable Minister of Health: Federal Republic of Nigeria.

Ranti observed that he refused to address her as Dr. Jare. She wondered how someone could be so stupid as to implicate himself by writing a letter to her on such a serious matter. She concluded that as with a lot of the vagabonds who ruled the country, he felt invincible.

A week later as Ranti was returning to her bungalow on the grounds of the hospital, she thought she saw a man who looked like Akanbi talking to one of the security guards. He was far away and she told herself that her mind was playing tricks on her, but it was not because half an hour later Akanbi knocked on her door. Ranti half opened the door to talk to him.

"Ranti, it's good to see you, can I come in?"

"No, you cannot come in, what do you want?" She asked him coldly.

"Is that a way to speak to your father? I traveled all the way from Ibadan to see you because I read in the newspapers that you are a big doctor here now, and the World Health Organization paid you a million dollars for the work you do."

She stared at him for a moment. "And did you also read that the money was never given to us in this village? And besides, Akanbi, you are not my father, neither were you Lana's father and he died. You remember that, don't you? I'm sure you remember that my mother died carrying your baby and you didn't help her.

"Esho came to you when they were sick and dying. She came to you for help, but you turned us away. She came back to you when they died so you could help her bury them, but you called her a crazy witch.

"I came to you when she was depressed after she lost a daughter and a grandson and she couldn't lift a finger to care for herself or me. I came to you for help so we wouldn't starve. What did you tell me, Akanbi? That was the only time you spoke to me, even though I saw you almost every day. You said to me, 'come here you bastard, I am not your father, I don't know where your mother the prostitute got pregnant with you. Don't ever call me your father again for as long as you live.'

"I carried shit on my head, Akanbi. I was six years old and I carried other people's feces on my head to care for my grandmother! Children stopped playing with me and started to call me 'Feces.'

"You are right. You are not my father, because a father wouldn't have allowed that to happen to his child. My father is one of the many men my mother the prostitute slept with. I tried to give you a second chance to be my father but what did you do? You stole my money. I was on my way to secondary school, but you stole my money. So, it is no thanks to you that I'm a 'big' doctor today. I don't owe you a thing, so please leave." Ranti started to close the door.

"I need your help," cried Akanbi. "I ask for your forgiveness. I was a bad person at the time but I have changed. I'm now a born-again Christian and I have realized the errors of my ways. God has put you in a position of power now; don't abuse it by not helping me. Don't repay me in that way. I am your father, and it is your duty to take care of me; without me, you wouldn't even be alive today. You owe me that much, I gave you life. I wanted to be in your life but your grandmother is a wicked witch, she prevented me.

"I borrowed money to come here to see you, and as I stand here before you, I do not have a penny on me. The last time I ate was yesterday. Please help me. Do not turn me away. I don't have anything anymore. I had to sell my house."

Ranti remembered him on the second-floor balcony of that building, standing like Zeus on Mount Olympus raining down acid of humiliation on her and Esho.

"My wife left me. All your brothers and sisters are gone. I have nothing. Even if it is a job you can help me find here, I will take it. Have mercy on your father," he pleaded with her.

"Akanbi, please leave or I will call the police."

She shut the door on him and went back into the house to call the hospital security. She could not believe that Akanbi had traveled over five hundred miles to come and beg her for money. "Wait until I tell Esho this."

A few days later, the surgeon at the hospital warned her not to go into the village at all, and if she needed anything from the market the hospital staff would get it for her. He heard rumors that the religious leaders were not pleased with her work because a lot of the young women she treated were working as prostitutes. They said she was corrupting their women.

Ranti asked her staff if it was true that her patients were working as prostitutes, and they confirmed the story. They also told her that the news in the village and the neighboring town was that she received a million dollars from some European countries for turning these girls into prostitutes, and a lot of the people were angry about that. They said white people who were Christians did not like them and sent her to destroy their society by corrupting their women.

They wanted her to hand the money over to them for the village to use on more important projects than that of helping these women whom the villagers described as mere beggars who were "nobodies." She was messing with the work of their god who had ordained it such that some women would leak urine and feces, and it was such women that the society needed to be beggars.

"If this doctor goes around curing everyone who would be beggars, who will be there for the holy people to give alms to on Fridays, and prove to god that they are pious and religious? This doctor is destroying the moral fiber of our community," they quoted the villagers.

"What do you think?" Ranti asked the nurses, clerks and the driver. She wanted to know since they were local people too. "Is the work we are doing helping these women, or turning them into prostitutes? Are we corrupting them? Are we destroying the moral fiber of this community? Please give me your honest opinion."

"Even though I'm a man, Doctor," the driver started, "what you are doing for these women is a great blessing in their lives. They adore you. I hear them when I take them home or bring them for their appointments.

"My mother died when I was ten years old. She leaked urine and feces most of her life and we were outcasts. The only people who would allow us to live amongst them were lepers in the lepers' colony.

"I ran away to Lagos when I was thirteen years old, and that was where I learnt to drive a bus. If you had come into our life when I was a little boy, I would have gone to school and I would have received an education. My mother was always afraid because of the smell. People used to throw rocks at her and call her a witch. She was not a witch. She was a woman who was just always afraid.

"You are returning these women into the human beings that Allah made them in the first place. I'm happy to drive you places, Doctor, and to drive your patients. It makes me feel as if I am helping my mother. One day I might become a father of daughters."

Fausa, her personal assistant, joined in, "And Doctor we know the government did not release the money from the World Health Organization. I type all the letters for you. We know you have been begging them to release the money or even some of it. We know you've been writing to your friends in America to beg for money to pay our salary. We, your staff, we know this and we appreciate what you are doing for these women. We try to explain that to the people in the village but they don't want to understand."

Ranti was relieved that her staff was on board with her. She acknowledged that her young patients becoming prostitutes was inevitable. The girls had no other options, they had no education and they were already outcasts who felt they were not good for anything else, so the only means open to them to support themselves was by prostitution.

She cursed the Ministry of Health for not releasing her money with which she could have helped the girls more by building shelters and beginning to train them in some profession, and even counseling for them to know they had other options in life.

She heeded the warnings of the surgeon and stayed on the hospital grounds. She asked her staff to bring the girls working as prostitutes to her, to prevent them from being killed as was the punishment in this people's culture for the alleged crime.

A week later, Akanbi returned to the hospital. Ranti was on her rounds when one of the nurses told her that a man who said he was her father wanted to speak to her. He started by appealing to her for help again, but Ranti reminded him that he was not her father and she did not owe him anything.

"I have not eaten in two days. I have not been able to go back to Ibadan because I don't have money for transportation. At least give me some money so I can go back to my people in Ibadan."

Ranti borrowed thirty naira she knew was enough to get him back to Ibadan, and give him three meals, from one of the nurses.

"Is this all you will give me?" He angrily demanded of her.

Ranti nodded. "Remember, Akanbi, I do not owe you a cent. If anyone owes anyone here, you owe me my money that you stole. This is just compassion money."

"Compassion money? He shouted, and his voices got louder. "Compassion money? You are sitting on a million dollars and you give me thirty naira and you call it compassion money!"

Ranti stared at him.

"You bastard!" Akanbi shouted. "You child of a whore! I have been talking to the villagers. They are going to kill you because of the prostitution you have been spreading around here, but I appealed to them, I promised them that you will give them some of the money from the Europeans. They want at least three-quarters of that money, because that is the only condition by which they will let you live, so, if you care about your life, you had better pay me a hundred thousand dollars now. Otherwise I will hand you over to them. They are bringing men from neighboring villages to kill you and your patients, because they don't want to do it themselves in case the government sends soldiers to retaliate.

"The killers don't know you, but *I know you*. I will bring them here, point you out to them and disappear. If the government sends soldiers, I will be long gone and so will the killers. You have till this afternoon." He pocketed the thirty Naira and walked away.

Ranti watched him until he disappeared. She turned to her staff and instructed them to begin evacuating her patients and they moved quickly. With her ten-seater van and the hospital ambulance, they had transferred most of the patients to a hospital thirty miles away by noon.

While she was anxiously looking toward the hospital gates for her assistant who had gone to town to look for transportation for them and the remaining five women, she saw an angry mob making toward the hospital with a variety of weapons in their hands.

She ran back into the big ward to warn the women as the mob made for the wards. She started to worry about the remaining patients, most of whom would not be able to run for their lives, because even though they had not had surgery they were weak and sick from malnutrition and other concurrent illnesses, but all the same she yelled at them to run.

The mob stormed into the ward and started to attack the women as they were trying to run out through the doors and windows. Ranti had a moment to be thankful that the ward was on ground level. She was pleading with the mob when she saw Akanbi among the men. He pointed his right index finger at her. "That is the doctor who has been turning your women into prostitutes. Her mother was a prostitute and so was her grandmother."

Ranti was convinced she was dreaming. The men started toward her, chanting some words she could not understand as they were speaking in their language. She ran to the window behind her, jumped over it and into the woods.

There were lots of people running in the woods as well, trying to escape the killers, so she made sure she ran with them so her pursuers would not be able to identify her. She ran for about an hour, afraid to stop, even when she could not hear her pursuers or the people trying to escape them.

At some point she started to feel a severe pain shooting from her left foot and when it became unbearable, she stopped and looked down at herself. Her white coat was in rags, having been torn by the bushes and shrubs she ran through. Her surgical scrub was still in fairly passable condition. She had cuts all over her arms and face, and her left ankle was throbbing with pain.

She looked in the direction of the hospital and could see smoke. She realized that the mob had set the hospital on fire and killed her patients. She took off her white coat, tore it into small pieces to bind her throbbing ankle and continued on her way in the bushes, limping for another hour until she arrived at a truck stop.

A driver was getting into his semi full of cows. She ran up to him, begging him to take her with him. She pointed at the smoke they could see. "Those people will kill me, there is a riot going on there. Please help me. She offered him her stethoscope as well as her wristwatch and earrings, which were gifts from her friends.

"Please, I had to run for my life. I couldn't even take money; this is all I have on me. The watch and earrings are made of real gold, please help me, I beg you in the name of God."

He looked at her for a long time as his eyes traveled over her body, taking in her bound left ankle. He looked in the direction of the smoke. "These people become crazy when aroused. A Yoruba woman does not belong here, didn't you know that?"

Ranti continued to plead with him. He took the watch, earrings and stethoscope from her. "Hop in. I'm going to Lagos."

Ranti had a moment to wonder what he would do with the stethoscope as

256   *Feasts of Phantoms*

she climbed into the truck to sit next to him. He drove for four hours without stopping and she was grateful because it took her far away from the village.

Eighteen hours later, at about six o'clock the next morning, he dropped her off on the outskirts of Lagos. He did not ask her any question through the long drive. She smiled at him as she profusely thanked him. As she was hobbling away from him, he called to her. She turned around. He came toward her and gave her back her wristwatch, earrings and stethoscope without saying a word.

An hour later, Efunwunmi screamed when she opened her door and saw Ranti in rags.

Two days later, on a Friday, when Depo picked her up from JFK airport, he took her straight to the hospital and a few hours later she was in surgery. She was told that her ankle had broken in four different places. She had pins inserted to hold the bones together and her surgeon instructed her to stay off the foot for three months.

37

The following day Depo brought Esho, who had been helping Moradeke with her two small children, back to the loft. Ranti could not talk with her grandmother because of the sedation from the pain medications. Depo told her as much as he knew, and Esho started to cluck around the house cursing Akanbi as she had always done.

On Monday morning, Moradeke took the day off work since Esho was not available to help with her children, she brought them with her to visit Ranti who was more alert and was able to tell them the details of the incident.

Esho became very quiet. She did not curse Akanbi and her silence was more disturbing to Ranti, but she assured herself that even though she knew Esho would like to kill Akanbi, thankfully he was thousands of miles away in Nigeria.

Ranti repeatedly asked her what she was thinking, and Esho kept saying she was not surprised at the behavior of the man.

The following day, after Moradeke dropped her children off on her way to work, Esho told Ranti she wanted to go to Nigeria to visit her friends. "I haven't been back in eight years, I miss my people."

Ranti knew she wanted to go and kill Akanbi. She had anticipated this and on her way to America had even formulated a lie she would tell her, but when she saw Esho, some regression set in for her, as well as the disappointment that not only had Akanbi refused to acknowledge her as his daughter, he wanted her dead.

She had found it difficult to accept that a man who had fathered her, at least by his final admission for the first time, one week ago, and a man who had been her mother's lover for many years, would want her dead because of money. But then she reminded herself that he had watched Oshun become sick and die while she was pregnant with his child, and had watched Lana get sick and die too.

She finally admitted that he was a very cruel man and such cruelty was possible in the world and they would kill without batting an eyelid. But the pain of the disappointment was there, and that was why when she saw her grandmother's ever loyal and reassuring face, she broke down and told her the truth. But she felt that Akanbi was safe from Esho where he was in Nigeria.

"Esho, please listen to me, you can't go to Nigeria, especially now. You are too angry with Akanbi. Please, I beg you, if you have any love for me, don't go to Nigeria now. Wait for two months until my ankle has healed some, and we will go together."

"No, Iranti, you have been through enough already. You need to rest here. I will go alone. I can read and write, I can travel alone to Nigeria and I will be back before you know it. I don't even want you going back there at all. I want you to stay here with Depo where it is safe."

"Esho, I can't let you go to Nigeria. I just can't. Give me two months and I will come with you, please. Haven't we always done everything together? You are the only family I have and I don't want to lose you."

"Lose me? What are you talking about? I just want to go to Nigeria to visit my friends. Who is losing who?"

"Esho, you and I know why you need to go to Nigeria so desperately. What friends are you going to visit? Akanbi will meet his end in his own way. I hate the man and I want him dead too, but he can't hurt us anymore. You are not the young woman you used to be. He could kill you and then what will become of me? I will become a motherless child, and when I have children they won't have a grandmother. You wouldn't be there to hold and take care of my children as you have been taking care of Moradeke's children. Is that what you want for me, Esho?" Ranti pleaded with her.

"If the likes of Akanbi continue to prowl the face of this earth, Iranti, you will not live long enough to have those children you are promising me. Your life will always be in danger. I worked hard for us to get where we are now, and I refuse to have him take that from me. He has taken too much from me already, no more!

"I killed men who did not even rob me of a tenth of what he has spent his life robbing me. As of today, this earth is too small for the two of us. He and I cannot exist on the face of this earth at the same time. One of us will have to leave and I am not leaving," Esho asserted.

Ranti was at a loss. She could not let Esho go to Nigeria to kill Akanbi because she might die or be imprisoned. But at the same time, Esho was determined to go.

Depo, Moradeke and Gboye joined Ranti in appealing to Esho, and for days they begged her not to go, but she was adamant.

Finally, two weeks later, Ranti said to Esho, "I forbid you to go to Nigeria and I'm not buying your plane ticket until I'm able to come with you, and that will be in six weeks."

Esho surprised her by nodding her head in consent.

A week later, about six on a Thursday morning, when Moradeke on her way to work came to drop off her children, Esho was not there to open the door for her as she had always done. Depo was out of town on a work project that took him away during the week.

The persistent ringing of the doorbell woke Ranti and she stumbled out of bed. She and Moradeke went in search of Esho who had never overslept in her life but her room was empty. Her purse and small traveling bag were gone.

Ranti panicked. "She's gone Moradeke. She has gone to Nigeria to kill Akanbi. I might never see her again because he could kill her or she could end up in prison." She started to cry. She ran to her room and started to dress. "I'm going after her. I have to stop her. I can't let her go killing people. I hope it's not too late." She stopped all of a sudden as it hit her.

"Oh my God! She left last night. I heard a lot of banging going on at about nine but I was too woozy from those damn painkillers I've been taking. I went to sleep at about eight last night. I heard the noise and something did tell me to get up and investigate, but I was just too sleepy. Damn those pills, I am never taking painkillers again in my life. Damn!" She explained to Moradeke, who appealed to her to calm down and let them call JFK first.

"They won't tell us names of passengers on the manifest for security reasons, and we don't even know which airline she's traveling with," said Ranti.

Moradeke tried to stop Ranti, urging her to take a breath and let them call Depo first, and he might come with her, but Ranti did not stop as she quickly got dressed in a pair of jeans and a sweat shirt. She hurriedly stuffed some underwear and two tops in her purse, as well as her wallet and passport. She grabbed her crutches where they were by the front door, and giving Moradeke a quick hug said to her, "Esho is capable of killing him, trust me. I'll call you as soon as I can."

At JFK airport she bought a ticket at the KLM booth. They were boarding a flight for Amsterdam, and they happened to have empty seats.

She arrived in Nigeria eighteen hours later at about six the next morning. She took a taxi to Ibadan and arrived in their rented one-room accommodation at about ten that morning. She asked the driver to wait for her.

When she tried the door to their room, it opened, and Esho was sitting on the bed with that spaced-out expression that Ranti remembered from when she was a little girl.

"Esho!" She ran to her as she started to shed tears of relief. Esho raised her hands to hug her and there was caked blood on them. Ranti suppressed a scream.

"Esho, this is not the time to space out. Snap out of the fog, we have to get out of here, now." She started to pull her up from where she was seated on the bed but Esho would not budge.

Ranti could hear the neighbors speaking excitedly in front of the house. She ran to the back of the house to get some water in a bowl and started to wash Esho's hands.

She removed most of the blood from her hands and arms, and as she quickly inspected her to make sure there was no blood on her clothes and shoes, she picked up her bags and pulled her off the bed. She dragged her out of the house and into the waiting taxi while some of the neighbors tried to stop them, so they could greet them.

"We'll be back soon. There is someone we just have to see urgently. They're going out of town in a few hours. We'll be back soon. It's so good to see all of you," Ranti explained to them as she pushed Esho into the taxi. She gave some of the neighbors quick hugs, but as she tried to fly into the taxi after her grandmother a man pulled her back and whispered into her ear, "I'm sorry this is a bad home-coming for you, I just saw him yesterday morning and he was fine. I'm sorry but they found your father's body by the river. Someone must have beaten him to death with a club. Don't tell Esho yet. We will be here when you get back."

Ranti thanked him and rushed into the taxi, "We are going back to the airport, we are late for our flight, so please step on it," she yelled at the driver.

"I don't want to go back to America yet, I still have some business I need to take care of here. I need to go home to my father and mother's village. I want to pay them a visit," Esho asserted.

"No, Esho, you have taken care of enough business as it is. No more revenges, okay? We are going back to New York, now!" Ranti yelled at her.

They arrived at the airport two hours later and Ranti ran into the departure lounge to scan for flights leaving in the next few hours. She did not care where it took them so long as they got out of Nigeria immediately.

Ghana Airways was leaving for Accra in forty-five minutes, so she ran to their desk and bought two tickets. She was relieved when the plane started to taxi.

She looked at her grandmother. "Esho, Esho, oh Esho," she called to her as she hugged her and held her in her arms. Esho stayed in her granddaughter's arms with that spaced-out expression on her face.

In Ghana, after Ranti bought tickets on a British Airways flight that was leaving three hours later for London, she took Esho to the bathroom to inspect her more closely and make sure there was no blood on her. As she started to take off her skirt, Esho snatched her skirt back. "Do you think I'm an idiot? I washed up after."

"Yes, Esho, I think you are. What were you thinking?" Ranti yelled at her. "And when I found you spaced-out in the room, you had blood on your hands. You could have been killed or ended up in prison. And was that a time to space out? You are in the habit of spacing out at the wrong moments. Jesus, Esho."

Ranti still inspected her and made her change her outfit. She threw her skirt and blouse into the garbage. She too changed her underwear and top. When she came out of the toilet stall, Esho snapped at her, "Didn't the doctor tell you to stay off your foot for three months, and where are your crutches?"

"The patriarch is burning and you are asking about his beard?" Ranti rolled her eyes in disbelief. "I took them with me when I left New York but I must have lost them somehow. I'm fine. My foot is not too painful."

"Don't you want to know how I did it? I went to…" Esho started,

"Hey, hey, hey, hey, Esho, No, not now," Ranti yelled at her as she raised her right hand to stop her from speaking. "I don't want to know anything, not here. When we get home you can tell me, but you are not to speak of it while we are in transit okay? *Walls have ears*, otherwise you will be telling the police."

Esho gave her a dirty look, but she kept quiet.

Twenty hours later, and after a two-hour lay over in London, they arrived in New York City in the early hours of Sunday morning. Ranti did not realize how tired she was until she walked into the loft and Depo, looking so relieved, hugged her.

She had been able to catch only snatches of sleep on the planes, about four hours in those four days. She had been too afraid to sleep or even doze off at the airports, constantly watching out for the police and developing anxiety attacks each time a uniformed person lingered too close to them.

Esho on the other hand had had hours of the sleep of the innocent, sleeping throughout the duration of the flights. When Ranti made the observation, Esho said she had not slept in two weeks prior to going to Nigeria, and that was why she needed to go so desperately.

"What happened?" Depo demanded of them. "I leave you two alone for a few days and you are gallivanting around the world. What the hell is going on?"

"Esho this is a good time to tell your story, and please say everything in Yoruba, no English at all, *walls have ears*."

Esho sat down next to Depo and grateful for the audience she started to narrate her story. "No one has ever offended me and gotten away with it. I never allowed it, because if you let such a person get away once, they will come back again and again. I more than anyone know that. My father raped me four times before I stopped him by stabbing him in the chest. And the mad man that gave me Oshun before I was ready? The second time he came at me, I killed him. I should have taken care of Akanbi the first time he slept with Oshun. If I had done that, he wouldn't have taken so much from me." She paused for a moment and then continued.

"After Iranti came back from Nigeria when those barbarians wanted to kill her for taking civilization to them, and Akanbi was the one who pointed out my child, I said to myself, "Esho, you have always known this, people who take precious things from you will keep coming back to take more and more, until you stop them."

"I died at the age of thirteen after I killed that mad man who gave me Oshun before I was ready. I stopped being afraid, and a person who is alive should be afraid. It is what makes us human. But then children were born and they breathed life into me, and I started to be afraid again, because you love children and that makes you vulnerable and you are not as vigilant as you should be.

"I was not able to keep my children alive because I was not as vigilant as I should have been, and children died. Akanbi killed two of my children because I loved my children and I started to be afraid again.

"After he did that, I stopped feeling. I went to hell. I came back from hell and I said to myself, "This one remaining child, I will do everything in my power to keep her alive. I will stop feeling if that is what it will take." And I did, but then I almost killed her too.

"And the two of us, Iranti and I, we worked very hard so we would be allowed to live in peace and not be afraid. We sacrificed and we suffered." She paused again and looked intently at Depo.

"Iranti was a small girl but she knew how to fight to stay alive. She sacrificed as much as I did. She became my partner and no more my child. She became the father and the mother I never had. She kept me alive at a time when I wanted to die after Akanbi killed my children."

She turned to Ranti, "I know what you did Iranti, even though that time was like a dream to me. I wasn't in this world at all but I know what you did. Some things penetrated and came through to me. I know that you carried feces on your head for that good-for-nothing Aremu by the mill and he cheated you. Even though you never told me, and we never spoke of it, but I knew. That was why when armed robbers killed him fifteen years ago, I rejoiced. People like him do not deserve to be on this earth with the rest of us.

"Iranti was not seven years old when she knew she had to go to work to keep her grandmother alive. The truth is, I wanted to follow my dead children at the time, but Iranti would not let me go. She kept calling me back. I used to hear her voice calling to me, even though it sounded so far away, "Esho get up and take a shower, it will help you feel better," "Esho get up and eat, you have not eaten in two days," "Just try Esho, a little, just a little taste," or "Esho, do you want to hear what I learnt in school today, this is what they taught me in school today Esho.

"She kept calling me in those ways. She would not let me follow my dead children. Nobody has ever taken care of me. No one has ever worried about me or tried to keep me well and alive. Nobody has ever run after me to bring me back, all my life. I left places, and I didn't look back and no one ever said, "Let us go and get Esho and bring her back," no one except Iranti. I appreciated it then, and you did it again this time. The doctors said to you, "Stay off your foot for three months," but you did not listen to them, you ran after me to bring me back.

"You took care of me when I was sick with depression. You at the age of six went out to get a job, so I could eat to stay alive. You worried about me and you knew what to do to keep me in this world.

"You have suffered too much, Iranti, far too much for me to allow Akanbi rob me of you, or deprive you of a good life. I should have killed him a long time ago. I should have done it after my children died or even when he stole your money. I had so many chances. It was my mistake that I didn't.

"Here I am, a person who didn't believe in ghosts or black magic or any god, and yet I thought that cursing him and wishing smallpox on him would kill him. I became weak and vulnerable. If I didn't kill him, he would never leave you alone, Iranti. He wouldn't, not until he killed you, and I couldn't let that happen. Not anymore."

Tears sprang into Ranti's eyes as she continued to look at her grandmother.

"I died at the age of thirteen," said Esho, "but children have kept me alive. I haven't been living for myself at all, but children came along and tried to heal me and I force myself to live for them. Look at Moradeke's children. They love me, and they laugh when they see me. I want to live for them, but I need to keep a part of me dead, the part that will help me defend and protect that which is mine, because it is difficult to kill a man unless a part of you is dead already. I remember what it was like to die at the age of thirteen." She paused and was quiet for about a minute.

"The question you asked me. I left on Wednesday night. I had gone to the travel agent down the street on Monday when I couldn't take it anymore. I bought a ticket on South African Airline. It stops in Lagos. I left after you took your medication and I knew it would make you sleep."

"So she had about ten hour's head start on me." Ranti thought. "She did not have to go through Europe at all. By the time I discovered she was gone, she was almost in Lagos."

"I took a taxi to Ibadan," Esho continued her story. "When I got home, I met Mama Oye." She paused. "Iranti, do you remember her? I used to buy kerosene from her, she was very happy to see me and I was very happy to see her too. That was when she told me what had been happening in the neighborhood.

"She told me that Ajao died, that Isaac's mother by the bus stop died too. So she is telling me all these things, and how Iyabo by the dispensary had a baby. I was impatient to get going because '*when you go somewhere, you face what you have gone there to do, and not waste time on distractions.*' But I'm happy I did not cut her off. I patiently waited for her to give me all the news of the neighborhood.

"She even told me that the woman who sold palm oil close to the police station was a witch. One night, the year before, she just started confessing to all the people she had killed with witchcraft. She said she killed a lot of children who died in infancy, and that she and her fellow witches ate them at their meetings. So the people of the neighborhood, especially the families of those children she claimed to have killed and eaten, stoned her to death."

Depo was horrified, "That's not possible! How could she have killed the children and eaten them? Did she kidnap them? Did their families not bury them when they died?"

"I don't know, Depo. We hear a lot of crazy things like that in our neighborhood. Those children died of some illnesses, and their families buried them, but we are very superstitious and the families believed she used black magic to kill them. I don't care for such nonsense, I am too practical."

Ranti explained for Depo's sake, "The poor woman probably had a clinical depression. Some women, after menopause, which usually occurs around the time their children have all grown up and left home, become depressed. It is double loss, so to say; not only are the children gone, so she doesn't have to be a mother doing hands-on care anymore, and then her periods stops too, telling her she can't have any more children, so they become depressed, develop delusions of guilt and are suicidal, and they start confessing to things that were impossible for them to have done. But since our culture has no understanding of mental illness, and we believe in witches, they stone such people to death. It is '*suicide by neighbors.*'

"That is just terrible, just terrible, couldn't the police have intervened?" Depo lamented.

Esho continued, "So, Mama Oye was bringing me up to date, and I'm happy I didn't stop her, because she finally started to talk about Akanbi and his family. She told me a lot of things I didn't care to know, but then she told me he had sold his house, and moved to a shack by the river. I wouldn't have known to look for him there at all. I thanked her and promised to visit her the next day.

"I went to the riverside right away. Iranti, since the economy has gone bad, a lot of people have built shacks there, it is a slum now. I asked around and a woman pointed Akanbi out to me. I couldn't believe my eyes; he'd aged in a terrible manner. His teeth were gone, and he was bent. He used to be a solidly built handsome man who stood up straight and though he wasn't all that tall, he looked so tall, but it's like he had shrunk. He used to have good teeth too. He looked forty years older. Anyway you saw him not too long ago.

"Do you know what he did when he saw me marching toward him? He ran! The coward ran! But he couldn't run faster than me. I caught up with him and I said to him, "Akanbi, you scum, you armed robber; I am going to kill you today. I listed to him all the ways he had robbed me, and he started to cry, to beg for mercy. Can you believe that? He went down on his knees and he was crying and begging me. He even prostrated himself on the ground, as he continued to beg for mercy. I had my knife in my shawl but I couldn't kill him. So I just spat in his face and went back home, but I couldn't sleep.

"I kept thinking of you. I know you love the work you do. You want to go back home, and you should be free to go back when you like, but I know this man would not leave you alone. I couldn't fall asleep all night. I was tossing and turning. Would you believe that at about three in the morning, he tried to break into our room?" She paused with disbelief written on her face.

"He had broken the front door and was in the hallway picking the lock to our room. I had the pestle that I used to make pounded yam in the corner by your bed, so I picked it and waited for him to finish picking the lock. Somehow I knew it was him, I can't tell you how I knew. He opened the door and as he tried to sneak into the room with a machete in his hand, I turned on the light and we stared at one another. I tried to hit him on the head with the pestle but it hit him on the back. He screamed and ran out, so I followed him, and he kept running but he couldn't run fast.

"I followed him and made sure we were close to the river with all the bushes there. I caught up with him and hit him on the head with it, five times, until he stopped moving.

"What did I tell you about people like him? They keep coming back! I forgave him because I looked into his eyes and took pity on him. I took pity on him even though he had tried to kill you. But what did he try to do to me? He came to my room to kill me with a machete.

"That is what happened, Iranti. I came back to the house and like I told you, I hid my knife in case the police came, and then I just sat there until you came for me. Thank you for always coming for me. You have been a wonderful child and now the world is free of danger, I have cleaned it for you. Iranti, go on with your life and live to the full, the world is yours. You have worked too hard not to enjoy a good life.

"Remember what I told you a few years ago, after you left that bastard Brian? I gave you back what you read in your books and quoted to me, '*as you go about the way of life, you will see a chasm, it is not as wide as it looks, jump.*' And please keep jumping until you get it right."

After a few moments, she continued, "Depo may not know this. My mother, I never knew her, but her name was Wura, it means Gold. My name is Esho, it means Treasures, I gave birth to Oshun; she was named after the goddess of fertility, a businesswoman and a political leader. Her message to Yoruba women is that they should not condone abuse and they can be all the things she was. My child was named after her. My child Oshun turned around and gave me a child and I named her Memory.

"Iranti, I used to tell you when you were growing up that the gods were laughing at us, at our line that was cursed. I was wrong. It was a dead woman talking to you. I was wrong because there is nothing like destiny that is written in stone. You use your own hands to sculpt the destiny you want.

"You have been proving me wrong since you could talk and you refused to call me 'Mama' and have been calling me Esho, and you have ascended to a height I did not think any one in my line could ever get to. Everything was coming to fruition in you. My mother that was Gold, me that is Treasure and your mother that was a powerful goddess, all of us have come together in Memory to produce you.

"Look at you Iranti. You have created a community of good people for yourself. You went out into a world that I told you was hostile, and you found good people to become your friends, and they are now your family. Moradeke and Gboye, they love you like a sister. Depo, he loves you too like you are his sister. You have done very well, Iranti. I couldn't make any friends. You are the only one I have.

"People came to me, they wanted to marry me. People continued to come to me to ask me to marry them until I came to America, but I refused, because to me the world is a hostile one. I don't have one single friend. I have neighbors that I lived with for many years but they are not my friends. They don't write to me when I am here and I don't write to them. They speak to me when they see me and when I am not there they forget about me.

"Our line was not cursed at all. Our physical beauty that I thought put us in danger was not a curse at all. We were just derailed, and you, our Memory, have been trying to put us back on track since you were born, and I know you will succeed, so the future generations of women born to us will use their attributes to become queens, as was our birthright before we were derailed. I was just shortsighted when I taught you that the world was hostile. Thank you, Iranti. Thank you."

She turned to Depo. "Thank you for being my child's friend all these years. Thank you for loving her and giving her a home with you. I'm happy you are in her life because I can be assured that you will continue to look out for her," Esho finished her story.

The three of them were quiet. After about five minutes, Ranti moved over to Esho and took her in her arms. She hugged her and kissed her on both cheeks. "I love you very much, Esho. Thank you for staying alive to take care of me. Thank you for always doing your best."

Depo looked dazed as he blurted out, "Wow, someone just confessed to a murder in my house!"

"We are not going to speak about this anymore. Okay, Esho?" Ranti warned. "We are not speaking of this anymore and we are not going to repeat it to anyone else. Not to Moradeke and not Gboye. It stays in this room and it dies with the three of us.

"I'm sorry Depo that you are involved, but this is who we are, my grandmother and I. This is the tragedy that is our life. When Moradeke arrives, because I'm sure she is on her way, this is what we will tell her. Esho, we will tell her you did go to Nigeria to try to retaliate, but I found you and I brought you back here, and nothing happened. You didn't even see Akanbi at all. Okay?" Ranti asked Esho and Depo and they both nodded.

Later in the night Depo came to Ranti's room. "I can't believe that woman, and she is so petite. I hope I have never offended you in any way because I don't want to be on her hit list." He still looked dazed.

"She adores you Depo. She loves you too much. You can never do any wrong as far as she is concerned," Ranti reassured him.

"You know what? For the first time I'm thankful you told her I couldn't have sex, because then I could never become an enemy. I have a list of people I wouldn't mind to have taken care of though. Do you think she can help me?" He laughed.

38

The loft was disturbingly quiet when Ranti awoke at about noon the next day. She was exhausted and wanted to sleep some more, but remembering Esho's escapade of the week before, she bolted out of bed and ran into the living room. Esho was not there. Ranti went into the kitchen as she called out her name, but there was no answer. She panicked and ran into Esho's room at the other end of the loft, crashing into the door to open it. Esho was on the bed.

Ranti knew as she stood by the door, long before she touched her, that she was dead.

She replayed the weeks preceding Esho's death over and over in her mind for months after. Her friends opined that she died of pulmonary embolism from the long flights.

Ranti refused to have an autopsy done. Esho had not lain down for anyone after the second time the mad man who gave her Oshun before she was ready raped her, and she never let a doctor touch her either. Ranti did not want a doctor cutting into her body when her soul was not present to protest, so she protested on her grandmother's behalf.

She agreed with her friends that pulmonary embolism could have physically killed her, but Esho had been dead since she killed her father at the age of nine. That was when she became a wraith.

Children did arrive and breathed life into her, and she survived for a while, especially when Lana arrived. He was going to be her knight in shining armor. He brought with him the phallic power she never had, and he would have become her avenger had he survived.

When Lana died, she went back into being a ghost. The tragedy of two dead children drained her of the blood of life they had lent to her, because when they died they took their blood with them.

Iranti tried to bring her back again because she was afraid to be alone in a world she had been taught was hostile. The shade that was Esho hung around for Iranti's sake, though shades and ghosts have no business taking care of children and that was why she did terrible things to her granddaughter. She said it was for Ranti's protection. It was not. It was because Esho was dead and the dead bring about again and again that which killed them in the first place. That was why she destroyed her granddaughter's genitals.

Esho the wraith was the first person to rape her granddaughter because rape was all she knew. She wanted Ranti to die so they could both go away, and then she would have no need to be alive anymore.

Esho could not accept blood from Ranti to turn her into a human being. She remained a shade, sustained by her hatred of Akanbi, who actually kept her alive all those years. It was as if she and Akanbi were living from just one heartbeat like siamese twins. The gratitude for Esho's survival should go to Akanbi. Her plotting and planning the many ways she would kill him gave her sustenance.

The prosperity of later years, as well as the world opening up for her in a magnificent manner after she learnt to read and write were not enough to give her the juice of life. They were just balm.

Moradeke's children who laughed with joy each time they saw her? They just gave her a temporary respite in their attempts to seduce her to stay with the living. She did not accept blood from them either; she refused to allow them to turn her into a dear grandmother. She could not leave the desert into which she had been cast, and which she had accepted as home.

She had continued to use Akanbi for sustenance even in America, in the forms of the vengeful parts of American movie culture she could participate in. They made it bearable for her to live amongst the benevolent living.

Her hatred of Akanbi continued to be a festering sore in her heart that would not heal, and even a transplant of fresh flesh in the form of the laughter of children could not assuage her pain. She killed Akanbi in cold blood because she was dead herself. It was a premeditated murder that she traversed almost six thousand miles to execute.

She did not kill Akanbi in self-defense because he broke into her room in an attempt to kill her first. Akanbi broke into her room to expedite what he had always known she would do to him. He had always known that Esho would eventually kill him because she had promised him death too many times, and the weapon that changed from a knife to a pestle was just opportunistic.

'*Murder is a wandering mourning.*'

Murder had been in Esho's heart long before she was nine years old and her father first raped her. Murder had been in Esho's heart when her adopted parents died and her family and village rejected her and made her into a scapegoat. And she had been killing since.

She could not mourn because there was no one to help her mourn the death of her mother who was Gold, the most beautiful woman in her village, but the village blamed her instead.

So she killed her father and the mad man who gave her Oshun before she was ready.

She killed Oshun, because she was angry with her mother who had been Gold, but she could not be Gold to her own child that she abandoned to a cruel world.

She killed Lana too, even though she had loved Lana so much. Oh, how she loved him! But she was a dead woman. How can a dead mother love her child? How can a dead mother protect her child from harm? A dead mother cannot make use of available information from neighbors just as she cannot make use of nourishment. That was why she did not know to take Lana to the hospital early enough.

She tried to kill Iranti when she cut her genitals, because Iranti was a woman too; she was that Gold, who in memory did not stay around to care for her child.

Esho's touch was the touch of death. Her kiss was the kiss of death.

Akanbi was last on her list and after she killed him she no longer have any reason to stay alive. It was all done. She could go and rest in peace.

It reminded Ranti of *Moby Dick,* and the malevolent bond that existed between Captain Ahab and the white whale. Ahab was bound to the whale in hatred, and even though on his way to kill it he became conscious of the malignancy of his feelings and knew it might be the end of him, he could not stop until he took the whole ship down with him. That was Esho and Akanbi; she was Captain Ahab and he was her Moby Dick. Akanbi was the devil part of her, the incurable festering hatred for all people of the world inside of her, her heritage from Alebido Ekiti and the need to take her revenge on the world.

She could not have stayed alive after she killed such a huge part of herself. It was her heart that she cut out. That was the pact they had together—Esho and Akanbi.

For many years she wished him the calamity that befell Job without the redemption that Job enjoyed in the end. But she did not know she was the one who endured the trials of Job without the salvation that came for him in the end. She did not know that Akanbi whom she hated so much *was* herself.

The Sunday that Ranti brought her back from Nigeria to prevent her from being thrown into prison, she said her good-bye to her grandchild. That long speech that night to her and Depo was her deathbed farewell.

The following weeks remained foggy for Ranti. She remembered going to her doctor and he was not happy with her. He said her ankle was not mending, as it should. He threatened to confine her to a wheelchair.

Gboye, heavily pregnant with her second child, stayed for a long time in the loft with her and Depo, and Moradeke was there a lot as well.

Depo made all the funeral plans and it took Ranti a long time to decide where to bury her grandmother. She thought of burying her in New York City. That would be very convenient, but then she wondered if Esho would like to be taken back home so she could be buried close to her dead children.

She entertained the idea of taking her back to her home village in Ekiti, but no, she decided, all Esho wanted with that village was to take her revenge.

She toyed with the idea of burying her in the village to give Esho the chance to do just that. Her ghost could exact her revenge on the people by haunting them till they were out of their minds, but Ranti wanted her to rest in peace. Esho had been haunting people since she was five years old. She had earned the right to rest in peace.

Her friends insisted it was her decision to make. They told her they would support her in whichever decision she arrived at. She begged them to think for her, but they refused. They told her whatever she decided on would be the right thing.

Ranti was very tired. The heavy load on her shoulders from the time she stabbed her ex-husband returned, and all she wanted was to be allowed to stay in bed, but they would not let her.

Gboye kept intruding on her, yelling all the time and even sharing the bed with her on many nights, poking her with her big pregnant abdomen as she attempted to fall into a sleep that had deserted her.

Ranti finally arrived at a decision after a week. She would take Esho back home to Ibadan and bury her close to her children, Oshun and Lana. It would give her a chance to pay those departed ones a visit as well. Her family would be in one place.

She could not cry, and she wanted to cry for so much. She wanted to weep that she never gave Esho great grandchildren. Esho never asked for them, but had she given them to her, they might have healed her of her hatred and seduced her into staying with the living.

Ranti wanted to weep because Esho was too young to die at the age of sixty. She wanted to weep that Esho never married and never had a lover, and it was not for lack of opportunities because she had continued to turn heads in her own way until she died.

She wanted to weep for her grandmother whose only intimate connection with another human being was not one of being held lovingly in a mother's arms and breastfed, not one of being hugged with a lot of affection by a doting mother or father, but one of being raped, repeatedly, and at a tender age.

Ranti wanted to weep for her own pain and anguish. She wanted to be able to forgive Esho for the mutilation and for wiring her brain in such a way that she was afraid of men, and had learnt to pick rapists as lovers, but she knew it would be so difficult to forgive her grandmother.

"Who is to blame? Is it fear that made a whole village turn its back on an innocent newborn baby girl, when the placenta did not separate and it took the mother with it? Who is to blame? Esho's father? My great-grandfather who was a child molester and a rapist?

"Should we blame the mad man who gave Oshun to Esho before she was ready? What was his story? We did not even know his name. We did not see his face. We do not know his people, and we do not know his god. He remained faceless and nameless and came to be known as the 'mad man that gave Oshun to Esho before she was ready,' or just 'the mad man.'

"He was the mad man without a face, a story, a people and a god. He was invisible and he disappeared into thin air, but he left an intractable malignancy behind. What did he give me in terms of DNA? I know what he gave me in forms of emotional tools: Fear. My grandfather's name was 'the mad man.' He was a rapist too.

"Who is to blame? Is it Akanbi? Akanbi, who was much older than Esho but chose to molest Esho's twelve-year-old child? He too was a rapist. He molested his own daughter according to the neighborhood gossip.

"What a legacy! All the men in me are rapists and pedophiles. Great-grandfather, grandfather and father, and Esho killed all of them!

"My grandmother was a murderer. She killed three times. What a legacy!

"My mother was a prostitute. What a legacy!

"My grandmother killed my father and I was a part of it! What a headline and what a legacy! Who are all these people living in my house? With them there, I am not the master of my own mind."

Ranti could not weep. It worried her friends, and they cried buckets because they had known the "pretend" Esho. She had kept the festering wound of hatred well covered with a superficial scab from them. They never smelt it on her, and they did not know she was a wraith.

Moradeke especially wept at the loss of the adopted grandmother of her children. She had grown to love Esho who had loved and cared for her young family so much. She was convinced her heart would never heal.

The sisters and brother Ranti had adopted went with her when she took her grandmother back home to be buried ten days after she died. This time they did not allow her to throw away her crutches. Depo held on to them and they forced her to sit in a wheelchair. She was grateful for that because of the tiredness.

Efunwunmi met them at the airport in Lagos and she was in tears. It worried Ranti that everyone around her was in tears except her. She remembered Esho asking her why she cried when she was a little girl. It was a sign of weakness to her grandmother. She forbade it, and she would hit little Ranti when she cried.

"I'm going to give you something to cry about," Esho, who could not mourn, would promise, and she would deliver on the promise by giving her a physical reason to cry.

"You know Ranti, its okay to cry." Depo knew that lack of weeping, of not acknowledging that which has been lost, leads to accumulation of stench and trauma, so he gave her permission many times, but she could not cry.

She was like Esho after Oshun and Lana died. No, she was worse than Esho. Esho did not cry but she had shrieked a lot and she had gone crazy, but Ranti did not shriek. She did not scream and she did not speak unless she was spoken to. But she was very, very, tired.

"Death begets death! My patients were killed in the northern part of Nigeria, five of them. Akanbi was killed. Esho died because she killed Akanbi and there was no one to keep her alive anymore.

"I remember reading that suicide and murder are one and the same thing. It does not matter who dies, the subject or the object, but someone has to die, and this is because the actual murder we need to commit is not of an external person out there, but of what is inside of us, our internalized foe that becomes projected onto an external object; that is why object and subject become fused into one.

"Akanbi must have known this as well. He must have known there was death in the air. He too knew it did not matter who was the subject or the object. He and Esho were too intimately connected. That was why he went after her with the machete.

"I wish I could confess to the murder of Akanbi. I wish I could tell someone I took part in it. I drove the 'getaway' car when I got Esho out of Nigeria quickly. I didn't go to the police as a good citizen should have done because I wanted Akanbi dead. Me too, I am a murderer and a father-killer like Esho."

Ranti took her grandmother to the only one-bedroom home she ever had in Bere. Even though Esho's body had been prepared for burial before they left the US, she insisted on carrying out the rituals of properly burying her.

"Lana and Oshun were not properly buried when they died. I didn't have the good fortune of washing their bodies and touching them, I couldn't send them off on their journey at the time," she reminded herself.

Her friends respected her wish, and they helped. Depo and the neighbors took Esho's body out of the casket and placed it on a plank of wood on her bed.

Ranti went down on her knees as she laid several towels on the floor under the bed. The floor on which Esho slept for thirty years, on a mat because she could not afford a bed.

Ranti hugged that floor of their room. She was born onto that floor because Esho could not afford to pay the hospital fees for Oshun to deliver her babies. She had crawled on that floor, played with her brother on that floor, cried on it, ate on it, slept on it and sat on it facing Esho as she listened to her many lectures.

Moradeke and Gboye joined her as she lovingly washed Esho's body with soap and water. She massaged it with lotion, powdered her face and lined her eyes with kohl, as Esho had loved to do. They put her best *Aso-Oke* outfit on her, the outfit she wore at Ranti's graduation from medical school. That was her proudest day.

Ranti remembered the poverty of their lives. She remembered Esho's struggle to make ends meet. She remembered Esho's fears that she tried to hide from her granddaughter, but still came across the way she was anxiously hovering over Ranti especially when men were around.

She remembered Esho sitting on her mat with her back against the wall listening to her radio. That was how she spent her evenings, alone in her room leaning against the wall, listening to her small radio.

She felt gratitude well up in her toward her grandmother. "She lived for me. She didn't live for herself at all. She went to her job, came home, leant against the wall and waited for me to come home from running errands or from the bookshop, or she waited for Saturdays so she could come visit me in school.

"I am thankful that I did not disappoint her. I am thankful that I could give her some good years, years in which she did not have to worry about food or money in case I became sick. I am thankful that I was able to show her a benevolent world of good people like Depo, Efunwunmi, Moradeke, Bode and Gboye. She died knowing there are other kinds of people in this world. She died knowing that I would be fine, that my friends would take care of me. I am thankful for so much.

"This is the last time I will be in this room, in this house, and in this dirty cauldron of a neighborhood with the chthonic mingling of people, smells, colors and noise that I love so much. I will not return here anymore because this is my past, but I will carry this place in my heart forever. Esho thank you for so much."

She buried her grandmother. The neighbors came. The contractor who for many years employed Esho to carry cement for him, as well as the bricklayers and the carpenters. Over a hundred people were at the graveyard.

Ranti gave them a party after. Efunwunmi arranged it.

People had a lot to say. They had loved Esho. She had respected them and they respected her in turn. They admired her tenacity and energy, especially the way she raised her granddaughter and ensured she received the best education available. They admired her integrity. They regretted she was not more to them. They tried to bring her into the world of the living but she could not go with them.

Ranti soaked in the kind words and thanked them. They sang, wept and danced but the tears abandoned her.

Curiously enough, but kindly too, no one brought up Akanbi's death. No one seemed to have suspected that Esho's quick trip home had anything to do with it, or maybe they just did not care.

People did speak of the flying visit home though. "It was like she came to have one last look and to say good-bye," Mama Oye from whom Esho used to buy kerosene told Ranti. "It was as if she knew."

"Esho, you had a community of people but you did not know because you were a shade, and so you couldn't enjoy all these people who wanted to love you. You would have been surprised at the number of people who came to see you off. They danced and sang and wept, Esho. People loved you," Ranti informed her grandmother in her mind.

Depo, Moradeke and Efunwunmi took her back to Lagos immediately after the party, while Gboye went home to visit her parents. Depo and Ranti stayed with Efunwunmi for another week before they returned to New York City.

Ranti kept thinking to herself on the way to America, "I have no one anymore. I have no one related to me. I am alone in this world."

It was as if Depo could read her mind because he surprised her by hugging her at some point as they flew over the Atlantic Ocean, and whispering into her ears. "Ranti my love, you have me. You have had me since the first day I saw you and you have me for the rest of our lives."

Ranti stared at him. She told herself she had always known that. She had always known she could count on his love in the way he was able to give it to her, and she had become grateful for it. She continued to look at him and finally the tears came. She welcomed them with a smile, and they did not cease for the next year.

Initially it was everything that made her cry. Every act of kindness or meanness done to her or witnessed anywhere. Catching glimpses of Esho's movies of revenge made her cry.

A month later, as she lay in bed unable to get up on her own, as had been the case since the day her grandmother died, the smell of urine and feces arrived.

She had been expecting them and had wondered what took them so long. She welcomed them as you welcome old companions.

39

A month after the smell arrived, she was invited to the World Health Organization to discuss issues that had to do with the million-dollar grant awarded for her project. She was afraid to meet with them at the World Health Organization because she might be thrown into prison for fraudulent practices.

She wondered if she was delusional because she had not committed fraud. But she reminded herself that she was guilty. She was guilty of Akanbi's murder and that was enough as far as her mind was concerned, because her mind did not care for particulars.

Depo offered to go with her, but he had just been made team leader on a construction project, and it meant a lot for his career. She did not want him to lose the opportunity.

She spoke firmly to herself that she was guilty indeed, "Iranti," she called aloud, "separate the issues the way Mr. Edwards taught you to separate the membranes when you repair a damaged genital. Separate the urethral membrane from the vagina membrane first, and separate the rectal membrane too. Then, suture them so the membranes stay with their own kind, where they are supposed to be. In that way, the urethra would not melt into the vagina, and the vagina would not melt into the rectal. Everything would be in its place, performing the job it is supposed to do. Then, if a problem occurs, you deal with it on an individual basis. This is because the histology of the urethral membrane is different from that of the vaginal mucosa and the histology of that mucosa is different from the rectal mucosa. Even though they are very intimate neighbors, they are individuals with separate boundaries.

"You are guilty! But you are not guilty of fraud. You did not steal the money from the World Health Organization. You did not receive a dime of that money. What you are guilty of is patricide, and even though it is a very serious crime, that is not what they invited you to discuss in Geneva. Everything and everyone should stay in its place, Iranti.

"Do not go to Geneva to confess to Akanbi's murder, just like if the police in Ibadan were to arrest you for the murder, you would not talk to them about the million dollars from the World Health Organization you never received," she repeatedly warned herself.

When she arrived at the World Health Organization headquarters in Geneva on the fourth of June 1995, an American met her at the reception room and smiled at her as he introduced himself as Grant Phillips. He was the lawyer in charge of the investigation.

He had a very friendly manner and tried to make her feel at ease because he could sense she was nervous. He offered her a wheelchair because she was on crutches. She declined and thanked him. He walked slowly with her to the conference room.

In the room were five people, and Ranti's heart started to beat very fast. She wanted to burst into tears as she was convinced they could smell her. How could they not? The smell was making it difficult even for her to breathe.

The men stood up when she hopped in with Grant, and they took turns to formally shake her hand as they welcomed her. She felt reassured by their friendly attitude.

They asked about her project and she started by telling them of the part Jamba had continued to play in her life, and why he got the ultimate revenge by withholding her grant, when she refused to go to him in his big office in Abuja to beg for the money.

She told them why she wanted so much to help these women, for at the age of nine, she too was mutilated for her grandmother's ignorance and fears.

An hour later, she concluded her story by telling them that it was when she ran for her life from the village that she fractured her ankle.

She did not tell of the part played by Akanbi; that he indexed her to the mob, and she did not tell them that her grandmother made him pay by murdering him, and that she died after.

She did not tell them that seven people died as a result of that one-million-dollar grant: five patients, her grandmother, and the vehicle by which she came to be, the man whose sperm fathered her.

She commended herself for separating the issues, and letting each membrane go with its kind. She did not give the men in Geneva the confession that belonged to the police in Ibadan.

She wondered if she wanted to be arrested and punished for Akanbi's murder. Punished as an accomplice? Perhaps it would help her feel better, even if she went to prison. Would punishment coming from outside be easier to endure than the punishment coming from within one's mind, from within one's conscience? "Who is the worst executioner, the police or depression?" She asked herself repeatedly.

The men listened without interrupting her. Grant stood up at some point to get her some water. They were quiet for about three minutes after she was done.

The Indian team leader whose name Ranti could not remember, broke the silence to thank her for coming to the interview.

"You are absolved of all responsibilities, Dr. Jare. We still love to fund your project because we believe that what you have to offer African women is priceless. You are working from your own trauma, what more could make a person a good doctor?

"Nigeria has a very hostile government at this time. They told us you refused to cooperate with the Ministry of health, and that is why they did not release the money to you. Unfortunately at this time, the World Health Organization does not give out independent grants of such magnitude, not attached to a university or the government. That is a thing we need to change, especially when we have to deal with hostile dictator governments. We can give you some grant as an independent contractor, but the limit is about fifty thousand dollars a year. That will still do a lot of good. When you feel ready, please send us a proposal and we will honor it."

"What happened to the million dollars? Has it been returned to you?" Ranti asked unnecessarily.

He shook his head. "Your government claimed they spent it on building health facilities in some rural part of Nigeria. We sent our auditors to inspect the facilities but they received a very hostile reception. We had to call them back in a hurry. I'm sorry to say, Dr. Jare, but the money just disappeared."

"I'm sorry too." Ranti said. "But I know where the money went. I don't know if you are interested in pursuing it, but a million dollars is a lot of money." She opened her purse and brought out the letter that General Jamba wrote to her the week before the mob attacked. She handed it to Grant.

He took the letter, read it and had a look of disbelief on his face. "Is this possible? Could he have implicated himself by putting this in print? Can anyone be this stupid?" he asked as he handed the letter to his boss.

"Oh yes, that is the invincibility of the entitled there for you. The entitled don't think it's stupid to put such things in writing. He believes he is a god and he is a god, he had gotten away with worse," Ranti answered.

The Indian man had a look of incredulity on his face as well. Ranti handed him the postal envelope with the federal government seal.

"This is unbelievable, he is going down. We are going to pursue this to the end. Thank you, Dr. Jare, thank you very much. In fact, you should be working with us here in Geneva. You are on our team; just say the word and you have a job with us. Thank you very much for this." The Indian man continued to flap the letter and the envelope against his left hand in his excitement.

They shook hands as they thanked her for coming to the interview. Some of them wished her luck. Grant offered to take her to lunch, but she told him she was too tired to eat; she just wanted to return to her hotel to sleep. He offered her dinner, but she refused.

"What about tomorrow? When do you go back to New York? You've got to see Geneva before you leave. I won't take no for an answer." It was as if Depo had spoken to him.

She gave in and the next day he took some time off to take her out. He mostly drove her around since she was on crutches, and in spite of the way she was feeling she did have fun with him.

"Do you know what the men said about you after the meeting?" He asked her at some point.

"That woman is a nut case," Ranti offered, "and she made a total ass of herself. Who cares about her pathetic life?' I must have lost my mind. Actually, I have *lost* my mind. I have a psychotic depression at this time. What I didn't tell you guys is that my grandmother, who raised me from the day I was born, just died, less than six weeks ago. I hope it excuses my weird behavior in there yesterday."

"I'm sorry to hear that, you are going through a lot."

Ranti said to herself, "There is more but I'm not telling you. I'm not telling you of the crime we committed together, my grandmother and I; my partner in survival and in crime. You are not the one I need to confess that to. I'm separating the membranes and keeping the boundaries clean. No touching please."

"No," said Grant, "the men, after you left said, 'That woman is so beautiful and brilliant, she is so genuine. She sure makes one lucky man very happy.' One of the guys said you are so classy. They love you, Ranti, and they will continue to fund you as much as they can." He paused. "I'm sorry about your grandmother. These past few months must have been hell for you. I may be out of line here, but who is the lucky man you make happy? Why isn't he here with you?"

"There is no one, Grant. There used to be, but he didn't feel so lucky. He abused me, so I left him. You did hear my story didn't you? My brain has been wired such that I pick men who abuse me. It's a tragedy."

"You are alive, you are well, except for your ankle, and it will heal. I am a realist and I predict that you will meet the kind of guy who will treat you like his queen because that's what you are, a queen."

"That's very kind of you," she told him with a smile.

"It's the truth," he tried to convince her.

The following day he came to take her to the airport. Ranti had told him she could easily take the airport shuttle from the hotel, but he insisted. He made her promise to keep in touch as he kissed her good-bye.

Two weeks later, Grant called to tell her he was coming to New York City in a few weeks, and would like to have dinner with her. She marshaled the energy she did not have to commit to a dinner date with him.

On returning from Geneva, Depo forced her to return to Dr. Obed, the psychiatrist she saw when she left her ex-husband. He put her back on the medication that helped her at the time, especially to sleep, and with her being able to sleep, a lot of the confusion she felt abated. He insisted she see him at least twice a week.

She had the dream again. The dream about her giving birth to a baby alien. The same dream she had when she left Brian four years earlier and the psychiatrist put her on that medication. She wondered if the medication was provoking the dreams.

She was in the hospital after she had a baby. She was very happy. It was a baby girl but she was a biracial child. She was surprised she had a biracial child. They told her she could not take the baby home with her just yet. They said something was wrong with the baby and they had to keep her in the hospital a few more days.

Ranti refused to leave the hospital without her baby. The hospital wanted her to leave because it was costing too much money to keep her when she was not sick. She told them Depo would pay, but she needed to be with her baby.

At some point they took the baby away, telling her they were going to run some tests on her. They did not tell her where they were taking her, so she snuck after them.

They took the baby into an operating room. They put her on a table and spread her legs apart as four people bent over her. Ranti panicked and started to shriek.

She woke up terrified, screaming and drenched in sweat. Depo was in the room holding her, and reassuring her that it was just a dream.

Dr. Obed said it was a hopeful dream, even though it scared her. He said she was getting to her point of trauma and it was good. It would give her an opportunity to do the work of mourning that she needed to do. He continued that she was probably the baby in the dream. That being biracial could mean she was changing from who she was into someone who would be more in charge of herself; someone different. Her inner life was changing.

He too thought it was a continuation of the first dream she had four years before. He pointed out that she was more accepting of herself in this dream; she had moved from being an alien to being a biracial child.

The other dreams returned as well. *The dreams of being excluded, but most of the time she dreamt she was not allowed to see Dr. Obed in his Park Avenue office. The doorman shut her out, and at another time, a woman who said she was Dr. Obed's secretary accused her of smelling and shut the door in her face.*

Ranti started to spend most of her days in bed and when Depo came home from work he would drag her out of bed, and she would sit blankly in front of the television. He made it a duty to get her out of the house every day, if only for a walk.

Two days before the dinner date with Grant, she told Depo. He became excited that she had met someone, but she was not.

"He's a great guy, Depo, but he's not for me. It would have been too easy and too good to be true, and such good things do not happen to the likes of me. He is either married or he is gay. I think it's the latter; there was something about his level of comfort with me that reminded me of you. I can't explain it.

"You know me, if a man comes after me, he is gay and all he wants is my friendship, which is a wonderful thing, but you know I want more. And if I go after a man, he is a rapist. I have it figured out! Wow! What an insight! The men that pursue me are gays and wonderful friends. The men that I pursue are rapists. Uhn! Isn't that something? There is no middle ground, none at all. What a wonderful solution to my problem of sexual trauma! I need to tell the shrink that and I-need-to-learn-to-leave-unwilling-men-alone!" She yelled at herself.

"Whatever, you can be as pessimistic as you like, no one is asking you to marry the guy. Just get dressed, do your hair, put on some makeup and go out with him. That is all I ask of you," Depo told her.

Depo came home early to make sure she went on the date. Ranti lost a lot of weight and it took them a while to find the appropriate outfit. They settled on a pair of jeans and a white shirt that still looked stylish.

Her braided hair had matted together because it needed to have been re-braided six weeks ago, but Depo tried to whip it back to bouncing by brushing it for a long time. By the time he was done, she was so tired that she wanted to crawl back into bed but he would not let her.

When Grant and Depo saw one another, Ranti confirmed that she had been right; he had been too good to be true for her. She knew they fell in love with one another at that moment, though it took both of them a while to come to that realization.

"Depo, why don't you throw on a shirt and come with us?" Ranti said after the introduction and the shaking of hands was over.

"Oh no, that won't be necessary," Depo protested shyly.

"I think it would be a lot of fun. Come on, the more the merrier," Grant insisted.

The three of them went to dinner and walked around the city for another hour. Ranti and Depo hung out with Grant for the rest of his stay in New York before he returned to Geneva.

A week after he left, Depo finally admitted to Ranti that he found him very attractive. Ranti called Grant to tell him, and Grant in turn admitted that he was attracted to Depo.

A month later, Depo went to Geneva to visit him after he shipped Ranti off to Moradeke in Delaware. Grant returned to New York to visit them the following month, and seven months later, Grant quit his full time job with the World Health Organization to become a contractor, and he moved in with them.

Ranti was happy she had found the love of Depo's life for him.

40

Ranti spent the weekend writing. She had continued to see Abe at nights. He was busy during the day as well, working on his photo book.

"It's like we both had to escape to this peaceful island to put the wrecks of our lives back together. During the day, he is busy with his stories of horror and I am busy with mine, and at night we find poetry in each others arms," she observed.

On Sunday night, as she lay in Abe's arms, the phone rang. She excused herself to get it from the living room. She had refused to have a phone in the bedroom when she first arrived on the island, because she did not want to receive calls that bore bad news like Fausa's call of the month before.

Gboye was yelling on the line, "Ranti, Moradeke and I are coming tomorrow at noon."

"Okay, Gboye, I'll be at the airport. You could have given a girl some warning."

"Why do you need a warning? Your sisters are coming to see what you are up to. Depo says you are feeling much better and eating more. Well I didn't have much warning either. I think Moradeke is having a nervous breakdown. She called me on Thursday and suggested we visit you and she wanted to leave right away. Her mother is arriving tomorrow and she doesn't want to be in the same house with her. That's weird, don't you think? She wouldn't give me details, so anyway, I agreed, and I need the time off too. I know you and I will get to the bottom of why she's avoiding her mother."

"Gboye, how are you? How are things between you and Olu? I'm sorry I haven't called, but you've been on my mind."

"You had your own stuff to deal with. Actually Olu and I are fine, we talked, we are getting a divorce."

"I'm sorry."

"It's for the best. I'll fill you in when we get there. See you tomorrow."

"I love you Gboye, and I'm glad you are flying down, I know how scared you are of flying when pregnant."

"Yes Iranti. You've always made me fly when I'm pregnant. That tells you how much I love you."

Ranti wondered why Moradeke was avoiding her mother. They had a good relationship as far as she knew.

"I hope they won't take you away from me." Abe volunteered to go with her to the airport.

She assured him they would not. She promised herself she would continue to spend her nights in his arms, because she was not ready to give up the way he had been making love to her.

Ranti was shocked when she saw her friends. Gboye had dropped at least twenty pounds and she looked subdued, while Moradeke had dark patches all over her body, though her eyes still sparkled.

They were very happy to see Ranti, and they both commented that she looked great, especially since she had gained some of the weight Gboye lost and her face was fuller. They took turns to hug her, as they caressed her face and abdomen.

"You look like that time you came back from England in 1982, free and buoyant. This island must be magical," Gboye said and Moradeke agreed with her.

Ranti introduced Abe to them and Gboye winked at her, saying she could see why she was buoyant. "How is he in bed?" She whispered into Ranti's ear as Abe loaded their luggage into his truck.

Ranti shook her head, paused for a moment and then smiled and whispered, "He is fantastic. For the first time in my life I'm having orgasms. It's heaven."

"Are you in love with him, is he commitment material?" Moradeke wanted to know.

"No, he's not, he's a nomad. He's a freelance photojournalist. But I'm having a ball. I've learnt to accept unwilling men as they are, and just enjoy them and love them the way they want to be loved. Don't worry Moradeke, I'm not going to fall hopelessly in love with him and then spend the next fifteen years getting over that. I'm fine this time. But he makes me so happy," Ranti quickly reassured her.

Abe pulled Ranti aside after he dropped them off at the cottage. "Do you want me to come tonight or do you want to spend time with your friends?"

"Of course I want you to come," She told him as she gave him a peck on the cheek.

"I'm so glad to have you guys here," Ranti hugged her friends again. "How long are you staying?"

"About two weeks. I need to get away, my mother is here and I don't want to spend time with her. She's going to Canada in two weeks to see Bola. I'll explain later." Moradeke said.

Gboye started, "I needed a vacation. I haven't taken a vacation in five years. Can you believe that? No wonder I was going crazy. I'm like a woman possessed or pursued, and I don't even know what's chasing me. The kids aren't going to miss me anyway. They hardly ever saw me to begin with." She paused for a moment, looking pensively at the ocean. "This place is beautiful! So I might stay longer than two weeks, let's just take it a day at a time. We should buy this cottage from the Sanchezes, I'm serious girls. It's breathtaking. I have never lived close to an ocean before. Do you mean to tell me some people see this every day of their life?"

282   *Feasts of Phantoms*

After lunch, Ranti suggested they go swimming but Moradeke declined.

"I'm glad to see you Gboye," Ranti thanked her as they swam.

"I needed my sisters too. I need you and Moradeke."

At about five in the afternoon they sat on the deck looking out at the ocean. Gboye continued to exclaim at the beauty of the ocean, saying she had never seen a more peaceful place in her life.

"So girls what's going on with you two? We are together again, let's catch up and share our pains," Ranti said.

Gboye started, "You know I returned to Boston the next morning after you collapsed at the restaurant. I went to work, it was my surgery day, so I didn't get home until late at night as usual, and of course the kids had been asleep for a while; story of my life. I probably see my kids for a total of ten hours a week. It's sad. Olu was there as usual waiting up for me, and he had dinner ready and he just wanted to make me comfortable. I was very tired from the trip to New York, with you so sick and running into Irish. I just wanted to go to bed and not wake up for a week, but I couldn't sleep. My head would not shut down.

"He fell asleep right away. I kept looking at him and I couldn't believe who I had become. Here is this wonderful man. All he ever wanted was to love me and take care of me and the children and all I have been doing is cheating on him. I realized I didn't deserve him at all, that the boys are very lucky to have him and if he wants a divorce I wouldn't fight him over the kids. He should have custody of them. I kept thinking, so I just woke him. I said I wanted to talk.

"He wondered why it couldn't wait till the morning, but he sat up, turned on his bedside light and said, "Okay, shoot." And I did. For two hours, I spoke. I confessed everything to him, that none of the kids was his.

"Even saying it now, I want to cut off my tongue. You know, he didn't interrupt me once. He just sat there calmly and listened to me. So I told him I had an affair with this Chinese brain surgeon who came for a fellowship at Harvard, and I was pregnant. For a moment while I was confessing everything, it occurred to me that he could get a knife and kill us both.

"He was quiet for about fifteen minutes. He just sat there. Finally he said, 'The best thing will be for me to divorce you. This cannot be good for the boys. Take the weekend off and we'll talk to them, and I want you to move out of the house as soon as possible. You will not tell them I'm not their father, but you will tell the older three you had an affair. I'll call a lawyer in the morning.'

"I said I was sorry. He said 'Me too, Gboye, I'm very sorry too. I am sorry I'm not the man you wanted. I love you very much, but I was never enough for you. I've always known about the affairs. I walked into this marriage with my eyes wide open. I've always known the boys were not mine. But they are mine, so don't you dare fight me on that."

"I said I had no intention of fighting him on anything, but 'Why didn't you stop me when you knew?'

He said, "Gboye, I'm your husband and I tried to be that. I'm not in charge of your body. I show you I love you when you allow me.'

"And he is right. It's not his job to control my body, but he is scary, isn't he? How could someone know that his wife cheats on him and keep quiet? He could be one of those guys who just wakes up in the middle of the night and murders the whole family, and then friends and neighbors are surprised and everyone would come on television and say, 'He was such a good man, he went to church every Sunday, always polite and kind too.' That is the kind of person he is and that is very scary.

"But you know, at the same time, he is very kind. So we spent the rest of the night talking, and I'm not going to contest anything, he'll get the house and the kids. He said he would let me see the kids whenever I wanted to see them, and then he blew my mind. He said, 'I know you are very busy at work. When this baby comes, I'll help you with it.'"

She paused and looked at her friends. "I was so enraged, so I cursed him out. I called him names I can't even repeat. Is he for real? He's killing me with kindness and that is very sadistic. It is the fucking sainthood that drove me mad and made me sleep with everything I saw in the first place. I know it isn't his job to control my body but the man is not real. Who wants to live with a saint? Give me a fucking sinner anytime because saints don't belong amongst us!" She paused.

"For the first time in years, I called in sick the next morning, and I took the weekend off. I slept until late in the afternoon and I spent time with the boys. So on Saturday we told the older three I would be moving out of the house because dad and I are having some problems, but I'm still their mom and I love them and I'll continue to see them as much as I have been.

"It broke my heart because they just said 'Okay' they did not cry or ask any questions. I deserved that." She was quiet for a long time.

"You know, they don't run to me when they are in pain. They go to him. When they need a parent in the middle of the night, they wake him. They talk to him about their day, school, sports and friends. I ask them and they say, 'its okay, mom,' but they don't tell me anything.

"So that's what's going on, girls. I moved out a week later. I'm renting an apartment, and he filed for divorce that week. I still go home after work to eat the dinner he continues to prepare for me, and to see the boys. After they go to bed I leave and go to my apartment.

"Olu looks at me and I read sadness in his eyes. I have never stopped loving him. I picked a good father for my sons.

"Four days ago I asked him, 'Why aren't you angry with me that I didn't have your child?' He said he didn't know. But he called me two days ago. He said he wanted to answer my question. He had always asked himself the same question but he thinks he was afraid to give birth to his own children.

"I was shocked. I thought I knew this man so well. You guys are never going to believe this." She paused. "He said, 'My mother was mentally ill all my life. She had schizophrenia. She never had a good day. I took care of her till she died. Schizophrenia is hereditary you know, why would I risk giving birth to that? Maybe that is why I didn't stop you Gboye. I knew when we met that you were more aggressive and domineering. I must have known you would be unfaithful to me.' Jesus fucking Christ!" She yelled.

"Hey, hey, hey! Are you out of your mind?" Moradeke warned her.

"Can you believe this guy? He used me. He wanted to be a father but not to his own biological children. We were in it together. We knew what we wanted. I tell you, that is *the* perfect marriage if there is anything like that."

Ranti asked Gboye, "What was your reason, why didn't you want his sperm to father your children?" She had come to the realization that a parent is first of all only a vehicle by which you come into this world like Esho used to tell her. The parent can then decide to be more to the child.

"I don't know. I think it's this competitive streak in me. Olu is not the most intellectual of people. He is an instruction man, you give him instructions and he follows them. He is not a creative person on his own. I want my children to be smart. I grew up with brilliant brothers, I didn't know about the schizophrenia business. When we met in Boston, he told me his parents were dead. I knew he was not ambitious. He told me on our first date he was happy being an elementary school teacher because he loves to teach kids. I didn't have a problem with that but I didn't want my children to inherit his brain."

"So you both agreed for you to bring home illegitimate children," Moradeke said. "As long as you keep it within the Negro race, you could lie to one another, but you being Gboye, you had to overdo it, so you crossed the Pacific Ocean and boom! The whole thing explodes in both your faces."

"Yes, it did. I probably wanted it to stop. I was tired of the lies."

"But there is something called birth control you know. You could have asked the Chinese to use condoms. There are deadly diseases out there, Gboye." Moradeke could not hide her disgust.

"Haven't you heard a word I've been saying? It's more than just the sex. I needed him to stop me. I was tired of the lies." Gboye paused.

"So there you have it. That's the story." She continued. "It's important for him to save face. So the divorce is the right move."

"Why have you lost so much weight? Are you depressed?" Ranti asked.

"I don't think I'm depressed, but I'm eating less. Somehow, I just don't have the need to be that big anymore. It's going to sound crazy to you guys, but all my life I have always needed to be the biggest person around. It's as if were I not the

Kehinde Adeola Ayeni 285

biggest person around, someone would exploit me.

"Maybe it's because I grew up with five brothers who are giants and I had to take care of myself with them. I'm always ready to do battle. I had to be fearless. Do you know that, as strange as it sounds, the only thing that scares me in this world is flying in an airplane when I'm pregnant? But why, who is fighting me? No one is fighting me, but I'm always up in arms.

"When I was a resident, each time I walked into the emergency room to see a patient, everyone would stop talking and get out of my way. People were afraid of me and I knew it, but I told myself since I'm an immigrant to America, no one would dare be racist to me, but the thing is no one had ever been racist to me.

"My weight is an armor I wear around me. I'm like a Mack truck charging down a suburban road and everyone better get out of my way. It doesn't make sense." She paused.

"My obstetrician warned me that I run the risk of gestational diabetes. I'm not in my twenties anymore. So I just cut what I eat by half and the weight has been sliding off. The baby is fine. Almost ten weeks now."

"I love you Gboye, and you will be fine. It'll work out for the best. I'm glad you are keeping the baby, and you came clean with your husband. The truth is always a good idea, no matter how painful or scary it is. It's the lies that drive us crazy," Ranti offered.

"Me too," Moradeke reluctantly added. "I'm here for you though I might give you grief but I love you. The three of us have been together since medical school. That is almost twenty-four years girls. We are a tradition."

41

The next morning while they were having breakfast, Jack called. Ranti smiled as she went out onto the deck to speak with him. As usual he wanted to know when she would return to the City and she told him she would be there in another four weeks.

"Maybe I need to come and take you away from that place. I'm sure it's so beautiful you don't want to return to a concrete world, I don't blame you."

"I will return, I'm just enjoying myself and feeling so much better," she laughed.

"I can hear it in your voice. I hope there aren't some undeserving men bothering you. If there are, let me know and I will drop everything and come rescue you," he laughed.

"Okay, I'll let you know."

"Promise?"

"I promise."

"I have to go in to work early today so I decided to give you a call first."

"What do you do?"

"I'm a chef, but my cooking is not as good as Boris'; that's why I still go to his diner, and besides when you are a chef you want to eat someone else's cooking. I'm part owner of a restaurant here in town but one of my assistants called in sick today so I have to go in early. Usually I do the graveyard shift, working till two in the morning. What about you, what do you do when you are not hanging out by the ocean?"

"I'm a gynecologist. I work mostly in Nigeria."

"Wow! Does that mean you will be going back to Nigeria? I don't want you to go, or I might just come with you."

Ranti laughed.

"I would love to be with you right now to see you laugh. I have never seen you laugh. I have seen you give a very reluctant smile. I bet seeing you laugh is a wonderful sight."

"Thanks, so you are not a dog walker. I thought that's what you do. You were always with dogs."

He laughed again. "I do that on the side. No, I'm not a dog walker. I help these elderly people in my apartment building. Walking the dogs forces me to walk too, so that way I get my daily exercise. I love dogs but I can't live with them."

"That is so sweet of you," Ranti said to him.

"Make sure you remember I'm a sweet man who volunteers to walk elderly people's dogs." He laughed again. "Well, I have to go. I can call you again tonight can't I?" He checked before he hung up.

Gboye smiled at her as she said. "This is good for you Ranti. I was worried about you. I was afraid that like Esho you had given up on men and sex, but I can see you just took time off to recuperate. Two men at once, it's like you are exploding. It must be the pregnancy. It's either a man magnet, or all those progesterone and estrogen is finally allowing it to penetrate your thick head that you are a desirable woman."

"Yeah, after Brian I was like, I don't need this at all, I'm better off on my own. I even told myself that Esho lived without a man all her life, but I wanted to be in a relationship. Esho was lonely. How could she not have been? And she was bitter. I didn't want to be bitter.

"After I met Grant and he turned out to be gay, I said to myself; 'That's it. It's the curse, forget it, we are playthings for men.' That's what Esho used to tell me. But I didn't want it to be so. It's like in my attempt not to have it be so, either I link up with rapists or men who are gay. And though Depo and Grant are wonderful men and I will not trade them for straight men, they are not going to have sex with me no matter how much they care about me. It's like either no sex at all, or rape, no middle ground. So I didn't date or let any man touch me for twelve years. I might as well have joined a nunnery. But in my heart, I continued to hope and wish for a good man.

"I needed those twelve years of celibacy after Brian to heal. I've been working on convincing myself not to end up like my grandmother, though you know these things are very tenacious because your brain is wired that way. Unless you fight it, you end up doing exactly what your parents did.

"I think Boris coming into my life helped. After I became friends with him, he repeatedly pointed out that men were always checking me out, but I never saw it before. I started to pay attention and he was right. But I didn't see it before because I didn't want men to check me out.

"When Jack came to talk to me at the diner, I didn't blow him off, and I didn't frown, though I was feeling too sick to smile, but I told myself it was okay, I can smell rapists now, all I need is just to shake hands with them. Is the grip too tight? There is some need to dominate in the man. Can I smell gay men yet?" She laughed, "I think so but they are always welcome. I have two in my life and they are just the greatest.

"When Abe ran into me at the store and offered me a ride, the old Iranti called him a pervert, but it was my grandmother's voice inside my head. I didn't accept the ride from him. He came back and invited me to a barbecue and I went.

"When he asked me if he could make love to me, I said yes though I was afraid. And his touch has been so gentle; it's like whispers. Abe is a nomad, he made that clear, but I love him for what he is able to give me and I will not ask for more.

"This Jack, he wants to come and get me. No man has ever come after me to bring me back in my life. No man has ever wanted me that much. The only time a man came looking for me, was to point me out to killers to kill me, and that was the man who fathered me. I want Jack to come and find me. Donald Winnicott once said: *'It is a pleasure to hide but a disaster not to be found.'*

"Jack is a chef. He nourishes people like Boris does. He shook my hand at Boris' diner and his grip was very tender and gentle. I'm happy," Ranti told her friends.

"And I'm very happy for you Ranti. This is the least you deserved. Keep dating the two of them to be sure of what you want," Gboye said.

"I don't know Ranti, just be careful, the two of them? I don't think you should see two men at the same time. Don't listen to Gboye. What if Abe wants a life with you?" Moradeke wondered.

"He doesn't want more Moradeke. He made that clear. I'm not going to set myself up to be disappointed by hoping for more. I love being with him and I love the way he holds me, and I'm settling for that for now. It's more than I ever had from any man in my life. When he leaves, it is good-bye. He made that clear.

"Jack and I are just talking. I like the way he calls to talk to me. We are getting to know one another. There might be something there and there might not be. Time will tell. So I'm not seeing two men at the same time."

"I just don't want you to get yourself into a big mess. I've never liked the idea of affairs or of people dating more than one person at a time. It's depressing because everyone loses; no one really has the other person." Moradeke explained while giving Gboye a knowing look.

The look was not lost on Gboye who demanded, "Okay, we're here now, what the hell is going on with you? I asked you before we left New York and you said you would tell me when we got here and I can't stand your irritable attitude, it's spoiling the fun."

"Bode might be having an affair," Moradeke blurted out and started to cry.

Ranti and Gboye looked at one another in shock.

"What happened?" Ranti in confusion went to hold her.

"The operative word is 'might' and not 'is." Gboye pointed out. "What makes you think he might be having an affair?"

Moradeke between sobs explained, "I'm not sure. This girl joined our church two months ago. She's a graduate student, and you know how it is in the Nigerian community, you make the effort to welcome a new arrival. I invited her to lunch one Sunday afternoon. Bode stared at her the whole time.

"Each time we see her in church it's the same thing, he is unable to take his eyes off her. Two weeks ago, he said, 'You know Yinka has skin that looks like velvet, and I'm sure it feels like that too.' I became angry and accused him of sleeping with her. He denied it and we had this huge fight, so I kicked him out of the bedroom.

"Then three days later, he told me he wasn't having an affair with the girl and he had never had an affair since we got married, but he had been tempted. He said when we met, I had skin that felt like velvet and looked like hot chocolate drink, and he had enjoyed drinking it many nights, but since I started to use the creams to lighten my skin, he misses that, and when he sees women with my old complexion, he is attracted to them. He said he loves me as always but he misses my skin." She continued to cry.

"That's why I don't go to church," Gboye blurted out.

Ranti gave Gboye an irritated look, as she said to Moradeke, "That's what I thought the first time I saw you, I thought your skin looked like a comforting cup of chocolate drink."

Moradeke continued, "He begged me to stop using the creams. He said he wants the woman he married back. I stopped using the cream and that is why my skin is all patchy."

"I don't think he's having an affair. He told you the truth, he was tempted, but he hasn't done anything yet," Gboye tried to reassure her.

Moradeke continued to cry.

"Moradeke honey, I never liked the idea of you using those creams like Gboye and I have been telling you for years. You are one of the most beautiful women I know. You never needed those creams. Look at your beautiful daughter; that is what you looked like when you had your old skin. I'm glad you stopped bleaching it and you are allowing it to come back," Ranti said to her.

"Whatever gave you the idea that your skin wasn't beautiful?" Gboye demanded of her.

Moradeke went to stand by the railing of the deck. She looked out at the ocean for a long time, sighed, and turning back to look at them, started, "That's why I don't want to be around my mother this time. She did not offend me, but when you are in psychotherapy, it dredges up a lot for you, and for a while you are very angry. I'm not blaming her for things; that will not do me any good, but I'm angry with her and I need the space from her.

"Do you guys know that my father always had affairs? Yes he did, every day of their married life there was always another woman in the wings. And my mother would put up a brave front. It used to make me so angry. I would say to her, "You are a doctor for goodness sake. Leave him." She would say, "I can't leave him because I love him." And because he was so much in the public eye they continued to be Mr. and Mrs. Pretend. Pretending everything was fine, but they were not."

"What has that got to do with you bleaching your skin?" Gboye asked in exasperation. "There are people who cheated on one another in my family. I'm not sure about this, but I think my parents must have cheated on one another. I know they don't have sex. They keep separate bedrooms, but I'm not bleaching my skin."

"No you are not bleaching your skin but you are sleeping with everything with a penis," Moradeke yelled at her.

"Okay, sorry, continue," Gboye raised her two hands in apology as she gave in.

"You know my sister Funmi?" Moradeke asked.

"The most lethal weapon in Nigeria, the pen is mightier than the sword." Gboye chuckled, unable to resist teasing Moradeke about her Newspaper editor sister.

"Funmi has always been the princess in the family. 'Funmi this,' and 'Funmi that.' Bola and I grew up in Funmi's shadow. We were always compared to her and we always fell short. My father loves her so much because she looks exactly like his mother, and his mother is a saint. We all worship at Saint Grandma's altar, though we never met her since she died ten years before any of us were born. He used to go on vacation with Funmi leaving my mother behind and she stood for that nonsense.

"And of course Funmi is light complexioned like my father is and like Saint Grandma was. My mother and I on the other hand are very dark skinned. Bola is kind of in between. I look exactly like my mother. She was never happy with her looks. She didn't think she was much. In fact she used to say my father wouldn't have strayed from home if only she had been light complexioned like the women he went after.

"She would berate herself, and after a while she stopped bothering to take care of herself. And I look exactly like this woman. When I was a little girl and she would start to say she was unworthy and ugly, and the next minute a visitor came to the house and on seeing me, exclaimed, "You look just like your mother!" I hated it. I didn't want to look like this woman who was not beautiful, I wanted to be beautiful like Funmi.

"I even used to wish that one of my father's girlfriends was my mother. So I guess even though you guys and Bode tell me how much you love my skin, I couldn't hear you. I wanted to be light complexioned. I was afraid that if I wasn't, Bode would get tired of me and start running after light-skinned women, like my father, and we live in a country of light-skinned women.

"Bode told me several times that he wasn't blind when he married me, he could see I was very dark skinned, and that's what he loved the most about me, and he is happy Yejide looks just like me. But my father wasn't blind either. When he married my mother, he must have noticed she was dark skinned, and yet he was chasing after every light-complexioned woman in Lagos, why didn't he marry a light-skinned girl in the first place?

"That day, five weeks ago when we ran into Irish at the restaurant, and he accused me of wanting to be a white woman, it was a turning point for me. I felt so small that I wanted to crawl into a hole and die. That was the last day I used those creams, even though I had been seeing a therapist for the past six months.

"My dermatologist said it would take about six months for the skin to go back to what it was, and though I look like a freak now, I am never using those creams again for as long as I live. What lesson am I imparting to my daughter? Though she is luckier, Bode always tells her that her dark skin is her best feature."

Gboye emphatically agreed with her, "And black girls these days are luckier, more and more they see beautiful very dark-skinned women on television and in magazines as role models, not so for us when we were growing up. You can imagine how it was for me in secondary school in England. The standard of beauty in that place is a white woman."

"I'm sorry Moradeke. I had no idea. I love your mother and I think she is a very beautiful woman. She was so kind to me in secondary school," Ranti added.

"I love her very much too. Some days I feel sorry for her that she couldn't appreciate herself and she put up with my father's nonsense. But then I'm angry with her for making me hate myself. I'll get over it, but I don't want to be in the same house with her now. I might end up yelling at her all the time. She's to blame yet she's not to blame. Do you guys know what I mean?"

"It's like with me too," said Ranti. "I've been spending my time here writing my life story. It has helped a lot. Dr. O suggested I do that when he came to see me in the hospital. I wasn't going to do it. But then I wanted to work on the proposals for funding and I couldn't write a thing. Speak of writer's block! It's a terrible thing for a writer to have considering their livelihood depends on writing. But I had it for three days here. Then it dawned on me that I couldn't write because the pains in my life were getting in the way.

"So I took Dr. O's advice and started to write my life story and that was when I truly started to feel better. Abe just crowned the good feelings. It's like for the first time, some parts of me were finally able to breathe.

"But then the question arises, who is to blame? And what is the point of blaming anyone? It's like a car wreck has occurred and several people were injured in the accident. We could start blaming the driver or the condition of the car or even the road. We have to do that to prevent the accident from happening again but what is more important is to take care of the wounded. Blaming is retrospective. It isn't going to cure the present situation.

"Eventually, the responsibility is with you. You know, "*We cannot control who brings us into this world. We cannot influence the fluency with which they raise us; we cannot force the culture to instantly become hospitable. But the good news is that, even after injury, even in feral state, even, for that matter, in an as yet captured state, we can have our lives back*"

"*Fallible parents and societies raise us.*" Most of the time, ignorance is to blame. But we have to take the ultimate responsibility for whatever challenge life has dished out to us before we can begin to live our life.

"And if we are able to do that, we break the generational transmission of pathology. Moradeke, I don't know your mother's or your father's tragic story that made them behave in those ways. Why does she think so low of herself? But I hear her.

"Esho stood me in front of a mirror when I was eight years old, after a man complimented her on my looks. She cut off my hair and asked me to take a good look at myself. She told me I was an ugly girl, and that if anyone told me I was beautiful, they wanted me dead. So while I was married to Brian, and he called me ugly, I wasn't surprised. I believed him.

"When we met people and they complimented me on my looks, he would say to me, "Don't listen to them, they are lying." How can someone be that cruel? But I believed him because long before he came along, Esho had already stood me in front of the mirror and told me the exact same thing. "If anyone tells you that you are beautiful, Iranti, know they are saying it for one reason and one reason only, and that is to ruin your life, because you are not beautiful." And she followed it with concrete actions too. She cut off my hair and she destroyed my genitals. That was God! Esho was the only parent I ever had. She gave me the tools to create my world. Whatever she said to me became written in stone because it wired my brain there and then. She was my fountain of life, so for me, God spoke and it became so, '*Orisa bi iya ko si*,' you guys know the proverb, '*there is no god like mother.*' If Esho hadn't told me that, I would not have married Brian, or picked the rapists I dated in medical school. I would have known I deserved better in life, and chosen kinder men.

"It's only in the past few weeks that I look in the mirror and think that I am a beautiful woman. You guys and the whole world have been telling me that I'm beautiful, even my enemies told me I'm beautiful, though in warnings. Brian's aunt said it. Jamba the minister of rape said it. But I believed my grandmother and my ex-husband and I disbelieved the rest of the world.

"And why would Esho do such a terrible thing? She tried to take her words back before she died, but it was too late, my brain had been wired already. She did it out of fears and because she believed it would protect me from harm, from men. I'm forty years old now, and it took me that long to believe that I might be a desirable woman after all.

"Moradeke, maybe one of your mother's parents told her she wasn't a beautiful girl, I don't know. Maybe your father is looking for his mother, who died before he was ready to let go of her, in all those light-skinned women he is chasing all over Lagos. But he married your dark- skinned mother because some part of him knew that a dead person is gone forever, and the living have to bury them and move on with their lives, but the part of him that wasn't ready to let her go continues to chase light-skinned women. They are both victims of their circumstances.

"But we have to know our family history in depth, and even the history of our society, and take responsibility for it before we can live a fulfilling life, otherwise we would be dead and we would just be shades, doing these crazy things the three of us have been doing to ourselves."

They were quiet for about five minutes.

"I have a confession," said Ranti. "I had a brother who died when I was six years old."

Gboye and Moradeke stared at her in shock.

"His name was Lana. He was nine years old. He might have been in your brother's class, Gboye, I'm not sure."

Gboye shook her head. "I didn't know you had a brother."

Tears sprang into Ranti's eyes, "I'm sorry I never told you guys. He died of tetanus infection. Esho forbade me ever to speak of him again. "*We will never speak of him again!"* She pronounced. The pain, even in memory is still so terrible. It is still terrible. I missed him so much I thought my heart would stop. It is still so painful."

Moradeke and Gboye had tears in their eyes as they hugged Ranti. The three of them started to weep.

A few minutes later Gboye suddenly asked them, "Do you know what our problem is?"

They looked at her.

"Phantoms! That is what we are," said Gboye. "We are phantoms and that is why we are crazy women. We truly are insane. There you are Ranti, one of the most accomplished and beautiful women I know and you thought you smelled of urine and feces and wouldn't let men touch you. You go around thinking people will laugh at you if you tell them of the miracles you have been performing at home.

"Do you know that my father loves you? And he has a lot of respect for you, right from when we were in elementary school. He continues to be admiring of you. And yet you see yourself as the opposite of what you really are. You are a millionaire who thinks she's a pauper. If that is not crazy, I don't know what is.

"And you, Moradeke, with your sparkling eyes, lovely figure and delicious skin, thinking that until you were light complexioned, you wouldn't be beautiful and taking such a wonderful gift from god and pouring acid on it, everyday?

"And me, here I am, six feet tall, still thinking I needed to be bigger than other people, otherwise my life is in danger. I am bigger than most people in the world because of my height already, so what more do I want? I married a wonderful man but I continue to run the streets looking for what? Irish actually did us a favor that day when we ran into him. He pushed us to confront the craziness of our lives.

"I've been an orthopedic surgeon for ten years, but it never ceases to amaze me each time I amputate a limb on my patients, and they begin to complain of pain in the limb that is gone.

"The limb is gone! The area where they feel the pain is air! Space! So how can you continue to feel pain in something that is not there?" She asked in exasperation. "How can you? It's gone! *Vamoosed! Finito! Capische! Ofifo!* In how many languages can I say it? There is nothing there! It is air!" She waved her hand in the air to emphasize her point.

"It just made sense to me now that we are talking about our pains. Our difficulties and craziness are our phantom pains. The issues are not there anymore, but we continue to behave as if they were still very much present. And they continue to be destructive. It's like those neuroscience studies that are able to explain that experiences actually wire the brain in a certain way, and even when the experiences are gone or over, the brain continues to behave as if they were still present. That is what happens in phantom pains. The area that is gone is still represented in the brain for a while. I'm going to have more respect for phantom pains from now on, because I just got it," Gboye explained.

"It's the same explanation for post-traumatic stress disorder," Moradeke added.

Gboye continued, "You know, I learnt a lot of crazy stuff at home too. You guys know that my grandmother lived with us until she died in our second year of medical school. She was a remarkable woman in a lot of ways, and she had the memory of an elephant. She was a genius, but she didn't have the opportunity of being educated.

"This woman single handedly raised six children and they became accomplished men and women. She raised three doctors, two lawyers and my father the successful businessman, and she did it alone.

"Ranti, you remember she had the poultry? She was a tough businesswoman; she kept track of every egg from that poultry. When Goke started to truant from school? I tell you guys, the way she dealt with him? I knew I had better not miss a day of school. When my parents discovered he was skipping school and they told her, she gave him such a tongue lashing, and for days too, and boy, she can nag!

"Then she started to follow him to school. She would go to his classroom and announce to his classmates that she had to come with him so he would stay in school. She called him a baby who needed his mother to come to school with him.

"She embarrassed him so much, and then she would sit under a tree across from his classroom until the end of the day. That cured him of truancy forever. To her too, like Esho, education is the most important thing in life and you are getting it whether you like it or not.

"But tragically, when it came to relationships with men, she failed, and woefully too, as well as her three daughters, and me, her granddaughter.

"You guys remember my aunt Yemi? Her case is the worst. Her husband is the most pathetic man I know. He never had a job, and she is a lawyer. He would take her money and car and disappear for weeks.

"Each time that happened, my aunt would become depressed and return home to her mother. She would move back to live with us, with her three children. Every day, when she came back from work, she, my mother and my grandmother would sit in the kitchen and lament about this man. The three of them would curse him out and wish all manner of ill to come to him. My aunt would cry, and my grandmother and mother would cry with her. If any of my other aunts came to visit, they would join them and cry too. This would go on for weeks and then suddenly, this man would reappear.

"What do you imagine these women did? Initially, I used to think they would let him have it, or even beat him up, but Noooooo! They would welcome him with open arms.

"My grandmother would start to run around the house preparing his favorite meal. They would wait on him hand and foot, offer him cold beer, and pamper him! Most unbelievable thing I've ever seen in my life.

"My aunt would start to smile. My grandmother would 'lend' him money. She was always lending him money, which he never repaid. And that would be it, he was forgiven and then when he disappeared again in one month, the same scenario would be replayed.

"Initially I was confused, and then I became convinced that my grandmother was crazy. Here was this woman, so capable in all areas of her life except when it came to men, and her daughters learned very well from her. It's a big disconnection, like the right side of the brain does not know what the left side of the brain is doing.

"They had split personalities. Like inside each of them was another woman who was the opposite of the woman they were in their career. Like inside a fantastic lawyer or a brilliant ophthalmologist was a stupid wife who endured humiliating abuse from her husband.

"Once I confronted my grandmother about the madness. I said to her, 'Mama, why do you pamper uncle when he reappears, after he has disappeared for weeks, making everyone so afraid and miserable?'

"I asked her to encourage her daughter to leave him because he was abusing her and her children. 'Mama, I said, Auntie is a lawyer for goodness sakes. She's a very brilliant woman. She's a professor of law at the university. She doesn't need this lowlife scumbag. Mama, you single handedly raised and educated six children and they are very accomplished men and women. She can raise her three kids by herself. I'm going to speak with auntie about this.'

"Mama said to me, "Gboye, you are a small girl, and you don't understand how these things work, that's why you are talking like that. You see the most tragic thing in life is for a woman to be without a husband. And it's even worse for a woman who is well educated like your aunt. It would have been better for her not to have any education at all.

'A man is the crowning glory for a woman,' she said, "Without a husband, a woman is nothing. I can't encourage your aunts to leave their husbands, what would people say of me? They would say my daughters are cursed and they would blame the fact that they are well educated. As you know, all your aunts have problems in their marriages. But we are making do. Like I keep telling them, they should just pamper their husbands." That's what she told me. She was nuts!

"Those are the women I grew up with, they were my role models. Explains a lot about me, doesn't it? I refused to be a victim, so I took the domineering role. But the thing is, I married a man who has a job he loves and comes home to take care of my children and me, he doesn't disappear at all, and he doesn't abuse me in any way.

"I am competent in my career like my grandmother and aunts, but I refused to be a fool for any man. It's like I will break their hearts before they break mine, but I'm not married to my aunts' husbands. I married a very good man. But all the same I ended up doing exactly what my grandmother and aunts did."

They were quiet for a long time.

"We didn't let the dead bury the dead as Jesus advised in the Bible," Moradeke added.

Ranti agreed with her. "I more than anyone know that, I lived with a ghost all my life. Esho was one, but it still took me forty years to get it. Yes, that is what we are, we are phantoms."

Gboye went to the fridge and returned with a bottle of apple juice and three cups. "We have to toast to a new beginning. We have to toast to the determination to keep fighting to let the dead bury their dead, and that we will not interfere so we can go on to live our lives with joy.

"We are going to toast to Moradeke's shedding of her skin, and rebirth, as her beautiful chocolate drink of a skin is growing back and that she will see it as the most beautiful hide in the world. She will believe that Bode, a real sweetheart of a man, loves to drink in it before he goes to sleep at nights. And she will let him return to the bedroom so he can have his fill."

Moradeke gave Gboye such a grateful smile that her eyes sparkled like diamonds.

Gboye continued, "We are going to toast to me giving up my armor of needing to be the biggest person in a room because I'm not living with my giant brothers anymore, neither am I married to my scumbag uncles-in-law, and no one is attacking me, and if they try, there are weapons like knives and chairs and tables or baseball bats that I can use instead. We are going to toast to me realizing that I love my soon to be ex-husband very much, and even though he is not the most intellectual or creative man around, he has a heart of gold, and hopefully he can forgive me enough to take me back as his wife, and if he is not able to do that, I will cherish his friendship.

"We are going to toast to my having the courage to keep this pregnancy, and when I give birth to this Chinese baby, that I will have the courage to be a good mother to it, by standing up to a world that will have lots of questions.

"We are going to toast to Iranti, my dear sister, that she is healthier, stronger, and getting it every night as is her God-given privilege. That she fought demons and hardship, she descended to the lowest a human being could descend in an attempt to survive and at a very tender age too, and she emerged to climb to the highest mountain possible in the world. I am honored to be a spectator to this transformation."

Tears sprang into Ranti's eyes as she looked at her oldest friend.

"We are going to toast to Depo and Grant. I know I call them names, I'm angry they are not sleeping with women, but the truth is I love those guys and I'm glad they are my friends."

"I just got it!" Moradeke exclaimed, interrupting Gboye's toast. "You know I'm a born- again Christian and I know you make fun of me, but you see, since I've been seeing my therapist, I'm getting a better understanding of the Bible.

"It's like the Bible gives you these instructions and therapy actually shows you the way to follow them. With the Bible alone, you keep trying to do your best to follow God's commandment but then you fall short and you feel guilty. But why are you falling short? It's not because you are a hopeless sinner or a bad person, but it's because of all these phantoms, this post-traumatic stuff we are talking about.

"But with therapy, you are able to understand why it is difficult for you to follow God's instruction and the purposes of the commandments. Then you are free to obey them, and you are not caught up in the web of guilt and remorse and sin. They are both talking about the same thing.

"Now, do you guys remember that story of the Israelites, and how they left Egypt and wandered in the desert for forty years? Forty years! Look at the three of us. We are in our early forties and we are finally getting it. We are finally getting it that we are the sculptors of our lives. It's like we've been wandering in the desert for forty years too, doing the work, and it is finally making sense.

"The story is a metaphor that I finally got. I used to wonder why God made them wander for so long. Why didn't He just take them straight to the Promised Land? After all, He has all the power and He is all seeing. But they had to work hard for the Promised Land. Its like a land promised to them alright, but it is not empty, it is occupied by forces that wouldn't give it up easily and the forces are these phantoms of ours. They had to fight for it and earn it. That's what we are doing girls, and it's like we just found our way. We are just coming out of the desert here, and we are on our way to the Promised Land. We are almost there. Isn't that something?" She smiled.

Ranti smiled, enjoying Moradeke's sparkling eyes, as she said to herself. "I am Sleeping Beauty just waking up from my hundred-year slumber. I'm thankful that my hundred years were up so soon."

"I have just one thing to say about that," Gboye started. "I'm happy I had my sisters with me while I wandered aimlessly and lost in the desert. Thank you for never judging me Ranti. And Moradeke, you judge me all the time but you have never turned your back on me, thanks for your loyalty."

"Who am I to judge you Gboye?" Ranti thought, "My mother was a prostitute, that was her desert, and my grandmother was a murderer, and that was her desert too. It isn't my place to judge you or anyone at all."

"No, we didn't wander aimlessly in the desert," She corrected Gboye. "It was purposeful wandering with a lot of pain and hard work, it was toward a goal. We just didn't understand the purpose of it and our goals because we were shortsighted. It was not aimless wandering at all."

Gboye smiled at her in gratitude.

They clinked glasses, drank and hugged one another with tears in their eyes.

42

One and a half years after Esho died, Ranti continued to nurse the depression. She did not return to Nigeria, or to work in the free clinic in Brooklyn where she was always welcome.

She spent the time lying in bed staring at the ceiling for hours on end, going on the mandatory daily walks with either Grant or Depo, going to visit one or the other of her friends for one or two weeks, and then returning to Depo in New York City, and to her bed.

Efunwunmi visited for a month at some point and she dragged her along as she went shopping. The tearfulness was still very much there as well as her companions—the smell and sometimes the phantom genital pains and crawling sensations in her anus.

Her friends were patient with her as they took care of her. They insisted she get up every day and eat at least a meal, and she had to go for a walk and take a shower. Outside of that they left her alone.

In February of 1995, Depo had to go to a conference in Florida. Grant had gone to Geneva the week before, so he forced Ranti to go with him. They arrived in Miami very late on a Monday night, and they just had time to eat a quick dinner in the hotel restaurant before they went up to their room for the night.

Depo left early the next morning to go to his meetings, but he called at about ten to wake Ranti, and to insist she go to the beach for a walk. She promised she would. She turned over in bed and though she did not fall asleep, she just lay there. She only got up to use the bathroom. She did not eat the breakfast room service had delivered before Depo left.

She must have dozed off at some point because suddenly she heard Depo yelling at her. She took the cover off her face and he was very angry with her. She looked at him but she could not be bothered, she just wanted to be left alone. She was surprised that it was eight at night already.

He dragged her out of bed and into the shower, at the same time saying it was a good thing he brought her with him to Florida, otherwise she would have lain in bed for the one week he would have been gone.

They went down to the restaurant for dinner, and after they went for a walk on the beach. It was dark but the cool air felt good on her skin.

The next day, Depo returned at about ten from his early meetings to get her out of bed. He walked her to the beach this time. "Ranti, look at the beach, it's beautiful, look, the sun is out, isn't it a glorious day?"

She could hear fear in his voice. She gave him a sharp look, and felt guilty that she was making him afraid. She nodded, agreeing with him that it was a beautiful day. "I promise I won't go back to the hotel just yet. I'll walk around," she tried to allay his fears.

"You *will* walk on the beach and you *will* go shopping. Look at all those stores. Buy anything; buy the things you don't need, though you do need a lot of things. You need some new clothes. Buy clothes that fit better, please, just be like a normal woman for once, and spend too much money so I'll have a reason to yell at you." He handed her his credit card.

She accepted the card, nodded her thanks and started to walk toward the ocean.

"Ranti," he called to her.

She looked back at him.

He came toward her. "You are not thinking of doing anything stupid," he hesitated, "like killing yourself, are you?"

She looked at him and tears sprang from her eyes. "No, Depo, I am not, I will never kill myself. I love you too much to do that to you or to Moradeke or Gboye or to Grant. I just want to feel better."

He hugged her as he kissed her on the lips, "Please spend too much money. I love you."

She walked toward the water and for the first time she did notice that it was a fabulous day with the sun shining bright. She could not remember the last time she had noticed the sun in that way.

Something jumped in her as she looked at the people around her. They were happy and enjoying the ocean. They were smiling and laughing as they frolicked in and out of the water. She felt alienated and wanted to be part of that beautiful humanity.

She walked amongst the people enjoying the look and sound of them. She arrived at the edge of the ocean, took off her shoes, rolled up her jeans and walked into the water. The waves lapped at her feet.

She suddenly felt hunger pangs. They were new. She had not felt hungry in a long time. She walked back toward their beachfront hotel and into a coffee shop close by. She ordered a cup of coffee and a bagel, sat out in the sun and ate. She drank her coffee and it was very refreshing, because she could taste her food. She suddenly realized she could smell the ocean and taste the salty air on her lips. She guffawed so loudly that the people around her gave her a strange look.

She smiled and said to herself, "Welcome back Iranti, welcome back from hell."

She wanted to call Depo to tell him that the smell of urine and feces which had been her companion for the past eighteen months were gone, but she decided to surprise him instead.

She took his advice and she hit the mall. She bought two pairs of jeans in her size that was two sizes smaller than the jeans she had on. She felt so rich that she threw her old pair into the garbage.

She bought tops and a beautiful fuchsia sleeveless dress. She bought two pairs of shoes, makeup, lipstick, a pair of gold earrings and necklace and she went to the hairdresser where she put a perm in her hair, and had it stylishly cut.

When Depo returned to the room at about six that evening, he was stunned at the sight of the new Ranti that greeted him, as she stood with hands on her hips, waiting behind the door.

She leapt across the room into his arms as she breathlessly told him the smell was gone. "I have eaten three times already today. Do you want to know what I ate? I went shopping. I bought this beautiful dress and shoes. I also bought two pairs of jeans. I had my hair done. I love you so much, Depo, thank you so much, thank you." Tears continued to stream down her face.

"Then we are going dancing. A group of us are going to some clubs in the city and they invited me but I didn't think you would want to go. But we are going. Give me a minute to change my clothes." He kissed her again as he hugged her tight.

Ranti accepted a temporary appointment at the free clinic in Brooklyn while she started to write proposals for grants. She also continued to see Dr. Obed and to have the recurring dreams of being locked out of his office by different people, his doorman, his secretary and even once his wife. But in the progression of the dreams she noticed that she started to fight with these people more and more each time they told her she could not see the doctor.

Dr. O. liked that about the dreams that she was fighting for her right to come and go as she pleased.

Six months after the smell left, she was given a fifty-thousand-dollar grant by the World Health Organization after an interview over the phone. She packed her bags and returned to Nigeria, but this time to a village outside of Kano, to a small clinic where a friend of Gboye's was the general surgeon.

For the next few years, Ranti was able to help these women as much as she could with the limited amount of grants she continued to receive from the World

Health Organization and other organizations sympathetic to her cause. For the most part she felt gratified, but she realized that much more was needed to properly rehabilitate these women, and even more in preventive education to spare newborn baby girls from the trauma. But she did the little she could.

Her friends took turns helping her out, buying her plane tickets when they missed her and wanted her to return to the US to visit them. She returned to the US early in 2003 to visit Gboye who had just given birth to her sixth son. She spent a month with her helping Olu care for the boys, while Gboye as usual remained very busy at work.

The weekend after she arrived in Boston, Moradeke and her family drove up to spend time with them. On Saturday, the three friends left the children with Olu and Bode, and went shopping and for lunch to catch up on their lives.

Gboye was eager to tell her friends that she had run into Brian's ex-wife at the hospital. "I didn't know her but she knew me. She remembered me from when I beat the living hell out of Brian. She was the blonde on the bed. Do you remember her Ranti?"

"No I don't, I don't even remember that she was a blonde. I remember a woman on the bed but that's all."

"It was the weirdest thing. This world is not only small, it is round and that's why people keep bumping into one another. So this is what happened. I was in the clinic and she brought her grandfather. He had complications from diabetes and we had to amputate some of his toes.

"I didn't recognize her, but she kept giving me this look that made me very uncomfortable. As they were leaving, she asked, "You don't remember me?" I said I was sorry; could she please refresh my memory? She said her name was Mrs. O'Connor, and I was thinking, okay this is Boston. My mind didn't even go to Brian at all. Most of the time, I don't remember that's his name.

"Anyway, I still looked vague and she said she was married to my friend Brian O'Connor. She was the woman on the bed that day when I taught him a very good lesson. That was how she put it. She said 'the day you taught him a very good lesson.'

"I stared at her, because she was so young. Her grandfather, my patient, is just seventy-two-years old. I asked her how old she was and she said she was twenty-seven. I said, so nine years ago, you were eighteen. She corrected me and said she was seventeen years old at the time.

"I said to her, 'That day in Brian's room you were seventeen?' She nodded and said she was an idiot at the time, but she thought she was the wisest thing around. I said to her, 'it's nice to meet you.' She asked if she could speak to me. I was like, what about? But curiosity got the better of me. So I told her I was going to the cafeteria to get some coffee and she was welcome to walk with me.

"Anyway, shortly after your divorce was final Ranti, he married her. She hadn't turned eighteen yet, but she was pregnant. He had been seeing her for a year while he was still married to you."

"That is statutory rape!" Moradeke yelled, interrupting Gboye. "He was like--- how old at the time? We were twenty-seven, and he is three years older than us, so he was a thirty-year-old man sleeping with a sixteen-year-old. Gosh, where were her parents?" Moradeke was disgusted.

Gboye continued, "She said she knew he was married. He told her he was in the process of getting a divorce from his wife, and she was making life difficult for him. He had a lot of sob stories to tell her and she bought everything. Then, that day when we appeared suddenly and I beat him up, after you had stabbed him and he almost died, it convinced her that he had been right, that you, Ranti were really crazy.

"So, she took good care of him after the beating and when he proposed to her a month later she eagerly accepted. You know he lost his visa when you divorced him, so instead of him applying for an exchange visitor's visa, she filed for him. Anyway, the marriage lasted three years. The same things that happened to you happened to her, the same repeated rejections of her when she wanted him to make love to her, and then the rapes, the same paranoid accusations and the same demands that she should not have anything to do with her family, but she should focus only on him.

"The Yorubas have it all figured out with that proverb, '*The whip used on the first wife is waiting for the second wife.*' It was like your marriage all over again, Ranti, there was no difference. He abused her, rejected her and repeatedly raped her in the exact same ways.

"And she did try to focus on him. She didn't work, she kept home for him. They had three children in that three years of marriage, but she said that with the birth of each child he became more and more difficult to live with. While she was pregnant with the third child, the beatings got worse, until he broke her left arm. So her parents removed her and the children from his house.

"Her father made her file for divorce from him the following week, and sent her and the children to Boston to live with her grandparents. She told me a lot of details, but that's the gist of it.

"He remarried two months after the divorce was final and he married a nineteen-year-old girl, so he was cheating on her too. She had a daughter by him, and the following year they were divorced. Brian is on his fourth marriage now. He married a twenty- one-year old girl the fourth time. She said it's a struggle to get him to pay child support."

"So why was she telling you all this?" Ranti asked.

"I asked her the same question. She said she didn't know, but when she saw that I was her grandfather's doctor, she recognized me right away, and she debated whether to talk to me or not. She said she was happy that I gave him that beating, because I stood up to him.

"Her first child is a boy, and then two girls. She said the weirdest thing is that he gave his three daughters the same name. Her first daughter is named Omowale, the second one is named Omowaleola, and the daughter by the third wife is named Omowaleade. She wanted to know if it's a cultural thing for us.

"I told her it is not, but it shows that Brian has no imagination at all, since he can't come up with original names for his daughters."

Moradeke looked confused. "That's weird, what's that about? I thought he would give his children Irish names or at least American names, since their mothers are Caucasians. Is that the only name he knows?"

"That's his mother's name. Her name is Omowale," Ranti volunteered.

"That is another thing this girl told me. His mother, Oh my God! If I had a mother–in–law like that, I would have pushed her down the stairs. She said that Brian's mother had a say in everything that went on in their marriage, and she was there most of the three years she was married to him. He consulted her on everything. Do you know he's not practicing medicine anymore, Ranti?"

Ranti shook her head.

"He is in some kind of business that involves exporting goods to Nigeria. He registered the company in his mother's name. That's why this girl hasn't been able to get him to pay child support. She hired lawyers but he doesn't have any assets in his name. Everything is in his mother's name, even his house. She said he is doing very well, that he is a millionaire now but nothing is in his name. It's like he's unemployed because he doesn't even file income tax. Can you guys believe this man? Jesus!" Gboye exclaimed.

"I'm not surprised. After all he suggested we commit tax fraud when I was married to him," Ranti thought.

Gboye continued. "So I gave her the name of a good lawyer I know here, because there are laws that have to be obeyed, and the lawyer would go after his mother's assets; after all these children are her grandchildren, and if her son is a deadbeat, then she should be made to step in." Gboye looked around at her friends.

"Is that the juiciest news of the year or what? Ranti, since I spoke to that poor girl, every day that I remember her, I'm thankful you got out of the marriage," Gboye said as she squeezed Ranti's right hand.

"Me too, I'm glad I got out of it," Ranti said. "He's a very wicked man. It was difficult for me to believe someone could be that wicked. Guys, there are times I dream that I'm still married to him and I would start to panic. I would really break out in sweats. And then when I wake up, I'm like, 'Oh thank God, it was just a dream.' Good luck to these young women he continues to marry."

"That is not a dream. That is a nightmare," Moradeke shook her head sadly.

43

On a Tuesday morning a few weeks after Ranti returned to New York City from her visit to Boston, she received a package from Funmi, Moradeke's editor sister in Nigeria. It was a copy of a newspaper that was a week old. She started to read it wondering why Funmi would send her the paper, but the centerfold was an obituary of General Jamba. She caught her breath.

She got her coffee and sat down at the dining table to enjoy the article. The obituary itemized all the "wonderful and great" things Jamba did for Nigeria over the forty years he was in the army. It concluded that he was killed in a motor vehicle accident, 'he and his only son, a forty-three-year-old businessman who lived in England.'

Ranti laughed out loud. She stood up and did a little dance around the kitchen in celebration. "Thank goodness that I don't have to commit murder, because as I promised myself, if I had one more encounter with the man, I would have had to kill him. Being party to one murder was too much for me, because it took me almost two years to recover. Now the world is clean of my enemies and I am safe."

She called her friends to share the good news with them, and later in the day she went out to shop in celebration. She took her laptop with her, with plans to drop it off at Computer Warehouse that was close to Depo's office for repairs.

She walked in and out of several shops without buying anything, because she was too afraid to spend the money she did not have. At some point she decided to go and meet Depo at his job, so they could go to lunch.

She called him but he was in a meeting and he would not be able to break for lunch. She was disappointed, so she called Grant in case he was free. He was not and he apologetically told her he needed to stay at his desk, otherwise they would not see him at home for another week.

She walked around some more, when suddenly it began to rain. "So much for my celebration," she said in resignation.

She tried to catch a cab to take her home but she could not get any. She decided to go to a diner ahead of her for a cup of coffee and wait out the rain. As she started to walk towards the diner, three young men walking toward her from the opposite direction suddenly started to run at her. She tried to get out of their way but two of them crashed into her. She reeled back, hitting her head against the building wall.

One of them slapped her hard across her face as they pushed her into an alley and against a wall.

"What is it about my face that people just slap me around?" She wondered.

The other one flipped open his knife and it glinted at her. The third one stood at the entrance of the alley, watching out for the police and yelling at the other two to hurry up.

They demanded her purse. She handed it over to them. She wanted to ask them to let her take her laptop out of the purse and they could have the money, but the robber with the knife screamed at her, sputtering saliva on her face as she tried to speak. She kept quiet.

The other one took her purse and went through it. He saw her laptop and commented that it was so small. The scout kept yelling at them to hurry up.

The two robbers with her started to argue with one another. The one with the knife wanted to see the laptop; the other one wouldn't give it to him and in the scuffle it dropped on a rock and shattered to pieces.

Ranti closed her eyes in pain. A lot of important information about her patients was stored in the computer, as well as the proposal she was working on.

The three of them started to argue and yell at one another.

"Just take the damn purse and leave me alone," Ranti suddenly yelled at them.

They stopped and looked at her for a moment.

"You don't give orders around here bitch, I do," the one with the knife yelled into her face.

"How ironic," Ranti thought, "there I was celebrating that Jamba and his son are dead and the world is safe, and the very next minute, I'm being mugged with a knife pointed at my chest. Is Jamba going to win?"

"I could stab you, bitch, I could even kill you. Don't think I can't," the robber with the knife informed her.

Ranti kept quiet.

"You want a demonstration? Here, here is a demonstration." He slashed at her left arm. She could feel the knife going through her jacket, a gift from Moradeke, and she could feel blood running.

The assailant noticed the jacket after he cut through it. "This is cashmere!" He exclaimed. "Give it to me, now, before I cut you more."

Ranti quickly took off the jacket and gave it to him.

The scout yelled at them to hurry, and they ran after him with her purse and her jacket. Her laptop lay on the ground shattered to pieces. Her arm was bleeding.

"This one's for you Jamba, congratulations," she said aloud and started to cry.

She walked slowly out of the alley onto the sidewalk, and stood in front of the diner. She was drenched with rain and the heel of her left boot was broken. She tried to think, but could not because she needed to catch her breath from the adrenaline that had poured into her bloodstream.

She stood there as the gravity of what she had just escaped hit her. She started to tremble and continued to cry. She told herself she should call either Depo or Grant to come get her, but her cell phone was in her purse.

"I should call the police," she suddenly said aloud to herself. But she stood rooted to the spot, unable to move.

"I should move away from here, walk away, as far away as possible in case they have a gun and come back," she instructed herself but she did not move.

"I should go get a gun and come back here and hang around until I see them again. I'm sure they will come back here. Predators usually do. I should take care of these offspring of Jamba once and for all like Esho would have done. She took care of Akanbi that last time. But I can't kill. I can't even kill the mice that harass me all the time in my house in Nigeria, I just shoo them away." She remained standing there, with tears running down her face.

An elderly man came out of the diner toward her. "Please come in out of the rain. You are crying in the rain," he said in a Russian accent, as he held out his right hand to her.

Ranti shook her head. "No, thank you."

"It's safe in my diner, please come in, please, you are bleeding."

Ranti refused.

"It is raining, it is cold, it is March, come in please."

Ranti stood there as she stared at him. "He has a kind face," she told herself.

"Thank you, I'm fine here. Thank you."

"Okay, I stand in the rain with you then, I stand and we both catch cold and pneumonia." He folded his arms across his chest and stood next to her.

Ranti stared at him. "Is he crazy? If he catches pneumonia, he will die. He is so old and frail," she thought.

She took his left hand and pulled him toward the diner. He gave her a towel to wipe her face.

"Boris," he pointed at himself as he handed her a cup of coffee.

"Ranti," she smiled at him. "I like him, he came for me." She smiled at him again.

She called the police and the telephone company to disconnect her cell phone. She was grateful she did not have a credit card, and she had just a hundred dollars in her wallet. She reminded herself that she had to go to the Secretary of State to report her driver's license stolen, and they would have to change the locks to the loft.

Grant picked her up twenty minutes later from Boris' diner to take her to the hospital to treat the stab wound. On the way home they stopped at the police station for her to sign her statement and look through the police files for pictures of the muggers.

Ranti started to go to Boris' diner to hang out with him and to help him out sometimes. A month later, she asked Boris about a man who always sat outside the diner. She had seen him there almost every day, and Boris would take food and drinks out to him and talk to him for a few minutes. Regardless of the weather, sunny, cold, snowy or rainy, the man never came into the diner to eat.

"That's Harry; he has to sit out there because he cannot come into the diner." Boris paused and looked at Ranti. "Harry doesn't take showers, and he does smell. People don't like to sit around him and definitely they wouldn't want to eat with him smelling in the diner."

Three days later, when she arrived at the diner at lunchtime, Boris and his assistants were swamped serving the customers. Harry sat outside in the cold, looking expectantly into the diner.

The expression on his face tore at Ranti's heart. It was a combination of hope, longing and expectation of disappointment. She sat in her corner of the diner and stared at him for a long time. Boris remained very busy. When she could not take it anymore, she went out to Harry. She sat next to him though it was too cold for her, and a few moments later the smell hit her. She almost gagged, but she controlled herself.

"What would you like to eat Harry? As you can see, Boris can't tear himself away to serve you just yet. I'm a very good friend of his, I help him out sometimes, I can get you whatever you want and I'm sure he will come out and say hello to you as soon as he can. My name is Ranti." She held out her right hand to him.

He continued to stare into the diner, ignoring her.

She waited for about a minute. "Okay, I'll go ask Boris what it is you like to eat and I'll bring it out to you, so you won't have to wait."

"Oh, no, he won't take the food from you," Boris told her. "He doesn't trust anyone. He will only take food from me. I will serve him in a minute, he doesn't mind waiting. He knows the drill."

Ranti went back to her seat but she could not resist the urge to keep looking at Harry. His expression continued to tear at her until she could not take it again. She went back to Boris where he was behind the register. "Okay Boris, please go and serve him, I'll take care of your customers here."

Boris took food out to Harry where he was seated in the cold. He sat next to him for about five minutes, talking to him. At some point, Harry smiled as his face relaxed.

For days following this, Ranti plagued Boris with questions about Harry, but he did not know much about him. "He started to come to the diner about five years ago, and initially he would come in, but then customers started to complain, and some of them even left. I didn't have the heart to ask him not to come. So I suggested he sit outside. I stopped charging him four years ago when I realized I'm probably the only person he talks to. He comes even on days I'm not open like on Sundays and holidays. Every day I cook for him, otherwise he won't eat."

"Is he mentally ill, is that why he refuses to take a bath?"

"I don't know Ranti. What I just told you; that is all I know, I exchange pleasantries with him and I don't probe."

Three months later Ranti went to Nigeria for six months. She returned early in 2004 because she ran out of money, and started to apply for more funding. She spent her time in the usual ways she spent it while waiting for money to come through, working in the free clinic in Brooklyn three days a week, and visiting her friends and Boris.

At about ten one Saturday morning in February, while she was at home alone, Boris called her on the phone. "Ranti, I need you to go to Bellevue hospital immediately, please. I cannot leave the diner but Harry has been taken there by the police and I'm sure he's afraid."

"What happened?"

"I don't know, but the hospital just called me now. He gave them my name and number. Can you go for me please?"

"Sure, I'll go. I'll leave right away and will let you know what's going on as soon as I find out," Ranti told him.

Forty-five minutes later when she was let into the psychiatric unit, Harry was in a very agitated state. He was weeping inconsolably as three orderlies tried to remove his filthy clothes so they could get him to bathe.

When he saw Ranti, his agitation decreased some, and he made toward her. He clung to her as if, were he to let go, he would die. She was surprised because he had always ignored her.

She held on tightly to him as well because she could feel his fears in his trembling body. He was crying and muttering some things she could not make out.

The orderlies let them be for about five minutes. Then they asked Ranti to convince him to remove his clothes and bathe.

"Harry, I'm going to be here and I'm going to stay with you, but listen to me, everything will be okay, you are going to be fine. This is a hospital, you haven't done anything wrong and these men are not going to hurt you. They would like you to take off your clothes so they can wash them for you, and they will return them to you later.

"They also want you to bathe. It always helps. There have been times when I was depressed, taking showers helped me a lot. I'll be here with you. Boris will be here as soon as he can, he asked me to come here for now," she tried to explain to him.

He clung to her as he continued to tremble and whimper, like a wounded animal. When the orderlies tried to pry him from Ranti's embrace, his agitation increased. Ranti asked for more time to convince him to cooperate so they would not have to exert force on him.

They gave them another ten minutes but all Harry wanted to do was cling to her. He refused to let go of her or agree to take off his clothes or bathe. The orderlies finally pried him from her and led him away. He struggled with them as he started to shriek. It reminded Ranti of Esho in the days after Lana died when she was a little girl, and she burst into tears as well.

She called Boris, asking him to close the diner and come immediately. She could smell Harry on herself as she returned to his room to wait for him.

Twenty minutes later, when the orderlies brought him out of the bathroom, Ranti did not recognize him. They had cut off his shoulder-length hair and shaved off his beard. He was a very pale man, but he had become about ten shades darker because of the grime on his skin. He remained agitated as he continued to whimper. His eyes darted around fearfully.

Ranti walked over to him, taking him from the orderlies and he clung to her again as he continued to cry.

"They took her away. They took her away from me. She is not dead but they took her away from me," he repeated between sobs.

"Who Harry? Whom did they take away from you?"

"My wife Diana, they took Diana away. They took her away. It's not fair. It's not fair at all," he sobbed inconsolably.

A nurse offered him some pills and water. He refused to take the medication.

"You have to take it Harry, it will help you rest. If you don't take it, the doctors will give you an injection, so please take the medicine," the nurse appealed to him.

When he heard injection, he quickly took the pills and swallowed them. He held on tightly to Ranti. His whimpering and sobbing slowly subsided and after a while he started to doze off. She did not have the heart to disturb him so she held on to him.

Fifteen minutes later, when Harry heard Boris' voice as he whispered into Ranti's ears so as not to disturb him, his eyes flew wide awake. He resumed the sobbing and whimpering, "Boris, they took her away, they did, the bad men, they took my wife away, it's not fair."

"I know Harry, and I understand. I know. It's going to be okay, you are going to be fine, I'm here with you, and I'll stay with you for as long as the doctors say it's okay." Boris tried to reassure him.

He disengaged himself from Ranti and clung to Boris. Within minutes he was fast asleep in Boris' arms. The orderlies moved him onto his bed. They allowed Boris to sit next to him and hold his hand.

A few minutes later, Ranti returned home because she could not stand the

310 *Feasts of Phantoms*

smell of Harry that had stuck to her. All she wanted to do was throw away her clothes and take a long shower.

At about six that evening, Boris called her from the hospital. "He just died Ranti," he announced, "and he was just forty eight years old, he was so young."

When Ranti picked Boris up from the hospital an hour later, the older man was in tears. "He didn't have anyone. He left my name as his next of kin. He didn't have anyone. I'm always afraid too, you know I don't have anyone either. I don't have children and my wife died three years ago. It's not good to die alone."

"He didn't die alone Boris, you were with him. You held him. He had you, and you took care of him for many years. You did not let him die alone. He had you." Ranti tried to comfort him.

"And you are not alone either Boris. You have your friends and you have me."

She remembered how she found her grandmother's dead body. She had always wished she were there to hold her hands too. She had always wondered if she just died silently and peacefully without any pain, or if she thrashed around on the bed, gasping and clutching at her chest at the point of death.

Was she scared? Did she wish that someone was there to hold her hand? Did she wish for her granddaughter, the companion of most of her life at that time? Esho, who did not have anyone to hold her in life, did not have anyone to hold her at the point of death either.

Ranti wished she had continued to share the same room with her like she did until she came to America. At least that way she would have heard her if she had gasped at the point of death. Harry was luckier. He had Boris sitting next to him, holding his hand.

She took Boris home to his apartment above the diner and sat with him till Depo came for her at midnight. At some point she asked Boris, "Who was he? I mean Harry, who was he?"

"He told me about three months ago why he stopped changing his clothes or taking showers. They evicted him from his apartment at the time because of the smell. A shelter refused to take him unless he changed his clothes and took a shower, so he came here late at night. I couldn't let him stay here either because of the smell. The department of health would have closed my diner.

"A friend of mine had a room to rent, and he accepted him even though I warned him about the smell, but luckily my friend didn't have a sense of smell. On the way to my friend's apartment, I asked him why he stopped bathing."

Boris shook his head regretfully and continued. "Six years ago, he came home from work to his wife. He was working in construction. He held his wife and they made love. When he woke up the next morning she was dead, in his arms. She was very young. She was thirty-six years old. He said that he loved her so much. He said that she made him happy all the time.

He became afraid that if he took off his pajamas, or washed his body, he would be washing her away, and so he never did. He told me that as long as he did not take off his pajamas, which were under all his clothes, and as long as he did not bathe, she remained with him, he could still smell her, because his body had just entered her body before she died." He paused again and he looked very sad.

"When the hospital called me this morning to say the police brought him there because some neighbors complained about the smell, I knew they would force him to take a bath, and take his pajamas off, and I knew that it was only a matter of time before he died.

"I understand his pain. I too lost my wife three years ago. I did not want them to take her away either. I wanted to keep her with me. But I did not lose my mind like Harry did, so I knew that they had to take her away, and I had to change my clothes every day, and bathe every day."

For the next month Ranti could not get Harry out of her head. She became afraid without knowing what specifically she was afraid of. She started to have a sensation of time rushing by her, the way the wind rushed by when she rode on the subway.

She started to feel as if she were rotting away, that she would die and her life would have been meaningless. She developed anxiety attacks and was terrified that the depression would return, but she fought it by getting out of bed every day and going about what she needed to do. She made a list of her chores and followed it faithfully, using it as an anchor, so she would not slip and not be able to hold herself from falling into that hellhole of depression again.

She continued to see Dr. Obed as she had always done each time she was in New York, but she increased the frequency of seeing him to four times a week because of this new fear. She kept reminding herself that it took her eighteen months to come back from hell the last time, and she could not afford to go back there.

She continued to have the repeated dreams of being shut out of Obed's office and life. And sometimes within a week she would have the dream four or five times.

She dreamt *she was not prevented from seeing Obed by his staff, because she had fought them on that, but Obed was having a party at the time of her appointment, and he did not invite her to the party. He asked her to leave since he was busy enjoying himself at his party.*

Another time, she dreamt *she arrived for her appointment, and he was seeing someone else on her time, and then he told her the person was more important than her, because that person did not smell of urine or feces.*

She continued to discuss these recurring dreams with him and they kept working with them. Obed repeatedly told her it was her past intruding on the present and preventing her from having a future.

She became obsessed with Harry. "He stopped living because his wife died in his arms after he had just made love to her. Couldn't he see that he gave her a wonderful farewell? No, he could not because she was too young to have died, and he did not have anyone to help him mourn her, the way I had my friends who helped me mourn Esho when she died.

"Esho stopped living at the age of thirteen, after the mad man that gave her Oshun before she was ready raped her and she killed him. I have stopped living too. I am not living my life. I am just going through the motions. I have not allowed a man to hold me in almost ten years. I have not let a man make love to me. I want to be loved. I want to get married and have children.

"I do not want to die alone. I want someone to hold my hand on my deathbed. I want to have people who are related to me, my own blood. I have to go back to the world of the living. I came back from hell that time when the depression following Esho's death lifted, but I have not joined the living yet. I have been standing on the edge like a shade looking at people living their lives. I want my life to have a meaning.

"Gboye has been living her life. She is the mother of six boys now, she has continued with her career and her affairs. Moradeke is a mother of three beautiful children. Depo and Grant continue to adore one another more and more each day, and I am just a spectator to their lives. I want more, I need to have more. I do not want to end up like Esho. I want to live a life, not pretend at a life.

"One of my guides, Joseph Campbell said: *'The world is a match for us and we are a match for the world. And where it seems most challenging lies the greatest invitation to find the deeper and greater powers in ourselves.'*

"My greatest challenge is to become a lover and a mother. I need to be those two things so that I can truly love. I know I can become that important to a man. I refuse to be a plaything for men. I want to jump back into my life."

A few nights later she had the dream of exclusion again. *She had gone to Dr. Obed for her appointment. He was having a party in his office. The doorman told her she couldn't go in since she was not invited to the party. Ranti turned around to go back home but then she suddenly became very angry. She went back to the door and when the doorman tried to stop her, she yelled at him that she was invited to the party because Obed was having it at the time of her appointment.*

"He is on my time, because I am paying for the time." She pushed her way in through the doors, daring the doorman to stop her, but he did not stop her. Rather, he ran ahead of her to hold the elevator for her.

The next day, when she told Obed the dream, he smiled at her as he said, "That's more like it. It is your time and it is your right."

On a Wednesday night in early May, while Ranti and Depo were watching television she thought of telling him about the anxiety attacks. While she hesitated, a quotation about anxiety being a symptom of unrealized dreams and potential jumped into her mind and she recited it to herself: *"Anxiety occurs at the point where some emerging potentiality of possibility faces the individual, some possibility of fulfilling his existence; but this very possibility involves the destroying of present security, which thereupon gives rise to the tendency to deny the new personality."*

"That's what it is!" she yelled at herself. "The anxiety is about what I have to let die, so I can move to the next stage of my life. The old has got to die. It is scary stuff, I know, because I wouldn't have the security provided by the old ways of avoiding life anymore, just like I have been falling in love with gay men to prevent me from confronting my sexuality. It provides security but it is also stagnation, a prison, and I've got to move on, I have got to live my life. I have to take what looks like a risk and jump. It has to be done."

She looked at Depo and was shocked to hear herself say to him, "Let's have a baby."

He was shocked too, and he gave her a long worried look.

"Isn't that what you've always wanted? That was what you said to me when we met in 1981, "I want you to be the mother of my children." That's what I want Depo, I want to be the mother of your children. I don't want to wait anymore for a man who may never come. I want to go on with my life. I want to keep living my life. If I don't, I will die and rot."

Depo continued to stare at her. "Are you okay?"

"Never been better," she realized that suddenly she felt great. "I want to do this. It will be an honor to be the mother of your children, Depo."

He turned sideways to give her his full attention. "But what if you meet someone and decide to get married?"

"I haven't met a man in ten years Depo, I'm not waiting anymore, I want to go on with my life, and if a man comes, he will be welcomed. Please let's do this. Esho wanted it too."

Depo stared at her for another minute. She continued to look expectantly at him. He stood up from his seat and came over to her. She stood up too and they hugged each other tightly.

"Are you sure you want to do this?" he checked with her again.

"More than anything in the world," she laughed out loud, she felt so light headed and giddy with happiness. It felt to her as if it was the most natural thing in the world to do.

He kissed her on both cheeks and on the lips. "Thanks Ranti. Jeez, you have always made my dreams come true. This is unbelievable, thank you." He still looked surprised as he kissed her again.

Ranti continued to laugh out loud. The weighty feelings, and the feelings of time swooshing by her, were gone. She felt as if this was where she should be, doing exactly what she was doing, talking to Depo about having his baby.

"I will call my gynecologist in the morning, and you will discuss this with Grant. He has to be on board."

314   *Feasts of Phantoms*

"Oh, he's on board alright. We've been talking about adopting a baby. I've even discussed it with my mother, asking her to look into it for us, but this is much better. Grant adores you Ranti." He kissed her again.

The next morning when Ranti ran into Grant in the kitchen as he was hurrying off to work, he kissed her as he thanked her.

Later, when she reported her decision to Dr. Obed, he was as shocked as Depo had been and he asked her, "Where did that come from?"

"I have no idea," Ranti laughed. "I opened my mouth and the words just tumbled out."

A month later, in mid-June, she completed all the necessary medical examinations to clear her for the in-vitro fertilization and implantation procedures, but she convinced Depo to let her return to Nigeria to tidy things up with her staff and patients before having the final procedures done, as she would not be returning to Nigeria until after the baby was born.

It took them over a year and three trials to get pregnant. It was emotionally draining for her but with her friends and Dr. Obed's support she was able to endure the disappointments such that when her pregnancy test was positive in October of 2005, she warily allowed Depo and Grant to hold a small party to celebrate.

44

The two weeks Gboye and Moradeke spent with Ranti on the Island went by fast. Moradeke was eager to return to her husband and children and she told her friends that the talks helped her a lot, and she would be able to face her mother without any fears.

Gboye too was eager to go back home and return to work. They promised one another that they had to get away at least once a year to reconnect, as they had been able to do in the past couple of weeks.

The following weekend, Grant and Depo came to visit Ranti, and Grant had not seen her since her first weekend on the island and was amazed at the changes in her.

On Saturday, Abe invited them to a barbecue and gave them a slide show of his work. They started to talk about all the chaos going on in the different parts of the world, when Grant suddenly exclaimed, "How could I have forgotten to tell you this, Ranti? I pulled some strings with my connection through the World

Health Organization, and you have been invited to address the World Women Congress on the issue of genital mutilation. You will have the floor on June 9. It's at the Rockefeller Center."

Ranti stared at him. "What are you talking about, Grant? You are not making sense."

"The World Women Congress is inviting you to speak to all the representatives of the different countries in the world on the issue of genital mutilation. This is the least you deserve, Ranti. You have spent the last thirteen years of your life doing this work, and the world has a right to know. I will not let you hide anymore. This work is far too important for you to hide it. The date is June 9 2006, a Friday, and I told them you will be there."

"That's around the time I will have the babies. What if I go into labor the day before?"

"I thought the babies were coming in July." Grant was confused as he looked around. "Am I missing something here?"

"Yes, that's when they are expected, but they are twins and twins come early, sometimes four weeks early. You should have warned me before you committed me."

She knew he meant well, but she was anxious. The fears returned that she was an imposter or that they would laugh at her, telling her she did not belong in such hallowed halls.

"If I had checked with you, Ranti, you would have refused. That is why I went ahead and scheduled the time. You are not getting out of this one, and make sure you don't go into labor the day before. I'm warning you," Grant asserted.

"The babies will wait, Ranti. There is no reason for you to go into premature labor. You are doing so well now, and you deserve this honor," Depo reassured her.

Abe nodded, "I'm with them on that, Ranti. You should scream from mountaintops about what you have been doing in Nigeria. It's a wonderful opportunity and I'm proud of you."

Ranti was quiet. She started to chastise herself for allowing the ghosts she had been trying to lay to rest rear their dead heads again. She told herself the men were right. For the sake of her patients and in the memories of her eight patients killed so far since she started this work, she should shout about her work from mountaintops. The world should know that some women are deprived of the gift of having wonderful poems sung to them, and of enjoying the pleasurable zones of their bodies.

She hugged Grant.

Abe spent the following Tuesday night with Ranti in her cottage, but she noticed that he was subdued. She caught him looking at her on several occasions with a very sad expression. She asked him what the matter was, but he shook his head and forced a smile.

On Wednesday morning while they were making love there were tears in his eyes. Ranti sensed such sadness about him that she repeatedly asked him if he was okay. He kept reassuring her that he was fine.

They had their morning swim and he returned to his cottage after he kissed her for a long time, longer than usual for him, and with a casual, "I'll see you later."

Ranti was worried. She tried to settle down to do more writing but she could not concentrate. Abe continued to nag at her. She thought of going to check on him but was reluctant to disturb him while he was working. Finally, at about eleven o'clock, she could not take it anymore, so she walked over to his cottage.

She knocked on the door on the deck, but there was no answer. She started to panic. She walked around the cottage to the caretaker's lodge.

"Mr. Abe left about thirty minutes ago. He took an earlier flight." The woman told her.

Ranti was stunned.

"He might still be at the airport. The plane is not leaving till noon, but he wanted to be there early."

When Mr. Sanchez dropped her off at the small airport, she ran straight for the departure lounge. The only plane leaving the Island was boarding. She scanned the passengers and spotted Abe. He was holding his bags as he stood in line.

"Abe?" she called to him.

He gave her the despondent look he had the day before. He was quiet.

"Abe, I..." she started.

"Ranti, look I don't want a scene. I told you at the beginning that I can't make a commitment and that I move constantly. Let's not make a scene please," he interrupted her.

Ranti shook her head. "I'm not trying to create a scene Abe. I'm just glad I didn't miss you. I wanted to thank you. I don't have the words Abe. I never do and that's why I always borrow other people's words. I don't have the words that could convey the gratitude I feel toward you. Thank you for saving my life. The manner in which you've held me these past four weeks and loved me, you have told me in ways that other people have not been able to convince me that I'm a desirable woman. The words are inadequate. I wish I were a poet. Thank you for the ways in which you loved me. You cured me, Abe. I would have hated it if I were not able to let you know that.

"You need to know Abe, because you and I, we are the same, looking for healing and you gave me that, and may you meet someone who will be able to do the same for you. Have a safe trip. Providence will smile on you as you have smiled on me."

It was Abe's turn to be stunned as he stared at her. She turned around and started to walk away from him. She was almost at the Sanchezes' car when he pulled at her shoulder. He had tears in his eyes, and he looked like he had the first time they made love. Ranti stared at him and tears sprang from her eyes too, because he looked so beautiful to her. She smiled at him through her tears.

"I'm a coward, Ranti, a jerk, and that is why I didn't say good-bye to you. I was afraid of a scene, but now I realize that I am the one who would have made a scene, not you." He paused.

"I need to go away. If I stay, I will hurt you. I'm running away because I always end up hurting those I love. I'm a fool and you are too kind. I'm sorry."

"I understand. You have no idea how much I understand, Abe. Thank you, your gift to me is priceless. You blew years of sexual trauma away by loving me. You cured me. You didn't hurt me; you cured me. I understand that you have to do what you have to do."

He bent toward her and kissed her on the lips. "I am a fool, a sick fool and that is why I'm walking away now, but if I stay, we will both regret it, and I do want to stay. I will email you, and you will let me know when the babies come, won't you?"

Ranti dreamt that *Obed invited her to attend a party at his office. She was very happy, and when she arrived at the office with Depo as her date, the doorman, the secretary and Obed's wife were there. They smiled at her as they welcomed her and told her they were happy to see her. "It's like you are part of the family, welcome." They said to her in unison.*

She smiled and went into the office. Obed was talking to another man. When he saw her and Depo, he excused himself from the man and came to them. He shook their hands and hugged them, "Ranti, I'm glad you came. It's good to see you as always."

She smiled to herself when she recalled the dream in the morning. "I am welcome among the quality people of the world. That is where I belong as a result of my hard work. My principal in St. Ann's School was right when she told us that each woman's worth shall be measured by her own accomplishment, and not by the accomplishments of her parents.

"How interesting that I had this recurring dream again and now it is one of finally being invited to Obed's office, on the very night that Abe left me. I have come very far. The first hallucination or dream I had about Obed was one of being asked to leave his posh Park Avenue office because I smelled of urine and feces.

"Abe did not reject me. He has to go away to heal his own stinking wounds, because the sadness that I feel now as a result of the way he left is the stench from his wounds. He must cater to his wounds so the stench will not hurt more women, so he will be able to work hard to prevent the one fear he has from happening—the fear that in his old age he would be alone.

"I know too much about smells that drive people away. I used to smell myself even though other people could not smell me. And I prevented myself from associating with good people even when they invited me with open arms. It was my way of keeping hope away. They promised me life but I was used to death, because that was all I knew at the time. That was my cave of fear. Those were my thorns and hedges.

"And my patients in Nigeria, those women I christened Sleeping Beauties, their smell kept society away from them and turned them into outcasts and victims, but I have been working hard with them to turn them back into princesses by containing the smell for them, because when nature created them it contained the smell where it should be, but trauma spread it to where it should not be.

"I remember Harry whom I met through Boris. He was one of life's lessons to me. He concretized his dead wife in the form of his smell and he refused to let her be buried. His smell drove away the people who could have helped him. He refused to give up his smell and as such he prevented women from loving him and curing him. He prevented life from helping him mourn his dear wife. He died the moment his smell was aggressively taken from him.

"I also know a lot about wounds. I remember our neighbor Oke's festering wound. I remember how the smell from his wound tortured the neighbors. His parents were so afraid. Oke had to let his wound be opened as many times as necessary to drain of its poison so he would not lose his leg that was supposed to take him places, and so he would not lose his life.

"It was very painful, but he stuck by it and allowed it to be opened several times, until all the poison was drained off. And in the end there was no more pain. There was a scar but no more pain. And Oke was able to go places with his legs, and neighbors were not tormented anymore and his parents stopped being afraid.

"Wow! There is a lesson to be learnt everywhere. Life is full of metaphors to guide us. Oke's wound and healing, that is a huge metaphor about enduring the pain of healing. It just made sense to me now. That he was my neighbor, and I had the opportunity to learn this lesson from him, that was a gift to me," she concluded with a smile.

Ranti spent the rest of the week swimming, reading and catching up on Grant's DVDs. There was an inner security she realized was hers. She told herself she had worked hard for it and had earned it. "No one can take this away from me. Not all the Sharas of this world or all the Jambas, or the Akanbis or the Brians can take this from me. My wound is healing. It was covered over by a scab before and that was why I chose rapists as lovers. It had to be re-opened and drained of the poisonous pus festering inside it.

"I was able to allow it to be reopened and debrided in spite of the pain. It took twelve years of working with Obed, and two trips to hell. And it is healing with secondary intention as physicians would say, and that is why there is a scar. I know the scar will hurt sometimes and that is just fine. I know that when the scar hurts I will cry and so what? But it is my scar. The scar I earned as courageous soldiers earn medals. I am proud of my medals. I will be able to tell the difference between its hurting because of the change of weather and the original wound.

"This one is mine because you do not just happen into joy, and it is not something that is handed to you. You work very hard to attain joy. And this is joy. I may be unhappy because of the circumstances of life and I should be unhappy when it is called for. I should weep when it is a situation in life that calls for tears, and there will be plenty of situations in life that is being well lived that will call for tears, but I will always know that at my foundation I have joy.

"I know I will be despondent in certain situations, because I am alive and I have developed more compassion for myself and for my fellow human beings, but I will not be depressed. My smell could come back in tough times but I will see them as old companions that have come to remind me of where I came from, and to advise me there are dead things around me to be debrided and buried, and that when I did it before, I triumphed, and because of that, they will not stay for long. They will come back as a reassurance to let me know that though life is full of pain, I have the means to deal with it and I will be fine again.

"I need my scars and my smell around me all the time. They have made me the fine physician I have been so far. I'm like Chiron the Centaur, that mythological healer who had a wound that would not heal. That was what made him a great physician because he was working from his pain. I need my pain and my history with me in memory to assist me in being the best human being I can be.

"I am now in good relations with my internal demons, and that has freed me from external demons. I am the boss of my own head, the very thing Esho always wanted for me. I was in captivity. I was a slave of my history and circumstances. I wandered through the deserts of pains and agony, and I hid in caves of fears, but I am emerging onto the Promised Land.

"I have awoken from the hundred-year slumber. Time has been very kind to me. I did the work and helpers came and helped me. All the ghosts and the wraiths and the ghouls have been banished to their resting places. I do not have to cast angels in the role of demons anymore and I do not have to pretend that devils are angels.

"I'm like a sturdy seafaring ship on the Atlantic Ocean, that tempestuous sea. My ship is solidly built, and whatever storms the ocean can conjure, let them come, I will withstand them. All the help and all the teachers I can ever need are present in this world. The world is at my service. The world gave me the means to save my soul. It is a wonderful, wonderful and benevolent world.

"Esho is right. I have combined Gold, Treasure and a fearless goddess in Memory to make Joy. Our line was derailed but I have put it back on track.

"And Depo is right. I do not need a man to make love to me in a way that will make me feel like silk, all I needed was to know I am IT. I am a desirable, beautiful woman who has forged her own identity with her hard-earned accomplishments, a woman welcome amongst the quality people of the world."

Even though she missed Abe's touch, she continued to smile at the knowledge of what he gave her. She was happy she could let him go. She realized that she was able to love him and let him go because she was finally able to feel true love for a man, and she did feel true love for him. She did not use him to soothe some tired spots in her life. She did not use him to replace Lana at all because she had been able to let Lana go as well. She tried to use her boyfriends in medical school as well as Brian to replace Lana, to pretend to herself that Lana did not die and that was why she failed.

"I have taken Lana's love inside of me now. I took in his gifts for me. I have a good man in me now. Before I had rapists, child molesters and murderers in me but now I have a good man there as well and that is why I could respond to Abe, and when the time came for him to move on to take care of his life, I could let him go. I don't need a man to choose me or complete me anymore, because now I have a benevolent man in my head."

45

Depo was surprised Abe had left when he arrived on Friday. Ranti told him he had to leave in a hurry. He wanted to know if she was okay and she assured him that she had never been better. He suggested she return to New York with him the following Sunday but Ranti explained to him her need to spend the remaining two weeks of her time on the island to consolidate things, and be with herself. She realized that it might be the last time she would have that luxury for a long time to come, because once the babies were born, for the rest of her life she would always have to think of at least two other people.

On Sunday morning they set out at about seven for a restaurant that was some forty- minute walk from the cottage for breakfast. It was a cool and misty morning. They had to walk through the woods, and as they emerged into a clearing of leveled fields, they witnessed a most glorious sight that stopped them in their tracks.

There was a dead crow on the road. A flock of crows were flying around, above the road and the dead crow. They were making a sound that was mournful, yet beautiful. They flew around for a while and finally formed themselves into a circle. They started to fly around in that circle as they slowly descended toward the dead bird. They undulated in a moving way, as they pointed their beaks in unison toward the dead bird. They took turns to touch the dead bird with their beaks. Some of them picked it up and still in that concentric circle started to fly up with it. They continued with that mournful song as they carried the dead bird away.

Ranti and Depo stood side by side in awe as they watched the birds. They still stood there for about five minutes after the birds had completely disappeared. Depo moved closer to Ranti and hugged her. Chills ran down her spine.

Ranti started: *"When I turned her around, her whole body was covered in bright pigment. Herbs and stones and light and the ash of acacia to make her eternal. The body pressed against sacred color. Only the eye blue removed, made anonymous, a naked map where nothing is depicted, no signature of lake, no dark cluster of mountain as there is north of the Borku-Ennedi-Tibesti, no lime green fan where the Nile rivers enter the open palm of Alexandria, the edge of Africa.*

"And all the names of the tribes, the nomads of faith who walked in the monotone of the desert and saw brightness and faith and color. The way a stone or found metal box or bone can become loved and turn eternal in a prayer. Such glory of this country she enters now and becomes a part of. We die containing a richness of lovers and tribes, tastes we have swallowed, bodies we have plunged into and swum up as if rivers of wisdom, characters we have climbed into as if trees, fears we have hidden in as if caves. I wish for all this to be marked on my body when I am dead. I believe in such cartography—to be marked by nature, not just to label ourselves on a map like the names of rich men and women on buildings. We are communal histories, communal books. We are not owned or monogamous in our taste or experience. All I desired was to walk upon such an earth that had no maps."

Depo was quiet. They continued to walk slowly toward the center of the island.

Ranti continued to think of the book, *The English Patient.* "Almasy hatched out of the schizoid defense he constructed around himself to hide from life because of his pain. How did he sustain the wound? That was his cave of protection. But he ventured out when love beckoned to him in the form of life symbolized by the woman Katherine.

She died, but he was saved because he was able to love. She gave him that treasure. His body was finally able to go to rest when his mind recounted the story and brought everything to consciousness for him, and for those around him. He died rich, because his ghosts and phantoms, they redeemed him. Phantoms are full of treasures after all. Ah! That's why I've always been fascinated by that book."

"What in the world was that?" Depo finally asked. The look of wonder remained on his face.

"The birds are burying one of their own Depo. They are taking it into the palace of the winds, so it may rest in peace and allow the living to live their lives in prosperity."

"I have never seen anything like that in my life. I have seen ants carry away their dead, but I didn't know birds do that too. Did you know this Ranti?" He remained baffled.

They were quiet as they continued to walk toward the center of the town.

Five minutes later, "I am a father! I am a father of two unborn children," Depo said suddenly. He kept quiet again.

He continued a few moments later, "I have to bury him. I have to let him go too, so I can be a father to my own children. I just buried him like those birds just buried their dead in that ritual that is a gift for me to witness. I'm free Ranti, free to be a good father to my children." He squeezed her right hand that was in his. "That is the most beautiful thing I have ever seen, that funeral ritual of the birds, and who better to see it with but my dearest friend in the world!"

Ranti nodded. Mr. Jacobs had partially disowned Depo when he dropped out of medical school to pursue his passion of being an architect. He stopped paying his tuition then. But he fully disowned him when at the age of twenty-one Depo told him about his sexual orientation. His father told him he never wanted to see him again, and if he came around, he would kill him.

"Depo is finally able to bury his father so he can be free to become a father." Ranti thought. "Is he a terrible man? Depo's father, is he evil? No, he is not. I know he abandoned Efunwunmi when she could not give him more children and he married a younger more fertile woman, but he paid for the surgery to reconstruct my genitals. Efunwunmi went to him at the time and told him of my plight and he gave her the money—twenty-six thousand pounds sterling!

"Efunwunmi thinks he did it out of guilt at the way he treated her when he divorced her. But I think he did it because there was some good in him. He was able to empathize with a girl deprived of her womanhood. He knew that women hold the future of mankind in their wombs and it is something to treasure.

"He could not love his family unconditionally. He could only love Efunwunmi if she gave him lots of children, and even the child she did give him, he could only love him if he conformed to some ideas he had in his head, and because of that he threw away the love of two wonderful people. It is his loss. He deserves our pity.

"He deprived himself of the opportunity of meeting the grandchildren he made possible, because without his money I would not be an expectant mother today. He continues to deprive himself of so many treasures, and he is not able to enjoy the fruits of his labor. He is hiding in his cave of ignorance and fear. Where was his point of trauma?

"No, Depo's father is not a terrible person. He is just a scared person who is still wandering in the desert, a desert full of caves. Providence, please smile on him.

"But I know Depo has got to bury him so he can be free to father his own children, to be able to love them unconditionally, in the same way I have been spending my time on this island burying all my dead, and carrying them out into the palace of the winds, so that I can bring these babies to life and be free to be a mother to them too.

"My dead will continue to walk with me. They form the foundation on which I stand each day. They provide me a springboard. Without them I will not be me. Because of them I will not be shaky. They are in me, not at me like a foreign body. They are no longer wraiths or ghouls demanding the sacrifice of human meaning, but they are my companions, my allies.

"What did Esho give me? She gave me the sense of industry and the spirit to go on in spite of obstacles. She taught me courage, perseverance and loyalty. She taught me not to give up and just die even though that could be a very attractive option. She taught me to squeeze life-giving waters out of rocks.

"Esho who refused to give up her child, a child thrust at her in such a violent manner, and even though she was not mothered, she knew not to do the same to her child. Esho who wanted to die after two children died but returned from the land of the dead so I would not be abandoned and become a motherless child.

"Esho was not a bad person. She just did not have help, and she was so afraid. She could not even mourn her dead children, and for the rest of her life she could not bring herself to mention Lana's name. She could not revel in the memory of the only member of the male species that she loved. How could she have forgiven? The one love of her life that could have healed her, she could not even hold him in memory. What a painful sore it must have been in her heart.

"Why? It is because were she to mention his name and talk about him, she would have to mourn his death. And were she to mourn his death, then she would have to forgive Akanbi. Because that is what happens when we mourn effectively, we come to understand fully and we forgive. But she did not want to forgive. She needed to kill Akanbi because death was all she knew. She did not know the only 'Akanbi' she needed to kill was the hatred in her heart, and that even when there has been horrendous tragedy and pain, life is still a possibility.

"Yes, she wired my brain in a way to be afraid of the world, and of men. And yes, she destroyed my genitals, and that made it, oh, so difficult to become a lover. But she taught me how to battle when it is called for. I healed my genitals in a physical way and it's healing in my mind now. My brain is rewiring itself to live in a benevolent world.

"What did Oshun give me? Oshun that I never knew, Oshun the product of rape and murder. She did not have a prayer in this world because she was dead before she was born, and yet she tried her best in her own way. She was a prostitute but she chose the best man in her horror of a world to father her children. She chose the only man with a government job in our very, very poor neighborhood. She must have believed he would point the way out for her children, a way out of the cruel poverty that was our lives.

"Akanbi was the proverbial one-eyed man in the village of the blind. Oshun saw that and she chose him. What did she see in Akanbi? She must have seen something. What should I be grateful for in Oshun's choice of a father for me?

"What did Akanbi the pedophile, thief, murderer and scumbag, whose cruelty was worse than the cruelty of the pinching monkeys give me? I probably got good DNA. I got my looks from Esho's line but if truth be told he was a handsome man. He had good teeth. He was in good physical health. He didn't give me a congenital disease and I am grateful he refused to be in my life. That spared me from internalizing his psychopathic ways.

"He inadvertently pointed the way out of poverty to me like Oshun wanted by making thousands of books available to me, and sages both departed and with us still, spoke to me from time long gone. They raised me into maturity by imparting their hard-earned wisdom to me. It was as if in some ways Akanbi realized his limitations and asked others to do the work he was not able to do. Akanbi the scumbag did give me a lot.

"Lana? He taught me about a brother's love and I have found it in three wonderful men, Depo, Grant and Boris. He introduced me to the world of books and taught me to fight for an education in whatever way I could get it, even though it cost him his life. He helped me become the successful gynecologist I am today. What a sacrifice!

"He gave me my first doll, though he had to carve it out of a plank of wood. He actually was the first person to tell me I had the right to become a beautiful woman and a mother. He gave me permission to identify with the mothers in the neighborhood. Lana in his short life gave me so much.

"What about my teachers, those people whose gifts to their students cannot be quantified? They helped Esho and I bid farewell to poverty. Where are the words adequate to thank teachers?

"Even some of my teachers in medical school, who side by side with imparting such marvelous knowledge to me; sexually harassed me. I hated them for the harassment but they gave me so much, they gave us so much. My classmates and I have been performing miracles as physicians because of these teachers.

"Did the sexual harassment take away from what they imparted to us in terms of priceless knowledge? I don't know, but I am grateful to them. And I know they sexually harassed us out of their own stinking wounds. They are not any different from Esho who gave me so much and yet destroyed my genitals.

"Dr. Obed? Dr. O as we have started to affectionately think of him. What a wonderful guide he has been through my valleys of fears and doubts.

"Even Jamba, that raping minister of Nigeria, he gave me a lot too. He pushed me to tap into my fighting spirit, and he gave me Boris. If he hadn't died when he died, I wouldn't have gone out to celebrate his death. I wouldn't have been mugged and Boris wouldn't have come into my life.

"In spite of everything, I have a lot to be grateful for in my ancestors and in the world. The rest is up to me now. I have learnt my history and I can live with it and stand on it, and now the rest is up to me.

"My root goes deep, because our history begins for us eons before we were born. The words of wisdom I read in the many books are making sense to me more and more now, *"History is that which had happened and which goes on happening in time. But also it is the stratified record upon which we set our feet, the ground beneath us; and the deeper the roots of our being go down into the layers that lie below and beyond the fleshy confines of our ego, yet at the same time feed and condition it—so that in our moments of less precision we may speak of them in the first person and as though they were part of our flesh-and-blood experience— the heavier is our life with thought, the weightier is the soul of our flesh."*

"I am made of all those who came before me. I am Esho, the hardworking, persevering woman, the loyal mother and the murderer. Me too, I killed my unborn baby and I almost killed a man. But more important is that I have learnt to kill off the internalized undesirables in my mind.

"I am Oshun, the prostitute, the seductress, the seeker who sought the best man she could find to father her children. Me too, I chose the best man in my world to father my children. Oshun gave me her beautiful body, only I could not celebrate it until now. Now I can celebrate it and I am grateful for it.

"I am Lana, the conduit of Esho's love, who because of her love, on tasting life, fell in love with life. He was a connoisseur who took all that life could give him and made such a joy out of it and for me too. He taught me to welcome new experiences and as such he taught me open mindedness. I have learnt from him and I have wonderful friends in my life now.

"And I am Akanbi the thief and scumbag. I stole before, but I stole for my mental survival. Lana and I, we stole education in the big bookshop when we read the books without paying for them. We learnt to steal an education. We must have learnt that from our father the thief.

"It is true that no one can save you except yourself. I have been meeting with Dr. Obed on and off for the past twelve years, and he has been helping me delineate the past from the present and from the future. He repeatedly impressed on me that the past has to be mourned and buried so we can live in the present and so the future can unfold in freedom. This is his message to me for over twelve years. But I still had to take the leap. I had to jump over the chasm that looked so wide. I had to bury the past so I can let the present be, and allow the future to unfold.

"I stayed in my marriage because I could not let the past die. I tried Akanbi on for size in form of Brian, Jide and Tolu. They even physically resembled him.

My God! I tried all of Esho's men on for size. I wanted to repeat Esho's life and that is why I hung around in spite of warnings from friends until I almost killed Brian. I was on my way to becoming Esho, the killer of fathers. And I did kill my unborn baby by staying when friends anticipated that very tragedy and warned me against it. Like my grandmother, I committed that one murder and almost succeeded at a second.

"But I have to let go of the past. I have to carve my own path and not follow the path of those before me. Tragedy results from following the path of those before us instead of carving our own path. I get Dr. Obed now.

"Moradeke could not let the past die. She wanted to repeat her mother's life and that is why she tried to push her husband into extramarital affairs, so he would cheat on her like her father cheated on her mother, but Bode did not buy into her retrospective script and yet what did she do? She accused him of extramarital affairs anyway and chased him away from their marital bed.

"Gboye has been living out her dead script since she could differentiate between boys and girls. She was beating up boys in elementary school and in medical school, and she treated them like shit the moment she could date them. She too was acting out a dead play. She anticipated unfaithfulness where there was none, and because there was none there, she took it upon herself to act it out.

"Gosh! What feasts of phantoms we've all been having!"

"And the husband I married in my attempt to deny history," Ranti continue to mourn. "I married him in an attempt to pretend that Wura did not die in childbirth abandoning her newborn child. That Esho was not raped and that she did not murder the rapists. That Oshun was not a prostitute and that Akanbi was not a scumbag. That Lana did not die of tetanus, and that I did not carry feces on my head for other people, that I was not infested with intestinal worms, or that I did not have my genitals destroyed at the age of nine.

"I tried to deny these in my choice of a husband. I did not even tell him my history. I did not actively lie to him. I just omitted to tell him. I tried to deny these events that gave me a solid foundation.

"I wanted Brian to re-invent me and save me so my history would disappear. I wanted to be someone else and not Iranti Jare anymore. I wanted to wipe out my name that was formed out of a wrenching history of torment, terror and tears.

"How could Brian have loved me? I did not even give him a chance to know me. How could he have loved what he did not know? How could he have loved a lie? It is not possible to love a lie, just as it is not possible to love the things we are afraid of.

"I did to Brian again what his parents did to him when they sent him away to a monastery and his identity was negated when they changed his name and raised him as an Irish Catholic boy. I re-traumatized him again by not telling him my story.

"I did it out of fear. I realize that now. My identity was stolen from me as well when Esho destroyed my genitals, and when she cut off my hair and told me I was an ugly girl. Esho tried to negate that I was a girl who would grow to be a fruitful woman.

"We were the same, Brian and I. We were two lost souls in a turbulent world without the roots and anchors that are our identities. How could we have loved one another? How could we have made a marriage work? That is why a little breeze came and blew our marriage into smithereens. But Brian was looking for a savior too. We were the blind trying to lead the blind. He too got caught in my hedges and shrubs and in a way he was killed because the marriage died.

"Over the years I have come to develop compassion for Brian. I am not angry with him anymore, because he was as much a victim as I was. He too in his own way was and still is a sleeping beauty, and we both killed off prospective suitors because we believed that someone else would do the work to save us.

We did not want to do the active work of sleeping on our sorrow, pain and trauma for a hundred years, because it is painful work but it must be done. We did not want to own our pain and live with it. We tried to dump it on someone else.

"Brian was not parented because his parents abandoned him at the age of five when they divorced and sent him to a monastery as if he were an orphan. How he must have yearned for them. How he must have been terrified and cried himself to sleep on many nights. Who comforted him on stormy nights in that monastery full of men? Who answered his plea for help at a stage in his life when he should still have been in the arms of a doting mother?

"Who cherished him so he would learn to cherish life, and woman as the symbol of life?

"Who went after him to bring him back home, so he would learn to go after loved ones and bring them home when they leave in fear?

"Who celebrated his prowess when he was a young boy, so he would learn to admire friends and lovers?

"Who welcomed his curiosity and answered his questions, so he would know that in this world it is okay to accept those who are different from us, and that new experiences make us richer.

"Who assisted him as he created this world in his own way, so he would know that he stands in the center of the world, just like everyone else in this world stands in the center of the world too, and tolerance is the only avenue to love.

"He was asked to forget who he was when they raised him as a good white Catholic Irish boy though he was a black boy born in Ibadan, Nigeria. What a head fucker? Why would he not fart at the world? Why would he not repeatedly rape life? He raped me, killing our unborn baby. He was a terrified little boy surrounded by his hedges and shrubs, and they also pricked me so terribly, and pricked our marriage to death."

Tears sprang into Ranti's eyes as she thought of her marriage to her ex-husband. Her insides twisted and her heart ached as she felt his pain and internal torments because the doors she had nailed shut on her own pain had been opened, and she remembered when her brother died, and she was not yet seven years old.

It was as if a parent had died for her too, because at the time he had been taking care of her and raising her. He was with her twenty-four hours a day. He played with her and made sure she ate. He answered her questions and allayed her fears, and he made her first doll for her. Because at that time Esho had to work twelve hours each day, six days a week, at her laborer job to feed them. And it was Lana who brought Esho's love to her. Esho loved him so much but where Ranti was concerned, Esho was angry at the female that she was, and she was afraid.

Ranti remembered her fears after he died. Her world came to an end there and then and that was when she stopped being a child. She could not even cry for him. Esho forbade it, so she did not cry, but how her insides used to twist together in fear all the time, and she was terrified. And it was then that she became a target for exploitation.

"Oh my gosh! That is how Brian must have felt when he was sent away from all that was familiar to him at the age of five. How he must have been scared."

She wept for his anguish and how he must have suffered from his experience of being abandoned and how he continues to suffer. She recalled how each time she went on call as a resident doctor, he felt abandoned again. He picked a fight with her all the time.

"I didn't get it then. I was baffled that a person who is a physician himself would find it difficult to understand that other physicians go on calls, especially when they are in residency training. He behaved as if it were my choice to go on those calls, as if I could choose my schedule. It baffled me so much, but I get it now. He didn't want me to go away because each time I went away, that scared abandoned five year old in him felt the pain of the abandonment all over again.

"Who wants to revisit a painful period in his or her life? Isn't that why we start wars? It is easier to manage a war than go back to that horribly painful place. That was why Brian, a physician, who married another physician, could not tolerate it for her to go on mandatory calls. I get it now.

"He waged a lot of battles with me. The return of that terrible abandonment feeling was responsible for him constantly accusing me of having affairs with other men. What a joke, me who couldn't even bring myself to talk to other men. It explains why he used to go crazy each time a man paid me a compliment. I remember his admonitions, "Don't let it go to your head, you are not beautiful, he was just being polite." He was afraid that if I truly saw myself as the beautiful woman that I am, I would leave him for another man. Just like his mother left him at the age of five.

"Age five for a boy? Isn't that the time they are trying to negotiate their Oedipal situation with their mothers? Yet she abandoned him before he could resolve it in his own way, with her present, surviving it, and not running away from him. He couldn't arrive at a healthy resolution that his mother would remain his mother, and that it was okay for him to grow up to become a man and love his own woman.

"Rather, she removed herself and one wonders what explanations he gave himself for that action of hers. Did he tell himself she removed herself because she did not want his love? Or as a punishment for loving his mother, so he was in a way castrated? Or, the reward of loving a woman is you would be banished?

"He continued to yearn for her. She became a goddess in his mind and she came first in our marriage, and continues to be so in his other marriages. Isn't that what we do with what we have been deprived of, we idealize it. What is idealization anyway? Idealization is not true love. We idealize when there is a hidden fear we need to exorcise. We idealize when we are afraid of the person. We do not idealize that which we love because we have to be at par with the object of our affection to truly love them.

"That is why Brian, the father of three girls today continues to name his daughters after his mother. It is not that he isn't creative and could not think of new names to give his daughters, but he continues to yearn for the mother he never had, and to hope she would return and re-mother the five year old in him that was rejected. He is determined to coerce the world into becoming the caretaking mother, and he continues to look for her in his innocent children.

"He doesn't know the days of getting are over and he has to allow himself to be angry with her for the injustice she meted out to him, because she did do terrible things to him by abandoning him. He doesn't know he has to weep those assuaging tears over his stinking wound, so as to heal it; the way Oke healed his festering wound when I was in medical school.

"Brian has to do that so he would not keep punishing the young women he continues to serially marry for his mother's sins. So he could assist his ex-wives in taking care of his children by meeting his financial obligations as their father. So he could let his five children have their own lives.

"He was afraid to love me because if he did, his mother might become angry and leave him again. So, though she did not live physically with us in the US while we were married, and though she remained thousands of miles away across the Atlantic Ocean in Nigeria, she ruled our marital home. And our marriage ended the very night she arrived to visit us for the first time. He was too afraid to let her see him with another woman. She might leave him again.

"I understand his fears of being poisoned as well. How he used to accuse me of wanting to kill him. That used to baffle me too. Why would I kill a man I fought so hard to marry?

"He refused to eat Esho's food, and Esho's food was delicious. He accused Esho of wanting to kill him several times. He accused her of being the one who made him fail all his examinations.

"He was so primitive in his fears because he was stuck at the primitive age of five, as that was his point of trauma. He did not know how to be around a mother. In his deep experience, mothers are witches, after all one abandoned him at a very vulnerable stage in his life. How could he trust any mother? How could he trust any woman? That would be asking the impossible of him.

"I understand why I constantly had to be the bad guy in the marriage and he had to be the good guy. He needed to put all his fearful feelings of inadequacy into me, so he would feel that he was fine, and if he were good, then no one would abandon him again.

"How he used to tell me, "Ranti, I am fine, you are the one with all these problems because of your past and your crazy grandmother." What a laugh? How about his own abandoning mother?

"He had never been helped to own any feelings that were his, be they good feelings or bad. No one had ever helped him contain his tantrums and fits by holding him lovingly until it was over, and not running away from him, so he would know that it is okay, sometimes we hate and at other times we love, but we remain the same true reliable people.

"He could not hold me in tenderness. Where would he have learnt that? So he raped me. He rejected my sexual advances when I offered them, but at other times he forced himself on me and raped me. I didn't get so many things then. I get them now. He didn't know how to connect in tenderness. It was too scary for him. What if I rejected his tender overtures? It would be that abandonment again, so he took charge and he took me in a way that I couldn't have rejected him, and that is why the only form of lovemaking he knew was to rape me. Then, he was in charge, and there was no room for me to say no. He had the power then because at other times he was a powerless, castrated, terrified man.

"And all I wanted was to love him and have him love me, but he couldn't, his ghosts and phantoms would not allow him to write a prospective script. They wanted to keep acting out those retrospective plays.

"All his cruelties now make perfect sense. And the only time we almost became parents, I was pregnant and sick in the hospital. He did not come to visit me. We lived ten minutes away from the hospital for goodness sakes! He could drive a car and yet for two whole weeks he did not come to be with me, to reassure me and comfort me. My husband, the father of our yet to be born baby could not hold me in the time of my need.

"Esho could not drive a car, but she braved the January cold every day to come and sit with me. She walked the five miles each way, every day. I didn't know she was walking those ten miles each day until the third day. Yet my own husband could not get into a warm car and we had two cars at the time. He could not get into one of them and drive the ten minutes to visit his wife, who was pregnant with his child!

"Depo came from New York City after work, every day. Gboye, a busy surgical resident, came down from Boston once a week to be with me, and she called me three or four times a day. Moradeke as well, she came about three times a week from New York City; she too was a resident doctor and the mother of an infant at the time. Yet my own husband, who was ten minutes away, did not come to see me for two weeks!

"When confronted, he said he was studying for the third part of his examinations, and he had to work as well. We could not understand the inexplicable wickedness. But I get it now. It was revenge. He was taking revenge on me, and the world that had hurt him so much.

"He never learnt to go after anyone. He never learnt to look for anyone. He is the one that should be found. He is the one that should be pursued and comforted, and he could not become a father at that stage in his life. How could he be ready? He wanted to be the baby in the house and have me re-mother him, so how could he have welcomed another baby? No wonder he harassed and nagged me and raped me until I lost the pregnancy." Ranti shook her head in sorrow.

"He was so irrational that I thought I had married a psychotic man. No, he was not psychotic, and psychotic does not mean wicked. He was wicked because he was in so much pain from his stinking wound.

"*For in married love we will seek to reclaim the loves of our early yearning, to find in the present beloved figures of yore: The unattainable parent of Oedipal passion, the unconditionally loving mother of childhood and the symbiotic unit where self and other meld, as we once did before. In the arms of our own true love we strive to unite the aims and objects of past desire. And sometimes we hate our mate for failing to satisfy these ancient impossible longings.*

We hate [him] because [he] hasn't ended our separateness.

We hate [him] because [he] hasn't filled up our emptiness.

We hate [him] because [he] hasn't fulfilled our save-me, complete-me, mirror-me, mother-me yearnings.

And we hate [him] because we waited all these years to marry [daddy]—and [he] isn't [daddy].

We do not, of course, enter marriage with the conscious intention of marrying daddy—or mommy. Our hidden agenda is also hidden from us. But subterranean hopes make for seismic disturbances.

"That is why our marriage was such an earthquake. Ha! I get it now. If I knew all this then, I might have tried to help him metabolize some of his fears, but how could I? I was equally sick and weak.

"I was innocent of so much but at the same time I was guilty, and so was he. He was guilty of a lot but yet he was innocent too.

"How did I hurt him with my pain? How did my thorns prick him? I don't know, but if we were to ask him, I'm sure we would get an earful. I know in the end I almost killed him. I didn't walk away from the marriage like I should have when it started to get really ugly. I had so many chances to walk away as my friends encouraged me to do. But I stayed around until he cut me again and I almost killed him. I was like the dead bringing about again what killed them in the first place. I waited for another son to die and be mutilated again. OH!

"I told myself that I loved him, but the truth is, I couldn't forgive him and I wanted to kill him for hurting me in so many ways, so I hung around to give myself a good reason to kill him. That is why I didn't leave after he raped me and I lost the baby. Did I need more convincing that it wasn't a good marriage for me? No, but I stayed around to find a good reason to kill him. I was becoming my grandmother.

"Did I really love him? Or was I using him with the hope that he would save me? I believed that if I married him, a man from a solid traditional and respected family, it would erase my traumatic history. To be honest with myself, that is why I married him. I used him too, only that he didn't save me. Depo had my heart and my love the whole period I was married to Brian. How could I have been present in the marriage?

"No, I didn't love him, I needed him just like he needed me, and need is not love. This is because when we are in need we are not in a position to reassure the other person, but in love we are able to reassure the other. Brian needed me to reassure him and I needed him to reassure me. I used him, just like he used me. I exploited him too. I wasn't innocent at all. I was guilty of a lot.

"Am I guilty because I couldn't stand firm and demand that he treat me decently? I remember I was afraid that if I demanded accountability of him he would leave me, and I didn't want him to leave. My sense of me as a human being was dependent on having been chosen by a man, any man. Not to have been chosen would have confirmed that I was trash, because in my history men have always left me. I idealized him so much, I was grateful he married the unworthy woman I was. Maybe therein lies the ways in which I failed him. I didn't call him to order at all. I didn't help him be a decent man.

"Guilt and innocence are rarely obvious. They are unapparent, interwoven intimately with each other in a marvelously convoluted design."

Tears ran down Ranti's face as she continued to think of Brian. "Both of us were guilty and innocent at the same time. My share in the failed relationship is a hundred percent. He did to me what I wanted him to do to me. If I didn't want him to act out some script that was already in my head, I wouldn't have married him and he wouldn't have treated me the way he did.

"I get so many things now. All those wonderful passages in the books I read that made such huge impressions on me, I didn't get them then, but they impressed me so much that I made notes of them, and read them aloud to myself from time to time in private. I asked them to speak to me and finally they are speaking to me, almost overwhelming me. *'Be patient towards all that is unsolved in your heart and...try to love the questions themselves like locked rooms and like books that are written in a very foreign tongue. Do not now seek the answers which cannot be given you to because you would not be able to live with them. And the point is to live everything. Live the questions now perhaps you will then gradually, without noticing it live along some distant day into the answer.'*

"I have been able to live into the answers now, and everything makes absolute sense. Wow, it's like those mythological stories where light is suddenly shone into dark places. I can see clearly now.

"I hope Brian will allow his hundred years of slumber to assist him into finding joy so he can reclaim his wounded soul as his own and nurture it, and not continue taking revenge on the world and on women. I pray that providence will smile on my ex-husband."

She looked around her at the island, "Nature is wonderful. Nature is perfect. Nature is on time. If birds can bury their kind with such a beautiful ceremony, taking it into the palace of the winds, why should we not bury our dead and allow them to rest in perfect peace? We have to bury the dead, so the phantoms, wraiths, ghosts, and ghouls will not torment us, but then we will be able to inherit their blessings and earn the freedom to live our lives.

"*The kingdom of the father is spread around the earth and men do not see it'.* That was the kingdom of the father we just saw, the birds burying their kind in the same ways the lessons of nature are around us in the weather, storms, animal life, and plant life. Snakes slough off their skin periodically to teach us about rebirth and about another chance, just like the spring comes with its reassurance every year. Ants teach us about industry and cooperation. Baboons teach us about fidelity. Dogs teach us about loyalty, vultures teach us to clean up after ourselves, and lions teach us about well-deserved pride."

She stole a glance at Depo walking silently beside her. He was looking at her too, "Are you okay Ranti, you are in tears."

She shook her head as she quoted to herself, "*The familiar faces of friends, who in spite of their own pain and sorrow continue to reach across the incalculable gulf that separate us, they reach out in love and in hope, and we touch one another and reassure one another.'* Depo, the enduring love of my life, how did he come to be such a great human being? What is his secret? His secret is that he had to live in a world that refused to take notice of him, a world that rejected him because his god made him in a different way. His wound is in his biology in this world that could be closed minded and prejudicial. That is his source of strength.

"Depo must have taken this journey that I'm now taking, that Gboye and Moradeke just realized they have to take too. Depo was forced to retrieve his golden fleece in his twenties, but unlike the mythological Jason, he held on to the love of the feminine in him. He held on to the love of his mother and he held on to my love, and it made him into the wonderful man he is today.

"How can anyone see the world and this earth as just malevolent?" She concluded, as she moved closer to Depo and took his hand in hers.

46

Depo left later on Sunday after he tried unsuccessfully to convince Ranti to return to the city with him. She spent the week in her usual manner of swimming, walking, eating Mrs. Sanchez' cooking and reading her life story that she was able to put together. She thought of working on the proposal or her address to the World Women Congress, but told herself she would get to that later.

She did not receive an email from Abe and she was not expecting to hear from him, ever. She understood his plight only too well. She had been there herself. She continued to smile each time she remembered the ways he held and loved her. She hoped he would realize what a wonderful person he was, and soon enough.

Jack called a few times and kept encouraging her to return early. She reminded him that she would be in the city in less than two weeks and they could have dinner.

Gboye called too to say that she had an ultrasound test and the baby was fine, and it was a girl. She was overjoyed that she was finally having a daughter. She and Olu were still proceeding with the divorce, but they were talking more to one another than they did before.

On Friday morning, a week before Ranti was scheduled to leave the island, she returned from swimming to find Boris and Jack standing in the living room. She screamed with joy as she ran to embrace Boris. For a moment Jack looked different to her.

"What are you guys doing here? What? What are you doing here?" she exclaimed, unable to conceal her excitement.

"Well, *if Mohammed won't come to the mountain....*" Jack started. "I wanted to come get you. I didn't think I could survive one more week without seeing you, and I was worried you might extend your stay, but then I was afraid you might call the cops on me so I convinced old man Boris to come with me."

"It is a pleasure to hide but such a joy to be found," she quoted to herself.

Ranti still held on to Boris. She looked at him and he nodded confirming Jack's story. She hugged him again and kissed him on the cheeks.

"What? I don't get a hug? I brought him here, he didn't bring me here," Jack told her as he opened his arms to her.

She shyly went to him and hugged her for a long time. He kissed her on the cheeks. "It's so good to see you, Ranti. You are even more beautiful than I remember."

She smiled her thanks.

"You look fantastic, Ranti. It is a joy to watch you. I'm glad you are doing so well." Boris spoke for the first time.

Ranti looked at the two of them and she laughed out loud. "Could things get any better?" She asked herself. "My 'father' and a man who loves me finally came after me. Two men came for me, to bring me back home with them. They want me that much. Two men! Not one but two!" She laughed out loud again.

"Thank you so much for coming, both of you, thank you for coming to get me, you can't begin to imagine how much this means to me," she told them.

She settled them into the cottage and later in the afternoon they went walking on the beach.

Boris left her and Jack after a while to return to the cottage, "My work here is done, I brought you here Jack to let Ranti know that you are a good man and that I approve. Ranti, I approve, Jack is a good man."

Ranti smiled as she kissed him again.

She and Jack spent the afternoon on the beach swimming, and at some point just sitting on the deck talking.

"Esho, a man came to get me. He wanted me so much that he came to get me. There are great men in the world, Esho. Once I opened my heart to them they came. There are lots of men who are descendants of Noah," Ranti repeatedly told her grandmother in her mind.

Boris and Jack did not have to do much to convince her to return to the city with them. She gladly packed her bags and gratefully thanked the island and the Sanchezes for caring for her.

Ranti had fantasized many times about what it would feel like to be in a relationship with a man that she loved and who truly loved her, and the feeling was everything she anticipated, but it made her understand the Yoruba proverb, *'ayo abara tintin,'* which seems to appreciate that when true joy finally arrives, one is still one, and not a person who has expanded. The mind has expanded, and has stretched such that it can never regain its original dimension, and it should not. But the body still remains the same. The person has not suddenly become ten feet tall. The mind has. It is not a letdown feeling, but one that leaves you unable to imagine the alternative. It is a feeling that says to you, *"This is the way it is supposed to be, how could it be otherwise?"*

Ranti's relationship with Jack seemed to take such wings. It was as if she had been practicing for the role of being his girlfriend and lover all her life, because it just felt natural. She told herself she had been practicing all her life so that when he appeared, she would be ready, and she was. If he had come into her life a year earlier or even six months earlier, she would not have been ready for him. She would not have seen him. She would not have noticed him on the streets even if he had a million dogs with him. Her hedges would have blocked her vision and her thorns would have pricked him to death.

"How many Jacks have passed me on the streets in my life?" She was sure thousands had but she was not ready for them and so she did not see them and they did not see her. "That is why Depo is right. I needed to heal and see myself as a truly desirable woman, because that was the most important battle of my war. I have gathered all of myself into a wholesome unity. I am living in fragments no longer because I have connected the prose with the passion. I am sufficient unto myself, I don't need someone to complete me, and I don't have to provoke rejection or rape. I don't have to take revenge on the world anymore. I can let other people be whom they want to be."

It was as if Jack took lessons from Abe or Abe took lessons from him. Or as it later occurred to her, this is how kind men make love to women. His touch was so gentle that they left her in tears of gratitude. And she could appreciate *Rainer Maria Rilke's 'It is a great unending experience, which is given us, a knowing of the world, the fullness and the glory of all knowing.'*

Her first night in Jack's apartment, after he held her and loved her, *She dreamt she was about to have a baby. She was prepared for caesarian section. Esho stood by her bed as the doctor got her ready. She reassured her that when she came out of the general anesthesia, she would be there waiting for her. Ranti nodded. She felt she could trust Esho.*

She awoke from the anesthesia, and she had the baby. The same doctor was there with Esho by her bedside. She asked to see the baby. Esho and the doctor exchanged a strange look. Esho said to her, "You had a very beautiful baby girl, but she died."

Ranti panicked as her heart dropped.

She looked around her and right by her bedside was a beautiful baby girl who was sleeping peacefully. Ranti could feel the baby's breath on her arm.

She gave Esho a questioning look and Esho in turn gave the doctor a nasty look.

"Why would you lie about such an important thing Esho? Are you out of your mind? This is my baby here. She is alive and well and she is very beautiful. How dare you lie about that Esho?" Ranti yelled at her.

"I asked you to give her more sedation." Esho in turn yelled at the doctor.

Ranti gave Esho such a forceful kick with her right foot that she went reeling to the end of the room. "You are not to fuck with me ever again, okay!" She yelled at her grandmother.

When she awoke, "I got my body and my mind back, and when my prince finally arrived, I was ready for him, my hundred years of slumber—of very active sleep, not passive sleep, but a sleep of hard work and toil, of inner growth, of creative waiting paid off in just forty years. No one is to fuck with me ever again!"

Efunwunmi arrived a week before Ranti's presentation and she shed tears of joy on seeing her pregnant with her grandchildren. "My prayers have been answered, Ranti. I'm a very happy woman. I'm happy that my son is happy in his life. The first time I met you, I wished for this, to see you pregnant with my grandchildren, but then my son told me of his sexual orientation and I despaired that this day would ever come. Thank you my daughter."

Ranti's response was to burst into tears as well. She had never been a person who could ever find the words she needed to convey her feelings in any situation. That is why she envied poets the same way she envied birds their ability to fly, but at the same time she was grateful to poets because she had continued to borrow words from them.

She looked at Efunwunmi and thought, "This is the grandmother of my children. A woman dispatched especially to me by an act of heavenly mercy to lift a curse off my head some twenty-five years ago. Not only did Efunwunmi made it possible for me to become a doctor, she gave me back my sexuality. She made it possible for me to be a woman, to be a human being.

"Efunwunmi raised me from the dead, because by her act of kindness she put death that was Esho and that hovered over me to shame, because without her, the shade that was Esho would have taken me with her to the land of no return, and Wura's line would have failed and perished. Efunwunmi prevented that from happening.

'Our line, Wura's line, is cursed, our beauty is a curse, we are either play- things for men or we are always afraid,' had been Esho's lesson to me. But Esho did not realize that Gold is incorruptible and imperishable. I knew that we were always afraid because we were dead. But Efunwunmi stepped in and changed that. She gave me back my stolen femininity and as such my ability to continue the fight for life.

"I did not succumb to fate. I gave destiny a run for its tenacity. I did not follow the paths of Wura who died at childbirth because her placenta did not separate, or of Esho who died at the age of thirteen but whose ghost hung around haunting everything in sight, or of Oshun who passively laid there, letting fate twist her around as if she were in the eye of a tornado.

"Perhaps Efunwunmi helped me out of selfish reasons so I would be able to give her grandchildren. Perhaps she did it out of love for her son who had told her that I meant the world to him. Whatever Efunwunmi's reasons were, one thing I can say for the woman is that she recognized the importance of transmitting blessings from generation to generation and she lent a helping hand to a girl of the generation after her own. She gave me life and liberty even though at the time, she herself had just been discarded for a younger more fertile woman.

"Efunwunmi did not respond to that with bitterness, but she responded with astounding generosity. Words are not enough, how could they be? Because most of the emotions I want to convey are from a place where language has not yet penetrated."

The two women held on to one another and wept tears of gratitude together, and Ranti's throat closed on her so she could not even utter borrowed words to thank Efunwunmi. "You are my mother," was all she could say.

On the eve of her presentation, Ranti had a dream she christened "The Dream of Rebirth and Triumph," especially because she woke up singing, and felt like dancing and rejoicing.

She dreamt that *she had driven herself to the Rockefeller Center for her presentation, but she arrived too early. They told her she had to come back later. She decided to go back home and wait. She told herself there was no need to be in a hurry, and she had to follow the procedure because you could not rush these things.*

She had to drive on a freeway. The traffic was backed up and the drivers were angry. They were yelling at someone in front of her. The traffic moved slowly until she arrived at the point of the congestion.

Three little children were walking on the freeway. She stopped to talk to them. She was concerned that it was too dangerous for them to be walking on the freeway. The oldest child was about seven years old. She could not remember if they were boys or girls, it did not seem important.

She picked them up with plans to take them to the police station, but they told her they were going to the fair, and that if she took them to the police station they would miss the fair.

She asked for their mother and the children told her she was asleep at home. They were in charge of taking care of themselves, and their mother didn't have a problem with that. Ranti decided she would return them home and have a serious talk with their mother.

She saw an exit on the freeway that read 'Nigeria.' She was surprised there was an exit on the freeway in New York City that pointed to Nigeria. She was seeing it for the first time and she had driven on that road many times.

She took the exit to investigate. She arrived on the road with the name Nigeria and there was a building, one block long, with the Nigerian flag in front. She parked the car and taking the children with her, went into the building and she was amazed.

It had a lot of works of art on the history of Nigeria, from pre-colonial time to date. They were so beautiful that she was speechless. She kept looking at them, admiring them and soaking in their beauty.

She walked up a flight of stairs and there was the most beautiful music she had ever heard coming from a room. She looked into the room and it was a very big hall. People were dancing in celebration, both women and men. She stood in awe as she watched them. They were so beautiful. Tears sprang from her eyes.

A woman came out of the hall. She was one of the dancers. Ranti asked her what was being celebrated, and she smiled at her as she told her it was the festival of Rebirth. She pointed at the sheaves of rice in the dancers' hands. "That is the symbol of Rebirth. Someone has just been Reborn." She smiled again and left.

Ranti enjoyed the music and the dancers for a while and she left to continue to explore the building. She went down some flights of stairs toward the basement and three women sat on the stairs, each woman sitting on the stair below the previous woman.

Oshun was the first woman. She smiled in a welcoming manner at Ranti. She did not yell at her or give her a knock on the head.

Esho sat below Oshun. Ranti happily embraced her.

Below Esho was a woman whom Ranti did not recognize though she looked familiar to her.

"Esho, what are you doing here?" Ranti asked her grandmother, "I thought you would be in heaven by now, not still hanging around in Nigeria."

Esho smiled at her. "Iranti, we were waiting for you, we wanted you to show us your children before we leave. Did you meet Wura? That is your great-grandmother." She pointed to the first woman who had looked familiar to her.

Ranti smiled at Wura. "Esho, she is so beautiful."

Esho nodded, "I told you she was the most beautiful woman in our village. Thank you for coming to show us your children. You have done very well and made me very proud."

Ranti wanted to explain to Esho that she picked-up the children off the freeway and they were not her children, but then Esho along with Oshun and Wura had joined the dancing celebrating the Rebirth and they did not hear her.

Ranti shrugged and said to herself, "What the heck? They are my children, I finally picked up all of myself scattered all over the place and I made it into a wholesome unity. They are me and they are my children." She held on to the three children and joined in the celebration as well.

"I'm like those Russian dolls with one inside the other and inside the other and on and on. In my inner most core, the doll is Wura, my inner gold, indestructible and enduring. She is enveloped by Esho, my treasures, because of gold, treasures

340   *Feasts of Phantoms*

are born, those potentials capable of making us whole only if we knew how. Then comes Oshun, my indispensable instincts that make life possible in that they are natural and always right. And encompassing all of these is Iranti, Memory, this is what activates all of them and make them dynamic to nurture my soul."

Friday, June 9 2006. There was a lot of excitement in Depo's loft, as they got ready for the noon presentation.

The week before, when Moradeke and Gboye came to New York City to welcome Efunwunmi who had just arrived from Nigeria, a lot of discussion had gone into what clothes they should wear.

Gboye suggested that she, Moradeke and Ranti wear the same outfit, the Yoruba traditional *Iro, Buba and Gele* made of the same fabric in the same color. "Because we are sisters and this is our proudest day so far. We are going to have many more days to be proud of, like at our children's college graduation and weddings and when they give us grandchildren, but so far this is our proudest day, the day the world recognizes my dear sister's triumph."

Efunwunmi had informed them, "I'm wearing *Iro, Buba and Gele,* that I bought and had made especially for this occasion. My headgear will be the tallest in that room, because the height of your crown reflects the intensity of your pride and I am one proud woman."

Moradeke ordered the clothes from a Nigerian tailor in Brooklyn.

Moradeke and Gboye arrived in town the day before with their families. They checked into hotels, but the two women came to the loft very early in the morning so they could get ready together. It reminded Ranti of her friends' wedding days, when the three of them had gotten ready together.

They helped one another with the outfits and when they emerged into the living room, Grant burst into tears. He claimed he had never seen three more beautiful women.

They took pictures to put the moment on record.

Thirty minutes before they were to leave in the limousine, a package arrived for Ranti. It was from Abe. He had sent it from Indonesia.

It was the book of pictures he was working on while they were on the island. Ranti's picture was the front cover. She was in her lime green bikini set and she was coming out of the ocean; the waves could be seen as they crashed onto the shore. Her pregnant abdomen protruded massively in front of her. Her wet hair covered half of her face. The book was entitled *Hope Out of Despair.*

Tears sprang from her eyes as she opened it. They were pictures of despair from around the world. There were pictures of human tragedy, of wars fought and lost by many.

There were pictures of child soldiers in Liberia carrying guns and submachine guns, bigger than them.

There were pictures of beggars from Niger republic, with amputated right hands—"they must have stolen food with those hands," Ranti told herself.

There were pictures of a toddler in Sudan pulling at its dead mother's breast.

There were skulls, the symbols of what Rwandans did to one another.

There were pictures of children playing on the street where dead bodies lay around from South America.

There were tragic, but beautiful because human souls were in the pictures. And the tears continued to stream down Ranti's face.

She flipped the book to the end and read: *"Ranti, thank you for trying to let me know there was some good in me. I did not give you a gift. You gave me a gift.*

Now, even though the pictures contained in this book is the way I see the world, more and more these days I am able to see the world the way you looked that time when I took your picture as you came out of the ocean. That was the morning after we were first together.

There is hope out of despair and I believe you that I will find what I seek, so that in my old age I will not be alone, because I'm seeing the world differently already.

Go on to the World Women Congress today and give them stories of hope.

Abe.

They arrived at the Rockefeller Center at eleven o'clock, and Boris, Jack, Olu with his and Gboye's six boys, and Bode with his and Moradeke's three children were there.

Ranti kissed Olu to thank him for coming, "I wouldn't have missed it for the world and I don't think the boys should miss this at all. It's about the best part of their education," he told her.

She smiled at him, thinking, "And this is the man my dear sister accused of not being creative. Their sons are lucky young men."

The chairperson of the occasion offered her a seat for her presentation because she was over eight months pregnant with twins, but Ranti reassured her that she would be fine, and that she wanted to stand up to speak to the world because genital mutilation was not a sitting matter.

At five minutes after noon, Ranti walked up to the podium to address the world on the devastating effects of genital mutilation on the women and the societies where the practice was still active. She did not have to prepare the speech that had always been a part of her, but which she was able to consolidate with her stay on the island.

"Good morning, ladies and gentlemen. My name is Iranti Jare. Genital mutilation is practiced for many reasons, but the reasons all have the same denominator—fear. When I turned nine, and my body started to change into that of a young woman, my grandmother who had been a powerless victim of sexual exploitation on many occasions and at a very tender age too, decided to protect me from…."

Forty-five minutes later, at the end of her slides presentation, pictures and stories with the souls of her patients, she was rewarded with a standing ovation. She was thanked by many of the officials present, and lots of promises were made to support her work.

As she walked through the throng of people who milled around to shake her hand, hug her and congratulate her, she thought to herself, "I'm grateful I can tell my story. I'm grateful the world listened to me. It is true that my sufferings were real. The world has become my witness, and they are joining me in healing my hurts. What a wonderful opportunity I have been given. What a lucky woman I am. My suffering has not been in vain because I have been allowed to tell my story. I am heavily indebted to this world."

An hour into the party at Jack's restaurant, Ranti's water broke. Depo blamed it on the fact that she had been on her feet for hours and she had too much excitement for one day, "The pregnancy is just thirty-five weeks old, and I didn't think the babies would come so soon. We haven't talked about names yet, and the hospital will demand names from us…."

Ranti gave him a hug of reassurance. "It's going to be okay, Depo. We will be fine."

The party moved to the hospital and Ranti smiled because everyone in their excitement reminded her of the celebration in her dream earlier that morning.

She delivered a girl and a boy by caesarian section, and the hospital did ask Depo for names minutes after the babies were taken out of her.

He brought the babies one by one to her. "Ranti, my love, here is our daughter; she was brought out of your first. Her name is Wura, and here is our son, his name is Esho."

Ranti took both babies from him and held them in the crook of each arm. She smiled at them and even in her sedated state was able to recall:

"We shall not cease from exploration,
And the end of all our exploring
Will be to arrive where we started
And know the place for the first time."

Bibliography

A Chorus of Stones by Susan Griffin
Women Who Run with the Wolves by Clarissa Pinkola Estes
Howard's End by E. M. Forster
The Writer and the World by V. S. Naipaul
Peer Gynt by Ibsen
Wasteland by T. S. Eliot
A Hero with a Thousand Faces by Joseph Campbell
Letter to a Young Poet by Rainer Maria Rilke
Home Is Where We Start From by Donald Winnicott
Discovering of Being by Rollo May
Freedom and Destiny by Rollo May
The English Patient by Michael Ondaajte
Joseph and His Brothers by Thomas Mann
Necessary Losses by Judith Viorst
The King and the Corpse by Heinrich Zimmer
Little Gidding by T. S. Eliot

Fisher King Press is pleased to present the following recently published Jungian titles for your consideration:

The Sister from Below	ISBN 978-0-9810344-2-3	
by Naomi Ruth Lowinsky	Jungian Perspective	
The Motherline	ISBN 978-0-9810344-6-1	
by Naomi Ruth Lowinsky	Jungian Perspective	
The Creative Soul	ISBN 978-0-9810344-4-7	
by Lawrence H. Staples	Jungian Perspective	
Guilt with a Twist	ISBN 978-0-9776076-4-8	
by Lawrence H. Staples	Jungian Perspective	
Enemy, Cripple, Beggar	ISBN 978-0-9776076-7-9	
by Erel Shalit	Jungian Perspective	
Re-Imagining Mary	ISBN 978-0-9810344-1-6	
by Mariann Burke	Jungian Perspective	
Resurrecting the Unicorn	ISBN 978-0-9810344-0-9	
by Bud Harris	Jungian Perspective	
The Father Quest	ISBN 978-0-9810344-9-2	
by Bud Harris	Jungian Perspective	
Like Gold Through Fire	ISBN 978-0-9810344-5-4	
by Massimilla and Bud Harris	Jungian Perspective	

Learn more about the many Jungian publications available for purchase at **www.fisherkingpress.com**

In Canada & the U.S. call
1-800-228-9316
International call
+1-831-238-7799
info@fisherkingpress.com

Also Available from Genoa House

Feasts of Phantoms
  by Kehinde Ayeni
ISBN 978-0-9813939-2-6
Literary Fiction

Main Street Stories
  by Phyllis LaPlante
ISBN 978-0-9813939-1-9
Literary Fiction

The RR Document
  by J.G. Moos
ISBN 978-0-9813939-0-2
Literary Fiction

Requiem
  by Erel Shalit
ISBN 978-1-9267150-3-2
Literary Fiction

Sulfur Creek
  by Thad McAfee
ISBN 978-0-9810344-8-5
Literary Fiction

Timekeeper
  by John Atkinson
ISBN 978-0-9776076-5-5
Literary Fiction

Dark Shadows Red Bayou
  by John Atkinson
ISBN 978-0-9810344-7-8
Literary Fiction

Journey to the Heart
  by Nora Caron
ISBN 978-0-9810344-3-0
Literary Fiction

The Malcolm Clay Trilogy
  by Mel Mathews
    LeRoi
    Menopause Man
    SamSara
Literary Fiction
ISBN 978-0-9776076-0-0
ISBN 978-0-9776076-1-7
ISBN 978-0-9776076-2-4

Beyond the Mask: Part I
  by Kathleen Burt
ISBN 978-0-9813939-3-3
Astrology

Phone Orders Welcomed
Credit Cards Accepted
In Canada & the U.S. call 1-888-298-9717
International call +1-831-238-7799
books@genoahouse.com
www.genoahouse.com

LaVergne, TN USA
03 January 2009

168688LV00003B/2/P